Praise for *The Lady*

"Halley Sutton's propulsive, delectable noir is one of the most thrilling debuts I can remember. With a pair of utterly captivating femmes fatales at its dark and twisty heart, *The Lady Upstairs* is sharp, sly, and crackling with erotic tension. I didn't just read this one—I devoured it."

—Elizabeth Little, author of *Dear Daughter*

"*The Lady Upstairs* is seductive and as sharp as a knife sliding between your ribs. Feminist noir that should scare a few awful men into better behavior. Loved it."　　　　—Lori Rader-Day, author of *The Lucky One*

"Halley Sutton's *The Lady Upstairs* is a haunting, unforgettable debut that sizzles with menace and charm. This dark noir is loaded with mesmerizing characterization and a taut, always-moving plot that left me thirsty for more. Packed with well-crafted twists and a hypnotic voice, Sutton evokes the work of authors like Alafair Burke and Megan Abbott while adding her own unique verve and fire. I loved this book."

—Alex Segura, acclaimed author of *Blackout* and *Miami Midnight*

"Sultry, captivating, and electric with tension . . . With sharp, magnetic prose, Sutton dives into the darkness of women's lives, illuminating how venom and vulnerability are often two sides of the same coin."

—Megan Collins, author of *The Winter Sister*

"Halley Sutton's debut crackles with the unmistakable voice of its heroine, a cynical, wisecracking femme fatale straight out of a Raymond Chandler novel, who becomes enmeshed in a twisty tale of greed, betrayal, and vengeance. As dark as Megan Abbott and as voice-y as Lisa Lutz, this astoundingly self-assured debut ranks its author alongside the best in her genre. *The Lady Upstairs* is LA noir at its finest."

—Amy Gentry, author of *Good as Gone* and *Last Woman Standing*

"This diamond-blade feminist noir is near-impossible to put down. . . . A stunning new voice in LA noir, Halley Sutton has set the bar high. I can't wait to see what she comes up with next."

—Wendy Heard, author of *Hunting Annabelle*

"Savvy, seductive, twisted—noir at its best. Shrewd women enact vengeance to fill their empty pocketbooks and hollow souls. Sutton's timely plot will chill and resonate beyond the page."

—Vicki Hendricks, author of *Miami Purity*

"A stunning debut, noir as hell, filled with complex and daunting characters, and just a real good time."

Tod Goldberg, author of *Gangsterland* and *Gangster Nation*

"Sharp as a stiletto and twice as sexy, *The Lady Upstairs* is the smart, sultry noir we need right now. Sutton's feminist femme fatale heroine will seduce and intoxicate you, and you'll love every second of it."

—Layne Fargo, author of *Temper*

"A twisty, perfectly plotted, feminist crime noir that juxtaposes the glittering LA social scene with its gritty underbelly, this thriller sizzles with tension."

—Samantha M. Bailey, author of *Woman on the Edge*

The
Lady
Upstairs

Halley Sutton

G. P. Putnam's Sons / New York

PUTNAM
— EST. 1838 —

G. P. Putnam's Sons
Publishers Since 1838
An imprint of Penguin Random House LLC
penguinrandomhouse.com

Library of Congress Cataloging-in-Publication Data

Names: Sutton, Halley, author.
Title: The lady upstairs / Halley Sutton.
Identifiers: LCCN 2020013916 (print) | LCCN 2020013917 (ebook) |
    ISBN 9780593187739 (hardcover) | ISBN 9780593187746 (ebook)
Subjects: GSAFD: Mystery fiction.
Classification: LCC PS3619.U8944 L33 2020 (print) | LCC PS3619.U8944 (ebook) |
    DDC 813/.6—dc23
LC record available at https://lccn.loc.gov/2020013916
LC ebook record available at https://lccn.loc.gov/2020013917

Printed in the United States of America
10 9 8 7 6 5 4 3 2 1

Book design by Laura K. Corless

To my parents,
who didn't even flinch
when their baby girl handed them this book

The
Lady
Upstairs

Chapter 1

I'd picked the hotel for the sting because the bar had one hell of a happy hour—if you liked your drinks cheap and strong, the glasses washed maybe once in the last week. It was down the street from the studios, the right type of place to entice a movie man to meet an obliging blonde for a quick afternoon pick-me-up.

And not the least of my calculations: the St. Leo let me have my choice of adjoining rooms whenever I checked in, and didn't mind early arrangements or a quick redecoration, for the right price.

By my second drink, the apricot-tinted windows were purpling with twilight—happening so early these days—turning the light in the bar a good soft color for sloppy bad decisions. I was waiting on my third when I saw Ellen escorting the mark through the lobby to the elevator.

She stayed cool, didn't toss me so much as a backward glance. It was harder to do than it looked. But Ellen kept her eyes firmly on the mark's face, fingers curled around the patched elbow of his tweed blazer—a gift from one of his grandkids, no doubt, or one of the grown children benefitting from his production company's rampant nepotism. When I'd researched him for Lou and our shadowy employer, the Lady Upstairs, it had been one of the things that sold me: he kept his grabby sons on set, even after numerous complaints had been filed. I'd read that and thought: *This one's perfect.*

He looked at me—a swoop of terror in my stomach, but it was no more than the passing glance of a man surveying the room. I met his eyes and looked away without smiling, letting my gaze go through him.

Once they got upstairs: showtime.

Even on a Saturday afternoon, prime drinking hours, the bar was nearly empty. It was big business when a young couple sat down by the windows, and I watched them as I waited for the mark to reappear. Distracting myself. Her long honey-brown hair was ironed straight and scissored over her face, while his fingers plucked at the neck of his sweat-splotched shirt. They ignored each other and the fact that neither one of them was having any fun. She'd ordered something clear— vodka soda, I bet, unfussy and low-calorie, *See how low maintenance I am?*—and watched it melt all over her napkin.

They hadn't slept together yet, I was positive. Perhaps tonight was *the* night. Another bet: between the heat and the poor hotel accommodations and the fact that they were working hard to ignore each other, it wouldn't be a night to remember.

Making up stories about strangers is not usually in my nature.

"Relax, Jo, would ya?" Robert Jackal had said that morning, buttoning his shirt collar and studying himself in my bathroom mirror. Eyelashes longer than any woman's, but that was the only thing womanly at all about that carved handsome face, eyes pure no-hazel green, dark hair in disarray like a sleepy boy's, crunchy between my fingers. "It's not like you to be nervous."

Even before the sun was up, my walls sweated little beads of condensation. I was enjoying the coolness of the pillow against my cheek, starfishing my limbs and trying to find some chill in the spot he'd left. I didn't answer him.

"By the time I'm done, we'll have so much footage we won't know what to do with it all," he said, then bent down to kiss me on the forehead, reaching down to tap his fingers against the bracelet he'd given me as a birthday present a few years back, a mistake he hadn't repeated since. I'd slapped his face away.

As I waited, I piled my fleshless lime rinds into dimpled green pyramids. Keeping the trash to mark time, how many drinks I'd had, keeping my fingers busy so I wouldn't start doing algebra about Klein's net worth on the bar top. Three hundred twenty-six million meant he'd pay how much for photographs of his nasty predilections? What about for a video? Six blockbusters scheduled to come out in the next year meant a reputation was worth how much exactly? Fifty grand? More? My 20 percent of fifty grand would just about do it.

Calm down, I told myself. *In less than an hour, you'll have the prints. And this time tomorrow, or the day after, say, you'll have what you owe to the Lady Upstairs.*

Every three minutes, I allowed myself one long swallow of gin.

I let the couple distract me as I waited out Ellen's seduction. The girl's purse had crept from the floor to her lap, and now she clutched it tight between her knees like a chastity belt.

There are women who can spend time with men and manage to keep smiles on their faces no matter what. She wasn't one of them and I liked her for it.

The man said something, too low for me to catch, leaning in close and intimate. I leaned forward, too. The girl tilted her head. He placed both hands flat on the table and repeated it again, louder, slower. As though the problem was with her hearing. The girl rocketed backward, a blush throttling her neck, and then, slowly, deliberately, she tipped the three-quarters-full beer he'd been nursing into his lap. He jumped up and flapped his hands at his crotch, squawking. I laughed out loud.

And then there was the flare of the elevator as it opened on a familiar face—the mark, the object of every stakeout I'd sat through for the last three months, first me alone and then later, when I'd recruited her, with Ellen. He looked flustered. Pissed. I snuck a quick peek around the lobby. Luckily, most patrons were still tracking the beer-foam bath, and no one seemed to notice one of the wealthiest men in the city barreling for the door.

My pulse jumping, I reached for my purse steadily, measuring my movements in slow seconds, thankful for the commotion. I signaled to the bartender, slipping out a credit card and the room key in one motion, the number *345* scribbled in thick black strokes on an attached Post-it, being very careful not to turn and look at Hiram Klein.

Behind me, I heard someone from the bar call out, "*Hey*, aren't you that movie guy—" and I turned my head, but the mark, Hiram Klein, billionaire movie producer and launcher of a thousand careers, was hustling out of the lobby. The bar patron sat back down, not enticed enough to chase after *that movie guy.* The bartender handed me my check, and I smiled, cozying up to him across the bar top, skin buzzing, trying to imagine what celluloid gold Jackal must have gotten if Klein was that fired up.

"Was that a celebrity?" I asked him, testing the waters. I have a reckless streak sometimes.

"Not much of one," he said, and passed me my receipt.

The door to 345 opened with a smooth *click.* The bathroom was barely bigger than a closet, and I could hear the erratic drip of a leaky faucet. The room was 90 percent bed—no use wasting space. The only art on the walls was something Lou had picked out, a shamelessly tacky Thomas Kinkade wannabe's whale scene Jackal had mounted before Ellen and Klein arrived. The eye of the whale could take up to sixty minutes of video, but the Moby-Dick we were chasing hadn't needed it—he'd finished within thirty-five flat. The bedside alarm clock housed a speaker that Jackal monitored from the next room, magnifying everything said or whispered or moaned in that bed to a mountaintop yodel when you played it back.

In the center of the bed in question, legs butterflied, sheet dripping down her chest, was my girl Ellen. Her fluffy blonde hair was a nimbus around her head, and a few strands of it had been tugged out and dangled across the grayish-white pillowcases. A black-and-orange duvet was crumpled on the floor, like it had been yanked off. Ellen's big black eyes were glassy—a little bit thrilled, a little bit tearful—and one bright red mark clawed across her face. I could see the outline of two fingers forming on her cheek.

So he'd used an open hand this time.

"How'd it go?"

Ellen shrugged. "Same as before," she said. "A few slaps, during. A bit harder today for the video. I told him to prove he was a real man." Ellen rubbed her jaw and a little squeak came out of her. I hissed in sympathy—it was easy to be kind with the chorus of *mon-ey, mon-ey, mon-ey* galloping through my veins. I tapped on the adjoining door, eager for Jackal's playback.

No answer.

I had a bad feeling. I tried to ignore it. Maybe he was in the bathroom. I looked over my shoulder at Ellen, who was slowly combing her fingers through her pillow-fluffed hair. "Was the room already set up when you got here?"

She nodded. I tested the door for myself and it opened. I pushed at its mirror twin to reveal a bed and a bathroom. No light on. No sign of anyone. Not Robert Jackal, not the recording equipment he should've set up to catch Mr. Casting Couch *in flagrante delicto*, not even a note.

I didn't bother to close the door before I climbed up on the dresser, grappling the Kinkade down from the wall. I threw it on the bed, narrowly missing Ellen, who shrieked. The whale's eye was empty. Just an eye.

I let fly a string of expletives that came out of me twisted and nonsensical—"Fuck, fuck, fuck, that *asshole!*" A perfect goddamn opportunity and Jackal had wasted it.

"What's wrong?" Ellen asked. "He didn't get it?" Her voice took on a slight hysterical edge. "That was all for nothing?"

I ignored her and looked more closely around the room. Klein hadn't left anything behind, not a watch or a button, nothing to prove he'd ever been there.

Goddammit, Jackal. Eleven thousand dollars. That was all I needed. Eleven grand, and he'd fucked me out of it. There were two options I could think of as to why—another woman, a poker table—and neither was a good excuse for fucking me out of the last bit of the money I needed to pay off my debt to our boss.

I pressed my knuckles into my eyes until little comets pinged around my lids. *Think, Jo.* It was a setback, sure, but as long as Ellen hadn't blown it with Klein, we still had him on the hook. What was another week when I'd been waiting nearly three years to be clear of the Lady? It was nothing. Absolutely nothing.

As long as I still had Ellen on my side.

I pasted a sympathetic smile on my face and turned toward Ellen on the bed. "You okay?" I asked, my voice sweet enough to maraschino an onion.

"Yeah," she said, still working her jaw. "Sometimes I almost like it." She smiled for me, maybe putting on a brave face, maybe not. She'd been a good pick for this particular job.

"That's good, Ellen. I'm really happy to hear that. Because I'm going to need you to tough it out for me a little longer."

Ellen's face froze, and she tugged the sheet up to her chin. "I thought you said *this* was the last week."

"Plans change. It's the nature of the job."

Ellen's face reddened, and she sat all the way up, the sheet falling to her waist. If she thought I'd be impressed with the view, she was mistaken. "I can't do this another week!"

On the best of days, patience was not my strong suit, and this was no longer the best of days. "You have a better acting gig on the books?" I snapped. "You have any other producers breaking down your door?"

Ellen glared at me from behind her puffy thatch of blonde hair. "It's not exactly *empowering* to be acting like his mistress all the time."

I bit my tongue. Loose tempers weren't what I needed; what I needed was a compliant Ellen, still on my side. I sat down on the bed. I didn't touch her, but I let my hand get close so she knew I was making the effort to respect her space. The mark on her cheek would fade soon, I thought, but those slaps would've cracked like gunshots in the bedside mic. God*damn*.

"Ellen," I said—a person's name is usually their most comforting sound, which is also true for dogs—"Ellen, I'm really sorry. An emergency must've kept Jackal today, but I promise you, we won't miss it again. I need you to do this one little favor for me, and then it'll all be over. You'll have your money and you'll never have to see him again. And guess what? I bet he'll never smack another girl again in his life. He'll be too scared of what you could do to him."

I wasn't sure that was true, but I *was* certain he wouldn't guide another extra to the casting couch without thinking twice, that was for damn sure. And Ellen would know that *she'd* done that, *she'd* been the one to change him. I could see her turn it over. She furrowed her brow and stared into her lap, hard. Not a yes, not a no.

A week earlier, that little speech would have been enough. But now, she hesitated, which meant she doubted *me*. Which meant she was more dangerous than she'd been thirty minutes ago. *Jackal, you have fucked me now.*

"Please, Ellen." I hated myself. I hated her for making me beg. "One more time, for me."

"That's all? You promise?" Ellen sniffled and wiped her nose.

I hid my smile. "That's it."

Ellen nodded, but she didn't look happy. "Why did he storm out of here?" I asked to change the subject, reaching for her shirt on the floor. I tossed it behind me and let her have a few moments of privacy. I poked my head into the bathroom. The trash can was empty. Klein was so paranoid that if he'd used a condom, he'd flushed it. Or taken it with him.

"Oh," Ellen said, her tone light. Too light. Without looking at her I knew she was about to lie to me. I hoped Klein didn't find her so easy to read. "I asked what his wife would think if she knew he was here with me."

"That was enough to send him running?" I turned to stare at her.

There was a faint pink glow to Ellen's face now, and she was chewing on a thumbnail. "Hy is touchy about his wife," she said, trying for worldly. An ingénue on the make.

Hy. My final bet of the afternoon: she'd wanted something from Klein—maybe a comparison between her and his wife that found the Mrs. wanting. *Is she this sweet and juicy?* Or a token, maybe, of his esteem.

Oh, Ellen. I tried not to let my disgust show on my face. Whatever crumb of affection Klein could offer her was nothing compared to the cash—50 percent of whatever the mark paid—that waited for her on the other side of the sting. If I was right, if she cared so much about his approval that she was willing to pick a fight, then I wouldn't be able to manage her much longer.

"Better not to mention wives at all."

"You promise it's only one more time?" Ellen asked, her dark eyes suspicious and lovely.

"I promise. Just one more." I kept my voice soft, clipping any trace of a threat from it. I didn't want her scared of me yet.

I could save my threats for Robert Jackal, for now. The lying fuck.

"Come see me tomorrow at the office," I told her as I headed for the door. "We'll figure out a new plan. Together."

The last I could see of Ellen was her head nodding jerkily up and down as the door crashed closed behind me.

I was out of the elevator, heading for the parking lot, ready to call Lou—wanting to hear her voice, ready to not think about the near miss of the blackmail photos and the money I still owed our boss— when the beer spiller caught my eye. She'd taken my seat at the bar and ordered a bottle of wine, which she was making quick work of. Her soaked friend was nowhere to be found.

Reaching into my bag, I flipped a card between my fingers—my name and my number, nothing else—and scribbled on it, *Men are assholes, but I like your style. Call me if you want a free drink.* Then, for good measure, I wrote *NOT A DATE!!!* at the bottom, underlining it twice. I dropped it in front of her without looking.

"Hey . . . !" she called after me, but I didn't stop.

If she was the kind of girl I had any use for, *she* would chase *me*.

CHAPTER 2

Lou had picked up immediately. Told me she was sober and tired of it and where did I want to meet her? No, wait, she knew exactly the place: a tonga-hutted skid mark not far from the St. Leo. I met her there, a hole-in-the-wall terror of a tiki bar, walls painted a ghastly labial pink, canned thrums of an absent ukulele clogging the air.

Lou had a knack for finding the last place I'd ever want to go.

Break it up into little pieces, I'd told myself as I was leaving the St. Leo. *Call Lou. Figure out the next meetup between Ellen and Klein.* I had to make sure there was no way to fuck *that* up, even if I had to record it myself. And then, a little treat for last: *Murder Robert Jackal in his bed.*

I'd spent the majority of the ride trying Jackal's number. The rage boiling inside me had simmered to a slow burn by the time I hit traffic, but my fingernails left dents in the steering wheel.

Blackmail was only as good as its evidence. I *knew* that. All the research in the world wouldn't make up for a missed opportunity, and this one had been golden. Without tape, Ellen was a nobody. Another girl who wouldn't be believed. A fucking nightmare.

I slammed the dashboard with the heel of my hand so hard that by the time I met Lou at the bar, I had a bruise.

Weeks ago, at the start of the job, Lou had passed the Lady's envelope to me, the one with Klein's name in it, and I swear, I *swear*, her eyes had been shining when she'd said: "This should close it, right?" She hadn't needed to elaborate. We were both keeping track of how much I owed, even if Lou pretended she wasn't. It was my debt and my problem, but I knew it hung over her, too. It was a secret we shared, even if only one of us was paying for it.

Lou sat at a table uncluttered by other admirers. She was the best-looking woman in the bar—I was big enough to admit that. She was one of those beautiful women who never took much care of her face at all; the humidity had caused her mascara to bloom under her eyes, and her bright copper hair was damp at the temples. The heat had softened her like warmed chocolate.

Here's my idea of a good bar: a clean, ill-lighted space. No pink drinks. No hula statuettes. Certainly no dangling stuffed parrots strangled by fairy lights. But this bar had Lou. She looked up, smiled. The drink in front of her was so orange it glowed, turning the underside of her chin the color of a sunrise. It looked like the sort of drink that made you hug strangers before you hugged a toilet.

"Is it spring break already?" I slid into the seat across from her, catching the glass with the tip of my finger and stealing a sip from her straw. An explosion of sugar and foam and one sickly zing of rum down my throat. I grimaced, and Lou laughed.

"For six dollars a pop, you can rewire your palate," she said, grabbing the little purple umbrella from the glass and tucking it behind my ear. I brushed the garnish out of my hair and onto the floor. Lou laughed again, a full-throated sound. I could feel the disappointment and panic still tugging at me, but it was easier to ignore now, as though one sip of her cocktail had washed the taste of Robert Jackal's failings right out of my mouth.

"I ordered you the Bombs Away," Lou said. "Since we're celebrating."

Celebrating. Right. "Oh, you ordered *for* me."

"You'll like it."

"You know what I'd say to Jackal if he decided what I'd have without asking?"

Lou dimpled. "I have some idea. You'll drink it because I'm buying." She took another sip. "You like the place?"

Behind Lou, some kid at the jukebox threw on a classic rock song popular at least a decade before he was born, and the carved wooden hula dancer in the corner swayed offbeat. Every time someone ordered one of the specialty cocktails—*Enjoy Our Blasted Good Bikini Atoll!*, a Jäger bomb in the center of a lake of curaçao—a cardboard volcano spewed tissue-paper lava and cardboard people at its base shook and danced.

"*Hate* it," I said.

"You never like anything I like!"

"I don't think that's true. It's just that I have better taste in most things."

Lou arched an eyebrow. "Robert?"

"*Most* things."

A briny waitress plopped a disturbingly pink mug in front of me, a wilted purple flower starting to capsize in its frothy depths. "Bombs Away," she said with a smoker's rasp. I crinkled my nose and looked up at Lou skeptically, but she was crackling with delight, waiting to see if I'd actually drink it. I sniffed it—grapefruit and something that made my tongue curl. I took a sip: mezcal. Smoky and bitter and juicy.

"Not bad," I said to Lou.

"See? I know you better than you think." Lou reached out with one finger and gently tapped the corner of my mouth with her nail. A bead of sweat rolled along the inside of my knee, tickling. "Is that a new lipstick? No need to dress up for little ol' me." Lou cracked that lopsided grin, and her hand went back to her drink. A little red smudge lingered on it, then on the glass.

I resisted the urge to swipe at my lips. "I might be paying Jackal a visit later." And it was true, I might do that. There were many things I might do later that evening.

"I don't know if that means he's a lucky man or a very unlucky one."

"Somebody's gotta keep him in line."

Lou chuckled a little. "Always a thing for the bad boys," she teased.

"What use do either of us have for *boys*?"

Lou smiled at me, her face glowing. "So? How did it go with Klein? Tell me, tell me."

Jackal didn't show, that's how it went. "He's rough with her," I said. Trying to think up the best way to break the bad news.

Lou lifted one shoulder in a half shrug. But her eyes were still twinkling, so I knew it was a challenge, not a letdown. "Bor-*ing*. Besides, that can be fun."

I took another sip of my drink—going down easier all the time. "Not when you're the man who's made a living as the kindly cardiganed grandfather of Hollywood."

It was a thing Lou had taught me to do well: walk through the pitch ahead of time. *So you've got pictures of me naked with some broad. What do I care? Let 'em see.* You always had to have an answer. Besides recruiting and training the girls, it was the most important part of my job: crafting the pitch for maximum payout. And for Klein, I had the pitch down pat. Just no pictures. Yet.

Lou nodded her approval, drumming her nails on the bar. "It might not ruin him," she said, thinking her way through it, "but it'll mean he has to reinvent himself. And that could take years. He's, what—sixty-five?" I nodded, and Lou's nose crinkled, making the smattering of freckles across her nose dance. "I'm willing to bet he doesn't think he's got those years to waste. Oh, good work, my love." I choked on my drink, and Lou went on like she hadn't noticed: "This will set *her* mind at ease."

She didn't have to specify who.

I'd pestered Lou for years about details on the Lady Upstairs, the faceless woman who handed down our orders on the marks, and our paychecks. But there was a reason Lou was the only one who dealt with her directly. Even loaded, she was the soul of discretion. She never leaked any details, no matter how many drinks I poured her.

Jackal told me once he thought the Lady Upstairs was a retired movie star. I figured she was married to one of the old families of Los Angeles, those scions established a generation or two ago. She clearly had access to people with money. Maybe she wasn't even a she at all. Except too many of the marks, the names funneled to Lou and me in white envelopes, were bad men—cheaters, assholes, men who never heard a no. They weren't exclusively the men we targeted, but it was more than a passing coincidence. And I could understand why. Any woman could. I couldn't imagine a man sharing that vendetta.

But knowing the Lady had a personal hatred for bad men with money didn't really narrow the field.

I took a moment to wipe my chin with a tiny damp cocktail napkin. "Set her mind at ease?"

Lou stamped wet circles in the grain of the wood table with the bottom of her glass and didn't meet my eyes. "I didn't want to worry you. She told me— Anyway, it doesn't matter since you'll have the money tomorrow." Lou grinned at me, her dimples flexing.

I gulped the drink, wishing Lou had made it a double. I'd never had much of a poker face. My mother had always been able to tell when I was fibbing or upset—she said I looked like I'd swallowed my heart, exactly that phrase. Since my time as one of the Lady's girls, I thought I'd gotten better at hiding it, but Lou noticed. Lou always noticed. "What exactly did the Lady tell you?" I asked.

"What's wrong? You *will* have the money tomorrow, won't you?"

"By the end of the week," I said, trying to sound confident. It didn't convince either of us. "An equipment malfunction," I said. I didn't want to rat on Jackal, even as pissed as I was. "This time next week, we'll be laughing at him." I took another gulp of the drink and dared a glance at Lou's face. She was staring at me like she'd didn't understand what I was saying. I charged ahead. "I don't know what the big deal is, one more week when it's been three years—"

"Stop," Lou said. The fan above her churned hot air vigorously enough that little auburn strands undulated above her head. She was staring past me, and her eyes had gone glassy and dark.

In all the scenarios I'd imagined on the drive over, I'd pictured Lou irritated—pissed, more likely—but I'd also figured we'd talk it through together. Work out a new plan.

I'd never imagined the look on her face now.

"I know it's not ideal," I started to say, but Lou cut me off.

"The Lady wants to retire you," she said.

The sound that came out of me was between a cough and a laugh. "Yeah, sure," I said. "What sort of 401(k) is she offering?"

Lou's mouth was a tight, flat line. She reached for her purse and snapped it open. I watched her pull out everything inside—wallet, tampons, bullets and bullets of lipstick, even a piece of hard candy crushed into a thousand twinkling shards like a tiny butterscotch galaxy. Finally, she found her cigarette case and used trembling fingers to light up. It took her two tries.

She was scared, I realized. Lou was scared. I'd never seen it before.

"Come on, it can't be that bad—"

"What do you think, Jo, the Lady sends us off with a tidy severance package when things 'no longer work out'?" Lou gestured with her cigarette, and embers hopped onto the table where they flared and died. "Do you think girls like us get to go live quietly after this, dreaming of our wayward youth? Knowing what we know?" Lou shivered. It was infectious.

My head filled with water, like a kiddie pool inflating. A half-submerged memory, from my early days with the Lady: a woman, one of the Lady's runners, who'd dropped items from the Lady to Lou. She'd always stopped by Jackal's office, where she paused too long, laughing at his jokes, her mouth sticky like red vinyl, training her breasts on him like a sniper. We'd started up by then, but I wasn't jealous. I'd never be her, I thought, not with Jackal—my favorite thing about the man was that he didn't make me preen for his attention. But their familiarity had its own intensity, too, and I'd understood that he meant something to her—or maybe that she was trying to mean something to him. And then one day I realized I hadn't seen her around for weeks. I'd asked Lou, and she'd shrugged me off with some half-baked answer, some *don't worry about it* bullshit. I'd been dumb enough that I hadn't.

"She's done this before?" It was only half a question. "That woman. Jackal's ex. The Lady dealt with her, too?"

Lou stubbed out what remained of her cigarette. She didn't meet my eyes. Finally, she said, "Unpleasant business. Jackal understood."

I imagined that slick red mouth opened wide in a scream of terror, and I shuddered. So Jackal didn't mind that his workplace paramours had a shelf life. For all his assurances this morning, none of it had been as important as whatever shiny object had distracted him. The chills started in the pit of my stomach and moved up my spine to my scalp. "What do I do?"

"I'll talk to her," she said. "I'll beg her. But it has to be this week,

Jo. The money this week or"—she licked her lips and her eyes were pleading—"you'll have to leave Los Angeles. For your own good."

I gripped the edge of the table, trying to think. The ancient mariner of a waitress popped her head over Lou's shoulder to check on our drinks. Neither of us said anything. Eventually she got the memo and moved on.

Once we were alone, I promised Lou: "By the end of the week." She nodded and grabbed both my hands in hers, squeezing tight.

I didn't tell Lou the thing I'd noticed in Ellen, that Klein was more than a job to her now. It was our one unbreakable rule for the girls: don't get attached; never lose yourself in someone else. Once you developed feelings for the mark, you couldn't do your job. You couldn't see clearly, once you were attached. I should've told Lou then, but I had bigger concerns. So I was worried about Ellen, but not the way I should've been. I'd find a way to handle it, I told myself.

"I hope so," Lou said. "For both our sakes—I hope so."

The thing I wanted to say then, but didn't, was: *Lou, what we did all those years ago—we did together. I took the fall and I owe the Lady and it's my ass on the line, but it was as much you as it was me.* But I didn't say it. I wasn't even sure I believed it—that what had happened was as much Lou's fault as mine.

The glow of the evening had been ruined, and no matter how many of the Bombs Away I gulped, it couldn't quite lose its tarnish. By the time we decided to go home, get some rest, we were chattering about the usual things, both of us working hard to pretend nothing important had happened.

Lou leaned in to give me a hug as we reached her ride, and I could smell the lemon scent of her hair, her neck. I let go as soon as I could, but Lou clutched me tight. But when she broke the hug, her face was wiped clean of fear like it had never even existed.

"Headed home?" I asked, trying to ignore the feel of her still lingering in my arms.

Lou winked at me and turned away. "Tell Jackal I said hello," Lou called over her shoulder, her flinty grin a little cut beneath my breastbone.

"I don't think we'll have time to talk about you at all," I managed, feeling glad to see her go so I could process the Lady's threat on my own—even if it meant losing the plugged-in zip of her presence, of watching her face as I made her laugh.

At the last possible moment, I reached for her hand but caught only air and told myself it was for the best.

Jackal kept a key taped to the back of the fire extinguisher outside his apartment door, snuggled against the dry and gummy cobwebs that crisscrossed the back of the box. He trusted too much in the laziness of other people; it was a hiding place that would stop a determined thief for all of thirty seconds.

The apartment was still hot from the day, clammy almost, if walls can be clammy. I could hear the whirr-buzz of Jackal's air unit propped inside his bedroom window. I knew his place almost as well as my own. But I didn't want it to feel like mine. I didn't want anything of his to feel like mine.

I crept through his house on unsteady feet shucked of shoes. A small but tidy apartment. No stacks of books. Carpet always freshly vacuumed. He hired a maid to come in and clean everything twice a week, but that was never enough; he couldn't go to sleep unless he'd wiped down the counters and cleaned every dish. But the ceiling was pocked with asbestos and the tiles beneath the sink were mushy. Jackal was all freshly closed seams and tight corners, as though that could hide the rot underneath.

Robert Jackal: inveterate gambler, enforcer, and photog for the Lady, sometime paramour to me and any other disposable dark-haired vixen who strolled through the office.

I slipped through his foyer, past his kitchen, which smelled of lemons, like Lou's hair, and into his bedroom. Jackal's bedspread was tugged down to his waist. Wiry black chest hair rose and sank with each breath. I wondered how far down his body that naked went. I stood in the doorway for a moment, carpet swaying beneath me like a choppy sea.

It disarmed me to watch him sleep. Those shoulders I knew so well, pocked with glowing half-moon reminders of me, his dark lashes fluttering as he dreamt. Staring at him, I thought there weren't enough words in the dictionary for the things we were—not friends, lovers certainly, but something and nothing more, too. And then he stirred and frowned, a dark lock of hair falling over his perfect face, and the anger took root.

I wanted to slap him awake. I leaned down and pressed a kiss lightly to the corner of his mouth. He grunted and twitched but didn't wake up. I slipped my pantyhose down but left the dress on. In the dark, the gray-green of his sheets looked like swamp water. I eased back his covers and sat on top of him. Jackal's eyelids fluttered. He started to sit up and I pressed him back down, moving a knee over his most sensitive part as I dragged my nails around the edges of his jaw. I wanted to scrape him raw and eat the leftover bits.

He looked at me, groggy still, and opened his mouth to say something, but I leaned down and cupped my hands over his eyes, pressing gently at first and then harder when I could feel his eyelashes flickering back and forth. I kissed my way down his chest, stopping to tease his nipples first with my tongue and then my teeth, tugging until he yelped. I brought my mouth to his face and bit down on his lips. The mood I was in, I could rip one off and not notice. Farewell to that lovely face.

He tasted like night sweats and nicotine, and I could almost detect the tangy smell of well-handled cash, which gave me a clue where he'd been when he was supposed to be with me. I pressed down harder on his eyes. I imagined sliding my fingernails into his green circles. Jackal let out a strangled sigh. I wondered if he knew what I'd been dreaming of, but I slipped him into me so easily. One hand drifted up, reaching for me. I let his thumb hollow out in my collarbone, pressing hard enough to feel a sharp crack under my skin. He tried to bring his other hand to the back of my neck, bend me over him, but I wouldn't let him. I didn't want any sort of affection from him tonight.

I rocked on him, clamping my thighs against his ribs, until I could feel the old familiar sparks moving from my toes to my scalp. I didn't want to see his face, so I pressed it away from me, cranking his head into the pillow until he grunted in pain. I liked the feel of him underneath my hands, and I wished they were larger, like a man's, so I could really hurt him. I imagined him panicked and trying not to show me, wondering what I would do to him, how far I was going to take this, and it sent me over the edge.

As I came, I bit his thumb hard enough to draw blood. I could tell that he was close, too, by the hitch in his breathing, but there had to be some sort of punishment for standing me up at the St. Leo, so I slid off him with no warning. He gazed up at me, pumping recklessly for a moment, mouth gaping like a fish. I leaned down and slapped him, once, twice, until I could see my hand's red shadow on his face.

"Listen to me," I hissed. "I don't care where the hell you were or who you were with, but you better thank your lucky goddamn stars I convinced Ellen to see Klein again. If you fuck *that* one up for me, I'll do worse than this, understand?" He blinked up at me, mute, and I felt a rush of hatred. I wasn't sure if it was for him or myself or both of us.

I gathered my stockings and swayed unsteadily out of his bedroom into the kitchen, where the lemon smell was making me dizzy. It followed me all the way back to my car and into my own bed and even, it seemed, my own dreams.

CHAPTER 3

The Lady Upstairs' Staffing Agency was located in the center of Little Busan Plaza, on the second floor, above Fish Heaven Aquarium Repair and Seven Galbi BBQ, and between a nail salon that never did any business—I had my own theories about that—and a payday loan shop that had long since been closed.

You could say we brought style to the place.

Seven Galbi was the main attraction, and their delicious specialty beef kept me shampooing my hair every day, trying to get the smell out. It was not the aphrodisiac you might have supposed. On weekends and at night, the restaurant was so crowded that we had to give the valet our keys. But during the day, I could've parked my car across three spaces and there still would've been room to spare. That day, there were only two other cars parked in the lot, a gray Mercedes and an oxidizing Honda that had once been beige.

It was a habit from another lifetime, one I couldn't seem to shake, the need to be at the office by 8 a.m. Even when I knew Lou and Jackal wouldn't be in for hours still. Even when I was so hungover I couldn't remember my zip code. But that morning, having the threat of the Lady hanging over my head added an extra incentive. I needed all the time I could get to figure out Ellen's next rendezvous.

I could feel Jackal and last night between my legs with each stair up to our office—the pleasant soreness of the well fucked, a little throbbing ache that lives in you like a secret—taking the steps two at a time to feel it deeper. It gave me something to focus on while I gnawed on the soft guts of a croissant, my pantyhose already sweat-chafing my thighs from the single flight of stairs.

Even this early in the morning, the smell of browning meat wafted up with me. I suppressed a gag. The sun bounced off the aluminum roof and cast dusty rays into my hangover, subtle as a spotlight, and I kept my head ducked like I was trying to crawl up the stairs incognito.

I'd almost bumped into her before I looked up.

She could've been twenty-five or forty, depending on which part of her you were looking at, with the calves of a go-go dancer and the carefully moisturized lipstick lines of a well-tended woman battling the inevitable with grace. She wore a silk blouse the color of a ripe melon, and the inch of dark roots under her bottle job seemed exactly right—the obvious artifice making it clear how good she looked. Large smoky sunglasses shaded her eyes, and she had one hand on our door. I couldn't tell if she was coming or going.

"Hullo," she said. Her voice was low for a woman, and her fingernails were painted a bright blue. She tapped one against the door and then her hand dropped. Around her wrist, another slim circle of blue. I squinted. A tattoo, little stars inked in a faded denim color.

"Can I help you?"

She flipped her sunglasses to the top of her head and studied me for a moment. Her dark eyes were bright but flat, the way I'd always heard sharks' eyes described. Behind her ear, I could still make out the faintly tattooed outline of Perfect Alignment Massage's logo on our door, the business that had owned the joint until the Lady came along.

"No," she said, "I don't think you can." She didn't move. I didn't, either.

When the Lady had taken over the lease, back when Lou's and my little side project had gone wrong and we'd needed cover, she'd registered our business as a staffing agency. It gave us cover for the shuffle of girls coming by the office, and more importantly, it gave us respectability. We'd created our cover so well that occasionally, we got mistaken for a real staffing agency. Sometimes, when business was slow and Lou was bored, she'd even take jobs and place girls for the hell of it, adding the seventy-five-dollar check to her rainy-day fund.

Half distracted, digging through my purse for the key and wondering how quickly I could reasonably expect Ellen to reschedule with Klein, I started to say, "Are you looking for a temp? Because I'm about to—" But she held up a hand. She hadn't blinked since she'd taken off her sunglasses.

"Be a dear and give this to Lou for me," she said, handing me a white envelope embossed with a blue fleur-de-lis. My scalp began to prickle. "I'd prefer it go to her *unopened*," she added as she sashayed past me down the stairs, and I stepped automatically out of her way, then wished I hadn't.

"Excuse me," I called after her, but she held up a hand so I could see each cobalt almond perfectly. The diamond on her ring finger, big enough to anchor a small yacht, caught the sun, and little sequins of light burst across my face. My scalp prickled again, harder.

I dropped the croissant and followed her down the stairs, not sure what I meant to say, but she turned before I reached the bottom, one hand on the driver-side door of the Mercedes, like she'd been expecting me to follow, like it was a script, and said: "Lou told me you were pretty, but high hopes are such a bitch, aren't they? Nowhere for them to go but down."

And then she turned the engine and drove away.

Across the street, a congregation of women gathered on greenery in front of a flat-topped church. I watched her drive away, memorizing her plate number before I felt the eyes of someone else on me—one of the women clustered on the lawn, moving their arms in circles and slow spins, somewhere between kung fu and ballet. A sunglassed dumpling of a grandmother had her face tipped in my direction, and I held up a hand, dazed.

She gave me the finger.

I walked back up the stairs and unlocked the door. The massage parlor had left us with a small waiting area. Behind the front desk, there were three doors that led to separate offices for each of us. At the very back of the office proper, a bathroom, a sink, and a little balcony that afforded a view of dark glossy skyscrapers. At the front desk, a phone that almost never rang was nestled among neatly collated file folders.

At the front desk, I jotted down the license plate number on the back of the envelope in letters as small as I could manage. And then I peeked inside. It didn't disappoint.

I stood listening to the envelope chatter in my hands, and that was how Jackal found me, pushing open the now-unlocked door. He snarled something rude at me, a word I only liked to be called behind bedroom doors, but it passed over my head. It didn't matter. We would say and do worse to each other before our dance was over.

"Did you see her?" I asked.

"What? Who?"

"Blue nail polish."

"Are you still drunk?" He shouldered past me to his office, the massage table long since replaced by a desk, even though his door still bore a trace of a lotus-flower sticker.

"The Lady Upstairs wears blue nail polish," I said out loud, to no one.

Lou didn't get to the office until noon, which surprised me: she'd had less to drink than me, and said she was going straight home. But my morning hadn't gone to waste, at least: one call to Klein's secretary had confirmed an opening in his schedule—for a prostate exam, which wasn't exactly a lie—on both Thursday and Saturday afternoons. She'd promised to hold the spots in his calendar while she confirmed with him. I called the St. Leo and booked rooms for both afternoons, to be safe.

I sat at my desk, thinking about how the Lady's blue fingernails would look wrapped around my throat, when Lou popped her head into my doorway. Her hair was dark and slightly damp, and she grinned at me, fresh and not hungover.

"Guess what!" Lou chirped.

I winced, sliding the Lady's envelope into my desk drawer. "Good morning to you, too," I said drily. "Or, I should say, afternoon. You're in a good mood."

"I'm a miracle worker," Lou said, twirling into the seat across from me. I let out a breath I felt like I'd been holding for a month. "You've got until Friday."

I bit off a tight smile in Lou's direction. If I could convince Ellen, a Thursday afternoon rendezvous left a one-day turnaround. It was *just* possible. "Thank you," I said with stiff lips. If Lou noticed I was less than thrilled, she didn't show it.

"And," Lou said, "I got this." She held up another envelope, a twin of the one I'd tucked away in my desk. I jerked in my chair and tried to disguise it as a cough. "A new name," Lou announced, her lopsided smile turning wicked. "We're in a busy season." She chucked the envelope onto my desk and then draped herself in the chair across from me.

As I opened it, pulling out the folded note—one single line, not even a full name, no other information: *M. Carrigan*—Lou asked, "Have you set the new date with Ellen?"

I danced the mouse across the pad at my desk, waking up my computer and typing in *M. Carrigan, Los Angeles*. "I'm expecting her any minute," I said. "Where did you get this? Was it on your desk?"

Lou yawned, wide—goddammit, what *had* she been doing?—and shrugged. "Yep."

Maybe the envelope the Lady had handed me was a test, a way to prove that even now, deadline looming, I was still loyal to her. "Lou, wait a second, let me—"

"Mitch Carrigan," Lou went on happily. She was never as happy as at the beginning of the grift. All those possibilities still out there, all those different ways to ruin an asshole's life.

Then it clicked.

"Carrigan? Like the city music hall Carrigans, those Carrigans? Old-money founding-fathers-of-Pasadena Carrigans, *those* Carrigans?"

"One and the same," Lou said, her expression smug. "Ours. All ours. And once you're done with Ellen"—her smile wavered—"we can work it together. Like the old days."

"Like the old days," I repeated. A sharp memory of a bra-clad Lou clutching my arm, fighting down giggles. Our very first case all over again—only this time, we wouldn't leave any loose ends.

Lou came to my side of the desk so we could read the articles together on my screen. She rested her elbows on my back, sharp points that made me shiver as she shifted positions, shiatsuing my shoulder blades. *"Mayoral dark horse thunders into the lead."* She read the *Times* headline over my shoulder. Goose bumps rose on my skin each time her elbows slipped. *"Family name pays dividends for would-be mayor."* She read another, yawning again.

I shrugged her elbows off me and skated my chair backward so I could look at her. I could see each pale freckle on her nose. I could probably count them if I tried. I wanted to tell her I didn't have time to waste on a new mark, not when I had four days to turn around Klein or else leave her and this life we'd built together before the Lady put me down like a dog shot in the street.

"Lou, I should tell you— Is that the same blouse you were wearing yesterday?"

"Hmm?" Lou had moved to the bar cart she'd bought to celebrate my first anniversary with the Lady—the same day I'd paid off twenty large on the debt—and was fixing a cocktail, humming as she did. My mouth watered, not pleasantly, and I narrowed my eyes at her back. Black, linen, sheer—I was almost positive I was right. I heard the chime of the front door—Jackal leaving. Even better. I didn't want him to overhear what I was about to say.

"Never mind," I said quickly. "Lou, come here and tell me if—"

Lou turned around, toasting me with a tumbler of tea-colored liquor, capsizing a maraschino cherry. "It'll be tricky, but *Mitch Carrigan,* our biggest score ever—"

"Hello?"

Ellen rapped two small fingers on my office door and pushed it open, but she didn't step inside. Her hair was pulled away from her face with a clip, which was a mistake—it wasn't that kind of face. A small cluster of acne blossomed on her chin. She was wearing blue jeans and a tight pink sweater with embroidered pom-poms, and she looked younger than legal.

Lou's mouth dropped open, but she recovered quicker than I did. "Hello," she said, pulling Ellen in for a kiss on each cheek. "So nice to see you again." Ellen stammered something back, half dazed. Lou could have that effect on people. It was why I'd had Lou meet Ellen and me for drinks at the St. Leo back at the beginning of the case: she was still the best at making the girls see past the payoff and *want* to be involved with what we did. Lou could sell anything.

There's a magic Lou has, a certain kindness in her face. It's a small miracle, finding a nice face in this city. People respond to it, even when they shouldn't. Even when she was wearing day-old clothes and no makeup and hadn't gotten enough sleep because God knew why.

"Ellen, a little birdie told me you're *killing* this case. Jo says you're one of the best we've ever had." Lou smiled, warm and homey, and Ellen smiled back, a little uncertainly, making knots of her fingers and venturing a glance at me as Lou tugged her to my desk.

I was not smiling, not at either of them. I was wondering exactly how much Ellen had overheard and why she looked like such a flight risk.

I studied them as Lou chattered away at Ellen, tossing compliments her way, reaching out once to tuck some of Ellen's frizz back against her head. Something Lou taught me years ago, good advice to live by: never trust women who don't like other women. At the rate Lou was working Ellen, the three of us would be tangling together friendship bracelets by happy hour.

Finally, Lou pushed away from the desk and tossed a half-penitent shrug at me, as though she truly regretted leaving. "I'll get out of your hair now," Lou said, smiling over dazzled Ellen's head at me, widening her eyes so I knew she, too, was wondering how much Ellen had heard, and shut the door behind her. Ellen stared after her, ignoring me. She didn't want to meet my eyes, I realized.

Later, I thought about how it might have gone if I'd been wise enough to play nice, be the smart older sister with a plan. But I couldn't stop thinking about the Lady with her blue nail polish and her easy disposal of the girls she'd once worked with, and the envelope in my desk I hadn't quite managed to mention to Lou, and speaking of Lou, where the hell had she gone last night after the bar, and then there was that hangover to consider, no small thing, the mezcal that was refusing to play nice with the gin. Maybe if any one of those things had been different, everything would have been.

There's excuses, and then there's excuses.

Instead, I didn't say anything. I didn't get up from my desk. Ellen was frozen, half turned to the door. I kept my eyebrows raised, waiting for her to make the first move. Finally, she took a step toward the chair, moving tentatively. She searched my face for an invite to sit and, when it wasn't forthcoming, bypassed it and circled the room.

She paused in front of the drink cart. She turned the bottles this way and that, no doubt looking for something to do with her hands. Coming across like she'd never seen liquor before.

Maybe with Klein's money in her pocket, the knowledge of what she could do to a powerful man, she wouldn't always wait for other people to tell her what to do. I hoped so. I wasn't convinced.

"Is this a good time?" Ellen asked finally, turning to me and rubbing her pale lips together. Her fingers drummed against the cart. Nervous. She'd been thinking since last night. I didn't like it.

"As good a time as any. Pour me a drink and let's get down to business."

Ellen's mouth dropped open, a *who, me?* thing that made me want to slap her.

"A . . . drink?"

"Gin. Straight."

Ellen reached down on autopilot, hand hovering over the black glass bottle, and I felt a little smile in my chest, *aha*. I still had her. But then she pulled her fingers back like she'd been burned and said, "You want me to pour you a glass of gin?"

"Not all the way full. A few fingers, not the whole hand. It's still early."

She didn't like it, but because I'd done my job well and picked a girl who could take a few slaps but couldn't figure out if she minded, she yanked the top off the bottle like it had done something ugly and personal to her and dunked a few splashes into two separate tumblers.

She slammed the glass down on the desk, a few drops of gin splashing up onto my neck, and sat down in the chair across from me with even more force, crossing her legs and bouncing her foot up and down. It was a practiced move, not comfortable, like she'd seen someone do it in a movie once. She swirled her glass of gin and bent her face to it, sniffing. She took one big slug and her nostrils flared. But to her credit, she choked it down. I almost laughed.

"Oh my God," she said. "Do you have any ice, at least?"

"No," I lied.

She nodded, up and down, up and down, a little sad about the state of the world she'd found herself in. But I still had her. And even better, she was so distracted, she didn't seem to have picked up on anything she might've overheard between me and Lou. Good.

I kept it brisk and all business. "Klein's free Thursday afternoon. I've booked the St. Leo already so all that's left is for you to call him—"

Ellen was turning red, and she started to shake her head. She mouthed something, but no sound came out, and I watched her face as I talked until the words exploded out of her: "No! No, no, Thursday isn't going to work. No!"

The hangover was making it hard for me to focus on anything other than the blotchy red spots spreading across her cheeks.

"What, you have other *plans?* Okay, if Thursday's no good, we could—"

"Thursday isn't going to work because I'm not doing this anymore," Ellen said. "Any of it. I mean it. I'm out. Finish the job without me because I'm done."

CHAPTER 4

It was lucky for me that Ellen was not a good negotiator. After her outburst, she couldn't stop talking—she didn't uncork so much as explode.

"You can keep the money, that's fine, that is fine with me," she said. The more she repeated the word, the less I believed her, and I was right: "Although technically I've been working for weeks, so maybe we could come up with some sort of pro-rated— But all I'm saying is that I'm not doing it anymore. And that's final. Nothing you can say would convince me. Nothing. Zilch. That is all I'm saying. I mean it."

Mistake one: never speak first.

I folded my hands at my desk and watched her. She was breathing hard—emotional—no doubt scared of what I would say. Which meant I still had some power over her. That was good to know. The threat of the Lady's forced retirement beat in my head like a second heart, but I kept my face as blank as I could.

"You know, you said to me, two, three weeks tops. You made it

sound like it was going to be a lot of fun, like I'd be getting to play
dress-up and having great sex and eating fancy dinners and . . ."

My patience was a very dry well. What was dinner and dress-up
compared with bringing Hollywood's richest scumbag to his knees?
"He hasn't been feeding you? He hasn't made you feel real pretty?"
Easy, Jo. You need her more than she realizes.

"Do you know what it's like, having to fuck that old man? And
then he *hits* me," she said, as if I didn't know. "I'm not doing it again.
The way he *looks* at me. God." She raised a hand to her cheek—the
outline from the afternoon before had faded, but I was willing to bet it
was still tender. She bit her lip and sucked on her teeth. I remembered
she was trying to make it as an actress in this town. Well, who wasn't.

"Okay," I said.

Ellen was working up a good cry, her dark eyes glistening and
slick. She was so shocked, she choked mid-sniffle and gaped at me.
Now she didn't know what to do with all that effort.

Mistake number two: tears worked on men; they were wasted
on me.

"What? What did you say?"

"I said *okay*. It's been a tough case. We fucked up. We promised you
a schedule, and you've kept up your side of the bargain. We didn't.
Tough shit for me, but that's the way it goes sometimes." I even worked
up a smile for her, gnashing my teeth together.

"*Really?*" Ellen exhaled, and her shoulders dropped about a foot
from her ears to her knees. She beamed a beatific smile of relief in my
direction, like the Virgin Mary successfully pleading a headache to
the Holy Spirit.

"Sure, no hard feelings. I get it. He's a tough man to get it slick for.
We'll grab Lou and cash you out. But let's celebrate all your hard work
first. To your perseverance," I said, raising my glass. Ellen raised hers
in return, but she set it back down without taking a sip. The juniper

quieted my headache a little but not nearly enough. "You've been lovely, Ellen. Truly. Thank you for your service."

I paused the tumbler of gin halfway to my lips before I set it back down on the desk, as though I'd just remembered something. *Ka-thunk.* A solid weight to these tumblers Lou had bought, I mused. In a pinch, you could use 'em to murder a pesky blonde.

"It's too bad you won't get a chance to say goodbye," I said. "To *Hy.*"

Ellen flinched at the sound of his name—*aha*. "That's—that's fine . . . What do you mean?"

"I mean," I said, trying not to enjoy it yet—there were so many ways it could still go wrong, "we'll have to terminate your work on set. It's in your contract, a small clause—we rarely have to use it, but it seems these are exceptional circumstances."

"All right," Ellen warbled. "That's . . . all right."

"And you understand the precautions we'll have to take, of course. Calling the wife is never fun, but we have to be sure you don't see him again. You get it." I plucked my phone from the desk and held it out to her. Conspiratorial. Like we were girlfriends crank-calling local dreamboats at a sleepover.

Ellen blanched. "*What?* I'm not doing that!"

There was a near-dead part of me that admired her, clinging to the memory of her life before me, the time when I didn't call the shots. I'd seen Klein up close. He was doughy without being fat, which was, somehow, worse, an inch of pale flab separating him from the younger version of himself, with the skin of an unpaved street. I had the image of her cradled between his splayed legs, and it made me shudder.

But had my first mark been any different, or worse? You didn't do it to fuck men you liked.

"Lou's policy," I said, faux apologetic. "To make sure none of the girls run jobs with our marks on their own." I shrugged. "What can I say, it works."

"You want me to . . . to call her? You want me to tell his wife that we're—that we've been—"

"I promise you, he'll never bother you again after that," I said. "Plus, I thought you were so eager to know what she'd *say* yesterday at the hotel, about the two of you together. I thought you'd enjoy the opportunity." I held my breath, wondering if I'd tipped it too far.

Ellen's big brown eyes got watery, and she cocked her head, a kicked puppy. *No*, I thought. *She can take a bit more.* "Why are you so *mean?*"

"Here, I'll dial." I started to punch the numbers in, and Ellen practically vaulted over the desk to knock the phone out of my hand. She glared at me, more fire in her face than I expected.

"Stop it! Stop. I'm not doing it anymore, I told you," Ellen said, her voice squeaky but harsh. "I'm not calling anyone and I'm not seeing him again. That's final."

"Come on, Ellen, if you want out, you've gotta—"

"I can make calls, too, you know." Now she was standing straight, towering over me still seated at my desk. "What if I make a call to Mitch Carrigan's office and warn him about this, this, this *honeypot brothel* you're running here, huh? Tell him he better watch his back because I have it on *very* good authority he's the next target. What if I do that, huh?"

Her threat bounced around my office, getting bigger with each passing second. In the vacuum, just the sound of both of us breathing—Ellen, hard; me, barely at all. No air at all while I thought of what Lou would say, what the Lady would think, not only that I'd screwed the Klein job to bits—all those weeks of preparation and we'd end up with *nothing*—but that I'd managed to scuttle our newest job, too. "Mitch Carrigan, our biggest score ever," Lou had said, practically bouncing on her toes. There'd be no salvaging that fuckup, no matter how much Lou begged. And it was Lou she'd overheard. Lou would be on the line then, too. The thought struck me cold.

I stood up. Even in flats, I was taller than Ellen by more than an inch or two, and she stumbled back and almost tripped ass-first into the chair. But I bypassed her and walked to the liquor cart, grabbing the gin myself. My hand drifted over the bottles as I thought of what to say. No answers in any of them, but it didn't stop me looking. I topped off my own glass and then waved the bottle under Ellen's nose, but she twisted away like I'd raised a hand to slap her. I took a long deep drink, and when I came out of the glass, I knew what I was going to do.

I pulled the Lady's fleur-de-lis envelope from the drawer and held it out to Ellen. "For Thursday. On top of your cut."

"What?"

Ellen snatched the envelope from me so quick it sliced a finger. I popped it in my mouth and sucked on the welling blood as I watched her open it. Her eyes went wide. Inside: a folded piece of paper, the same weight as the envelope, the same embossed blue fleur-de-lis in the corner. Of course the Lady had a stationery set. When you rubbed the two halves of the paper together, they made a lovely *shish-shish* sound, like silk on skin. In thick marker strokes on the page: *A monthly courtesy for our brave blues.* Ellen tossed the paper and the envelope onto the desk without sparing either a glance.

Beneath the folded piece of paper, bundled together with a rubber band, a thick wedge of crisp green. The money, I'd realized when I'd peeked inside the envelope, must be the monthly bribe the Lady paid the cops. To ensure they looked the other way in case one of our marks decided it was worth the public humiliation to complain about what we did.

"There must be thousands of dollars here!"

"Eight large," I said, half wishing I could grab it back out of her hands.

"This on top of what I already get?"

"That's right."

It was more money than she'd make in at least three months any-where else and I knew it. More importantly, she knew it. I regretted offering it even as she shoved the money into her purse. I thought of her threat to tell Carrigan. I hadn't expected that.

"I'll assume this means you're free Thursday."

Ellen stood up and smoothed out invisible wrinkles over her mid-dle. Her cheeks were red and blotchy, but she wasn't crying anymore. "All right. One more time. *And that's it.*" Still trying to be firm, show me how in charge she was. I wanted to say her pique was wasted—that she should save it for Klein; that empowerment came from topping *him*, not me—but I couldn't. The weight of what I'd just done—and what I owed the Lady *now*—was stuck in my throat like a tumor. "Thursday, the St. Leo—and you *will* be there, right?"

"Yes." With Jackal in tow, dead or alive, and more than one cam-era, just in case.

She told me she'd call me with the time when they'd settled on it. I watched her face as she said it—she'd surprised me twice today, which was two times too many—and thought the odds were close to even that she'd try to find some way to wiggle out of it once Thursday came. I'd need a backup plan. But that's what the Lady paid me for.

As she was leaving, Ellen turned at the door, and said, "You know, when I first met you, I thought I wanted to be exactly like you. You were wearing these snakeskin pumps and leather pants, and it wasn't even 10 a.m. yet, you were at the *dentist*, for chrissakes, and I thought, *Now, there's a woman who knows what it's like to take what she wants instead of waiting to see what's left when the world gets around to her.* I thought, *What would it be like to be dangerous?*" She laughed again, unhappily, shaking her head. "And now I know you, this world you slither around in, and you know what?"

I wondered if she'd start crying again or tell me she wished she'd never met me. My lips twisted and my nail tinked against the crystal tumbler. In that pink sweater, she looked sixteen years old, the little sister I'd never had, except the coloring was all wrong. *She's too short-sighted to see what I'm doing for her, what we're doing together by taking down assholes like Klein,* I thought, right before she surprised me for the third time that day: "I still think I want it. It's the craziest goddamned thing."

And then she left, taking with her the Lady's bribe money for the police, and leaving me back in a hole that looked, from the bottom of it, exactly nineteen grand deep.

CHAPTER 5

After Ellen left, I tried to clear my head, get back to Carrigan. But it was no good. Nineteen grand now and a week to pay it back—my stomach dropped. Less, I realized. It wouldn't take the police long to discover their hush-hush money was missing. I couldn't count on more than a few days before they brought it up to the Lady and put their heads together and figured out where the cash had gone. If everything went *perfectly*, I'd have the money Friday. But now I'd need more from Klein, I realized. If we got fifty grand for the photos, that meant my cut was twelve point five. I needed nineteen now. Which meant I had to get seventy-five from him. The slaps might not be enough to warrant that kind of money. Ellen might have to deal with something worse than slaps. I tried not to think of what that might be.

It became a chant in my head—*something worse, something worse*—as I scrolled through different clips of the new mark, killing time so I didn't go crazy waiting to hear back from Ellen. Or imagining which would be worse: the Lady forcing me into "retirement" or what the police would do to all of us if I couldn't deliver their money quickly. *Something worse*, I thought, trying to focus on Mitch Carrigan's handsome face.

He was the best-looking politician I'd ever seen—one of the best-looking *men* I'd ever seen. A jaw like a lantern, dark blue eyes like a pair of sapphire earrings. A full head of graying hair, shoulders that filled the entire photo frame and then some. Movie-star handsome, but in a nonthreatening way, a believable way. I wondered how far that Carrigan ambition stretched.

It made me uneasy, that face. A face like that tended to mean a girlfriend at every campaign stop and a full team dedicated to crushing unseemly rumors. If the Lady had picked him, there were good odds he had *some* major flaw. The unimaginative one was easy to guess.

But that wasn't the only problem. For another thing, he was too connected.

Our marks had to be wealthy—whether they were handpicked by the Lady herself or chosen by those who hired her via gimlet-soaked referrals given poolside at the Beverly Hilton, the chic set dispatching blackmail orders from a cabana—or the marks had to be well connected and visible, able to lay their hands on tiny mountains of cash quickly. But Carrigan was another level of wealthy, a name synonymous with the founding of our city. There wasn't a cop, or an attorney, in this city who didn't know that name. You couldn't drive half a block without finding some memento of his family lineage. The Carrigans would be no strangers to blackmail. They wouldn't scare easy. They would have friends with the right connections.

That did worry me.

I filled a mug half with coffee and half with gin, then went back to my computer, clicking play on a video accompanying one of the latest news articles.

A perky reporter with the whitest teeth I'd ever seen was interviewing a woman in a navy-blue blazer, hair chopped into a frosty bob. The bottom of the screen identified her as *Tana Carrigan, Wife of Mayoral Candidate*, and then, in small letters, *Philanthropist.* Carrigan's choice of bride would tell me as much about him as anything I could find online. I turned up the volume.

"Tell me about your husband's plans, if he's elected," the reporter said.

Tana smiled, drawing a perfectly French manicured hand through her hair, which shook itself out and settled back into the exact same position. "He really cares about this city," she said. "The Carrigans have deep roots in Los Angeles. Who better to run it?"

"And has he always had political aspirations?" the reporter asked, seemingly not caring that Tana hadn't answered her question.

"He's always wanted to make a difference," Tana said. "It was one of the first things that drew me to him." I pictured Carrigan's cut-marble jawline, those steel blue eyes. *One* of the first things.

"Some have said it's your family's ambition, and not your husband's, that he run for office. Care to comment on that?" This reporter had finally grown some teeth.

I watched Tana's face creak under her Botox, but her immaculate smile didn't flag for a second. "*Some,*" she said. "Is it good journalistic practice to cite vague, unnamed sources?"

The reporter had the grace to look flustered. "I think your constituents have a right to know."

"Oh, by all means." Someone had taken plaster to Tana's face. She couldn't stop smiling if she tried. "Go on."

"Well, there's the fact that he made the nontraditional move of taking your name upon marriage. Which *some* have said is to cash in on your family's legacy and increase voter recognition."

Tana flicked a hand in front of her face, as if waving away a gnat.

"That was all Mitch's decision. I would say to those *unnamed sources*, you don't know my husband. No one can make my Mitch do anything he doesn't want to do." There was only a touch of murder in her voice.

The interview switched to a family picture of the wife, the candidate, and a towheaded cherub who was pink all over, like a half-cooked ham. It was unfortunate, the way attractive people never seem to breed well. I studied Carrigan on the screen. Those shoulders had my vote, and probably that was true for a lot of other women in this city.

So he'd taken his wife's last name. I kicked that one around in my brain for a bit but couldn't decide what to make of it. It could mean he didn't have access to the family money. But it could also make him more desperate to protect his reputation. He had a lot more than most men to lose in a divorce.

I stopped the video after a plug for an upcoming campaign fundraiser, to be held at Olvera Street in a few weeks. "Join us in the heart of Old Los Angeles," Tana had said, her sunny blonde beauty at odds with her trilling pronunciation of *El Pueblo de Los Angeles*. I had a hard time believing the Carrigans had any real Californio roots, but if she said it enough times, people wouldn't care. That was the magic of Los Angeles: over time, the artificial became as historic as the true.

Somewhere near the bottom of my ginned-up coffee, the booze too warm, the coffee only lukely so, I had to get a little honest with myself and admit I was avoiding looking at Klein's file, avoiding thinking about Ellen and the money I owed to both the Lady and the police now. I wasn't sure which was worse. The glands in my mouth started to sweat, and soon I had a mouthful of saliva that gin wouldn't wash down. I leaned over and spat into my trash can.

I couldn't let my guard down until it was over. Ellen would try to get the drop on me again. She had the cash in her grubby little fists—she'd won this round—but she'd tipped her hand, too. That was a bigger mistake than she knew. I couldn't afford to underestimate her again.

When Lou popped her head into my doorway to tell me she was leaving, my office was dark, the sun long since gone and only the glow of my computer illuminating my face, the bottle of juniper snugged between a coffeepot and a succulent on my desk.

"How'd it go with your girl?" Lou asked, fingers dancing along my door frame.

"She meets with him Thursday," I said, which wasn't really an answer.

Lou's face relaxed. I wondered what she had to promise our boss to get my extension. "Money to the Lady before you know it," she said, reassuring me. I let us both pretend it worked. She promised to pick me up the next morning at my apartment, and we'd start scouting Carrigan together. She glanced at the gin bottle on my desk and added, "I'll bring coffee."

The bottle was drying up by the time I powered the computer down. Damn thing must've been leaking. I put my head on my desk to rest my eyes and didn't open them again until I heard the faint tinkle of chimes on the front door. I sat up, wondering if the Lady had brought that sharpened shiv of a diamond ring back for the envelope. Or for me. But when I poked my head out into the hallway, no one was there. I shook my head. Just the gin making me jumpy. Time for me to be going.

On my way out, I paused at Jackal's door. I hadn't seen him since that morning, but I hadn't expected to. For the better part of the day, he'd kept his door locked and wouldn't even answer for Lou, because professionalism was a thing he'd left behind the day he bent me over the front desk to welcome me to the job, way back when. But he'd come around. Eventually.

His door was barely open, light slivering between the jamb and the knob, thin as the line dividing flesh from garter. From inside, a strangled bark of laughter—Jackal's. A different sound from when I made him laugh. I leaned my head closer and heard the crash of something falling from his desk to the ground and then the erotic hoot of a woman trying too hard. The sound made me tired. It was a nice thing to believe about myself after Ellen, that my instinct for sisterhood wasn't quite dead.

I listened, wondering what else I was going to hear—when you go to the trouble of listening at mostly closed doors, you do have certain expectations—wondering, too, what I would feel when I heard it. The fresh *zhish* of a zipper, the giggles swallowed between two mouths.

Jackal groaned, and I bit my lip, tasted blood. A feeling like a cold cloud of stars exploding in my stomach. I pressed a hand against the door and rested my cheek on it.

I let the fleshy sounds go on for a few minutes before I tipped the door farther open. Jackal had kept only one light on a desk lamp, and it looked like his paramour had attempted to fling a scarf over it to create a mood. She'd misjudged, and the scarf piled on Jackal's carpet. The girl was propped on his desk, her feet pushing against the desk chair's arms for leverage. Jackal's fist formed a ponytail in her long dark hair, his own body jammed between her and the chair. His pants were still creased in the back, and every time she tried to catch hold of his shirt, Jackal jerked away, not willing to grub up his starch. Fastidious, even in his one-night stands.

He moaned a name, too low for me to catch, and tugged the ponytail to one side so I had a clear view. Young, fox-pretty face, thick brows like slashes across her forehead. Lots of dark hair. Looked like me back when I'd started working in the office. I pictured sticky vinyl lips and realized she looked a bit, too, like the woman who had been retired. Jackal's ex. I shuddered. He had a type.

From her position on the desk, Jackal's new girl had a straight shot at my face, if she wanted it. But Jackal was good at this, I knew firsthand. She didn't look up until the whole thing came to the rather expected end. Jackal finally stepped back, tucking himself back into his pants, and she caught sight of me. The brunette shrieked and covered her unbuttoned chest with her hands, glaring at me.

"Feel better now?" I asked him.

"Robert, what is she doing here? Was she *watching* us?"

Jackal was still breathing heavy, but his eyes met mine, ember-hot. "Babe, I didn't know you were there."

I laughed, saluting him, trying to ignore the tightness in my chest. "Oh, I'm sure."

The brunette was looking back and forth between us, a growing horror in her eyes. "*Babe?*"

"I know," I said, sparing her a glance. A fine sheen of sweat glazed her brow, and a blush was vivid but fading across her chest. "I didn't much care for that term, either."

Jackal smoothed his mussed hair back. It wasn't that I was angry—though I was, but not because he'd brought another woman into the office. Or, rather, *exactly* because he'd brought another woman into the office and into our games—civilian casualties weren't my style.

"You proved your point," I said.

The girl jumped from the desk and jammed a finger into my face. "You sick bitch, what the hell do you—"

"Easy," I said. "He's not worth fighting over." I opened my arms, the gin zipping up and down my veins, looking at Jackal as I said it. "You want him? He's all yours."

She glared at me, still finishing her buttons, and I raised my eyebrows and let my arms drop. "I didn't think so," I said after a moment. I jerked my head to the door, eyes on the girl again. "I imagine you're a bit sticky. There's a bathroom down the hall."

Jackal made a show of watching her ass as she walked past, but she turned and glared at him from the door. "You sick shit," she said, and then she walked out, slamming his door behind her. The twinge of a conscience I thought I'd gotten rid of rose into my throat, but I pushed it down. Jackal had brought her into this, not me. And maybe next time, she'd be smarter. Maybe this memory would save her from the next pretty asshole who looked twice at her over a beer.

"Next time you're pissed at me," I said, "take it out on *me.*"

Jackal snorted, his perfectly shaped lips curling up into a sneer. "Please," he said. "You think you're any better, what you do with those girls?"

"That's *different.*"

Jackal didn't say anything, just stared at me, arms crossed. The wiry black hairs of his forearms fluttered with the fan overhead.

"They know what they're getting into," I said, not sure why it mattered to me. To Jackal, what we did was only a paycheck. I bent down and grabbed the abandoned scarf from Jackal's floor, twirling it around my own neck.

In the distance, I heard the slam of the front door, the chimes hitting glass sharp enough to crack. She wouldn't be back. But then, Jackal didn't need her to be. Expendable, I thought, all of us, even the ones who were his *type.* I perched on the farthest corner of the desk. What was it in me that wanted to wipe up all the traces of that girl from his desk with my own back? If my mother could only see me now, I thought.

"I show them what real power tastes like," I went on. "I'm not sure who you were trying to humiliate just now, but you're the one who looked like an ass."

Jackal stepped forward, his pants brushing against my knees on the desk. He dropped those arms on either side of me, caging me in, and leaned forward. "Whatever bullshit you need to tell yourself to sleep at night, *babe,*" Jackal said into my ear, sending traitorous shivers down my spine. "We're the same, you and me."

"You'll end up in some lonely place someday," I whispered. "Without me. And I'll be laughing."

"Liar," Jackal whispered, and leaned forward, kissing me hard.

Even in a city that worshipped beauty, no one was as handsome as Robert Jackal. More than handsome, he was beautiful, though not feminine. And he could be charming when he wanted—he must've sweet-talked that girl straight from the bar to flinging her panties on his desk in under an hour—but charm was cheap in this city. I never had to pretend to be any better than I was with him. The first man I'd ever loved, I kept waiting for him to find out the slimy, ratty parts of me. With Jackal, there was no waiting. He already knew.

I'd never mistaken it for love between us. Maybe it was something much worse. But it had been enough to solder us together all these years.

Or at least until he hadn't showed at the St. Leo.

I pushed him away, wiped my mouth, my head spinning. "You feel better now we're back to square? Ready to tell me why you fucked me at the St. Leo?" I distracted myself from his arms by looking around his office. My eyes were drawn down to his desk, stacks of file folders in neat piles, the edges so meticulously aligned that it looked like one thick brick of peach. Old notes from Lou, the word *albatross* peeking out from behind a folder—funny, I hadn't been so sure Jackal *could* read.

"I forgot," Jackal said. The handsome liar. I hadn't been able to talk about anything else for weeks—even, occasionally, in bed—and he'd forgotten? Not possible. "Sorry. What are you gonna do."

"You forgot," I repeated. On the ground, the wreckage of the file folders that had been pushed off his desk in the affair, which must've been the crash I'd heard. Glaring out from the edge of one, a black-and-white photograph of a man I'd never met before. Young, attractive—high cheekbones, rounded chin, the haircut of a cop, looking away from the camera. Nothing salacious.

I might not have met him, but I recognized him: a hero-kid cop who had a nasty habit of asking for favors from the women—junkies, working girls—he cleared off the streets. Lou had run his case last year. He wasn't the first, or the only, uniform in the city who partook in that particular indulgence, but he was easy pickings. After the Lady was through with him, he'd resigned, worked in insurance now. Lou had shared the photographs one bourbon-soaked night, the two of us laughing over the kid with an unloaded gun between the thighs of a girl I'd trained. Still wearing his badge, the dumb fuck.

"You forgot," I said again. "I don't believe you."

"Sorry, babe," Jackal said, shifting between me and the photograph so I couldn't see it anymore. "I owe you one. I fucked up."

Now I was sure he was lying. If he really had forgotten, if it had been an honest mistake, he would've picked a fight with me, tried to make me feel bad about what he thought wasn't his fault. *So I missed the show, big fuckin' whoop. I'll be there next time.* But an apologetic Jackal? I'd never seen it. He was trying to keep me from asking questions. Like if he'd been on a heater and decided the tables were more important than our case. Than *me.*

Or questions about what he was doing with evidence from an old case that should be with the Lady for safekeeping, like all the other photographs he took.

"What do I have to do to keep you from forgetting the time and place on Thursday?" I grinned at him, sticking my tongue behind my left uppermost molar. It did not feel sexy, but he seemed to like it. Thongs, practiced smiles, anal beads—what was it with some men and the allure of uncomfortable things?

Jackal reeled me into him. "Let me make it up to you."

We told the marks we destroyed the negatives and the SIM cards after they'd paid up, which of course wasn't true. But it was true that we'd never used the photographs against someone who'd paid—they were insurance, that's all. Lou gathered them at the end of every case and passed them to the Lady, one of our many rituals. If Jackal had copies, that meant he was running something on the side, had a buyer or was looking for one. Probably trying to pick up cash for a poker debt. The Lady wouldn't like that.

"Did you have something in mind?" I purred, inching myself forward on his desk, moving my legs apart.

Jackal nuzzled my neck. "I'll think of something." He started to stroke up my leg, massaging from knee to thigh.

In all the years we'd been whatevering, there were certain secrets I'd kept from Jackal. My debt to the Lady, for one. And what Lou and I had done to incur that debt. But—stupid me—I'd never considered he might have secrets of his own. Jackal seemed so easy to read. But continuing to blackmail old marks after the Lady's sting had ended, or else selling them to someone new—I hadn't guessed he had it in him. A reporter looking for a scoop, a rival business partner, an ex-wife with an axe to grind—pictures worth a thousand words and almost certainly several thousand dollars all told. Double-dipping would be an easy score.

"Come here," I said, guiding Jackal so close there was almost no space between us.

The nineteen grand in exchange for my silence would be a simple solution, if Jackal had it, but I'd already made one reckless decision that day that had backfired. With Lou and me, there was a code—we watched each other's backs and we took care of our girls, helped them to their fair share of the cut. But Jackal had brought that girl in here tonight, he'd let me down at the St. Leo, and he'd been complicit in whatever had happened to his ex. No loyalty to anyone but himself. Getting involved with Jackal's side business was one more bad bet I couldn't afford.

But maybe there was another way I could use the photographs.

Besides recording the footage, Jackal was the one who collected from the marks, keeping the girls out of danger and making the marks less likely to cause trouble. The Lady set the amount, but it wasn't like she followed up to make sure that the blackmail had met their satisfaction. If Jackal upped the Klein bribe on the sly, I could slip the excess back to the police before anyone noticed it was missing. And no one would ever have to know it had taken a detour first. Neat, easy, not even stealing, not technically.

Jackal's eyes were darker than normal, even in the half-light, and a fine sheen of sweat filmed his skin. I liked his eyes on me, and I liked the hate I felt for him even as I wanted him. Hate: an exciting emotion. I studied his face. Hair sticking up, combed by not-my-fingers. A little saliva hanging off the corner of his lip. Still more handsome than a man had any right to be. I smiled and reached for him, liking the feel of his shoulders beneath my fingers, his musky scent mixed with the sticky-candy smell of that girl's perfume. I kissed his cheek and melted into him, my hands at his belt now.

"Jackal," I whispered, and he brushed his nose against my clavicle, aligning my lips perfectly with his ear, "tell me about those old case photographs on your floor."

CHAPTER 6

Jackal didn't come clean right away. "What do you mean?" he asked, pulling back. Avoiding my eyes. Still keeping himself between me and the snapshot on his office floor.

"I don't think you'll be seeing that girl again." I rearranged myself on his desk, smashing papers under my ass. That seemed to irritate Jackal, and he shoved me off. I didn't mind. "Did you like her much?"

"What did you mean, about old photographs?"

"It doesn't shock me that you've got something on the side," I said. "Only I think you'd do well to remember the Lady Upstairs is less forgiving of sidepieces than I am."

His hands bunched, and he took two steps around the desk—he almost forgot the game he was playing and bent down to grab the photo before he turned around. There was a small smear of lipstick on his collar. Ugly, tropical-punch pink: a little girl's color. He was wild-eyed and trying not to show it, trying to think of something to say or do to throw me off, outsmart me. "I don't know what you think you've found out, but you're—"

"We both know you aren't as dumb as you like to pretend to be. So tell me. How long has it been going?"

His shoulders slumped. "Does Lou know?"

"Not yet."

"If you tell her anything, I will make you sorry, you bitch, you—"

"Oh, calm down," I said, dabbing my finger over the smudge on his collar. The pink blushed my thumb, and I sniffed it, then popped the tip in my mouth.

"If you tell her anything, I'll—" He closed the space between us. I put a hand on his chest, but it wasn't to stop him.

"You'll do what?"

His hand tangled in my hair and he pulled his fist forward so that we were both looking at the dark strands tucked between his knuckles. I leaned into him, wanting him to break the stalemate first. But he let go, taking a half step back. I watched a feeling pass over his face, quick like a summer storm, but I didn't know, did not want to know, what it was.

I reached out a hand for him, and his phone rang. Jackal's head jerked, and he stared at me, like he was waiting for me to tell him what to do. I blinked at him, and he cursed under his breath and answered.

"What." I watched his face as he listened to the other end, his knuckles turning white as he gripped the phone. Silently, he held his phone out to me.

Me? I mouthed.

Jackal shrugged, his eyebrows raised. *Lou.*

"What's up," I said into the phone, a small wash of panic rising in my stomach. Maybe she'd heard from the Lady that there was a second envelope floating around the office. Maybe she was calling to ask if I'd happened to see it anywhere.

"You weren't answering your phone." I could hear something going on behind her—the radio? A woman's crooning alto. Lou's voice had a tinny, disembodied quality, like she was speaking to me from far away.

"I left it on my desk," I said, picturing the phone next to the now-dead gin bottle. "Where are you?"

"On my way home," Lou said, which didn't entirely make sense—she'd left the office hours ago. Before I could ask about it, she went on: "I wanted to make sure we were all set for Carrigan tomorrow morning."

"Yes," I said, "of course. Ten. I remember."

There was a pause. I could hear someone honking in the background. "Don't be too hungover, okay?"

"Lou," I said, my voice waspish despite the fact that she had a point, despite the fact that I didn't want her asking me too many questions. "I won't fuck up. All right? Just because Ellen isn't—" I stopped. I could've bitten my tongue out.

Jackal was staring at me, his hands on his hips. I knew he was wondering what she wanted. If he should be worried.

"What?" Lou's voice was clipped now, panicky. "Did something happen while she was there, something you didn't tell me about?"

"No," I said. I didn't want her to know that anything was wrong. But Lou would jump to conclusions if I didn't say anything. "Nothing. But she's been in it too long. The feelings are starting to turn on her." *I think she'll sell us out to the police eventually, and by the way, while we're on the subject of law enforcement, the cops are missing their bribe money . . .*

"Jo," Lou said, her voice pitched low. "What's our number one rule?"

No attachments that can't be shed. Never love anyone more than yourself. If we had a manifesto, it would've been printed on page one and page fifty and the last page, too, for good measure. *Don't let the girls fall in love.*

"I know," I said. "Nothing I can't handle." I racked my brain and pulled out a detail about the new mark to distract her. "Carrigan's hosting a fund-raiser on Olvera Street. Perfect opportunity to study him in person."

Lou took the bait, perking up and asking questions about the event. But I knew she wouldn't forget what I'd let slip. We ironed out the last details of the surveillance—we'd swing by his office, maybe even his house, to get a look at his life up close. I hung up the phone, strangling a sigh of relief in my throat—she'd want to know more about Ellen tomorrow.

"What did she want?" Jackal's voice was strained.

"She wanted to know if I'd caught you doing anything *suspicious* lately," I said, biting my lip.

Jackal looked like he wanted to throttle me, and not in a way I'd enjoy. "You're not going to say anything," he said, too confidently. "You don't want to know what happens if you do."

I thought of Jackal's ghostly ex. It bothered me more than I wanted to admit, that he might've sat back while the Lady had her killed. And then the girl tonight—the next in his line of brunettes. "Of course I won't," I said, soothing him. "Because then who would help me with Klein?"

"I *told* you, I'll be there—"

"No. Not the usual. I need more than that from you this time."

It was difficult to explain why I needed the money without going into detail about the debt I owed the Lady, or the money I'd nicked from the Lady's envelope and given to Ellen. I didn't want him to know any of those things. Like my mother always said, *Knowledge is power.* So I decided to stick as close to a version of the truth as possible, which was: Ellen was getting squirrelly. I'd promised her more money to finish the job. I didn't want to tell Lou. Since it was Jackal's fault I was in this situation—and now, I added, because he didn't want me telling anyone about his little side business—he was going to help me make up the difference.

He didn't like it, but in the end, he agreed. I'd known he would.

It would be such a simple fix, asking Klein for a little more. As long as I had five days to spare. As long as I could keep control of Ellen long enough to get her back in the room with him. I could keep my end of the bargain. I had to hope that Jackal would, too.

On my way out, Jackal started to tidy the photographs that had fallen onto the floor, taking his time sorting them into separate piles.

"A woman used to work here," I said, taking a shot in the dark, "when I first started." I described what I thought I remembered: a round face, cheeks that creased when she smiled, dark hair long to her waist. I studied Jackal, looking for any clue that he knew what happened to her, or cared. "Very pretty. What was her name?"

Jackal didn't even bother looking up from the floor. "No idea. Now get the fuck out of here."

So I did.

Chapter 7

The listing for my apartment complex had called it "beachfront real estate," and I guess that was true, only the beach was pretty far in front of the real estate.

You couldn't hear the ocean over the planes, which swooped so low over the Gardens that when they landed in the morning, all the car alarms were set off like fussy newborns. Some mornings, I thought I could swipe my fingers along the undercarriage of those metal birds if I jumped.

You could smell the ocean, though. Even through the motor oil and the garbage left too long baking in the sun, even through the waxy, perfume-like jasmine bursting on the knuckled trees in the courtyard, you could still smell the vegetable saltiness of the ocean. That was the real name of the complex, Jasmine Gardens, for the trees—but those same trees attracted thick, hairy-kneed spiders. When Lou started calling it Tarantula Gardens after I moved in, it stuck.

Slinging my purse down next to the couch, I didn't bother to turn
the lights on—the bulb had gone out the week before, and I hadn't yet
bothered to replace it. My apartment wasn't exactly welcoming to
come home to—couch, carpet, and walls all a shade of Builder Beige
I hadn't bothered to update. A patio that was more like a two-by-four
plank of plywood taped to the side of the building. A wrought iron
fence with bars like loose teeth kept the patio this side of a personal
injury lawsuit. Luxurious living. Lou called my lack of decorating
"willful poverty," but then, she was always running up tabs to buy the
most expensive items, racking up class on her credit cards.

Style cost extra. What I saved in rent was more money that could
funnel back to the Lady to pay off my debt. I could move out if I
wanted something nicer, but why bother with marble countertops, or
a posher zip code, when I spent more time away from my bed than in
it? Tarantula Gardens was home, but it wasn't forever. I'd always
known that.

But I'd thought I'd have more time before it ended.

The last time I'd paid my own rent, I'd been a different woman.
That woman would've been depressed by this apartment. She would've
taken Builder Beige personally. Even with the debt and the threats, I
had much to thank the Lady for—murdering that woman was perhaps
top of the list.

As long as the Lady kept signing my checks, I didn't wonder, too
much or too often, about who she was, or why she did what she did. It
was enough for me to know that what I was doing made life a little
more difficult for men like Hiram Klein, for whom life had never been
particularly difficult.

But it did bother me that Lou had a real relationship with her, this
woman about whom I knew nothing. The two of them, bent heads
looking through the newspapers, picking out names. Networking with
the nouveau riche at galas, dressed to the nines. Arm in arm, sipping

from each other's champagne. How that would go on after me. Without me.

I stood up, my face hot, thinking I'd grab a drink. Instead, I went to the window and pushed it open, sticking my face into the warm night air that smelled equally of jasmine and festering garbage.

I wished I hadn't said anything about Ellen. I hadn't meant to. I'd wanted to take the words back as soon as they were out of my mouth. And she'd ask about it tomorrow. I knew that if I tried to smooth it over, like Jackal had with the photographs, Lou would see through it. She'd know I was lying to her, and then she'd start to wonder, and maybe she'd call the Lady and the two of them would put their heads together and figure out some *other* things before I had a chance to fix any of it.

The score from Klein would depend on the footage, and the story I could craft, what I thought I could use to trigger him. If it was meant to be fifty large, could I push it as high as seventy-five? Slip the eight back to the police for the bribe, a couple more to ensure Jackal's silence, and still pay off the debt. Playing fair, or close to it. The Lady would never know.

I took another sip of the warm night air, pondering it. Outside, the low rumble of the planes overhead set the glass in the window trembling. When I'd first moved to Los Angeles, I'd hated everything about the city, the traffic, the people. Everything. Los Angeles was an endless appetite, ninety-two smaller cities stapled together and consuming everything in its path. Even with my doors locked tight, I could feel the city trying to make its way *in*—the Santa Anas sweeping through freshly soldered seams, pale afternoon light spilling through blinds zipped shut, the sight of beautiful people on every corner turning you inside out against yourself. In the beginning, living in Los Angeles was like having a constant spotlight shining on you and at the same time like being invisible.

It had taken Lou, and the Lady, and even Jackal, for me to understand that the best part of the city was its artifice. Use the spotlight as a weapon. Wear the con like a coat. That's when Los Angeles became my city.

Somewhere a cat yowled, and I turned my back on the window. I'd never asked myself—I'd never *wanted* to ask myself—if there had been other girls before me. I'd never wondered what would happen if I didn't want the job anymore. How impossible it would be for the Lady to let someone with so much knowledge about her business leave it. It had seemed we could go on indefinitely, the three of us, carrying out the Lady's orders, making this little corner of the city our own.

Little pinpricks of cold danced down my arms, into my stomach. When I'd been fired from my last job, I'd been sure I'd never put my life back together. But then I'd met Lou—or, rather, Lou had found me. There were other cities in the world, but there weren't other Lous.

Even if I didn't close Klein and somehow managed to escape the Lady, I'd have to leave Los Angeles. Maybe even California. I'd have to leave Lou, and Jackal. I'd be back to square one: no references, no work history. Not as Jo. Not as the woman I'd been before Lou and the Lady, either. I'd made something of myself by Lou's side. If that was gone . . .

I turned off the lights and walked to the cupboard and grabbed a bottle of gin and poured myself a nightcap.

I fell asleep that night on top of my bed, sheets pulled up to my neck, sweating through the cotton. If I had dreams worth remembering, they were ghosts by the time I woke.

Chapter 8

Lou and I were outside Carrigan's office before noon. She'd picked me up on time, for once, and called me from outside my apartment building chirping, "Let's go, let's go!"

Lou, normally, was not a morning person. But the minute she had a whiff of a mark, the whole game changed. When we were on a new case, she had an engine that couldn't be stopped, and a cheerful, ruthless focus that had led to more than one marathon thirty-two-hour stakeout, me asleep in the car next to her, or else asleep in my bed, fielding phone calls with details on the mark's bathroom habits. "Possible piss fetish," she'd say, her voice bright and chirpy at 3 a.m. "Gotta go, I'll call back when I'm sure."

On my way to meet her, I passed the pool where kids were slapping pastel-colored noodles against the surface for maximum splash. Management kept the concrete crater filled to the brim with eye-stinging chlorine that tasted of salty, gone-off fruit. A bright blue light at the deepest end kept you from noticing, right away, the scrum

ringing the edge, the oil-like sheen the too-still water took on immediately. Instead, that light made it look almost healthy.

After I'd finished my very first case, Lou and I had sat around the
pool downing a bottle or six of champagne—"sparkle water," Lou
called it. I'd been so loopy from the bubbles that when Lou made some
half-assed joke I'd nearly tumbled into the water, laughing.

"Don't fall in," she warned me. "I can't swim, so I'd have to let you
drown." She looked at the water like an ex-lover.

"It's only eight feet," I said, my eyes burning from the chlorine
fumes.

"I'd have to let you drown," she said again, waggling her eyebrows
so I was in on the joke, and then she poured me more champagne,
finishing the bottle and tossing the glass carcass into the deep end.

The morning fog had turned into a miserable steamy mist that
hung in the air like a wet wool blanket. Before I'd managed to buckle
the seat belt, Lou stuck a freshly brewed cup of java in my face, and I
took a long inhale, groaning in appreciation. It knocked me about halfway toward human.

Lou didn't drink coffee. She smoked cigarettes (she said they were
too tasty to kick, and besides, did you know you put on ten, maybe
fifteen pounds once you did?—no *thank* you), and she drank—with
me, mostly. But on the whole, she didn't tolerate girls who blew shit up
their nose, or jammed junk in their arms, and she didn't even like caf-
feine, said the stimulants made her skittish. Instead she chewed gum
in the mornings, said she thought the minty freshness jump-started
her brain. And who was I to say she was wrong?

"So," Lou said as she braked into the 405 and we settled into the
stop-and-go, "Ellen. Is she in love with him or what?"

I'd known it was coming and I'd practiced my answer to minimize
Lou's concern. "Infatuated, maybe. She asked if we wouldn't mind if
she kept seeing him, once it was all over." It was bad news and Lou

would worry, but not as much as if I'd pretended nothing was wrong. And not as much as if I'd told her the truth.

"How big a liability is she?"

"Well, she told me," I said, hating myself a little for the lie. "So she still trusts me. It's nothing, I've still got her under control. I guess I wanted to tell you, be honest with you."

"Jo, tell me now if you think you can't handle—"

"No," I said, fast. Lou had stuck her neck out for me with the Lady. I'd find a way to handle it. Ellen had her money. She'd be in almost as much trouble as us if she went to the cops. Even just thinking of the cops made me shudder. "It's a little crush, nothing to worry about. I shouldn't have even mentioned it."

Lou looked at me from the side of her eye, not turning her head. I held my breath. But she didn't push it any further.

Carrigan's office took up three high-rise floors in an Art Deco jewel box of a skyscraper that was located in the apocalypse of downtown. On the forty-minute ride, I had time to fill Lou in on what I'd learned so far about Carrigan.

His favorite movies starred Humphrey Bogart. He'd grown up in Wisconsin. He'd been the college quarterback. Married to Tana Carrigan, Philanthropist and Wife. Not a bad-looking woman at all, more handsome than beautiful, with a square chin, and despite her evident Botox, she still looked mostly human. She was also seven years older than her husband, which I suspected might have something to do with the fervent upkeep.

Before Tana, there'd been another wife, the college sweetheart, pictured with him in an old notice about Carrigan's football prowess. A nice-looking girl—small silver cross around her neck; nails painted purity-ring pink; shiny, center-parted hair. Also blonde. They'd been married three or four years—maybe she'd refused to give it up without a diamond; she looked the type. Virginity can make a woman sound interesting to a certain kind of man, but it's an interest you can never earn back once you've spent it. A quiet divorce, no children. Then came Tana, the *I Mean It This Time* Marriage.

And after Tana, zilch. Not so much as a photograph within an arm's length of another woman. Surprising, for a man that handsome.

Two blondes in a row. I wondered if that meant we should look for a brunette—men never seemed to crave what they already had—or if it was a better bet to stick with the tried-and-true. Something to think about, when the time came.

Finally, I brought up the most interesting thing I'd found. "He's only a Carrigan by marriage. He took the wife's last name."

Lou was quiet for a moment, blinkering onto the 10. She didn't seem surprised. Maybe she'd already known. "And?"

"I don't want you to be disappointed, that's all. If he doesn't have access to all that Carrigan cash."

"He's still one of them," she said finally. Lou took a turn too tight, and the car rocked a little as she overcorrected. "If he married in, he's still one of 'em."

I had my doubts, but I held my tongue. Instead, I showed Lou the family photo and her eyebrows leapt up into her hairline.

"Yowza," Lou said, grinning at me. "He's almost handsome enough for me to consider coming out of retirement."

"Almost."

If Lou had run marks for the Lady herself, it hadn't happened since I'd come on board. She must have done several when she started out, when it was a hinky two-person operation, no Jackal as the muscle and photog, no me to help research and find new girls. And I did know that there had been a time in her past when she'd done things for cash she didn't like to dwell on now. But all that was a very long time ago, in a city with a short memory.

It had been years since I'd had much to do with downtown, but I still knew the area enough to correct Lou a few times as she drove, guiding her to the right spot. Lou parked in the empty lot across from Carrigan's law office and turned to face me. Her eyes were shining, even more than her normal excitement for cases.

"You know, I'd always hoped I'd find a partner. I mean, the Lady's great, but it's not like she's part of the day-to-day. She's not *really* in it, the way we are. It's everything I'd hoped for all those years ago—that day we first met, you couldn't stop crying, do you remember? But you still had all that cocky attitude underneath, waiting for me. I knew it immediately, I thought to myself, *There's a girl who goes the distance.*"

I started to say something, but Lou held up her hand.

"And now we're taking down one of the Carrigans, together—Jo, it's like a dream. That name's everywhere, and it's going to be us who topples him." She sounded gleeful. "It's like we're really the ones running this city." Lou smiled at me and shook her head, cheeks glowing in happiness.

Carrigan still made me uneasy—*No one can make my Mitch do anything he doesn't want to do*—and I had too much over my head to be excited about a new case. But I couldn't burst that bubble. Instead, I said: "I guess we are."

We studied the joint. His firm was located on the ninth floor. It wasn't like we could see anything from the outside, and Lou was a little bit nearsighted anyway, so she mostly alternated between squinting at Carrigan's office, waiting for him to come out, and flipping through photos of him I'd saved on my phone.

Sometimes, the things you don't find are the most interesting. Like the fact that Carrigan's office had hung no billboards, posted no signs, made no announcements about his campaign. That didn't square to me. A man who would take his wealthy wife's last name for clout didn't seem like a man who was ashamed of self-promotion. It might mean something. It might not.

But one of Lou's rules was to assume nothing. Making assumptions was a fast track to making a mistake.

For example, assuming that I knew exactly how far I could push Ellen. Assuming that she was too chickenshit to ever call my bluff. That had been a mistake. An expensive mistake.

After twenty minutes, Lou stretched and yawned. I was about to suggest we move on, drive to Carrigan's house, when she said: "You never did tell me how it went with Jackal the other night."

I choked on the cooling coffee, splashed some up my nose. Jackal's photographs were my first thought. "The other night?"

"You know. When you left me at the tiki bar."

My stomach twitched. On the radio, an old jazzy standard made new by a woman with the voice of a thunderstorm. I looked at Lou from the corner of my eye—she hadn't moved her head at all, and even parked, her hands were stuck on two and ten like they were glued, but she had a mischievous little smile on her face.

"What exactly did you want to know?"

"Did he . . . learn his lesson? To bring backup next time?"

She'd never asked for details before. I fluffed my hands through my hair—an old nervous habit, from the days before I'd drowned my tells in gimlets. I knew she noticed. "You want to know what Jackal's packing?"

"Hey, you don't want to tell me, don't tell me."

"He learned his lesson."

"Good," Lou said. If she was disappointed I didn't go into more detail, she didn't show it.

"What about you?" I surveyed her briefly—white T-shirt, blue jeans, sneakers. Nothing that would make me think she'd been anywhere other than her own apartment last night. "Seeing anyone new?"

Lou pursed her lips, let out a little hum. "Nothing special."

I smiled into my coffee, then reached over and put my hand over the key chain from Lou's keys, still hooked into the engine and ticking back and forth. "Let's go."

"Go?"

But I was already out of the car, checking the traffic, trotting toward Carrigan's office. After a moment, I heard Lou get out of the car, walking slowly, reluctantly even, behind me.

I wondered if she was thinking of the last time we'd been in an office building downtown together. How badly *that* encounter had ended. I was.

I gave Carrigan's name at the security desk, which directed us to the ninth floor. Once the elevator doors closed behind us, Lou turned to me.

"What are you doing?" Lou's eyes were smudgy and a little bit nervous and a lot thrilled.

"Trust me," I said, smiling.

The doors dinged open on a big glass desk where a woman was glaring into the screen of her computer, asymmetrical haircut shuffled behind one ear.

"Can I help you?"

A woman behind the desk; too bad. Women were much better at remembering the little details about other women—the way they dressed, how they wore their hair. To a man, I'd be some random brunette asking questions. A quick glance behind the desk showed a pair of pink pumps tucked behind her chair wheels. And on her lap, a copy of the *Paris Review* she'd shuffled guiltily off her desk as we approached.

I made a split-second decision. "We're here for an interview with Mr. Carrigan," I said. "The *Times* sent me."

That interested her. She squinted at me and then at Lou, who managed a smile despite looking a little green around the gills. I was right. Offices *did* still make her nervous. "The *Times* sent two reporters for an interview?"

"My photographer," I said. On cue, Lou waved her phone in the air. I kept talking quickly, to distract the receptionist from the fact that Lou's most advanced equipment was a phone several years old. I nodded at the journal in her lap. "You a writer?"

She gave me a slow grin, a little shoulder shrug. "When I'm not here." She looked back at the computer and frowned. At the corner of the desk, a tiny pile of Carrigan campaign brochures were nearly hidden underneath a paperweight. Interesting. "I don't see anything on Mr. Carrigan's schedule about an interview. You sure you've got the right date, hon?"

Hon. I smiled. The power of favors, Lou had taught me once, was to ask for them, not to give them. Making someone feel generous was more appealing than anything you could offer. I leaned closer to the secretary, like we had a secret. Lou leaned in, too. She was staring at me, not the secretary now. She had a small smile on her face, and I tried to ignore her, my cheeks burning under her gaze.

"I'll be honest with you. I was hoping to find him here when he wasn't busy. Thought I might be able to catch him off the cuff." Her expression shuttered a little and I added, hastily, "Nothing bad, I promise. He won't speak to the press directly, and I'm impressed with his campaign."

"Mr. Carrigan's campaign is very exciting, but unfortunately it is not something we can comment on professionally, as I'm sure you understand," she recited. But the way she'd said *campaign*, such distaste—it was more than the company line she was selling. Very interesting.

"I see," I said, watching her. "You don't like his chances?"

"I don't like sellouts," she said tartly, then clapped a hand over her mouth. "Don't print that."

"I won't," I promised. I leaned away from the desk, giving her space now. "Can I leave a card with you to pass along?" I could see her weighing the possibilities, her job versus helping out a writer for the *Times*. A favor that would be remembered.

"I can take a card," she said slowly. She looked torn, as though she was deciding between telling me something and kicking me out. I decided to take a gamble and not push it. I dropped the card—the same I'd left at the St. Leo, just my name and number—and headed for the elevator.

"Hey, wait a minute," she called as the door dinged. "He's not available right now, but I think he might be heading to Sole del Mare next week. For happy hour, maybe. It's sort of a regular Monday thing, for him and a few other guys around here. If your editor can wait that long."

I loved this girl, she was an open book. She pronounced *Sole* like the bottom of a foot and *Mare* like a female horse. The way she said *guys* gave me a certain flavor, too—at least the girl we hired wouldn't have to compete with dozens of snappy young interns at happy hour.

I almost wondered if I should shuffle her a card with an invite to meet up, see if she might be willing to flip on her boss; she was in such a perfect position to do so. But that could get complicated. Maybe she'd feel some loyalty to her boss, even if he was a sellout. Even if he wasn't present.

I knew something about that.

"Thank you," I said, with real gratitude, snagging a campaign brochure from underneath the paperweight before pulling Lou back to the elevator by the elbow. "You don't even know how helpful you've been."

CHAPTER 9

Lou and I grinned at each other, stupidly, arms intertwined, all the way back to her car. She kept leaning into me and giggling, giddy with possibility.

I couldn't stop myself from twirling in front of the security guard, flirting outrageously on my way out, giving him a little salute while I bit my bottom lip. For a moment, it didn't matter that I still thought Carrigan had too many red flags, that I got short of breath every time I thought of that nineteen grand I owed. There was magic in our work when the pieces started to drop into place.

As Lou drove, we talked out the things we'd learned: the lack of flyers in Carrigan's office, the lackluster support from the staff. A favorite restaurant and a date that he frequented it would make it so much easier for the first meeting between mark and girl to appear coincidental. The old boys' club mentality, even as he ran on a platform of progressive change backed by old money.

I read to her from the campaign brochure and showed her the pictures, the little details I picked up. The suit Carrigan wore in the first picture was navy blue, which I assumed Tana had picked to match his eyes. Even from the tiny brochure photo, I could tell the suit was custom-made. A well-curated swath of diverse city dwellers all looked eager to shake his hand. That suit probably cost their entire month's rent. It would've cost a few of mine. Most of the space was dedicated to those pictures—it seemed Carrigan was a man of few, if any, words. There was only the slogan: *Make Money Work for You!* Tana looked more approachable in print than she did on TV, sugar blonde and beaming. She could fill out a twinset, all right. They looked like any handsome, unhappy married couple.

But my favorite photo featured a graying man with a hand on both Carrigan's and Tana's shoulders. Tana held her piglet of a son against her thigh. The caption read: *Hollis Carrigan and family. Three generations of Angelenos: The past, present, and future of Los Angeles.* Nowhere did it mention that Hollis Carrigan was the father of Tana and not Mitch. That fact alone painted a vivid picture of the man we were tailing.

I wondered what Carrigan's first wife would think of the photo.

"A drink?" Lou asked, cruising back into Beverly Hills. "And then maybe we go by his house. See if he's headed anywhere else tonight."

I laughed uneasily. "I can't. I'm meeting Jackal," I lied.

"More lessons he needs to learn?"

"Something like that. I want to make sure we're all set for Ellen and Klein on Thursday." I knew she wouldn't argue with that.

But Lou was too keyed up to be cautious. She bounced in her seat, the yellow light of the afternoon sun setting her hair on fire. "C'mon, Jackal can wait for *one drink*."

Yes, he could. But I couldn't. "Sorry," I said. "Rain check."

"Oh." Lou's smile faltered briefly, but then it brightened again. "Well, what about tomorrow night? Head to Olvera Street, scope out the fund-raiser location?" I knew what she was thinking: if I could wrap up Klein within the week, maybe we could have a girl in place in time for Carrigan's campaign event in a few weeks. It wasn't likely, but it was possible.

I said yes, of course.

As she shot south, back to Tarantula Gardens, Lou turned to me and said: "You're not afraid of Ellen, are you?"

"What?"

"I keep thinking about it. Her feelings for the mark. Our biggest rule, you know."

I laughed uneasily, fiddling with the radio to have something to do with my hands. Scared of Ellen—I was, but she barely made my top five.

"Please," I said, laughing it off. I was so good I nearly convinced myself. "Like that puffball has the stuff to scare me."

"By the end of the week," Lou reminded me. There was a little steel in her voice.

"Money in the bank, baby," I said, making her smile. "I'll bring a camera myself."

Lou dropped me off at my place—she'd offered to take me directly to Jackal's, but I'd begged off, saying I'd need my car for a speedy postcoital getaway. She'd smiled at that and shook her head, and I waited ten whole minutes after her car rounded the corner from my complex before heading to Ellen's, hoping I wasn't already too late.

It wasn't feasible for me to stake out the Alto Nido Apartments, Ellen's complex, every night without Lou getting suspicious, but I had a hunch I couldn't shake. If gambling had been my vice and not Jackal's, I'd have laid money that she'd try to find a way to see Klein without

me. Ellen might have won our skirmish in the office, but that victory
had come with a price. Now I had a better measure of what she was
capable of, and I didn't plan to lose the war.

Her apartment faced an alley, which sounded good in theory. But
alleys were terrible for surveillance. There's no good way to camp out
in an alley and not be remembered, unless you're a bum, and there
were still some lines I wasn't willing to cross for the job.

I did drive through the alley as I circled the block, clocking that
Ellen's light wasn't on. It was still the afternoon, so it didn't necessarily
mean anything, but her car not parked in the garage sure did.

I kicked myself, wondering if I was too late. Maybe she and Klein
were already holed up at some hotel—maybe even the St. Leo. My
brain kicked up a number of scenarios, none good: Ellen picking a
fight. Klein deciding the current lay wasn't worth the trouble. Ellen, in
tears, reaching for his hands, trying to hold him. Too many scenarios ended with him giving her the brush-off, generously slipping a
C-note into her hand to smooth things over. And then all of our effort, all those slaps, really would have been wasted. I pressed my fingers to the bridge of my nose, squeezing hard, trying to think. I could
turn tail and drive there. Barge into their hotel room—*with what
key?*—and tell Ellen to hop off now, we had shit to discuss. If that's
even where they'd gone.

No, I'd wait to confront her here. I'd be able to tell by looking at
her if she'd been with him. All that unruly blonde hair held a pillow
imprint for hours.

I waited, parked at a gas station across the street, facing the en-
trance to Ellen's garage, for nearly three hours. Wishing I'd brought
something to drink, resisting the urge to go inside and pay for whatever six-dollar bottle of sweet red the gas station could serve me. Finally, Ellen's blue Dodge rattled around the corner, pulling into her

garage. I locked my car and crossed the street, creeping to the windows near the front foyer of the complex, lighting but not smoking a cigarette I'd nicked from Lou to give me cover.

Ellen had picked her living quarters with an eye to stardom. Through the gray smog that hung like smoke on the hot days, you could still catch a glimpse of the Hollywood sign, the *land*, the last third of it, long since knocked down. A block and a half from the Alto Nido, an old hotel where Houdini's widow had once held séances had been converted into an old folks' home, though they still called it a hotel. You could check in any time you liked, but you were only leaving with the coroner.

From Ellen's lawn, I could peer into the hallway. She'd come up from the garage, pausing to grab her mail, and was staggering up the stairs to her floor under the weight of several purple-and-white department store bags. She hadn't wasted any time spending that money.

I crept to the back of the complex and watched Ellen's light go on after a few minutes. She stopped in the kitchen and poured herself a glass of white wine. I squinted up at her face—no makeup. Hair tied back in a ponytail. I couldn't be sure, but I didn't think she'd been with Klein. For one thing, she was sipping, not bolting, the wine.

Ellen disappeared into the back of her apartment, out of sight. I wondered how long to wait, but she reemerged almost immediately in her skivvies, a peach wedge of rayon barely covering her butt, matching skimpy triangles holstering her dark nipples. Still sipping the wine, she bent over and came up with a black dress. Even from the street, I could see the sparkle of it. Ellen held it up to herself, smoothing it down her front. Sucking in her nonexistent gut. She made a face and dropped it and picked up another—a hot-pink number. With feathers. It almost would have been worth breaking my surveillance to call her, tell her to return the pink monstrosity this minute, no way was the Lady's money going to pay for that disaster of a dress.

While I sat there and watched, Ellen tried on a few more outfits and, although I couldn't see them, new shoes, too, judging by the way she changed heights. All party clothes.

I tried to picture the new life she was filling with couture and spandex and sequins. Maybe she imagined cocktail parties on Klein's arm—the memory of me, and the photographs, and what she'd done and who'd she been while doing it, long behind her. A stepping-stone, unpleasant but necessary, to this upgraded life.

Ellen would be free once we'd closed Klein. Nothing tied her to us. She'd be free and clear to put it all aside and go back to her normal life. But it wouldn't be stardom she'd be returning to. She'd spend more time telling people she was an actress than booking jobs, and instead of rich producers, she'd be half-heartedly screwing nice bag boys she met at the corner store. It would be a blessing when they never called her back—she'd never realize how boring all those nice boys were. But she'd be devastated anyway. *That's what waits for you on the other side, Ellen, without me*, I thought. *That's what you're so eager to rush back to.*

I stayed there until Ellen undressed for a final time, exchanging feathers for ratty gray sweatpants. The apartment went black except for the glow of Ellen's television. I could see her silhouette lean forward every now and then to grab the wineglass, her naked arm long and thin and white in the dark. I waited until I was sure she wasn't going anywhere that night, and then I crept back to my car.

As I drove away, I could still see the impression of Ellen's ghost-pale, near-naked body flickering behind my eyes every time I blinked. Somebody should tell her those pink feathers made her skin look sallow. But the smile on her face in that dress—it'd be like snapping a puppy's neck.

Every time I blinked, the feathers swished, like a curtain dropping on Ellen's old life. At the first red light, I picked up my phone and made a call. "Come over. I need to see you. I need *you*. Now."

He made a show of arguing with me—told me he had better things to do, he wasn't exactly sitting at home waiting for my call, didn't I think he had plans?—but I knew Robert Jackal would make it back to my apartment before I did. Some things never changed.

CHAPTER 10

So: the dirty stinking truth.

Like Ellen, I used to be a little piggy, oinking for love. There was a man, the usual kind: tall, handsome, terrible. We'd worked together; he wasn't my boss, but his pay grade was higher. I'd found something sexy even then in the art of the conquest. I'd wanted him so long, been waiting so long for him to notice me—trotting out all the obvious tricks, flouncing past his desk in my highest heels, the ones I could barely walk in, wiggling into tighter and shorter skirts every day—that when he did, I made it my mission to become exactly what he wanted me to be.

One word of criticism, one night begged off from my company, even one lukewarm look, and I pretzeled myself to become better. I could laugh harder; I could crack dirtier jokes; I could play the lady, be meeker, sweeter, sexier; I could change and change and change and change. I could do it, I could be the dream girl. And I was proud of it, how good a chameleon I had learned to be. You could keep anyone if you tried, I thought. Most women just didn't try hard enough.

Did I love him?

Oink.

The day that Lou found me, after it had all gone bad, I was a different woman, one on intimate terms with tears. She found me sobbing inside an unlocked car. Later, I'd find out she'd been with a mark on that street: serendipity for us both. But I didn't know any of that then.

When he told me it was over, that it had been fun until it wasn't anymore—and it was a real shame because I was a sweetheart and a helluva lay, but he had to be honest, even if it hurt him to say it, even though he knew it was the best thing *for me*—it hadn't been only the end of our relationship. It had been the end of my career on the straight and narrow, too, although I didn't know it at the time.

I'd moped around the office for days, bursting into tears at my desk at the sight of him. Trying to imagine which coworker he was fucking now, what she had that was better than me. And the whole time, he never seemed bothered. After all, he'd known the score all along.

Two weeks later, I got a summons to a conference room with him and the big boss.

Everybody did it, so I'd never thought twice. A dip into the petty cash here and there, change from an errand that covered a drink or two at happy hour. I never thought of it as stealing, because no one ever checked. And there was no way my boss, a man with the wounded entitlement of family money he expected everyone to respect even though he didn't, would have thought to look through the petty cash drawer on his own. That was clear to me immediately. He'd had guidance.

"I'm so disappointed in you," my boss kept saying, looking from me to my ex-lover and back again. "I've been so good to you. How could you do it?" When I hadn't said anything, not trusting myself not to cry, disappointment had turned to rage. He told me I was fired, that

he wanted me out of his sight, that I'd never work again in this town if
he could help it. And he had the connections to help it.

And the whole time, *he'd* sat there in the conference room, a little
smile playing across his face. Letting me know that he *knew* he'd won,
in every way possible.

And I'd thought he had, too.

I drove around for days. Being constantly on the road felt better
than staying put. All I could do each morning was get behind the
wheel and drive and drive, telling myself I was looking for *Help
Wanted* signs, telling myself I didn't mind serving jobs, fryer grease in
my hair, as long as it paid the bills, when really all I was doing was
driving in circles, passing by my old office too often even for my own
liking.

I even saw *him* escorting a group of people to lunch, or, once, chatting outside the lobby with a fresh new penny of an intern. Probably
some young girl who didn't know any better than I had.

So even though it was expensive and my bank account was turning
from pink to crimson, I kept driving until I couldn't anymore, until I
was choking on the tears and I couldn't see. Then I'd park the car on a
street and put my head down on my steering wheel and sob for a few
minutes.

That was how Lou found me, shuddering all over and parked next
to bushes sprouting tubed white flowers, beer cans clustered near the
roots like mulch. Heaving sobs into the air like questions.

Two fingernail taps on my window. "Everything okay in there?"

"Go *away*," I wailed. I waved my fingers in the direction of the
Good Samaritan.

"It's just that"—the voice was soft and low, the way you speak to a
startled pony—"you've blocked me in."

I looked up. I *was* blocking a driveway. The tubey little flowers
belonged to someone's garden. Amazing how fast even heartbreak

gives way to embarrassment. I scrambled for my keys, spewing apologies and snot all over my dashboard.

Another fingernail tick at the window. I looked up, finally. The Lou I didn't know yet, coiled auburn hair and bright friendly eyes, smiled back at me, a pretty crooked grin, the unevenness making it all the more special since the rest of her face was so symmetrical. She bent down and leaned her folded arms against my side mirror, so we were face-to-face.

"My name's Lou. I think I could be a little late to work, if you wanted to grab breakfast or something. Maybe talk?"

And then I was crying again for another reason, because there were still good people left in the world, because I was still a person in the world and someone had seen that. I unlocked the passenger door and she climbed in. Still crying, I let her guide me two miles down the road, left, right, right, parking lot, to a stop in front of a hot-pink neon sign that blinked *Paulette's Slices 24/7.*

"I hope you like pie," Lou said. "It's my favorite breakfast."

I did not. Especially for breakfast. "That sounds great," I said, hiccuping.

I followed Lou into the diner, smoothing out my jeans to have something to do with my hands. Lou looked fresh and cool in checked-plaid culottes and a swingy cashmere cardigan, no makeup on her face. She had a loop to her hips somewhere between a sashay and a hula dance. When I sat across from her in the booth, she smiled at me and darted a quick look up to my eyes before she pressed a menu into my hands.

"Apple cheddar," she said, like she was telling me a secret. "Can't go wrong with it." Then she swiped at her face, beneath her eyes. "A little smudge, there and there."

I dabbed at my face with the napkin. I'd had girlfriends back in high school. Girls on the spirit squad who invited me over to their

houses after class to watch their older brothers' friends flex muscles. I
was on passing acquaintance with our school's homecoming court,
most of whom married those same muscle flexers. They sent me
Christmas cards, with pictures of their fat naked babies tucked inside. I didn't even throw away the pictures. I guess you could say we
were close.

But it had been a while since I'd been really seen by another person, and even longer since I'd felt anything like sisterhood. I opened
my mouth to thank her and the whole sordid story tumbled out. A
waitress came to take our order, but Lou waved her away, her eyes
never wavering from my face. Around the time I was telling her about
the way HR had called for security guards to escort me out, salt in the
wound, she grabbed a cigarette from her purse and offered it to me
with raised eyebrows.

"No thanks," I said, trying to catch my breath as the full spread of
my misery unfurled before me.

Lou lit the cigarette. "By the way," she said, "I didn't get your
name."

And it was so ridiculous, so sad, that I lost it—laughing, whooping,
donkey-braying laughs, until I snorted the tears trailing down my
cheeks back up my nose. Lou sucked on her cigarette and watched me
across the table, that big dopey smile on her face.

"It's A—" I said.

Lou nodded. "You can think about that and tell me again later if
you want."

I wasn't sure what she meant, but then the waitress was back. I
ordered a slice of cherry pie, à la mode, even though I didn't like va-
nilla ice cream. Lou ordered two slices of apple cheddar—"one to go
if I don't finish them both"—and eyed me some more.

"That's a sad story," she said finally. "I'm sorry to hear it. What an *asshole.* But they're never the ones who pay, right?" She shook her head. "*Asshole.*"

"Yeah," I said, uncomfortable now that my volcanic spill was done and cooling between us. The waitress clunked three dishes down, and we sat and chewed our pie in silence. The whole time I was wishing I'd kept my big fat mouth shut and that I could leave, leave now, before I started crying again, but I'd driven her here and somehow, even in my embarrassment, the idea of going back to my car and the radio and no one else . . .

So I stayed.

Lou was halfway through her first piece of pie when she cleared her throat and put her fork down. I thought she was going to make some excuse, say she had to leave, and I'd know that I'd embarrassed myself beyond measure, that I'd ruined any chance I had of being her friend. Instead, she told me a sad story of her own.

The details don't matter much—they're always the same. A big town and a *well, he's not* so *bad* man and too much love that he didn't want, a hard fall from grace. When she was done, she finished eating her slice, and I ignored the fork quivering as it came up to her mouth. Some hurts don't let you go.

Later, with the girls, she'd coach me how to win trust. "Use her own story in a pinch," she'd say. "Change the details but give her something she can relate to. Then think of your saddest birthday. Tears, right away." And it was true. Not one of my girls noticed when I spoon-fed her own story back to her, if I did it right. If I smiled, if I touched her hand gently and told her, without words, *I hear you, I care.* And by the time they left our business, they had a new story—a better story—to tell. I'd helped give them that.

I surprised us both by reaching out and touching her wrist. She nodded at me, fast, like we'd established something. Lou rubbed her wrist, then held my gaze for a beat too long, long enough for me to wonder if I'd done the wrong thing by touching her.

"You know," she said, tapping the ash from the cigarette onto her gooey, empty plate, "you seem really sad about it."

"Are you going to tell me I'm better off without him?" My voice was more of a squeak than I wanted it to be. It sounded like the sort of thing my mother would've said, all well-meaning sugar in her voice, ignoring the fact that I couldn't stop crying.

"I'm saying I think you've got a lot to be pissed off about," she said, her eyes very green through the plume of smoke drifting toward me. "It seems to me like you should be angry, not sad. You've got nothing left to lose here, y'know? That makes you dangerous. Especially if you're angry."

I didn't know what to say to that, so I shrugged and dipped back down into my pie. But I couldn't get those words out of my head. *Dangerous? Me? To who?*

When the bill came, I fumbled in my purse for my wallet. My share was four dollars, but I was down to my last ten. Lou must have seen the panic on my face, weighing the half-uneaten piece of pie on my plate with the last few dollars I had and the prospect of rent in a few weeks, and all the meals until then.

"Let it be my treat," she said, smiling again, like it was no imposition, like it was nothing. But I liked her. I wanted to be her friend. That meant equal.

I slid the bill out of my wallet, watching it all the way down onto the counter. The cards were nearly maxed out; the cash was running thin. Part of me said I needed that ten dollars more than I needed a friend. Part of me said I should grab her money and run.

But I was different then, so I passed her the ten dollars and tried not to stare at the fifty she laid down. I couldn't imagine what it would be like to have nothing smaller, to have to pay for pie with Grant's face.

Lou asked me questions, but my eyes kept flicking down to the tab. I couldn't help it. It was a crawly panic at the back of my neck, the idea that I'd wasted something I needed. I could feel tears pricking my eyes. She had to keep repeating her questions before I answered. All I could see was the little tear in the top right corner of her bill and the faded red scribble over Alexander Hamilton's left eyebrow on my own. Like someone had used it as a coloring book.

The waitress swung by, reached for the tab. But Lou was quicker. She trapped the bills between her nail and the table.

"One more minute," she told the waitress, flashing a high-wattage smile. "We might not be done yet."

A stone dragged down the pit of my stomach. I opened my mouth, about to say that I was full, thanks, when Lou stopped me.

"What are you," she said, "about a 34D?"

"Excuse me?"

"I'm pretty good at this," she said. "Am I right?"

I could feel color creeping into my face, but more than that, I was disappointed. This was it, the reason she'd been so nice to me out of nowhere. People aren't just *nice*; they always want something. I should've known better. I crossed my arms over my chest.

"Tell you what," Lou said. "How about neither one of us pays for breakfast."

I shivered, and my nipples got hard against my elbows. "You mean leave? Without paying the bill?"

Lou snorted. "No way, this is my favorite diner." She jerked her head toward a booth on the other side of the diner. "You see that guy over there? Glasses, too much forehead."

It was a kind turn of phrase. He hadn't had hair in my lifetime. In the booth directly across the restaurant, nothing between us but miles of black and white tile, a lone man was reading a newspaper but really watching us. I'd noticed him when we'd arrived. A thick paunch rode over his waistband. If he'd been much sadder, he'd be flat on a pavement somewhere. He made me cross my legs, and not in a pleasant way.

I told her I did. "He's been looking over here pretty regularly."

"Very good," she said, pleased. "I have this idea he might be lonely. I bet he'd love to buy a girl like you a nice breakfast. Maybe you walk those 34Ds over there and see what he says."

But my face—I'd been crying, I hadn't slept, I wasn't wearing any makeup.

"You've probably looked better," Lou said. Another thing to like about her: kind honesty. "But so what? He's no prize himself."

It was true, but I'd thought only of the way he'd see me, not how he'd want me to see *him*. As my savior. My hero. And then Lou said something that stuck with me, even years later when I'd developed my own style, so separate from hers you'd never guess Lou trained me, that she taught me everything I knew—I was that good; I took to it that completely. Three years before all that, Lou said to me:

"You'd be shocked how many men want to save a wounded woman. For a certain kind of man, the worse you can make that pretty face look, the better."

I made my way over to him, trying to channel the hypnotic way Lou had walked through the parking lot. I forced myself to think of figure eights and the dance of Salome and the push and pull of the tide until I had a handle on the rhythm. Everything was manufactured and self-conscious then.

For so long, I'd tried to be the woman my lover wanted me to be. I did it quietly, taking down notes in my head of what he liked, what he didn't. If he smiled when I cooked, I Betty Crockered him with mountains of muffins until he couldn't button his pants. If I held on to him too hard and he became allergic to my touch, I backed away for weeks, pretending that my every surface was made of ice and one hot touch would melt me dead. It didn't matter if this was my death by a thousand paper cuts. I could be better. I could be perfect. If I noticed the right things, I could learn to be exactly who he wanted.

I tried to notice things about this stranger. He was eating eggs, no pepper, no ketchup. Nothing else on his plate. Coffee, black. I'd seen the waitress refill it at least twice while Lou and I were eating. So maybe he was stalling. Maybe he didn't want to leave the diner and go back to whatever waited for him outside.

He buried his face in his eggs when I reached him. A man like that, a man who doesn't even pepper his eggs, has no business trying to play it cool. He did try, though. Even though he might as well have been a billboard advertising loneliness, he did his best not to notice me for a good twenty seconds.

I didn't say anything. I waited until he looked up. When he did, I smiled at him. I traced a figure on my collarbone with one fingertip. I pressed my measurements together and tilted forward a little. I figured he liked a direct woman.

"What's your name, handsome?"

He shriveled into the eggs. A miscalculation. It was all a lie; I'd never been good at reading men. No wonder *he* left me. I couldn't unsay what I'd said, and the words got bigger and bigger and I saw myself as Plain Eggs must've seen me—some blowsy burnout, messy hair and loose hips, trying too hard to be sexy. Panicked, I looked for Lou, who was watching me, thumbing that cigarette, her face a big blank.

Of the three of us, I was probably the most surprised when I burst into tears.

"I'm *sorry*," I said, sobbing. "I don't know what I was trying to— You seem like a nice man, God, what am I *doing*? I've been driving for days and I don't—I can't—"

"Jesus Christ," he said, his voice rising high on an alarmed note. His eyes were watery and the color of weak tea. They say you never forget your first. "Jesus Christ, sit down."

It was more surprising than the tears. I sat. I let him feel useful and hand me some napkins to use as tissues. I told him a story, but not the same one I'd told Lou. A breakup, a broken heart, an empty checking account. I thanked him profusely. I told him I was there with my sister, and she said I should go talk to him—didn't he look handsome in that silk shirt?—but I didn't know what I was doing anymore, and he seemed like such a nice man, I needed a nice man, so—

In the end, he threw a bill down on the table. I told him I couldn't possibly take it, but he insisted. I think he wanted me to leave him alone. I pressed a hug on him, lingering with a swipe of the 34Ds, and hoped that'd be enough of a cheap thrill that I wouldn't feel guilty about taking his money.

But to be honest: I didn't feel guilty at all. All I felt was relief—it hadn't been pretty, but it had worked and now I could save the cash. I wobbled back to Lou, trying not to swagger, swiping at my eyes and feeling, for the first time in a long time, the freshness of being somebody I liked.

When I got back to the table, Lou was chewing on the end of her unlit cigarette. I plunked the money down as I scooted into the booth.

"Not great," she said.

"It worked."

Lou nodded. "You think on your feet pretty well."

"I didn't plan that!"

"Then you have good instincts. Or you got lucky. Either way, I think you've got some sort of potential."

Later, she'd take me shopping. She'd buy me red lipstick and six thousand pairs of stockings and pumps and handbags and filmy little undernothings. Later, she'd explain the importance of style, that I was selling a desire made flesh, and that it was our job to figure out the marks once we got them. The Lady Upstairs gave us the orders, and it was the better part of our job to learn to not ask questions. Later, she'd give me cases and walk me through them. The first step: tailing the mark, figuring out all his likes and dislikes, followed by the meet-up, something so manufactured it was able to appear totally serendipitous. The last stage: the sting. Learning to shake off the end like water off a dog. It was a three-act play, she told me, except we were also the play-wrights and the director and even our own audience.

But she didn't tell me any of that over the sticky pie plates and the sweaty crumpled twenty-dollar bill I'd pried out of the man who took his eggs plain.

Instead, she plucked the drooping cigarette out of her mouth, smiled at me, and said: "I think I have a job you'd be perfect for. But first, I've got an idea for how we can make him pay, this asshole who hurt you."

CHAPTER 11

Ellen didn't leave her house until late the next afternoon, when the sky was already inching to purple. I was getting itchy—I'd been there for hours, and I'd promised to meet Lou at Olvera Street for dinner, scope out the location for Carrigan's upcoming fund-raiser. I told myself that if Ellen didn't budge soon, then I'd been wrong, at least for today—that she was planning on staying put or going to see her mother or a friend or something. Anyone else except Klein.

I told myself that I was chasing her for nothing, and I kept telling myself that right up until a pearly black Jaguar pulled up across from her complex and purred for a full two minutes before Ellen bounded out to meet it, practically bouncing in her stilettos. She clicked into the car, not even pausing to look around to see if anyone was watching. That made me angrier than anything. It was one thing to flout my rules, another to do it so blatantly, without any discretion or fear of being caught.

The driver of the Jag turned his head so she could kiss him, full lip smack, a lover's kiss, and my blood ran cold. Ears like a jug. A jowly face that had always had enough money that he'd never needed to work hard at being handsome. Joel Klein, Hiram's loathsome creep of a son, peeled away from the curb with Ellen's hand down his pants, tires squealing.

I waited thirty seconds, long enough to put inconspicuous distance between us, and then followed. At the first stoplight, heading west along Sunset Boulevard, I could see her tilt down the driver's side mirror, tip her head, practice smiling. Gave the mirror her best bedroom eyes and checked her teeth for lipstick. Furry pink fronds poked up from the bodice of her dress and turned the underside of her chin fuchsia. Klein Jr. goosed her under her armpit and she jumped. The light turned, and she went back to practicing seductive expressions.

I guessed where we were headed before we got there. Paramount Studios sat between a country club and a cemetery. Most other studios had moved out of Hollywood years before, finding cheaper or chicer digs in other parts of the city. But Paramount held on, locked away like a castle from the small-time wannabes a few blocks over who cruised Hollywood and Vine dressed as Marilyn or Elvis or King Kong.

An industry party, I guessed. The film Ellen had been working on—although that was a strong term; she'd been about as involved as background scenery—was a Paramount picture. I thought of her face in the cramped room at the St. Leo—she really did feel something for Klein; I knew I was right. You couldn't hide an eyelash in those big eyes. But maybe she thought it would make Klein jealous, seeing her with his son. Maybe she imagined he'd realize how *special* she was. His dream girl. Or, worse, maybe she was trying to transfer those feelings to Joel. Neither option was good business for me.

As I looked for street parking, I was already imagining a cover story to bluff my way into the party—I did not have it in me to pretend to be a lost tourist, starstruck and wide-eyed by the memorabilia of Tinseltown—when the Jag turned away from the gates, circling the block. I was surprised enough that I let another car maneuver in between us and then rode their tail until they blinkered and jerked into the other lane, sending a one-finger salute after me as I followed Ellen into the Hollywood Forever Cemetery.

I idled behind the Jaguar, not caring now if she could tell that someone was following her, and watched Junior half lift a hand to a security guard, interrupting an argument with a billboard-handsome man in a rumpled silk suit. The security guard waved them through, continued his argument.

I took a glance at the guard and weighed my odds. He seemed preoccupied enough that maybe I could squeak by without a story. I rolled down the window, not stopping the car.

"Here for the party," I called, catching a glimpse of the two men in the dying glow of the afternoon. They didn't stop their argument—the guest (an actor, no doubt) wanted to liberate the caged peacocks for the festivities, and the rent-a-cop wasn't having it. They both seemed occupied and I was counting on it. I kept driving until I heard the shout behind me.

"Hey! Come back here!"

I checked in my rearview. Both men were staring at my car now, and the security guard had a hand on his two-way radio. That stopped me. I backed the car up.

"Cake delivery," I said, adding, "special for Mr. Klein." I patted a hand at my back seat, then gave them both a full smile. None of us liked the smile much.

"Name?"

The security guard was not having a good night. He clutched a clipboard that looked ready to snap at any second. He was red-faced, angry or ashamed, while the man in the silk suit had that above-it-all actor's gaze, the *nothing can ruffle me, sweet stuff* billing that had gone out decades ago, once men on celluloid had to pretend to act human. I didn't like him on sight. But then, I wouldn't have liked anyone at that party very much—including Ellen.

"Karen," I said, "with catering."

"Company name?" He glared at the keyboard. In the distance, Junior's taillights rounded a corner and disappeared. I cursed under my breath.

"Look," I said, "if you want to explain to Mr. Klein why the specialty cake he ordered—"

The actor stepped forward and peered at my face in the car. "Oh, *Karen*, I didn't recognize you!"

The security guard looked over, skeptical. I matched his expression. "You know her, Mr. Wexler?"

"Sure do," Wexler said, leaning an arm on my car window. He leaned forward and grinned into my face, showing all his teeth. Wexler wasn't particularly tall—actors never are—and his face was very handsome, every feature a hair too large, including his oversized upper body and rib cage. But never quite handsome enough to be the lead—even among Hollywood, that sort of handsome was rare, and it made me wonder, for a moment, if Jackal had missed his calling. "Good to see you, Karen. Say, can I catch a ride up?"

"Sure," I said, looking from him to the security guard, whose face wasn't so much incredulous as pitying: *You sure you want this asshole in your car?*

I peered into the half-darkness. Through the carefully tangled ivy and rotting silvery palms, I could see the red glow of taillights and, far ahead, sweeping purple and gold spotlights. Far off, I could hear a woman shriek with glee. I waited until Wexler had walked around to the passenger-side door of my car, and then I gunned it, shooting straight past them both and lurching forward into the boneyard. Behind me, I thought I heard the security guard laughing.

Hollywood Forever Cemetery shared a plot of land with the studio, a shortsighted mistake by the undertakers of the early 1900s, who'd assumed the newfangled movie biz would fold in months. It didn't take long before the stars hadn't been content with their half of the land: they'd taken Hollywood, and then started to overtake the cemetery, too. A century later, the two still rubbed shoulders, two ghouls locked together in eternity. It was fitting: you couldn't see the celestial stars in Los Angeles anymore, but you could find the earthly ones spackling the sidewalks or bricked up in marble.

You could step off the studio lot, walk across the street, and find yourself in the Garden of Legends, crawling on the final resting places of residents with names almost as well-known as Carrigan, dozing off a lifetime of largesse.

Hollywood Forever wasn't home to all the departed luminaries of Old Hollywood, but it had more than its share. Jayne Mansfield and her head rested near the lake, richly fertilized by duck shit and pond scum. Virginia Rappe and her cosmically cruel last name nestled underneath a tiny tree that had never taken root. Marion Davies had been entombed in an enormous mausoleum, as befitting the mistress of one of the wealthiest men in the city's history. The dowager empress of kept women, an inspiration to us all.

I parked near the peacock cages, winding my way through the clutter of graves carved with curvy Armenian glyphs. Out of the car, I could see that many of the headstones featured carved black-and-white photographs of the long-lost departed in their prime. I imagined an old Armenian grandmother flipping through her photo books, picking out the one that would represent her face for eternity. If it were me, I'd have picked a nude. But maybe that task went to the survived-by. It was unnerving, knowing exactly what the pile of dirt and bones underneath my feet looked like.

I crept toward the front of the cemetery, the big eternity pool where mean-as-fuck swans sipped chlorine-green water in front of the everlasting tomb of Douglases Senior and Junior, patron saints of celluloid. My shoes were sticky with champagne and clung to the pebbles underfoot. I stopped every so often to shake one loose, squinting into the darkness for a sign of Ellen and Junior.

Klein Sr. would send her packing as soon as he figured out she was fucking his son—maybe it would even be an easy out for him, a way to rid himself of an annoying mistress without any nasty recriminations. I couldn't let that happen. I needed to get her out of there before she could make a fool of herself in front of Klein, ruin any chance that he'd speak to her, let alone fuck her, on Thursday.

Far off, voices hooted in harmony, and I wondered if this was what the party was meant to be, a sprawling bacchanal over the bones of Old Hollywood. I followed the screeching until I reached an enormous black valentine that held the framed face of a golden goddess, one I recognized from magazine covers but more specifically as the lead of Ellen's film, with the words *Rest in peace, Tati's youth!* emblazoned across it in silver-tinselly glitter. Beneath that, the dates *November 6, 1984—November 6, 2012.*

Someone had driven a plastic butter knife through the center of the valentine, spearing the ski slope of the birthday girl's nose.

An altar was set up before the valentine, littered with Veuve Clicquot carcasses and champagne flutes abandoned half full or never used. Little lights had been strung up across the Douglases and the celebratory spotlights swayed over the lawn. I swiped one of the half-finished glasses in passing and downed it, then came up sputtering. Not champagne. Vodka, warm.

Out of the corner of my eye, I caught a quick flare of fuchsia, a tittering giggle—"Oh, Joel, you're incorrigible!"—and I couldn't help myself. I turned and barked, "Ellen!"

Something pink and fluttering cackled off into the dusk.

I jogged after her until I caught sight of warm light spilling out of the wall of mausoleums lining the perimeter of the cemetery. That'd be Ellen, all right. Looking to make a scene.

Inside the opened tomb, a woman plunked at an old wood baby grand that hadn't been tuned in fifty years, and a man leaned heavily against the side of the piano, trying to explain something to her. Behind them, two stupefied revelers swigged straight from their own bottles of vodka. I recognized one, glazed expression and gold sequins, as the birthday girl, although she looked different without a knife for a nose. As I passed by, I heard the man against the piano say, "You're flat, Cara, if I've told you once, then I've told you—"

All around us, enmarbled bodies. The acoustics in the place were perfect. The audience was even better. I shivered.

"A twenty-eighth birthday party in a cemetery," I said to no one in particular. "What a world you people live in."

No one said anything—I didn't think they'd even heard me—until the birthday girl said, voice slow as molasses, "As above, so below."

She stared up at me, gaze unfocused. I thought it was unlikely that she had ever said one word to Ellen. I was starting to feel the vodka already, slick and fizzy in my veins—no dinner planned until I met with Lou. (Oh God, I hadn't thought about Lou in hours. What was I going to tell her, what excuse for my lateness? Jackal tied me to his bed, then went to Burbank for a sandwich?)

Behind her chair stood Wexler, peacockless. He glanced at me and grinned. His teeth were so white they were practically blue. I decided I preferred the actors in the ground. "Where'd your catering platter run off to?" He made a big show of looking around. "Don't tell me—you're here to . . . showcase your various talents for the old man."

"Am I that easy to read?" I licked my lips and tried to surreptitiously crane my neck, seeking out Ellen's bright dress in the mausoleum darkness.

"You've got the Ava Gardner thing going with the face and the dimensions, but those clothes—" He tutted. "Besides, he's got a buck-toothed blonde rubbing carpets thin for him these days."

My stomach dropped at that, but I didn't say anything. Just because the affair was an open secret didn't mean Klein wouldn't pay—it only meant I'd have to work that much harder at crafting the right pitch. I shuffled it away—I'd consider that when I had hauled Ellen out of here by the frizz of her hair. I eyed the vodka bottle he was swirling and decided he wouldn't remember me the next day anyway. "You know Ellen Howard? My little sister. Frizzy blonde hair, about five-six, follows directions like she aced kennel school? Seen her tonight?" Instead of answering, he pushed the bottle up to my face. I grimaced and knocked it away. "Christ, get a grip."

"I have something you could grip," Wexler said, grinning.

I looked around, but nobody else even acknowledged my existence. Instead, I caught the low hush of murmurs from deeper in the tomb, voices moving like shadows. I walked away from Wexler without saying goodbye, leaving him calling after me. I crept forward, hoping I wasn't going to find Ellen's sweating palms pawing at the crotch of Klein's son in front of the old man himself.

Thursday, a few more days, that was all I needed. I was so close to paying the Lady back, to getting the money for the police. I held my breath with each click of my shoes against the marble. I had to keep her going until Thursday.

I got lucky. In front of Bugsy Siegel's tomb—covered in Tropicana pink and coral kisses—old man Klein was flanked by a tiny army of wannabe movie babes. No Junior or Ellen in sight.

"So tacky," said one of two Harlow-blonde hussies.

"Early in the night for it," agreed a squinch-faced brunette—pretty in a knockoff-Audrey sort of way. She'd be catnip for marks who wanted to consider themselves American blueblood royalty—yachters, polo players, the country-club set. I shook the thought away. Klein, self-satisfied master of the universe, was rhythmically petting her head like she was a puppy, while the peroxide twins pouted prettily, preening for attention and giving the squat old man all their power. *Nothing personal, ladies,* I wanted to say, my knees weak with relief. *He's already got a blonde.*

Who wasn't anywhere in sight. I turned to go—Ellen was still out there somewhere, canoodling; it was only a matter of time before *some-one* spotted her—but Klein's voice stopped me dead.

"Who the hell are you?"

I froze. If I turned tail and scurried away without answering, it would look worse, like I wasn't meant to be there. *Play it big,* I told my-self. *Be bold. There's no way he remembers you from the St. Leo. He barely no-ticed you.*

In the dark, Klein's face lit only by a flashlight held by one of the Harlows, he looked like a helpless old man. Eyes shrunken into the blue half-moons of his sockets. Long hairs curling out of his ears. Not so very many years removed from his own enormous mausoleum. He looked feeble. Not capable of getting it up, much less slapping anyone around.

I pictured the sharp pink marks on Ellen's face at the St. Leo. Looks can be deceiving.

"Sorry," I said stiffly. "I must've gotten turned around."

Audrey the Second glared at me. She'd cornered the market on brunettery and she wasn't looking for a rival. The blondes were staring gloomily at Bugsy. Klein raised his eyebrows and extended a hand, indicating I could remove myself anytime I wanted, or maybe offering me the chance to kiss a ring. I picked the former. As I left them behind, I felt a surge of hatred and thought: *Be careful, Mr. Klein. Be careful, and when it all goes tits up, remember:* cherchez la femme.

A jet crash wouldn't have disturbed the partygoers collected in the foyer of the mausoleum. The pianist was still plunking notes on the piano, ignoring the man leaning against it. The birthday girl burped vodka in her seat. Wexler had left, presumably off to hunt peacocks.

I stepped out of the mausoleum, glaring into the cemetery. Even in the near-dark, I should've been able to see some flicker of that bright pink dress.

Then I heard it: Ellen's voice, sharp and tearful. I followed the sound and found her slumped over Toto's shrine, sobbing into the puppy's metal fur. Not too far away, I could see the shadowy outlines of a small group of revelers, among them both Joel Klein, who wasn't even looking back at his date, and Wexler, who caught sight of me and gave me a small half salute. I glared at him and knelt next to Ellen, trying to be gentle.

"Ellen," I said softly, one hand on her heaving back, noting that the fuchsia monstrosity was already muddied and ripped near the hem, no chance for her to return it and get my money back now. "Ellen, come on, get up. Let's go home."

Ellen raised her head—I don't think she even registered my presence—and shrieked, "I don't even *want* to screw that old fuck—they're paying me to do it!"

The conversation among the group lulled, and I could see Wexler's head lurch up—he must've been standing on tiptoe—his eyebrows raised. I didn't wait to check Junior's reaction or to see if anyone else had heard exactly what she'd said. I dug my fingers tight into the flesh under her armpits and yanked her up, thrashing against me, then dragged her back to my car.

CHAPTER 12

I shoved Ellen into the passenger side of the car and slammed the door shut, guillotining a handful of pink feathers. I crawled into the driver's side and locked the door, but I didn't start the ignition. We weren't going anywhere until we had a little chat, Ellen and me.

She was crying again, this time for real—her fake eyelashes were starting to wilt and slide toward her cheeks. With the light from the streetlamp overhead, I could see two pink poufy feathers clinging to her lip gloss. Nineteen grand. The plan I'd worked out with Jackal. Even whatever future life she'd planned for herself. She'd done so much to put all of that in danger, for nothing. For Hiram fucking Klein.

"So," I said, conversationally, staring straight ahead out of my windshield. Counting to ten in my head, then twenty, the word *motherfuckermotherfucker* chasing its tail in my brain. "How long have you been fucking Joel, too?"

"How did you . . . How did you find me?" A feather quivered on her lip.

"We might make an actress of you yet," I said. "That was quite the scene you made back there. *Quite* the scene."

"Do you . . ." Ellen's eyes darted out the window, and I think it occurred to her for the first time how pissed I was, how much trouble she might be in. She licked her lips. "Do you have a tracker on my phone?"

"Please. You didn't make it difficult."

Ellen squished herself into the corner of the car, pressing a small glittery clutch into her chest like it would be some protection against me. As if I'd come there to hurt her.

"This is all so easy for you," she said. Her tears had slicked muddy glitter down her cheeks. "But for me, it's like . . . it's like . . ."

Outside, another whooping burst of laughter, the crystal clink of a bottle smashed on marble. I wondered if Junior had heard. I wondered if he would tell his father, what he would say.

I studied her face again. Beneath the tears and the emotions, she was clear, coherent. She wasn't that drunk. There was something else bothering her. I tried to think of what Lou would do, or say, in the moment. A million years ago, she'd been kind to me in a diner. I tried to remember how to be kind. "What, Ellen? What's it like?"

"It's like it's getting harder to remember that it's all fake," Ellen said, turning her nose against my glass window. "It's getting harder to remember that this isn't really me. I find myself doing things, *feeling* things, and it's like, who the hell am I? I don't care about this man. I don't care about this shit. But it's like I can't stop myself." She stole a glance at my face and sighed. "I know you don't get it. And I'm not fucking Joel. I was trying to . . ." She trailed off.

I felt a little sting in my chest and didn't want to name it. So it wasn't easy, her job. She wasn't doing it out of any good passion. And she sure as hell wasn't going to let Klein jerk her around, not on my watch, not on the Lady's paycheck. I ground my teeth. If Junior hadn't heard—or if he was the kind of ne'er-do-well who didn't want to rock the boat in case it affected his paycheck—then it was possible nothing irreparable had happened. *Just* possible. But it had been a close call, too close a call. I reached into the back seat of my car, pulled out a flask full of whiskey I'd stashed for an emergency. Ellen flinched, her eyes darker than I'd ever seen them in her very pale face. Afraid, like I might throw the flask at her.

"Don't worry," I said. "I don't waste booze." I turned in my seat so that our knees were almost touching. I leaned forward and held out the flask until she took it. "It'll make you feel better."

As I watched Ellen take long, deep swigs from my flask, I realized I didn't need Lou there to tell me the thing I was now sure of: I'd let Ellen go too long. She'd lost herself, she'd lost sight of the end goal, and now I was going to lose something, too. Except that wasn't the way I ever played this game. I didn't lose, not anymore.

Six months before, I might've convinced myself to go to Lou, admit to her and the Lady that I'd fucked up and we needed to find a new girl. That either the mark would take a lot longer than we expected or the case was dead, too compromised. Let Ellen off the hook. But now there was nineteen grand on the line and not only my debt this time, but the money for the police, too. That mattered to all of us, Lou and Jackal and me. To our little blackmail family, such as it was. And it wasn't an option when I'd found such an easy out, poetic justice practically, to fix it.

No. I couldn't let up on her now.

"Feel better?"

Ellen nodded, her chin wobbling. She gave me a weak smile, her eyes still watery.

I took a deep breath. *This is what the Lady pays you for, Jo.* "Okay, let me see if I can guess what happened tonight. You got invited to a party by the mark's *son*. You thought you'd go, hoping Klein would be there, he'd get jealous. Not bothering to tell me, I might add, despite the fact that the dead flamingo you're wearing was bought *with my money*. Then—surprise!—Klein didn't give a shit, and you got sloppy on two sips of champagne, made a goddamn spectacle of yourself. That about sum it up?"

Ellen slumped in the passenger's seat, curling her legs up underneath her. Making herself as small as she could. Her face looked puffy and a little raw from the tears. I was careful to keep mine as blank and bored as I could. I told myself that hers was the sort of crying I recognized, an actress's tears: conscious of the effect you're making; check the mirror a few times when you're home alone, to make sure you know what pretty vulnerability looks like on your face. Bright, brimming eyes: check. Swollen lips: oh, sure. Color in your cheeks but no snot running: perfect. And then think to yourself, *Yep, heartbreak, nailed it*. I told myself she was a better actress than I'd realized. I told myself she knew exactly what she was doing.

"Please," Ellen whispered. Her hands were clenched and red. "I don't know how to do this anymore. Sometimes it even feels like I . . . like I maybe even love him. Why does it feel like that?"

Dopamine. The thrill of a new adventure. Bourbon. Take your pick. "Maybe I love this whiskey," I said, gesturing at the flask. "You see what I'm saying?"

Ellen's nose twitched and she sniffled. "But he's not *whiskey*. He's a *person*. Have you ever even *been* in love?"

Oink, I almost said to her. Instead, I tried to catch my temper on its way out and failed. "It is a *job*. He is a *job*. Listen, love is a thing men invented as a convenient excuse when they're done fucking women they can't stand. *Sorry, toots, no more hide-the-salami, can't help it, don't love you anymore. Not my fault.* You see? Jesus Christ."

"Do you have to be so goddamn *ugly*," she said, bouncing the flask against the dashboard where it tumbled to her feet. But I could see it was the last of her fire, one last flash in the pan.

I kept on it.

"You know where he is right now? He's fucking some new blonde, or a brunette, or both. But don't worry, he's not going to leave his wife for any of them, either. They *never* leave their wives, Ellen. That's not just a lesson for this case, that's a good lesson for you to remember. If he tells you he doesn't want you but still fucks you anyway, don't ever forget: he never lied to you. You are *letting him treat you like this*, Ellen. That's the truth."

She was crying soundlessly, mouth open in a wet red *O*. Staring straight out the window, her nose practically pressed against it. The kill shot was close. I could sense it.

"The whole production knows about the two of you. He's screwing everything with tits, but they *all* know about you. How would they know, Ellen, unless you've been making yourself a spectacle over him? Pathetic." I shook my head. She was crying so hard she was trembling, each sob rocking her back and forth slightly on the seat. "You have him right where you want him if you can be strong for me for a few more days," I said, and I reached out and threaded my fingers through hers. She jerked away from me, but I was stronger and I held her tight when I said: "Make him *pay*, Ellen. We're so close. Get back some dignity and *make. Him. Pay.*"

She didn't look up as I turned the engine over, started to pull out of the cemetery and head back toward her apartment. She didn't move at all.

I didn't look at her again until I pulled up to her curb, and then I scanned her crumpled face. Her feet were curled under her like a little girl's, and she clutched herself around the middle, like she was trying to keep herself together. Pink feathers on the seat, the car's floor, her face. "*Thursday*," I said, and we both knew it was a threat I meant to keep.

Ellen sobbed for a moment or two, her jaw mawing at the air like a gulping goldfish. Then, in the tiniest voice: "I'll be there." She didn't look up as she clicked the car door open and climbed out. I knew she meant it. Thursday, she'd be my girl, and it would run smoothly, exactly the way it should have from the start.

Thursday would be fine. I just didn't know what would be left of her on Friday.

Olvera Street at night glinted with candy-colored Día de los Muertos flags, even weeks after the holiday. Mariachi strummed guitars at the mouths of different restaurants, while a host of people chattered over meals of varying levels of authenticity. Cielito Lindo was located at the front of the street, a small cultural wedge of the oldest part of the city, between Little Tokyo and Chinatown.

By the time I got there, the taquito stand was closed for the night, all boarded up.

I found Lou in the third bar I tried, a little wrought iron joint with a reddish glow and eight-dollar pitchers of margaritas. She had her back to me, slumped over a tumbler, the scarlet tint of the lighting catching the slinky satin sheen of her cocktail dress. She stiffened when she caught sight of me from the corner of her eye.

"Hey." I slid into the empty seat next to her. A nearly full glass of amber on the bar in front of her. She didn't look at me.

"I've never been stood up before."

"I'm here now, aren't I?" I was too tired, the ghost of Ellen still too near, to soften my tone. Lou had taken maybe two sips of her bourbon. I wasn't sure what was worse: that she wasn't drinking it, or that she'd ordered bourbon at a margarita joint. "So I didn't stand you up if I showed."

"Not once, never even with a mark. Never even *before*."

As a rule, Lou did not talk about her life before the Lady Upstairs. I knew what I knew, which was more than Jackal did, but it still wasn't much. She didn't share the details with anyone, not even the Lady, I was sure. It thawed me a little, that Lou was sharing something with me she wouldn't tell the Lady. I touched her shoulder. "I'm sorry. I should've called. I got stuck in traffic."

Lou was wearing a little scrub of makeup—darkened lashes, lipstick glossy and reddish. If she knew I was lying, she didn't show it. She stared sullenly at her glass. Finally, she said: "So what is it, you don't want to spend time with me or you don't want to work Carrigan?"

"*Neither.* I'm sorry, I lost track of time—" That old saw. I heard Jackal's excuses in the office as soon as I said it and bit down on my tongue. Lou stared straight ahead, unwavering. She might've been straining to read the tequila labels on the amber-tinted bottles behind the bar for all the attention she paid me. I decided on something that was a close cousin to the truth. "Okay. Fine. The truth is, I *am* worried about Carrigan. He's too rich, Lou. He's too connected. There's too many ways for it to go bad."

"You don't think you can do it."

"It wouldn't be the first time we got in over our heads together."

It wasn't something I liked to dwell on, what had happened after my pie diner breakfast with Lou. I didn't regret it—I couldn't allow myself to regret anything that had turned me from *that* woman into Jo, that had brought Lou and even Jackal into my life. But it wasn't a pretty chapter, what had come between apple cheddar and my first successful case, weeks later.

Lou turned on the stool toward me. She blew out her cheeks in a big puff, eyebrows skyrocketing. "Do you blame *me* for that?"

"I blame us both." I signaled the bartender for a drink, whatever was closest, any damn drink he wanted to pour. Behind Lou, a couple moved to the bar next to us. He put his hand on the small of her back and she stepped away. Not a good sign for the date, but still: I'd rather have been him than me at that moment.

Lou didn't say anything. She took, finally, a small sip of her drink and said, under her breath, "Shit whiskey." Wondering, I was pretty sure, if my cold feet about Carrigan weren't payback for the way things had gone bad all those years ago.

"Forget it," I said. "I shouldn't have said anything. It wasn't your fault. It wasn't really anybody's fault."

"If you say so."

It wasn't that Carrigan was so similar to the Asshole. They didn't look much alike, except in that way older white men who paid taxes above a certain bracket all looked a little alike—the style of clothes, the haircut, the cash even men needed to keep up the goods. *He* hadn't been a lawyer, but he'd—*we'd*—worked in an office a few blocks from Carrigan's. That was pretty much the extent of the similarities, on the face of it.

But that first one had gone so badly, so quickly. With even fewer red flags than Carrigan.

After our pie breakfast, Lou had taken me back to her apartment, to shower and change. I had three weeks left on my lease and was getting desperate enough to consider calling my mother, asking her to send me money for a ticket home or a loan—I hadn't worked out the details yet. I was trying not to think about it. When I thought about it, I imagined her soft exhalation into the phone, a mix of relief and condescending care. *Oh, honey, I knew it. Come home. Let me take care of you.*

At that moment, Lou had seemed like a godsend, a temporary balm against everything that had flipped upside down in my world in the last month.

Especially when she'd come to me after the shower as I was combing my hair, smelling her lemon shampoo on me, a twinkle in her eye, and said: "How bad do you hate this guy? Really. Bad enough to get even?"

I hadn't even hesitated. Of course I hadn't.

Not two weeks later, Lou was meeting him for drinks, having ser-endipitously met cute at the bar around the corner from the office where I knew he spent his weekday happy hours. I watched them talk as the happy hours stretched to closing, Lou laughing loud and throaty the way I already liked. One drink multiplied into four, and then she was all over him, kissing the corners of his mouth, squeezing him through his thin pants. I'd laughed out loud from my hiding place out-side, I'd been so shocked by what I'd seen and how it made me feel, the pulse between my legs mingling with the power of knowing that to-gether, Lou and I were dangerous.

It didn't take much convincing on her part to get him back up to the office—I could picture her whispering into his ear, sibilant as a snake, *I can't stand it, I can't wait, fill me up, please, please*—and I followed them, taking the next elevator, getting off on the floor below and creeping up through the internal stairwell, waiting in the dark to hear what Lou said to him, did to him.

When she'd finished her work, leaving the Asshole tied up and naked in his boss's office—the door bolted from the outside; I still remembered where the keys were—we'd leaned against the door sti-fling our giggles, Lou in her bra and jeans, as we listened to him cry and plead for her to "fucking end this, you sick bitch, not funny any-more, please, somebody, Jesus Christ!"

Laughed ourselves sick.

We'd thought we were so clever. We'd thought we were invincible that night.

Behind Lou in the bar, a mariachi strummed his guitar, serenad-ing a tourist. "I'm sorry," Lou said, raising her voice above the music.

"That wasn't fair of me. This week's hell. There's been a problem with—" Lou stopped herself, her gaze stony again. The hairs on the back of my neck prickled.

"What? What problem?" Oh God, I thought, the Lady knew about the money. And now Lou knew what I'd done, too.

Lou bit her lip, flicked her fingers against her glass, her nails clacking. "Nothing. Nothing to worry you, anyway." Before I could ask anything else, she rushed on, "But the worst of it is I feel like . . . I guess I feel like . . . lately you've been avoiding me. Did I . . . did I do something?"

I felt a rush of guilt strong enough to knock the worry out of my head. Before anything else, Lou had always been there for me. "Of course not." I reached a hand forward, hovered it over her own. Lou didn't move, and I pulled it back. "I've been distracted. By Klein, Ellen." I held up a hand as Lou started to say something, but I shook my head. If I closed my eyes, I could see Ellen's teary face, pink feathers clinging to her goopy lip gloss, peering over her shoulder at me for one last affirmation I wouldn't give before trudging up the stairs of her apartment. I sipped on my melting margarita. I was sure as hell not ready to talk about her yet. "Trust me. She's fine. She'll be fine. Thursday will be golden. She could win a goddamn Oscar for what she'll do."

"Okay," Lou said, a small smile breaking through the thundercloud of her face. "I can't wait to see those pictures. Tell Jackal to turn the video over." She took a deep breath, pushed her bourbon away. "And then we can celebrate. With a *real* drink."

"Let me buy you a drink now," I said. "To make up for being so late."

Lou shook her head, biting her lip. There was a glow in her eyes now. "I'm done paying for drinks." She rolled her shoulders and took a languid look around the bar. She spotted them, the same couple I'd noticed earlier and flicked her eyes at me. A challenge. A game we'd played before.

"Batter up," she said, and leaned forward and tapped my arm. *Tag, you're it.* The spot burned through my sleeve. I had to keep myself from rubbing it.

Lou told me she didn't keep score, but that was bullshit. I was currently up three drinks on her, but it had taken the nearly three years I'd known her to get there.

He was still talking to the woman, but his eyes found me, gave me an appreciative once-over—if I were a kinder woman, I'd tap his date on the shoulder and tell her to keep moving, her first instincts had been right. Instead, I smiled. Looked away, looked back. Smiled again.

But Lou was faster. She was out of her chair and bumping him from behind before I'd moved. This time, she wasn't letting me win.

"Oh, I'm so sorry," she said, all big eyes and innocence. She hadn't even given me thirty seconds to make a move. Her fingers lingered on his sleeve and she flashed his date a sympathetic smile. "Did I spill your drink?"

The man was looking like he didn't know where to look. Trapped between panicked and amused and not sure if he could believe his own good luck. I could almost see the wheels spinning in his head, the mental calculations of how many of us, and where, and when, and whose legs pressed against his face, his waist, his hips . . .

"My friend is a little clumsy," I said, and his attention bounced back to me, a tennis match between women. His previously bored date sure looked interested now. You could almost call us matchmakers, Lou and me. "You should make her buy you both a round to make up for it. First dates aren't cheap."

"It's not a—" The woman started but then cleared her throat

and stared daggers at the two of us. "How did you know it was our first date?"

I shrugged and winked. "A lucky guess. I'm good at reading bodies." I hid a chuckle in a cough. "Body language, I mean."

And then he was stuck, volleying between the three of us, taking an extralong glance at the forty-five-degree angle I'd given him down my top. Lou had a little smile on her face and she was shaking her head at me: *You amateur.* But it was working. He took a look at his date, who'd stepped closer to him, and then at Lou absentmindedly stroking the material of his tie like she wasn't even trying to do it.

"No need," he said. "Why don't you two join us. What can I get you?"

We would stay for two drinks slipped onto his tab, just long enough for the bartender to get comfortable putting our beverages under his name. By that time, he'd be slurring and she'd be as possessive as if she actually liked him. And because we'd picked a couple on a date, there was little risk he'd demand repayment, monetary or otherwise.

The date excused herself to go to the restroom, and her absence emboldened him. He leaned into Lou, shrugging his weight onto her shoulders and draping a hand across her knee. Without losing a beat, Lou clutched my chin, her fingers drink-chilled, drawing me in for a kiss. It wasn't a regular part of our routine, and I could feel my heart skid as her nails scraped lightly against my jaw. Her lips were soft like lips and her tongue slid in between my teeth. She was selling it more than I was. I kept my hands to myself and my eyes closed and tried not to think of anything. After a few moments, she uncorked her mouth from mine with a pleasant little pop, and smiled at the man, who was watching the two of us, slack-jawed.

His date came back from the bathroom, but he couldn't stop staring at Lou, breathing like he'd run a marathon, and I knew her: she wouldn't be the first one to look away, either. I grabbed hold of Lou's hand and we excused ourselves back to our table, her hot giggle breaths drifting over my shoulder, my neck. We made a good team.

The trick was in keeping an eye on the date. By the time they started to make restless movements—she'd gone to the bathroom twice now; he was sobering up for the 405 with glass after glass of water—we'd finished seven or eight margaritas. It was a challenge we'd issued to each other silently, to see how long we could last before we chickened out and left. We'd been caught only a few times before, but this was the real game, not the free drinks: which one of us could stand the heat longest.

Lou and I slipped out seconds ahead of him closing the tab, cutting it close, the reckless pounding in my chest a building volcano that spewed into guffaws as we tumbled out of the bar to the shower of expletives from behind us, the outrage at his racked-up bill following us into the street.

We put a little distance between us and him, taking the long way back to our cars. I waited to see if she would invite me to follow her, feeling a little foolish, not wanting to say goodbye. Lou stepped closer, hooking her arm in mine. I wondered if she was thinking the same thing I was, which was that it might be the last con we'd ever run together.

At her car, she turned to me and said, "Truce?"

I shook my head. "No need. Never any fight."

She smiled back at me with her soft pink lips. "You have my lipstick on your teeth." She leaned over and rubbed it away with her thumb. I didn't move. Or breathe. Then she said, "I'll think about what you said about Carrigan. I mean it. I know you have the best interests of us all at heart. I know you'd do anything for the Lady. For me."

I thought of Ellen's dark eyes, slick with tears, her red mouth open and trembling. Still in that pink party dress, shaking in her seat.

Things I'd said to her that even I had never said to another living, breathing human before. But then I thought of the money that the Lady might already know was missing, and Lou's big hurt eyes, roaming over the bar as she wondered where I'd been, why I was avoiding her, and knew I'd say those things all over again if I had to. I'd go to the end of the world to keep that expression from Lou's face. If I had to.

"I would, Lou. Really, I would."

Chapter 13

'd noticed it in the Seven Galbi parking lot in the morning: brown Crown Vic, a lumpy cow of a car, no lights and no stickers, but there was no hiding that cop shape and sheen. I glanced through the window. No one inside. Nothing on the passenger seat. Could've simply been parked there—the lot was almost always empty in the morning—while the owner interviewed suspects or looted a doughnut shop. No need to jump the gun. *Not every cop in this city is looking for you, Jo. Get it together.* If it was still there at lunchtime, I would start to worry.

"Is there a Crown Vic parked outside?" I asked Jackal as soon as he dragged himself into the office. Not quite lunchtime, but still plenty to worry about. I leaned in his doorway and watched him ignore me from behind his computer screen, giving me the chance to stare at him. I can't say it wasn't an effective ploy on his part—he was so handsome. Damn him. I glanced around his office, looking for the contraband photos. I'd warned him that, even if I wasn't going to say anything, he needed to get rid of them: couldn't afford any chances for Lou to notice them. We both knew where her loyalties lay. I wasn't sure if he'd taken my advice, or if he even intended to.

Jackal didn't look up. "Don't know. Didn't check."

"Some private eye you'd be," I said, "with all those keen observational powers."

He made a big show of tearing himself away from whatever he was working on and stared at me. Those dark green eyes fringed by lashes a mile long. Money eyes. "You look tired," he said finally. "You didn't call me last night."

"There's that silver tongue that charms all the ladies."

"It doesn't have to charm when it's skilled at other things," he said, a small smile quirking one side of his mouth.

He'd honed some talents in the workplace, for sure. "Have you ever thought of retiring? From the Lady's line of work. How would you go about it?"

"Are you trying to make an honest man out of me?"

I smirked, laughing despite myself. "Never. I just wondered if you'd heard Lou talking about that before. Retirement."

"Tired of the game?" Jackal squinted at me. "Or tired of the whole outfit? We could make a great team, you know. You could get back in touch with the marks, then I'd lay it on them . . ."

I shook my head. I wasn't touching his side business with a ten-foot pole. "Has anyone done it before?" Watching him. Maybe he didn't know what the Lady had done to his ex, either.

Jackal shrugged, looking bored. "Dunno."

He wasn't that good an actor. I picked at a splinter in the wood grain of his doorway. "What time are you heading to the St. Leo tomorrow?"

Jackal rolled his eyes. "Two thirty. As soon as the cleaners have finished. I'll set up the room, then wait. I won't even get up to take a piss. I'll wait with my eyes glued to the screen for the world's oldest show. You know all the years I've been doing this, it's almost not even interesting anymore?" Jackal shook his head like he couldn't believe it. "I guess after long enough, even screwing can be boring. Even *tits*."

"Send me a picture of the room as soon as you get there." Usually, I'd wait in the lobby to make sure Ellen and Klein were on schedule. But I knew I'd check the room more than once during the wait, to make sure Jackal was where he was supposed to be. "And then one every thirty minutes, so I know you're still there."

"You don't believe me?"

"Never," I said. No window in Jackal's room. I couldn't even check if the car was still there. I plucked at the splinter, pulling out a small chunk of his door. "I bet that goddamn car hasn't moved an inch."

"What do you care? It's not like they're here to talk to *you*."

I shook my head. I had to check or else I would go crazy, coming up with fantasies of the blues storming the office, demanding their money. Asking for Lou, asking for the Lady. I didn't need that today of all days. Like Jackal, I should be thinking only about Klein. "You're right. They're not here to talk to me."

Jackal stared at my face again. Lou would have known I was lying. Jackal might have. I couldn't tell. I didn't care. "I'll be there this time, Jo. Trust me."

"If I believed every man who told me to trust him, I'd be pregnant," I snapped.

I stomped to the front windows and hooked a finger over one of the slats of the blinds, pulling it down so butter-yellow sunshine briefly blinded me. The car hadn't moved. But I could see the outline of a body behind the steering wheel, a hand dangling from the now-opened window. I caught my breath and looked back at Jackal's door. Still open, but he hadn't gotten up from the desk. Lou wasn't in yet—I wasn't sure when she would be. I chewed my lip, watching the car. As long as he stayed put, I wouldn't go down there. *Nothing good will come of talking to him, Jo*, I thought, even as I imagined Lou pulling into the lot, stopping to chat with him.

As I watched, convincing myself to stay where I was, the door opened and a salt-and-pepper squarehead climbed out of the car, glaring into the sunlight and looking around the strip mall, searching for something. With his eyes behind sunglasses, I couldn't see what he was looking for, but he found something he liked and nodded once to himself, heading for the staircase that led up to our office.

The Korean barbecue was in full swing, and the smoke from the tasty beef stung my eyes as I rushed down the stairs. I could only make excuses, promise the money by next week, hope that would buy me enough time to get the money from Klein. *If* everything went smoothly, of course. Between the sting tomorrow and setting up the money drop, there were still so many pieces that could go wrong.

I headed the man off at the bottom of the staircase, gripping both sides of the railing so I didn't slip a heel and go flying down into him. His expression didn't change as I stopped on the step above the lot, so that I was a touch taller than him.

"Can I help you?"

He didn't say anything. Thick around the jowls, neck like the trunk of a tree. His white button-down rolled up to expose a not-too-nice watch. I'd bet he'd been a cop since birth.

I crossed my arms over my chest and decided to play it righteous and offended. "We had reports that there was a man sitting in his car, staring at some of the women across the street. It was creeping the other girls out in the office, so I said I'd come check. Everything okay?"

He stared at me, not moving a muscle in his face, sizing me up. Taking in my face—I could feel it was pink, pinker than a trip down the stairs warranted—my hair frizzing in the morning heat, sweat darkening my blouse.

"Sorry," he said finally. "I guess I should get going." He didn't

move, but his gaze turned thoughtful and his sunglasses flicked up to
the second story of the complex. "Looks like you were coming out of
the Lady Upstairs' Staffing Agency. Is that your office?"

Why had I said *office*? I could've bitten my tongue out. No choice
now but to play it out. "That's right." I chucked my chin at the second
story of the complex and shivered in the heat.

"So you must know Lou," he said, smiling, friendly. We were
chums now.

"I do." I kept my face as stony as I could.

To my surprise, he simply nodded and smiled again, turning back
to his car and lumbering inside. "Tell her MacLeish stopped by," he
said, "if you don't mind. Tell her I'd be real happy if she gave me a
call." There was a message that would never get delivered.

He didn't wait for me to respond. Instead, he rolled the car away,
not moving quickly, holding up a hand out of the window in a parting
goodbye. I breathed a sigh of relief, glancing quickly back up at the
office. No Jackal silhouette, no telltale retreat from the window. I'd
bought myself some time.

But only a very little bit. MacLeish had been friendly enough,
hadn't threatened me or even Lou. A simple request still. But then, it
had only been a few days. It wouldn't be long before the courtesies
were replaced by something brassier. I had to fix it all, pay the bribe
money back, before it ever came to that.

There would be no second chances this time. Because this *was* the
second chance.

I'd almost toppled her empire once before.

If Lou's and my little extracurricular excursion to pay back the
Asshole had ended there, the two of us pressed cheek to cheek against
the laminate wood of his boss's door listening to him beg for help that
wouldn't come, my life would have been different. But then again, I
might also have been an Ellen—a girl looking for a quick buck, an

adventure, simply passing through the Lady's enterprise on my way back to the straight and narrow. It could have so easily been that, if he hadn't heard us. If he hadn't found me.

But we must have been louder than I'd realized. Two days later, he was pounding down the front door of my soon-to-be-former apartment, yelling that if I didn't let him in *right the fuck now*, he'd call the police on me and my little friend and whatever grifter game we had running.

"You think I don't know the sound of your voice? You think I don't remember the sound of your laughter?" the Asshole said, nearly cross-eyed with anger, slamming his fist into my Formica countertops.

It was, hands down, the most romantic thing he'd ever said to me.

But that wasn't the worst of it. When he guessed I was involved, he'd followed me straight to Lou's place. He knew we were in it together. I'd led him right to her. And because he was an asshole but not an idiot, he had enough of the pieces about the Lady's agency to make real trouble. Lou hadn't taken pictures. He had no reason not to go to the police. Unless we paid him one hundred large. He'd smiled as my jaw dropped. I had been the office manager—I knew what he made each year. It wasn't even a drop in the bucket to him. But he might as well have asked me for a plane ticket to Mars, the sum was that far out of reach for me. And he knew it. He didn't need the money. He just wanted to remind me what power really was.

He'd won. Again.

What choice did we have? I'd asked Lou. None, she'd told me. The only option was to fess up, come clean, fall on the mercy of our boss. She'd handle it for me—after all, before that moment, the Lady hadn't even heard my name—but whatever terms the Lady set, I owed her.

The expense, Lou explained to me, hadn't been only the bribe. It had been the protective measures the Lady was now taking. Before, Lou and Jackal had worked freelance, picking up cases from the Lady and coordinating over drinks or other public spaces. But the Asshole had figured it out—what was to keep him from threatening to go to the police again, even now that he had his money? The Lady's arrangement with the police predated me, predated even Lou, but even *they* couldn't sweep it under the rug if he made a big enough stink, got to the right person, an honest cop.

Enter: Perfect Alignment Massage. The Lady had bought the ailing business, done the bare minimum to convert the space. Now we had a legitimate cover, even paid taxes, the whole shebang. Girls? Of course we had girls coming through our doors. Los Angeles needed *a lot* of secretaries. We were doing the fine, upstanding work of placing them. Check the books. All in order. Every last penny accounted for.

Lou put a good face on it when we moved in. "This makes us respectable," she told me. "It makes us more of a *team*." We could call it Jo's Place, she'd joked, since really I was responsible for the office in the first place, in a roundabout way. If only that wouldn't attract too much attention, too many questions from passersby. *Jo's Place? A massage parlor? What exactly was offered . . . ?* If only they knew.

At least the Lady hadn't made me foot the rent bill on top of the bribe.

When I got back to the office, I stood in the front lobby for a moment, shaking. I made myself take three deep breaths before I moved, before I said anything. "I'm going home," I called to Jackal. "Remember. The St. Leo. Two thirty tomorrow. *Be there* or I'll drag you from the racetrack myself."

"Take it easy on the bottle tonight," he retorted.

I slammed the door to the office behind me. It wasn't bad advice from him, for once, I thought. Only there was no way I was going to follow it. Not tonight.

_____

The phone ringing woke me up. Lou, I assumed, calling to tell me whatever new nugget she'd sussed out about Carrigan. I jabbed the button on my phone without bothering to check the number. "Too early," I moaned into the receiver. The gin from earlier in the night was sloshing in my gut. I wished I'd thought to set out painkillers and water for myself before I'd fallen asleep on the couch. Past Jo, never looking out for Future Jo. "Can't you ever call me at a normal hour, f' fuck's sake."

"Jo?"

Not the voice I'd expected. I sat up on the couch, rubbing my face. The TV flickered, an old black-and-white movie nearly muted. A woman dancing, singing, by herself in front of a crowd, a phantom partner she kept repelling and embracing.

"Ellen? What is it, what's wrong?"

Amado mio, love me forever . . .

I knew without her having to tell me it was bad. But I didn't know how bad.

"I think you need to come over."

"Ellen, *what*—"

. . . and let forever . . . begin tonight . . .

"I think . . . he might be dead. Klein. He's not breathing and there's . . . there's so much . . . blood. In my apartment, oh God, it's *everywhere*. Come over *right now*."

CHAPTER 14

Outside her front door, Ellen had set up a planter filled with fake succulents and a welcome mat that said *#BLESSED* in big block letters. Ellen didn't answer the door right away, so I stood on her *#BLESSED* doormat and made a bloody mess of my cuticles with my teeth. I waited another twenty seconds before I rapped again on the door, harder, not stopping until she swung it open.

"Sorry," Ellen said. "I was in the bathroom." She turned away before I could study her face, but the waft of sweat and vomit coming off her let me know she hadn't been in the bathroom prepping her face for me.

"Well, come in," she said, sitting down on the couch and staring blankly at the television, which wasn't on. "He's in there." She pointed in the general direction of the bedroom.

She seemed fairly normal, if a little stiff and pale. Better posture than I'd ever seen, spine perfectly straight like she'd been impaled on a board. Her hands were trembling on her lap, but otherwise, she didn't seem that fragile. In shock, maybe.

From the living room, I could see a dark lump on the bed, spread-eagled, a thick black stain beneath him, turning the sheets a gluey, rusty color.

"Ellen, what did you *do*?"

"Is he . . . Is he really dead?"

I stepped into the darkened bedroom. Klein was in the center of the bed. Freshly dead, he looked like a mannequin, waxy and unreal. The back of his ruined head lolled off the side of a pillow. Blood had puddled onto the Berber on his side of the bed, and I could see small clumps of bone and viscera on the fog-gray walls, as far up as the crown molding. That satin headboard was a goner.

I'd never seen a dead body before.

"Yes," I said, after a moment, leaving the doorway and turning back to Ellen. I didn't need to take his pulse to be sure. I wasn't going to touch that thing with my bare hands. "He's dead."

That's when Ellen unspooled, my pronouncement unlocking shudders that started in her toes and moved up, until I could see even that poufy blonde hair start to dance on end. The whole time, she was chattering away, telling me what had happened, giving me every excuse.

". . . said I was some dumb kid, a bimbo, not even worth the Viagra . . ."

How long had he been dead? How long had she waited to call me? I stared at the smudgy browning streaks on the Lucite coffee table between us, faint enough to have been chocolate if I didn't know better, if there hadn't been a man oozing behind me in the bedroom. Where had those streaks come from—Ellen herself? Had she touched the body? Had she been stupid enough to touch him?

". . . and then he, he, he, he *choked* me, and we'd never done that before and I tried to act like it . . . was fine, but he wouldn't stop, he was *laughing*, and then it was over and I don't know, I think I . . ."

I forced my attention back to Ellen, trying to get a read on her. Her face was so pale it was almost blue. She was gouging at the threads of the couch cushion underneath her legs rhythmically with her nails. Her eyes wouldn't settle on any one thing, but her glance kept being tugged back to the bedroom.

All those slaps. And that wife he wouldn't leave. I wondered which had mattered more to Ellen, in the moment.

Days ago, I'd been so eager to catch those slaps on Jackal's bedside mic. What great leverage they'd have been. I forced myself to shake it off, count backward from fifty until my head cleared. If I fell down that self-loathing path now, I'd be no use to Ellen or myself.

"... and *you* told me, you said, 'Make him pay,' and that's what I ... that's what I thought ..." She circled her hands in the direction of the ruined producer, fingers flopping and jerking from loose wrists.

"Wait, stop. Start over," I said. *Make him pay.* Jesus Christ. *Come on, Jo, get a grip.* "Why was he even *here?*"

But I knew the answer to that one, or could guess. Which way had the call gone—inbound or outbound? *Sorry, baby, let me make last night up to you.* The same script, from either party. In the end, it didn't matter. Here we were.

Instead of answering, Ellen's face crumpled and she sobbed into her hands.

I let her sob. I walked back to the bedroom door, staring at the thickening black pool behind what was left of Klein's head. One day before the sting. One day before I would have had my money back, before the Lady would have canceled the debt. I closed my eyes for a moment against the wave of nausea that burned my stomach. I'd been so close.

And now, instead of cash, I'd be laying a dead body at her feet.

From the corner of my eye, I saw something on the bed move and I flinched, but it was only his hand, made slippery with blood, settling. I turned away from the body and walked to Ellen's window, the one I'd been on the other side of a few days prior, and peered down into the street. No one congregating in the alleyway, making notes about a suspected murder. No one outside at all, in fact. A fire escape that looked like it had seen very little use.

I hadn't known what to bring, hadn't been thinking at all, in fact. All I'd wanted to do was get in the car and see for myself. I hadn't thought to bring anything to cover the body, and I didn't even stock cleaning materials in serious supply in my own apartment. We'd have to use whatever Ellen had on hand. I looked around the living room— not so much as a wheeled bar cart we could've used to move him. I left Ellen chattering away in the living room, confessing everything to the walls like someone was capable of absolving her, and poked into her bathroom.

"I asked him to come over, I wanted to make sure he would still come over, after the, the party—" Ellen's shower curtain wasn't as opaque as I would have wanted, and it was decorated by gold and pink glitter swirls and a cupcake print, complete with cherry on top. In the top corner, gold foil spelled out *Good Vibes Only!* I yanked the curtain off the rod and brought it back to the living room, where Ellen was still talking.

"—and it was like, like everything was fine, you know? At least for a little while. He brought champagne. And flowers."

With my arms still full of Klein's pastel makeshift burial shroud, my eyes found the big spray of birds-of-paradise in a cut-crystal vase on Ellen's mantel, which made me think of the duvet at the St. Leo. I wondered if Klein, too, had thought of the acrylic bedspread when he bought them, if that's what had triggered thoughts of Ellen. His last living joke. I remembered a thing I'd heard once: birds-of-paradise are the goriest flower to kill. Decapitate them, and you have to deal with thick gray-green sap all over your hands, your clothes, the kind that never washes off. Birds-of-paradise bleed like any living thing.

"We made . . . love. But then he started choking me, you know, during, and he's never . . . That was new, you know? I tried to play along, act like I was fine with it, like it turned me on even—" I caught Ellen's shudder at that one. She was starting to repeat herself, verbatim. She'd practiced her speech before I got there, I realized. More than once.

"Oh my God," she said, starting to hyperventilate. For the first time since I'd stepped into the apartment, I caught her looking at the body, *really* looking at Klein. Her mouth dropped open—maybe to start screaming—and her body rocked as she suppressed a gag.

I crossed the room in three strides and took her by the shoulders. I gripped her in a rough hug, pressing her face into my collarbone until I was sure she wouldn't make a sound.

I was stroking her hair without even realizing it and murmuring soothing sounds into her ear, like you would with any frightened animal. "It's okay, it's okay," I said over and over, the words like glass in my throat. "Don't worry, we'll figure it out."

I needed her to keep it together. There was no way I could get Klein's body out of the apartment by myself. It wasn't going to be okay, for me or for Ellen or for Klein, but I needed her cooperation for what I knew would come next.

On the drive over, before I'd been sure that Klein was dead, I'd thought of all the worst-case scenarios, my next possible play.

If Klein really was dead, going to the police was not an option. I'd suspected Ellen wouldn't be able to keep her mouth shut about the Lady, the operation, and she was confirming that belief more and more each second. Especially since they were still missing their bribe money. And now, with Klein dead, no chance to get it back. No chance to get *any* of it back.

And what would the Lady say when I brought her this conundrum? No money and one of my girls turned murderess, the body of a highly public figure, one who would be *missed* for the very same reasons we'd picked him as a mark, decomposing in her bed.

I couldn't see that playing well, either.

I started to rattle questions off fast and hard at Ellen, wanting to shock her into giving me the truth, wanting to keep both of us from fixating on the corpse in her bed. This time, her answers were less practiced. No, she didn't think she'd touched the body. Well, maybe she had—she couldn't remember; she couldn't be sure. He *had* screamed, a little, although no one had come to check—the shot had been so fast, muffled by the pillows, it hadn't been any louder than a television sound effect. The gun was a present, from her uncle. (I'd stared hard at her at that one, trying to tell if she was lying.) No, she was pretty sure he hadn't told anyone he was coming over.

It wasn't great, but we would make it work—we had to. I told her to grab all the cleaning supplies she could find. Ellen sprang into action, flopping to her knees and putting sponge to carpet. She'd always been good with directions. But I already knew that: I'd profiled her myself. *Make him pay.* Oh yes, she could follow directions all right. My ears began to ring, and for a moment I felt light-headed, almost like I was going to pass out, but I gritted my teeth and braced my arms against the door frame of the bedroom. My gaze leveled, and I gulped down a few more breaths, bending over until I was steady, until I could think again.

Ellen started scrubbing down anything she could get her hands on, places I was sure Klein had never touched—the TV, the doorway, her kitchen tile. Anything to avoid the body in her bed. But some part of me had already guessed that would fall to me.

I began winding the sheets around the body, peeling him up from the mattress, where a pinkish stain spread out beneath him, trying to think only about the next thirty seconds. I didn't let myself imagine what Lou would say. In my fingers, the body felt like rubber. His remaining eye was closed, but his mouth was open, a faint trace of pale peach sparkle slicked to one lip. Ellen's lip gloss. I covered his mouth with the sheet and rubbed gently, trying to clean him off. His lips stuck to the sheet, to my fingers, which wouldn't stop trembling. I gave up, shuddering.

"Miss Howard?"

The staticky buzz of the intercom in Ellen's living room made me jump, but it made Ellen shriek outright. I thumped her on the shoulder and held a finger up to my lip. She stared at me from the floor, where she was trying to soak up Klein's blood with a sponge, fingers curling and uncurling. *What do I do?* she mouthed.

"Miss Howard, it's the front desk. Pick up, please."

I nodded at her, and Ellen moved to the intercom on tiptoe, as though they could hear her on the other line. She pressed the buzzer with one trembling finger, staring straight at me.

"Yes? What is it?"

"Miss Howard, do you have a guest over tonight?"

Ellen's finger slipped off the button, and I couldn't suppress a rising tide of terror, staring down at the body next to me. Someone *had* heard his scream; someone *had* heard the shot. We were so fucked.

"Ummm . . . I . . . I'm not quite sure . . ."

"A silver Audi, parked in the guest spot? You have to fill out the paperwork ahead of time for guest spots, Miss Howard. We've been over this. Someone's already reserved that parking spot tonight."

I blew out a sigh of relief, leaning forward a little and then catching myself as I swayed too close to Klein's body. In the living room, Ellen was laughing, borderline hysterical, thanking the front desk over and over, telling them she'd have her guest move the car as soon as he was *no longer indisposed.*

"It's not a request, Miss Howard. Please move the vehicle *now.*"

"Hang *up,*" I hissed at her, looking around the room for where

Klein might have left his keys. His coat, tossed over a dining room chair. I jumped off the bed, Klein bumping up and down as I did so, and shook the jacket loose, searching through the pockets. Nothing. No part of tonight was going to come easy.

The dead man's pants were in the bedroom, crumpled at the foot of Ellen's postcoital bed. I avoided making eye contact with the body as I picked them up by the hem.

"What are you *doing*?" Ellen shrieked.

I shook the pants out, and Klein's keys jangled onto the floor. I fished them out and held them up to Ellen. She reached for them, and I had a sudden vision of Ellen flooring the gas pedal, driving off into the distance, and leaving me behind with Klein's body in the bedroom.

"Huh-uh," I said, snatching them back and shouldering past her and out the front door, checking both directions before I scurried into the lobby.

Ellen's apartment was located on only the second floor of the Alto Nido. It was a short elevator ride down to the subterranean parking garage, but I counted the steps between Ellen's front door and the lift: fifty-six. Three apartments on either side. One person stepping out into the hallway for a late-night drive, to take out the trash, and it'd be game over. No, it would have to be the fire escape. We'd have to try not to fumble Klein's body over the side on the way down.

It didn't take me long to find his car, a silver Audi with vanity plates that read *MOVIEMN*. At least he'd take his last ride in style. I checked before I slid in to see if anyone had noticed me—the last thing I needed was some witness remembering a tall brunette who didn't live in the building driving a car with vanity plates into the alley. At the last minute, I remembered the bungee cords in my trunk—I'd helped Lou move a bookshelf weeks ago—and doubled back to my car to fish them out, taking the steps three at a time to get back to Ellen's apartment.

When I opened the door, I recoiled back over the threshold, my eyes burning. The entire apartment reeked of bleach. I wondered if the smell could seep through the walls, if the neighbors would smell it and wonder. Coughing, I propped the windows open, then immediately shut them—that wouldn't help our low profile.

In the bedroom, Klein was still swaddled in patchy sheets where I'd left him, the rest of the bed naked beneath him. Ellen was crouched above his head, careful not to touch the body, sobbing as she scrubbed at the reddening headboard, making a frothy mess of herself.

"Ellen," I said, "we have to go."

It wasn't ideal—there was so much left to clean—but with the car parked in the alley, we had to move quickly. Tomorrow, when the clues started to pile up, I didn't want anyone remembering Klein's car parked behind the Alto Nido. *Hey, did he know anyone there? Wait a minute, a bit player from one of his movies lives here? Strange coincidence . . .*

She didn't seem to hear me, her breathing getting heavier, her sobs turning into hiccups as she scoured the fabric.

"*Ellen!*"

I grabbed her by the arm and yanked her off the bed. She kicked Klein on the way down and gave a faint yelp. I pressed a hand over her mouth, gripping her cheeks so hard they turned white.

"We *have* to go *now*."

Klein wasn't a big man, a little taller than Ellen but not as tall as me, and while not thin, per se, not exactly fat, either, but he was heavier than I'd expected him to be and more difficult to hold on to. The blood made him slippery, and the feeling of his guts on my hands made the hackles at the back of my neck rise so that I jerked and nearly dropped him every time I thought I felt a slickness on my palms. Soon Ellen and I were sweating, wrestling the bedding and shower curtain around the body—starting to smell, which wasn't helping matters, either—clipping Klein into place with the bungee cords.

"Oh God," Ellen muttered as the body slumped against the bed frame, neck jammed unnaturally against the wood. Then she bent over and threw up on the floor, most of the splatter hitting the shower curtain tucked around him and outlining his sunken face in wet bile. I didn't say anything as she apologized over and over again. I was too busy trying not to stare, trying not to get sick myself.

"Now or never," I said, as much to myself as to Ellen, and grabbed him under the armpits. He was heavy and sagged unnaturally between us—a human hammock—but we got him to the window. Before I knew it, I had my arms full of dead producer on her fire escape, feeling backward with my toe for the next step, trying not to breathe through my nose, not to groan or trip or make any noise at all.

Together, we bumped him down the stairs. The shower curtain slipped once, and I caught a glimpse that made me queasy. I stopped to cover him back up so that I didn't throw up, too. The entire time, a strange feeling in the pit of my stomach, like even as everything was lurching forward without my permission—the dead producer, having to bring the car around to the alley before we could completely douse the apartment in bleach—it was all happening exactly the way it should.

When we reached the bottom, Ellen propped Klein against the car, shuddering and crying, her face turned away as she kept him in place while I popped the trunk. A bungee cord snicked loose as we slid him into the trunk, and I grabbed it and threw it in the back seat. As he rolled into the car, the shower curtain, tacky with blood, stuck on the carpet and shifted, revealing the corner of his blown-apart face. Just days since I'd seen him at Hollywood Forever, alive, if not well. I cursed under my breath, panting, unable to look away for a moment.

I pushed the trunk softly closed and shoved Ellen into the front seat. She was starting to hyperventilate, to make a strange sound deep in her lungs somewhere between a whistle and a howl.

"Stop that," I said, my own voice harsh, almost unrecognizable. My arms were shaking from the effort it had taken to drag Klein down the fire escape, and my back was aching. I was crunched up against the steering wheel because Klein's legs were shorter than mine and I didn't want to stop to fix it until we'd driven him far, far away from the Alto Nido.

The glow of approaching headlights in the rearview blinded me for a moment. I turned the key in the ignition so sharply the car sputtered and died. Behind me, the headlights flicked their brights, annoyed. They'd gotten an eyeful of the vanity plate now, I thought. I ducked down in my seat and turned the engine again—this time, it caught. I stomped on the gas, spinning my wheels for a second as I screeched out of the alleyway, leaving scorched tire marks in my wake.

Ellen started to make a strange, high-pitched noise, unearthly. I couldn't think with that sound in my head. But one thing was becoming clear. On the drive to Ellen's apartment, I'd put off calling Lou. I'd had the fantasy I could handle it on my own. I'd already screwed up so many times. But now, with Klein decomposing in the car, I realized how mistaken I'd been. How much I needed her.

Lou would know what to do next. Lou would help me. I was almost positive.

Chapter 15

When Lou's car pulled up behind me in the canyon, spewing gravel, I let out a long shuddering sigh and nearly buckled over the steering wheel. *Don't cry*, I told myself. *Don't you fucking cry.* Ellen was doing plenty of crying for us both.

I climbed out of the car and held up a hand. Even before she was out of the car, I could see that Lou's eyes were big, enormous, and her lips were white. I walked to the back of the car, popped the trunk, and waited for Lou to meet me. There was a chill in the night air and I started to shiver, but I wasn't sure if it was from the dip in temperature or the twist of both relief and nerves I felt now that Lou was here. I knew she'd help me. She would. But there would be a price.

I'd told her I could handle Ellen. I'd told her I had it under control.

Even in the dark, I could see the body was leaking. The first thing I thought when I noticed it was that I was glad Klein's car was taking the hit. The carpet in his trunk would never be the same.

Of course, we'd probably end up torching the car anyway—wasn't that how people disposed of corpses? And Ellen would probably have to get rid of her bed. It was a thing of nightmares now. The balance of my eight grand she hadn't spent on party dresses would go to a new apartment.

Lou, chain-smoking beside me, hadn't said much since she'd arrived. Instead, we stood shoulder to shoulder, staring into the trunk of Klein's car. The light from the filter tip on her cigarette crackled, glowed, and shrank rhythmically next to me, like a series of tiny dying stars. A piece of ash was stuck to the corner of her lip like a gray snowflake, and every so often she tapped the butt of her cigarette against her brow.

In the car, Ellen began the wailing again and I shut the door, mostly for a little peace and quiet but also so I could avoid Lou's eyes on me.

"Did you check his pulse?" Ellen had asked me on the drive to the canyon. "Maybe they could still do something, maybe if we . . . took him to a hospital . . ."

I hadn't said anything. We both knew it was useless. Instead, I'd kept turning and twisting the car down different roads, my only objective to get as far from the city lights as I could.

"Please," she said, and then she repeated it over and over and over again until I gripped her wrist, one hand still on the steering wheel, eyes on the road. I told her if she didn't shut up, I was going to put her in the trunk with Klein. Her eyes got big and round, and she didn't say anything after that.

I'd waited until I passed an address I could read and counted my turns until I found a deserted stretch of arroyo seco to my liking. Then I called Lou.

In the dark the trickling liquid from the trunk might have been oil if it wasn't for the sucked-penny smell of Klein's blood. Lou turned her

eyes back to what had once been Hiram Klein, and she leaned in close
to his sort-of face, gone soft and mushy now, collapsing in on the crater
of what was once an eyeball.

"Good shot," she said finally. "Where did it happen?"

Somewhere in the distance a coyote moaned and Ellen mimicked
the sound. I still didn't want to think about her.

I told Lou everything I knew, which wasn't much. Somewhere in
the middle of my story, Lou's cigarette burned out, but she didn't make
a move to light a new one and she let it burn down to her fingers.

Ellen was keening from the car like something dying, and Lou's
gaze kept flicking toward the back seat. I could see it clearly in that
moment. I had a choice: pin it all on Ellen or decide that she was one
of our own. And Lou and me, we protected our own.

"Maybe he did it to himself," I said. "Maybe it was a suicide."

Lou's eyes glittered at me in the dark. I knew better than to get
close to any of the girls we worked with. And I never would have considered myself close to Ellen, but I couldn't stop thinking about it:
Make him pay. I shuddered.

"You think he got bored of waiting for her to slip into something
more comfortable and put one in his own eye? You think that's a story
we could sell?"

My hands were shaking. I put them on top of the trunk and
squeezed the metal with my thumbs. My nails rattled against the
paint. "He hit her, you know," I said. "Maybe it was self-defense." Lou
was silent. "She's fucked if she goes to the police, I promise you that.
She won't say anything. I know she won't say anything."

"Okay." Lou leaned closer to the trunk so that she was nearly eye
level with Klein. My arms bridged over them both. "Okay. So what do
you want us to do with him? Call Robert?"

I imagined Jackal coming to our aid in his fresh white shirt and
dry-clean-only slacks. I imagined the worry on his face at the stains a

body would leave. I imagined a scene in which he got hysterical and I had to slap him back and forth across the face screaming, *SNAP OUT OF IT, BE A MAN.*

But that wasn't Jackal at all. Maybe that was me. I didn't want to see his face, I thought, and then I realized maybe it was truer that I didn't want him to see mine.

"We don't need him," I said.

"How are we moving the body, then?" Lou straightened from the car and exhaled twin streams of smoke from her nostrils. For the first time, I noticed she was wearing a black dress, silk and tight. She'd swapped shoes that would've matched the outfit for sneakers. Whatever she'd been doing, she'd had enough time to grab the right footwear, but not to change.

"Bungee cords from my car," I said.

Lou's mouth dropped open. "You did *not.*"

"Back seat."

Lou walked around the side of the car and peered into the back seat, which caused a fresh eruption of wails from Ellen. When she turned back to me, Lou had an expression on her face I'd never seen before. She brought her fists up to her eyes and knuckled them, swaying back and forth until she swayed into my chest, her head against my collarbone for a few seconds, and that's when I realized she was laughing.

"This isn't funny, Lou. Come on, I need you." She pulled back, but I could still feel the weight of her against me. It wasn't a good feeling, the phantom heft of her. "Stop laughing at me and be helpful," I snapped.

I'd have been better paid if bodies were a regular occurrence in our line of work. In three years, this was my first. My fingers were accustomed to the glossy coating of hotel key cards and silky scraps of lingerie. Not the oil slick of blood and viscera and other things leaking out of Hiram Klein. Before this week, I'd never expected bodies to be part of our work. I wondered if Lou had ever handled any before this.

"We could drive him to the river. Push the car in," I said.

"There's no water in the river," she said. "And the ocean's too far. The sun will be coming up by then."

"Okay," I said. "Okay, okay, okay. So here are the facts. We have a dead body in the trunk."

"Yes."

"Along with this dead body, we have . . . we have some paper trail about Klein being our mark. We have someone who hired us, who knows that Klein was being professionally played. We also have a grieving widow who will want answers." Ellen's wailing hit a fever pitch, and I leaned forward and smacked the back window with the palm of my hand. "Goddammit, be quiet for one minute!"

"Jo."

"The body has to go," I said. "The car has to go. But they can't really *go*. Klein is too visible to disappear."

Lou nodded, her cheeks hollowed like she was sucking on a lemon. She was waiting for me. She was trying so hard not to tell me what she'd already figured out.

I pinched the bridge of my nose. "How much was the contract? Has it already been paid?"

"Jo." Lou stepped toward me, putting one hand on my shoulder, cupping the smeary mess I'd made of my face. "You're my girl who can sell any story. Think for a moment. What's the story we can sell here? One of the richest men in California is dead, and how? What will his wife say? What will the press say?"

I could feel my mouth starting to tremble. *Keep it together, Jo, you fucking crybaby.* "He was— Maybe it was a robbery gone bad, a c-carjacking—"

"Jo," Lou said, stroking my cheek. She cupped my face in her hands, a lover's move, and whispered, "You said *anything*. You'd do anything."

The answer was staring me in the face and I didn't want to see it. I didn't want to see it at all.

I thought of the Lady, with her stupid blue tattoo and so much money she could write a monthly bribe to the police for eight grand. The Lady, who held my life in her hands. And on the other side, Ellen, with too much information and too many reasons to turn over what she knew, the best reasons now. With each blink, I could see a different Ellen—the imprint of her arm in the glow of the TV at the Aldo Nido, then her face streaked with tears and pink feathers in the front seat of my car.

I closed my eyes, let my cheek lean into the curve of Lou's hand. Remembered Lou's lips on mine on Olvera Street. The brush of her fingertips as she tucked a cocktail umbrella behind my ear, Lou's face tipped to mine, telling me she knew I'd do anything for her, she could count on me. Telling me without telling me: we could always count on each other. If no one else, always each other.

And then again, for the last time, the sound of Ellen keening in the car.

The drop from the side of the road wouldn't be enough to kill someone if this were really an accident. But if you weren't paying attention. If you had the police in your pocket—or thought you did. I lifted shaking fingers to my brow. I tried to block out Ellen's face as it had been the day I first met her, that hopeful grin and large dark eyes, so unusual with her coloring.

When I opened my eyes, there was a very real Lou right in front of me, her face so pale I could map each freckle on her face in one glance. Expecting an answer from me.

"You don't have a gun, do you? No. That's too obvious. It has to be a plausible accident."

Lou stood there, watching me, smoking still.

"Put that out," I said quietly. "We're already going to have to pick up enough evidence as it is."

Silently, she reached into her purse and shook a plastic bag at me. She bent over and started collecting the spent butts. Then she went to Ellen's side of the car and tapped on the window with two fingers, as politely as she'd done once to me. That same friendly smile. Ellen opened the door, pushing her legs out, sitting sideways. I could see her hands shaking in her lap in the moonlight.

Ellen, who had already threatened our livelihood once. Who I still owed money to. Who had taken slaps from the dead thing in the trunk because of me. She'd irritated me, and she'd fucked up, she'd *killed* a man, but wasn't there some line I wouldn't cross?

Lou's hand was on her shoulder now, touching her hair, cupping her face. So kind. My Lou. So loving. Ellen's trembling was starting to ease under her gentle fingertips.

Lou straightened and motioned me over, and Ellen turned to look at me. Her eyes were red, so swollen I wondered if she could see me, and Lou's magic wore off—it wasn't only her hands shaking; it was her whole body now. Like she was scared of me. How could she be scared of me? I would never actually hurt anyone.

Lou's hands all over her, still.

And then I could hear the click of my own heels on the pavement, walking toward Lou with my arms outstretched, reaching for them both.

CHAPTER 16

I'm not normally this stupid, but I wanted to watch the sun come up over the ocean, because I was alive and I could. I could remember each toss and roll on the mattress, the buzz of the refrigerator like a live wire threading my veins, keeping me company. Even the hushed murmurs of the TV I switched on in the early hours couldn't soothe me back to sleep. When you remember it, that's not sleep. And I remembered every sleepless moment of that night.

It was a long enough walk from my apartment to the water that it made me feel warm and awake by the time I got there. I took my shoes off and trekked into the sand, the crystals smooth and sparkling as white sugar. A navy sky flickered with the jets taking off, and I sat there and looked at the gray-blue gush of the water for a long time. The curls of white spray like smoke over the waves. I'd gotten there early enough that dawn was still pinkening, rosy like the color of blood vessels popping in eyeballs.

No.

Rosy like the color of nipples or bubble gum or eyeballs or a *sunrise*, goddammit, that was all it looked like. Pink dawn, that was all I meant.

"Don't worry," Lou had said the night before, washing her hands in my bathroom sink. She worked up a lather with pale green soap, eucalyptus wafting from her wrists, then flicked the drops off and made handprints on her black silk dress to dry them. Lou stared at herself in the mirror for one long moment before she caught my eye and said, "None of this happened, not at all."

So it hadn't happened. Not the events of the canyon, or the return to Ellen's apartment, after, where we'd finished cleaning anything that might have had my prints on it and picked up my car. If none of that had happened, that meant there was nothing to worry about. And if it hadn't happened, then I was still me this morning. Still human.

I sat and stared at the ocean until I couldn't bear thinking my own thoughts any longer, and then I got up and walked along the beach until I found a 24/7 convenience store near the water. I told myself: no drinks or maybe just the one.

I grabbed some rotgut gin and a glass bottle of apple juice, wanting something punishing, and slapped down a twenty-dollar bill in front of the bored and sleepy cashier, who barely even twitched her ponytail in response. I left before she could give me my change. I didn't want to stare at her face, wondering what it would look like after six long minutes noosed by a seat belt. Her eyes popping out, her tongue lolling.

Be human, Jo.

I parked it on the beach, dropping down on the slightly damp sand and kicking back a swish of gin topped with a mouthful of apple juice. I made myself do it three times in a row, the sugary juice hurting my teeth while the gin fogged my brain. In the distance, I watched a woman march back and forth on the bike path, her arms behind her, touching an ankle to a wrist with each step. She moved slowly but with purpose, concentrating hard. Like, if she could get each step right, nothing else mattered.

I'd asked Lou to stay the night but she'd said no and I couldn't help myself, I'd said: "I didn't mean like *that.*"

Lou sighed—in my kitchen by then, my fingers already opening a bottle of something clear and not very cold—and then she shook her head and said, "Oh, Jo."

"But if someone comes asking us about . . . about Ellen. Maybe someone saw something at her apartment. It was stupid of me to move the body." My fingers scrabbled against the plastic protector on the vodka and I gave up, put it to my mouth and tugged with my teeth.

Lou ran her fingers through her hair, snagging. She winced. "She killed him. She wouldn't have waited there with him for the police to show up. She'd have tried to get away."

"So was it vigilante justice for our mark? What happened tonight?"

"No," she said patiently, like speaking to a slow child. "Nothing happened tonight. Nothing we know about. If we knew Ellen, it was only in passing, some girl we—*you*—grabbed drinks with once or twice. The only thing that happened tonight was a very young, very stupid girl killed her lover somewhere, in her apartment, on a dirt road, wherever. It doesn't matter. She was tired of—well, whatever. There will be reasons, but that's not our job. She killed him, and she put him in the trunk of her car. And then she lost control of the car. A fluke accident."

An accident, being strangled by your own seat belt. I wasn't sure anyone would buy that. But there wasn't anything we could do about it now. "I don't think anyone saw me," I said, but I couldn't be sure. I couldn't tell if it was only wishful thinking. Those bright lights flicking in my rearview.

Lou stood perfectly still, watching me. No one could stand as still as Lou, even sweating through a silk dress. Looking to see if I was cracking up. If I was a liability. I knew that look, but I'd never been on this end of it before. I pulled the feeling down into my spine, tucked it away in case I needed more nerve in the future.

"No one saw me. I'm sure of it."

"Good girl," she said with a brief, tight smile. "The police will have no reason to link the two of you. They won't be trying very hard, either."

"I've never heard of anyone strangled by their seat belt," I said, closing my eyes against what I saw as I said it.

"A midmonth bonus should make it more plausible," Lou said, grabbing her keys and her purse.

I should've told her then, that thing I knew and she didn't. A thing that might make all the difference in the world. But all I could think of was Ellen next to me in the car, teeth chattering, wailing and wild and *alive*.

"I don't think either one of us should be alone tonight. I don't want to be alone tonight."

"The oldest line in the book," Lou said, smiling and moving to the door. "It'll be all right, you'll see."

Because I hadn't been careful, a small line of sand had gathered around the mouth of the juice bottle. I didn't bother to wipe it clean as I chased more of the gin down my throat.

In front of me, the ocean was sluggish. Ghostly palm trees, fronds sharp as scissors, cracked apart the asphalt of the empty parking lot. In a few hours, a gaggle of sticky little waders circled by inflatable red tubes making a toilet of the ocean would descend upon the beach, and then you'd never find the space in your own head to not think about things. Far in front of me, the waves blued the air with salty reaching fingers.

Somewhere else, perhaps not very far away, Lou waited for the sun to rise, the black silk dress tossed over the chair next to her bed. Or maybe she was asleep still, nestled in someone's arms. From the beach to the hills to that canyon in no time at all—some spandexed do-gooder chasing a bichon frise would find her way to Ellen and the car soon. If they hadn't already. I could almost picture the scene—the puffball of a dog yapping at the edge of the canyon, pissing as it ran. It would know before anyone else did; it would know what a body looked like after six hours cooking in the new-morning sun.

For God's sake, be human, Jo.

At some point, I'd started crying and I hadn't even realized it. One of the signs of cracking up. I was going to go crazy, sitting there with nothing but my thoughts.

Lou picked up my call on the third ring.

"I can't stand this. Why didn't you stay last night?"

A pause. "Jo, where are you?"

"I mean, what's my alibi? We should've watched movies all night or something. Made a prank call to Jackal. Something with a time stamp."

A longer pause. Mentally, I put together my to-do list: *1. Alibi. 2. Make nineteen grand in a day. 3. Laundry.* I choked back a giggle. There was always the possibility I'd lose my mind before I found money for the bribe, and then I wouldn't have to worry about anything at all.

Lou's voice was soft, a little tired. "I was with someone else last night. As far as he knows, it was the whole night."

"Oh."

"It'll raise more questions if I have to tell him something else later."

"Uh-huh."

"Where are you? Let me come get you and we can discuss it," Lou said.

"I'm sure you already have plans with Mr. Alibi. I'd hate to intrude."

"I'll pick you up. We'll grab a drink."

I wanted to believe the worry in her voice was for me, that she'd realized she'd made a mistake. That she should've stayed with me. I said yes, a drink would be nice. I gave Lou the name of the convenience store I'd left, and she told me she'd be there in twenty minutes.

I waited another few minutes, working a little more on my bottles, thinking and not thinking, trying to make myself believe that what we'd done had been only a nightmare I'd concocted after one too many nips of bad gin. Time kept moving forward, never backward, no matter how bad you wanted it to, and after fifteen minutes that went too quick, I got up and walked back to the convenience store to wait for Lou.

Behind me, the ocean kept its own counsel because nature is far wiser than any of us and who knows what sleeps under its waters. I bet you anything the ocean itself couldn't even tell you.

CHAPTER 17

Lou's car shimmered like a mirage on the horizon, and I skidded into the passenger-side door, yanking at the handle before she'd even stopped the car.

"Hey."

"Hey yourself," Lou said, pulling away from the curb. She was a little pale, a red slash of lipstick making it more obvious, and she was wearing dark cat-eyed sunglasses. It didn't look like she had slept much last night, either.

"You look—"

"Better than you do," Lou said. She didn't take her eyes off the road.

"Where are we headed?"

"Chinatown."

"We never go to Chinatown," I said. An unpleasant idea, like cake smashed into cashmere: "Are we meeting Mr. Alibi there?"

Lou didn't say anything. If I were a different woman, maybe I could've left it at that.

"Who is he? A new mark?"

We stopped at a light. I studied Lou's profile, tipped away from me. The mussed hair. The long line of her neck, all smudgy with fingerprints I could almost see. Her silence was making my skin crawl. "Christ, an *old* mark?"

Lou checked her lipstick in the side mirror, slid a thumbnail around her bottom lip. "I wish I hadn't said anything."

Outside, the green palm trees were turning dizzy cartwheels against the sharp white sky. God, I hated the sun. I hated the heat. Of course I was wrong; he wasn't a case. She wouldn't have asked him to cover for her if he were. Well, there was now one thing between us he'd never have.

Lou's knuckles were white on the steering wheel, and she was tapping the brakes steadily, which made the car jerk and jump. Good.

I couldn't stop. The murder and no sleep, Ellen's bulging eyes and little blue neck—and now this. "What about me, Lou? I'm just hanging out here, twisting in the fucking wind, no alibi, nothing? It wasn't my idea to strangle her, if you remember. *That* was definitely not my idea."

Lou slammed on the brakes at a red light, practically making a trampoline of them, and I jerked forward against the seat belt, smacking my hand against the dashboard. I stared at her, and she rubbed her hand across her face, trying to smooth out the anger. "Drunk again," she said finally. It wasn't a question.

"Yeah, well." I stared out the window. It wasn't even noon. This day would never end. When we passed by dark buildings shimmering in the heat, the glare made a mirror of my window. Black smudges under my eyes. Lips chewed to bits. Dark hair pulled back in a low ponytail, an efficient style that wasn't doing my face any favors. "I don't think you can blame me for that today."

After that, we rode for a while in silence. Lou nudged us onto the freeway, and I stared up at each shrub-covered overpass, refusing to break the silence. It stayed frosty between us through the golden twin-dragon gate, past the street vendors hawking yellow, red, and pink fake flowers on the sidewalk, past abandoned concrete curly-maned lions protecting no one, until Lou parked, not waiting for me to get out of the car before she was halfway through the gates to Chinatown.

I scampered after her, catching the full force of the gasoline fumes in my mouth where it mixed with the gin and made a not-unpleasant sweet taste on my tongue, and I wondered if it had even bothered her at all. Last night. Ellen. Any of it.

She led me through a square bookended by pagodas, one red, one green, decorated with sun-bleached lanterns that shimmied with any puff of air. Right, left, left—she didn't slow down or check where she was going. The neon signs were quiet, waiting for a nighttime resur-rection. I remembered what Jackal had told me once, that Chinatown had been designed by Hollywood scenery artists, a sort of living movie set. Except that people really made their homes here. Lou and I knew it well: when you kept up the illusion long enough, it became real. This city knew it, too.

Once or twice Lou moved out of sight and I had to pick up the pace to find her again. It wasn't that she was faster than me, I realized. I had the longer legs. She was cruising on autopilot, finding her way back to some old haunt. Making a point of showing me the pockets of her life I didn't know. Finally, Lou stopped in front of a matte-black door, a name buried in the corner of the shuttered glass window. She held the door open and followed me inside.

Lamps with dark Tiffany glass along the sleek bar cast an orange glow into the corners of the space. It made the bar look muddy, like clay. Even with the lamps, the bar had that darkness made for drink-ing, the kind the best can manufacture no matter the hour. Lush leather chairs grouped in corners. It was a good spot to seduce a mark

"Uh-huh. Blue tattoo on her wrist. Not even a nice blue, like a navy. Ugly blue, ugly, ugly."

"What did she say to you? Did you mention anything about Ellen? Even her name?"

Lou tucked her lips between her teeth and glared at me, staring intently at my face. I liked having an effect on her.

"Wouldn't you like to know?"

"Jo . . . !"

"Temper, temper," I chided. "I didn't mention Ellen. I did not believe that Ms. Howard was relevant at that time." I unfurled each word carefully from my tongue. "Should we *mention* her now?"

Lou shot me a *what are you, crazy?* look. "You better hope she never finds out." She punched out her cigarette. "Jo, this isn't a joke. She'll say you've gotten lazy, that I've gotten soft. That I should've put you in that car with Ellen. Or at least left the two of you for the cops to find. She has a business to run."

The bar door swung open, and Robert stood there, framed in light. It was still bright outside, still daytime. That was surprising. It felt like we'd been in the dark for hours, underwater.

Lou turned to him, and she was standing now, smiling for him, absolutely nothing wrong, nothing weighing heavy on her mind. She leaned forward as he stepped closer, and I noticed crow's feet starting to tug at the corner of her eyes, gone when she didn't smile or laugh. And I couldn't help myself, him walking toward us, it slipped out, I said: "I'm glad, Lou. I'm glad it's going to always be there between the two of us. Forever. Just you and me."

for the first time—to make a not-so-random rendezvous seem like fate.

Lou picked a seat in the farthest corner from the door. She gave a nod to the bartender, busy polishing a glass, who nodded back. Without asking what I wanted, she held up two fingers as if to say, *Two of the usual.* Lou drew a cigarette out of the case in her purse, setting tip to flame, exhaling a feathery plume of smoke.

"You'll like the drinks here."

"I like the drinks everywhere," I said. "They treat you like a regular."

Lou took another long drag, blew it toward the ceiling. "I was, once."

The bartender set two whiskeys in front of us. I gulped half of mine in one go. She watched me drink and said, "Now, are you ready to talk about it like adults?"

"I'm surprised you didn't mention him before. I don't know why you wouldn't tell me."

Lou waved her hand. "I meant getting our stories together. What's bothering you?"

"The murder, mostly."

Lou cut her eyes at the bartender and back at me. She didn't have to say anything. I held up my hands, a half apology. Hours ago, if Ellen had made that mistake, mentioning the murder in public, I might have slapped her. But it wasn't hours ago anymore. Funny how that worked.

"The police won't find anything to trace"—Lou mouthed Ellen's name at me—"back to us for a few days at least, and once they do, they'll be less inclined to poke around. You know what I mean."

I took another gulp of my drink. I thought about Lou's face when she left my apartment, the look of knowing pity she gave me when I suggested she stay. I thought about that thing I knew about the police's bribe money that she didn't. What her face would look like then. I finished the drink.

Lou reached into her purse, drew out another cigarette. "After I left, did you go over to Robert's?" She didn't look me in the eye as she asked it, signaled to the bartender to bring me another. "Part of Jackal's paycheck covers alibis. If it comes to that."

"I didn't want to involve him in this. I don't want him to know about it."

"You haven't mentioned anything to him?"

"And I'm not going to," I said, starting to feel annoyed. "The bartender sure is attentive. When did you stop being a regular? Why didn't you ever bring me here before?"

"Does Jackal know Ellen's name?"

"*Yes*, he knows her name."

Lou leaned back in her chair, staring slightly above my head. The bartender reached in front of me, set down another drink. His T-shirt bunched up, and I could see the tattoo on his biceps, the white flesh pebbled like an uncooked chicken. He was looking straight at Lou. Staring at her, in fact.

"Thank you, that's enough," I snapped at him. He straightened and left.

Lou cleared her throat. "It'll be on the news. He'll want to know what happened. And," she said, looking me over, "you're half in the bag already." She drew her phone from her purse, punching a few buttons with her thumb. When Jackal answered, she told him the address and hung up. Seeing my face she added, "You know it's better if we tell him a handful of details. Get ahead of it. That way he won't be guessing."

"Sure," I said, not liking the idea of all of us together in a bar, socializing. One cozy murderous family.

After that, it all went quickly. What to tell the police if and when

---

they came to the office. If anyone asked, Lou had never met never seen her even once. That part I'd insisted on. I'd watched face as I'd said it, watched the way she opened her mouth and shut it before nodding.

I was nursing the last of my third whiskey. It was a nice bar, if it was the color of silt. Lou had excused herself to go to the room, and in my alone time something else occurred to me, s thing that seemed more urgent even than the police. When Lou back with splotches of wet on the front of her dress that could've water or tears, I cornered her.

"Will you tell the tattooed bitch about our"—I pulled one away from my glass so I could make air quotes—"*little problem?*"

Lou froze, half crouched above the chair. "What?"

"That tacky, ugly blue." I reunited with my drink and tickled ice with my teeth. It had been a long thirty seconds apart for us b "Woman with the blue tattoo, a.k.a. the Lady Upstairs, a.k.a. the b you refuse to tell me anything about. Your *hero*."

Lou frowned and leaned forward. "Blue tattoo? What are you ta ing about?"

"Might've told you, but you were probably busy with Alibi. Go old Alibi. Trusty old Alibi. I met her. In the office. What, you thin don't have secrets, too?"

The look on Lou's face made me grin. I stretched my arms ov my head—*pretty, pretty princess*. My blouse was slicked to me like it ha been painted on, but I felt in control of the conversation for the firs time, even with the softness of the booze in my veins.

"I bet you're jealous I met her and I didn't need you to do it."

"What was she doing in the office?"

That question knocked me close to sober. "I'm not sure. Looking for you. She said she'd find you."

"The two of you spoke?"

CHAPTER 18

I f there was more to Robert Jackal than met the eye, he did an awfully good job of hiding it, although truthfully I never tried to dig very deep. My favorite thing about him—besides that face—was that you never felt like you were missing anything. There was never any wondering what he was thinking.

When Lou brought up Ellen—the story abridged so that what had happened was between her and the ghost of Klein, but we'd all have to be careful about what we said to anyone dancing around the office—Jackal didn't even flinch. He slurped his drink.

"So if the police come to the office—" Jackal started to say, but Lou cut him off.

"*When* the police come, you tell them you never even met her," she said. "Because you never did. Right?"

"I told you he didn't," I said. Lou kept her eyes fixed on Jackal. Waited for him to answer.

"Not once."

"And"—here Lou hesitated, stared at me, tried to tell me something, but I wasn't reading it—"we're pausing our cases, everything we've been working on. We need to keep a low profile, until all of this blows over. We can't afford any attention."

Jackal frowned, and his eyes narrowed. He cocked his head and stared at Lou. "That comes from the Lady? She knows about this?"

"It's from *me*," Lou said, locking eyes with him. Something was happening between them, a power struggle that I couldn't read or understand. "We don't want the Lady knowing about *any* of this."

Jackal nodded, his lips twisted ugly into a sneer. He turned to me, eyebrows raised. If he was looking for backing from me, he wouldn't get it. The man looked the other way when his girlfriends took the long sleep. He finally said, grudgingly, "Fine by me."

That was the last the three of us talked shop that night. Instead, Lou and Jackal launched into a conversation about a movie they'd both seen, a talky shoot-'em-up Jackal couldn't convince me to sit through. Lou was loose with him, flirtatious and not meaning it, and Jackal, the man who never stepped offstage, wasn't always searching for his cue. He fumbled with words. He had a goofy laugh, a snorty *hyuk-hyuk*, when he wasn't trying to seduce someone. Watching them, I could see the dynamic that must have existed before me. They shared the happy-go-lucky manner of nonmurderers.

You're drunk, Jo, I told myself, and then realized that it was mostly true but could be truer. I looked around for the bartender. Somehow, the bar had filled up and I hadn't noticed. No bartender. When it wasn't Lou calling, he couldn't be bothered. I stood up to go look for him.

"Jo?"

Behind me, Lou's voice had taken on a worried pitch. But she didn't stand up and I didn't turn around. If she and Jackal were enjoying themselves so much without me, I could find someone to enjoy myself with, too.

I walked to the bar, happy I wasn't swaying, happy that to anyone who didn't know me I looked sober enough. I wandered around, swerving through conversations, looking for the bartender to grab his attention.

I thought of something Ellen had said once, when we'd gone to grab a drink after one of her first meetings with Klein. She'd wanted to order something new, said she didn't feel like herself. I'd worried that she was unraveling already, couldn't handle the heat of the game, and I'd asked her about it—why didn't she feel like herself? She smiled at me strangely, lips pressed together, not looking at all like the half-sure girl I'd always known her to be. "That's how I wanted it to feel," she said. "I'm so sick of always being myself." She'd ordered a dirty martini with blue-cheese-stuffed olives, and she'd only taken one sip of it before she sat back, dismayed. "That's disgusting," she'd said.

I leaned over the bar top, plucking at the bottles racked neatly behind the counter. I jostled the couple next to me, tipping a woman in heels into her date.

"Hey, what the hell?" I couldn't tell who said it. I didn't care. Then there were two big hands around my waist, gently pulling me back. The smell of Jackal's cologne in my face, even from behind. The man bathed in it.

"I wanted one more," I said. "Blue cheese."

"Time to go." Jackal spun me around, marching me back to Lou, who was standing with her arms crossed over her chest.

Lou walked behind Jackal and me, quiet until he poured me into the passenger seat of his car, and then she said, "Keep an eye on her. This was too sloppy by half."

She pushed the door closed in my face as Jackal moved to the driver's side. I wanted to press a finger against the glass, tell her something I knew she needed to know, but she was staring down at me like she'd never seen me before, like she never wanted to see me again. I don't think she looked at me like that even when I brought her to Ellen. And then we were driving away and I couldn't see Lou at all anymore.

The swaying motion of the car lulled me into a calmness that was like sobriety except for the disjointedness of my thoughts. Jackal tried to talk to me once or twice. He'd even, voice gruff and unsure, asked if I wanted to talk about Ellen.

"Don't you say her name to me," I snapped at him, and then I cranked the seat back and closed my eyes and pretended to sleep the whole drive back to his place.

The car rocked as Jackal's door slammed shut and I jerked awake, the ruse having turned real somewhere on the freeway. I could see him silhouetted, walking up to the gate of his apartment complex. He meant to leave me in the car to sleep it off. I stumbled out, the alarm cooing behind me, and followed him to his apartment.

Jackal hadn't even bothered to turn a light on before he wandered into his bedroom, leaving the door ajar. I could hear him prop his window open, start up the box fan, then lean out to click off the car alarm. He came back into the living room, went to the fridge, and stared inside for a moment. He closed it without grabbing anything. Went to the bathroom, started to brush his teeth in the dark. Like I wasn't even there.

"Are you going to make me sleep on the couch?"

Jackal leaned into the sink and spat. "I don't care where you sleep." Coming out of the bathroom, he stared at my face, and when he asked, "Are you crying?" it was a surprise to me that he was right.

"No," I said, and unbuttoned my pants, reaching for him. "No, no, no."

After, I went to the fridge, in search of anything. I was more in control now, fucked sober, but a sandwich would still help. I'd never cried in front of Jackal before, not real tears. Inside his fridge, there were two beers, a half-drunk bottle of red—in the fridge?—the wedged-inside cork grazing the humming yellow light. The only actual food a half-eaten wheel of cheese.

I'd never once been inside Jackal's apartment when it hadn't been clean. When things first turned extracurricular between the two of us, I'd wondered if he kept it clean because he wanted to impress me. Later, I'd realized that was just how Jackal was, like white teeth full of cavities. Nothing in the fridge, but not one item out of place.

"Do you bring other women here?" I asked, bare-assed in front of the Camembert.

"Jealous?" Jackal purred from the couch, his mouth still dewy from me.

"How much do those photographs go for?" What was the point of running your own blackmail sideshow if you kept the fridge three-quarters empty? It made me sad, the idea of some other woman seeing this pathetic excuse for a fridge.

"Not this again," Jackal muttered, folding his arms behind his head.

"Two hundred a print? Three? And who wants them? The Lady would know if they ever became public."

"They'll never become public," he assured me. "Stop worrying about it."

I couldn't, but I didn't have it in me to argue anymore, not that day. I'd press Jackal again in the morning. With Klein dead, so, too, was my hope of an easy recoup of the police's bribe.

"You need something to take your mind off what's-her-name. That's all you need." A smile crept over Jackal's face and he palmed himself. "Well, maybe not *all* . . ."

I didn't normally stay over at his place. I hated the ritual of waking up together, getting back into my old clothes like a paid woman but with no cash in my pocket. Or, worse, Jackal fixing breakfast in the kitchen while I slept, laying out the paper, starting our morning together.

That night I let him wrap himself around me in his damp thousand-count sheets, but there was no sleep on the horizon. When I could hear him snoring, I considered grabbing his keys, driving back to my apartment. But I didn't want to be alone again. Instead, I tossed and turned, thinking of the look on Lou's face as Jackal and I had pulled away from Chinatown. So I'd had a few drinks. After we'd left the canyon, she'd gone back to Mr. Alibi. I'd cried for Ellen in my cold bed by myself. That counted for something.

I couldn't sleep. Jackal kept wrapping his arms around me, and the box fan wasn't up to the task of keeping me cool with his hairy chest pressed to my face. Around midnight, I crawled out of bed and stretched out on the couch. I turned on the TV and passed through different shows, a rerun that I could tell was supposed to be funny, the way the laugh track was yakking on and on. The lead actress was making her life more complicated than it needed to be, but weren't we all. *Flip.* A channel that only half came in, tinsel hopping across the screen. *Flip.*

An old movie, black and white. Two women in a car with the top down, driving around winding cliffs—Italy, maybe. One of the women wore a scarf that blew in the wind behind her, and her chocolate-chip freckles reminded me of Lou. The one driving had her hands clenched on the steering wheel. Bug-eyed sunglasses covered half her face. She looked happy—she glanced over at her compatriot, and that was the word I was thinking, *happy*. She said something to her friend in lisping Spanish, and on the subtitles I caught the words *Costa Brava*. Around one turn, the unsuspecting women giggled together—lovers? in black and white?—and then the car swerved and they . . .

Flip.

The news. A shiny-toothed anchor announced a new development in the mayoral race. Somehow, Carrigan was pulling ahead—polling well with housewives, no doubt. It was only a three-point lead, but we were down to the wire. I studied his face on the TV, superimposed in the right-hand corner. We'd been so close. A late-breaking three-point lead, I could've done something with that. But Ellen had put an end to it. Like the television anchor had read my thoughts, his photo dissolved, replaced by Ellen's face.

A young reporter in a skirt suit stood in front of the St. Leo Hotel in the waning light of early evening. My heart stopped beating, and I pressed the volume up, up, up, not caring if I woke Jackal.

"And now, to the case that's captured the attention of our city, a small break in the investigation of the deaths of Hollywood producer Hiram Klein and his young mistress, Ellen 'Lenny' Howard."

Lenny. I tried to reconcile my Ellen with a girl who could be called *Lenny*.

"Sources tell me, in a Channel 7 exclusive, that Klein and Howard were known to frequent the St. Leo Hotel. It may even have been the scene of the last-known sighting of the pair alive together. The two checked into a room earlier in the week, and witnesses claim that Klein left in a hurry, looking angry. Ms. Howard left the hotel an hour later." No mention of her bruised face from these observant witnesses. Or of me. "Authorities are asking anyone with further information to come forward."

A hotline to call for tips flashed across the screen, and it panned away from the young reporter back to the desk, to a man and a woman who looked appropriately sympathetic for the loss of two lives but who broke into immediate smiles once the St. Leo was out of frame. How nice to have that option, to set it down.

The news moved on to other tragedies. But I couldn't get the picture of the St. Leo out of my head. I'd known it was only a matter of time, but still.

Here we go. It was really starting. I was almost glad.

CHAPTER 19

Four days later, early Monday morning, the cops found me.

Since Chinatown, I'd kept myself busy scouring the office, trying to erase all traces of her. I grabbed anything she'd touched—the
picture of buffalo in Golden Gate Park Lou had given me that Ellen
admired once, the tumbler I'd made her drink out of—and piled it all
on the chair she'd sat in the last time she'd been in the office, when she'd
tried to blackmail her way out of the Klein job. It took three sweaty
trips to dumpsters four blocks away from the office to clear her out.

It helped keep me from thinking about what we'd done. Or the fact
that I hadn't heard from Lou since Chinatown. She hadn't come to the
office; she hadn't called. I didn't bother calling her first. If I called and
she didn't pick up, I'd know for sure she was ignoring me.

In the picture the papers ran—the same headshot she'd given me,
that I dug out from a drawer—a big blue flower perched fatly behind
Ellen's right ear. A dahlia. A cheap mall headshot from a time when
she had hopes of being an actress who stayed vertical. There was a soft

halo of light around her head that wasn't doing her hairstyle any favors, and you could see where her lipstick was smeared along the corner of one tooth. *Make him pay*, I thought, staring at those dark eyes,
her stretched-mouth smile. *Make* him *pay*. I ripped the photo in two
and buried the pieces in a notebook on my desk.

The last time I'd seen that smile, her teeth couldn't stop chattering, and she'd looked from me to Lou, waiting for one of us to say that
everything was all right, waiting for either of us to say anything.

I was shredding the very last of Ellen's files, resisting the urge to
read them again, when I heard the tinkle of the chime on the door,
bringing with it a waft of frying beef from Seven Galbi. Then a voice,
almost familiar, asking Jackal's name. I stopped shredding, my stomach
tensing.

Leaning forward, I could see a sliver of two men, one in sunglasses.
Cops. A thunderbolt quaked through me, a shot of pure adrenaline I
felt mostly in my crotch.

"She's in there," I could hear Jackal say. His voice was smooth,
bored, but he'd spoken louder than he needed to—warning me.

I stared down at the shredder—what was in there would have to
stay put. The only thing left of Ellen on my desk was the notebook
holding her picture. There was no time to get rid of it and probably no
safer place to keep it. I sat down at my desk and smoothed my hair
with tremoring hands.

The two blues appeared in my doorway. Neither offered a hand
in greeting. The one in sunglasses was the squarehead I'd seen in
the parking lot a few days before—back in that magical time when
I'd been worried only about finding the money for the Lady, getting
back the police bribe, kids' problems. If he recognized me, he gave no
sign of it. He flashed his badge, introduced himself as Detective
MacLeish—as though I'd forgotten—and his younger partner as Sergeant Escobar.

"What can I do for you, gentlemen?" I asked. I wished I smoked. I wished I had anything to do with my hands besides drum them on that damn notebook. "I sure hope everything's all right." My voice came out thick and froggy. If you pressed on my skin, you'd find a small reservoir of gin underneath.

"We have a few questions regarding an ongoing investigation, ma'am," MacLeish said.

I didn't offer them a seat, but they sat. Escobar took Ellen's chair, and I stared at the younger cop a beat too long, wondering, with a sick-feeling stomach, if I'd picked all the frizzy blonde strands from the arms. She'd left so many of them.

Escobar reminded me of a smoldering modern-day Rudolph Valentino with his mascara-dark lash line. He didn't like my eyes on him, played with his tie, his pant creases sharp as a razor. Wearing a long-sleeve uniform even in the heat. I disliked him immediately.

Cops always smell a little different. Self-righteousness smells like sweat and pencil shavings covered up with woodsy cologne and stale mint gum. I waited for one of them to speak. They waited for me. We were all so politely waiting, hoping someone else fucked up first.

MacLeish was much older than his partner and, unlike the last time I saw him, he too was in uniform. He kept a placid smile on his face. He might as well have been shopping for groceries as investigating a murder. If he meant to be the good cop, it would be all too easy to lay your daddy issues right at his feet.

He didn't show any sign that he remembered me. I wondered if that meant his partner didn't know about the money.

"Tell me," I said, the silence getting to me finally, "you guys decide ahead of time who gets to be the bad cop? Do you take turns? Or do you decide when you meet—" I broke off and gestured at myself.

They exchanged glances. MacLeish spoke first. "We do appreciate your cooperation."

Didn't seem like I had much choice, I thought but didn't say. "I think I'd prefer to be the bad cop. It seems like more fun."

"You've heard about the murders of Hiram Klein and Ellen Howard," MacLeish said. *Murders* plural, I noted. That was quicker than I'd expected. I forced myself to take a deep breath. It would be better to look a little surprised, I thought, arching an eyebrow. Not sure if I was pulling it off. MacLeish watched me, waited for me to respond.

"I watch the news."

"So you're aware of Ms. Howard's demise," the younger one, Escobar, said.

"You're quick."

He blushed and glared at me. MacLeish had more patience, waited for me to collect myself before he started again.

"Did you know Ms. Howard?"

That damn hotel. "A little."

"*How* did you know the deceased?" Escobar again, still red and trying to recover.

It would be easier to be the bad cop, pushing and digging. It was much harder to make friends. I knew from experience. If that was true, MacLeish was the better policeman. The better cop, yet still the errand boy for the bribe money. And the junior officer to his younger partner.

"Not friends. Acquaintances." I caught my nail peeling the edge of the notebook, thumbing pages. I put my hands in my lap. "I wouldn't say we were friends."

"You don't seem too broken up about the fact she's dead," Escobar said.

I took a beat. I didn't want it to sound prepared. I heard Lou's voice in my head: *It's not a crime to know somebody who died.* "It was a shock to hear she'd passed," I said. "But I'm not expecting an invitation to the funeral. Like I said, we weren't friends."

"Someone at the St. Leo said you and the deceased were spotted there together. Frequently," Escobar said. His palms were pressed hard against the arms of the chair, like he was ready to spring into action at a moment's notice. *The deceased.* I imagined freshly plucked blonde hairs threading between his fingers, tugging at his knuckles. Winding up his arms to his neck, strangling him.

Be human, Jo. And stay focused.

The news had said her friends called her Lenny. "I went there with Ellen once," I said. "They have a good happy hour. Maybe the word I'm looking for is *cheap.*"

"So you admit you were at the St. Leo with the deceased." Escobar looked like he'd won a prize.

I didn't bother answering.

"Did Ms. Howard pay?"

"I'm sorry?"

MacLeish had asked the question casually, not even bothering to look at my face to see how it landed. "When you went to happy hour. Did Ms. Howard cover it?"

I'd paid with a card. Too traceable. "I believe I did. Why?"

"Ms. Howard came into quite a bit of money before she died," MacLeish said, this time glancing up from his notebook to watch my face. I was biting my lip so hard I could taste blood. "Some"—MacLeish paused here, drew the moment out, his partner looking bored—"eight thousand dollars. Any idea where that came from?"

There it was, the other shoe. I studied the older detective while I tried to think of what to say. MacLeish had leaned forward so his elbows were on my desk and doubled his fists under his chin. Like we were having a real conversation, old friends catching up. His eyes both dreamy and focused. Like he was casually, lazily interested. I suspected not a move I made got by him.

I took a breath. Decided to gamble. "How much confidentiality does this conversation have?"

MacLeish's face didn't change, but Escobar sat forward, elbows on knees. I knew this man. I knew this *type* of man. Titillated and ready to judge in equal measure. I brushed my hand against my blouse, pretending not to notice the way it drew tight against my chest, careful to make the move reflexive almost, refusing to look at Escobar to see how it landed.

"We're only looking for information on Ms. Howard," MacLeish said. "Not anything else."

The best bluffs have a little bit of truth, Lou had said when we'd been figuring out our official story. *And trust me, these cops don't care if a well-heeled white girl hustles a little extra on the side in this zip code. It ain't fair, but them's the breaks.* Then Lou had grazed my chin lightly with her nails, turning my face. *Besides, you could proposition the pope and get away with it, with your mug.*

"Occasionally I make ends meet as a working girl," I said. I turned to Escobar, tried not to scan the chair arms too obviously for any long golden strands. "You understand what I mean?"

"I understand," he said, but he'd gone red again.

"Ellen and I sometimes worked the same circuit. The other thing about the St. Leo, they have good rates for a girl looking to rent by the hour. Discreet personnel."

MacLeish was dutifully jotting notes in his flipbook, back to business. I let myself relax an inch. Escobar was trying to regain his composure, but I could see him wondering what it would be like to pay someone for a fuck, wondering my price. Men always think it must be special if someone's willing to pay for it. I winked at him. He coughed and turned away.

I'd waited long enough to ask it. I forced my eyes wide. "But hey, I thought the papers said she killed that movie man before she crashed his car. Do you think she was *murdered?*"

MacLeish deflected beautifully. "We're just trying to answer some questions about Ms. Howard's last days, what she did, where she went. Ms. Howard was a prostitute as well?"

I thought of all the care Lou had taken drilling our terminology into my head—we were *consultants*, and our girls, *specialists*. "A working girl. That's right."

"A working girl," MacLeish repeated, letting me know he'd caught the difference.

"We've spoken with her friends and family," Escobar said. "No one mentioned anything about her being a pro."

"It probably didn't come up at Christmas."

"Was Hiram Klein a client?"

I sucked on the inside of my cheeks, pretended to think about it. "Not if she killed him, no."

"Why not? You think the deceased was having an affair with Mr. Klein?"

I gave them both a *drop dead* look. "You don't murder *clients*. There's no money in it." *Unless he was violent,* I thought but didn't say. *Unless you'd been pushed past your limit.*

"You ever hear rumors about Hiram Klein? From the deceased or any other call girl?"

I thought about Klein's fingerprints, tattoo-fresh, across Ellen's face. She wasn't the first woman he'd tried that with. "Rumors? What do you mean?"

Escobar didn't answer. "Was Ms. Howard ever the violent type?"

I tapped my nails on the desk, pretended to think about it. Anyone could be the violent type, given the right circumstances. The right motivations. "No-oo," I said finally. "I didn't think she was. But you never know, I guess."

Escobar and MacLeish exchanged glances, and MacLeish jotted something in his notebook.

"Anything else I can help you boys with?"

"I think you've given us quite a lot today," MacLeish said. "We know where to find you, if we have any follow-up questions."

He rattled off my address, which shook me. Would I be there tonight, in case they wanted to swing by with further questions? I nodded.

"That's all?" I looked back and forth between the two of them.

"If you want, I can cuff you for the thrill of it," Escobar said.

"Thanks," I said, giddy, my knees weak with relief. I didn't realize, until they were rising from their chairs, how much I'd expected this interview to end with me in custody. "But I charge for that."

At the door, MacLeish stopped and turned to me. His downturned eyes were unhappy—like he was a little sad at what was about to happen. My knees locked up, and my palm came to rest on top of the notebook.

"Your book there," he said, jutting his chin at my desk. I flinched. He saw. "That a datebook?"

"A—a what?" My teeth were chattering. I pressed my lips together and tried to take slow, even breaths through my nose.

"You know, a datebook," MacLeish said. His partner was still outside the door, craning his neck to look in on Jackal. "My daughter got me one for my birthday last year, keeps track of all your appointments in a day. A little old-fashioned, I told her, most people nowadays, they use their phone for that sort of thing." He shrugged. "I thought maybe you were like me. A little old-fashioned."

I'd let myself forget he was playing the good cop. I'd let myself be lulled in. "No," I said finally. "Only a notebook. Nothing special."

"Ah," he said, nodding, smiling. "Then I don't suppose it has any old appointments with Ms. Howard scheduled inside. Dates, times, locations."

"N-no," I stammered. I cleared my throat. *Buck up, Jo.* "You can come back, if you want. Look at anything you like. With a warrant."

"No need," he said breezily, reaching over and knuckling the desk right next to my hand, right next to the notebook with Ellen's torn picture inside. "You've been very helpful." I realized he was giving me a taste of it, what he was capable of. Escobar, all puffed up, didn't know how to dig. I'd been right: MacLeish hadn't missed a thing. I'd practically been tapping Morse code on the damn book—of course he'd noticed—but he'd waited until his partner was distracted to deliver the message.

He stopped at the door. "Eight grand," MacLeish mused, shaking his head. "Such an interesting number. You have my card, if you think of anything else to tell me."

My throat dried up as he joined his partner in the lobby. A warning. I had to find that money *soon*.

I had my eyes closed, so I didn't see Jackal push the door to my office open. But I could smell his woodsy cologne.

"What'd they want to know?"

I popped my eyes open, stared down at my desk. "If I knew her. How I knew her."

"What'd you tell 'em?"

"What we agreed. That Ellen and I knew each other from 'the Circuit.' You know, for *call girls*." My head was pounding. I wanted to go home. I wanted to be somewhere cool, having a drink with Lou, listening to her tell me, *It'll be all right, we'll figure out a new plan. Together.*

"There's a *circuit*?"

"Of course not," I said. "But men always think there is." I squared the corners of the file folders on my desk and, in one motion, slid the notebook and Ellen's headshot into my purse. Then I crossed to my bar cart and poured myself a glass of gin, straight, my trembling hands spraying drops over my toes.

To Escobar, at least, I was almost certain I'd come off cool, unrattled. And MacLeish I wouldn't have to worry about once I had the money. That was all he'd been trying to do, I decided. Scare me, let me know how unpleasant he could make things if the money didn't make it back to him. I could almost convince myself.

Jackal made a noncommittal noise and studied his hands.

"What? Something wrong with that?"

"You and Lou were working Mitch Carrigan?"

That came out of left field. I frowned. "Starting to, yeah."

"Lou's idea?"

"The Lady's, I think. Why do you care?"

"Lou's talked about him for years. Always told her it was a bad idea, but she couldn't let it go. Kept saying how the Carrigans were the big score we needed. That taking them would make us real power players in the city."

I snorted. "That shows what you know. It was a note direct from the Lady."

Jackal nodded, chewing on his lip, staring through me.

I didn't like the idea of Jackal and Lou deciding on marks, talking through problems without me. That she might've listened to Jackal's concerns about Carrigan for years and ignored mine. "What? You have something to say about it?"

Jackal shook his head, coming back to earth. "Nothing. You don't mind that she called it off?"

The Lady had found Lou and Lou had found Jackal before she'd found me. I knew that much. She'd picked him because he was competent with the technology, smart enough not to ask questions. Decent muscle, no moral code. Plus: that face. In a pinch, he could be a lure for one of our girls. It all made sense to me—I hadn't bothered to ask if their relationship went any deeper than that. I'd always assumed I knew the answer. But I hated what the thought did to me, that maybe

Jackal was close enough to Lou to offer his opinions on the marks and that she might listen.

"It was the right call," I said. "Too risky." Jackal nodded, but I could tell he was still turning it over in his head. "You're so eager for another score? That side business isn't paying out to your bookie the way you'd hoped?"

Jackal's head darted out into the hallway, looking to see if there was anyone to hear. "Jesus, Jo."

"Go away," I said, and meant it, dipping the tip of my tongue into the juniper. Jackal's meddling had jump-started the first inklings of a plan. Maybe my Monday wasn't yet wasted. "I have better things to do and I'm sick of your face."

The gin kept me company while I pondered the pieces. If I got the money back and got it to the police, maybe the Lady—maybe *Lou*—would never know I'd taken it. It would have to be quick. There wouldn't be time to do it the *right* way, all the weeks of surveillance, choosing a girl based on the mark's preferences. No, this job would have to be faster, messier.

It wasn't the best way to work. The best stings took weeks to set up because you only had one shot to hook him. But Lou had been the one to teach me. And I'd taught dozens of girls. I knew the game as well as anyone—*better* than anyone. And, well, I had the name, didn't I? I'd already done some of the research. I still had my doubts about Carrigan, but that didn't matter anymore. I'd kissed caution goodbye in a moonlit canyon. I'd either pull it off and get the money—enough for the police, enough for the Lady, enough to put this whole damn city behind me if I wanted—or I wouldn't and I'd go to jail for the rest of my life for murder.

I could hear Jackal stomping around his office, making a show of his irritation. I didn't want to talk to him. And the only thing keeping me was waiting to see if Lou turned up. But I didn't have to sit around and wait, like a lapdog, for her scraps. She hadn't called since China-town. She hadn't come by the office. No reason I should wait on her.

I had other places to be.

Chapter 20

ole del Mare was the sort of address I didn't naturally drift to, all glass windows and whipped beef tartare and juicy dishonest cocktails. No soft dark corners to hide in. Outside, a deck featured a nice view of the ocean, but it was too hot to stare at something cool and not drink it, so I parked it at the bar, a long, glossy slab underneath a wall of alcohol lit up like a movie-theater marquee.

As I sat down, I slid my phone out of my purse, keeping an eye on the time. I put the purse on the stool beside me. If anyone asked, I was waiting for someone. Even after running home to change into a black pencil skirt and white silk blouse, I'd gotten there earlier than Carrigan. If he was coming at all. The secretary had told Lou and me that Mondays were his day, but that didn't mean every week. I could think of a thousand reasons he might not show.

I took a lap around the restaurant before I settled on the bar, walking out some of my anxious energy as I cased the place. Two bathrooms upstairs, and a more discreet one downstairs, by the kitchen.

The dining room, with airy planks of tables, wouldn't do: nothing quiet or intimate. Communal benches were not made for playing footsie. It wasn't the type of place I'd have chosen on my own, but I could make it work. I had to.

When he came—if he came—how to start it? *Aren't you the man I keep seeing on people's lawns?* He might like that, the recognition. But I didn't want to act like a groupie. You didn't make time in your schedule for groupies.

Don't say anything, then. Stare at him until he says something. Men liked that from a pretty woman, direct, friendly eye contact. Maybe throw him off—offer to buy *him* a drink. No, his wife's family had money—he was used to women buying him things. Let him start it, let him say hello. Smile, chat, be a little distant but interested. Make him laugh. Say goodbye before he did, make him work for it.

It was funny, how easily it all came back.

The first time, the very first real time after the disaster with the Asshole, Lou had shown up at Tarantula Gardens before I'd even made it home, before I'd even washed the smell of that man off me. I found her sitting, legs crisscross-applesauce, on my doorstep. A bottle of bourbon warming between her thighs.

"How was it?" she asked.

I didn't know what to say. I didn't know how to explain it—that I felt both different and exactly the same. I'd shed a skin I didn't even know I'd had. I felt tough, untouchable, even with the ripe nimbus of the mark's breath, heavy with nicotine and the rotting flora of unflossed teeth, in my mouth.

"I don't drink that," I said, nodding at the bottle in her lap. "I only drink beer."

I put my key into the lock of the apartment I was still getting used to, the one whose first and last months' rent Lou had paid. I pushed the door open, wishing she'd at least given me an hour to clean myself up, consider my feelings on my own.

Years later, when I was managing my own set of girls navigating their own first times with marks, I'd realized the strategy to what Lou was doing—not giving me enough time to think things through, to change my mind. I tossed my keys onto the table and set my bag down underneath it, heard Lou following me inside.

The high from the pie escapades, what we'd done to the Asshole, was starting to burn off. I'd done things in the last week that made me ask myself why I kept saying yes to her. Why was I listening to this woman I barely knew? Why did I let her talk me into the things I was doing? But on the other hand, there was this apartment. I wasn't sleeping in a car. I wasn't crying myself to sleep at night. Not every night, anyway.

And there was that money I owed her boss. I couldn't forget about that.

"Beer isn't gonna cut the mustard tonight," Lou said, following me inside and plopping herself down on my couch. She was always saying things like that, that made her sound like she'd come out of a different era altogether.

I went to the kitchen that I still didn't know, searched a moment or two for a clean glass, and ran it under the tap. Lou's eyes tracked me as I took long deep gulps of water, trying to wash out the taste of him.

"How was it?" Lou repeated.

"Well, it's the first time I've ever fucked someone for money, I'm not entirely sure how it was," I snapped. My hands were shaking as I refilled the water glass.

When my back was turned, Lou had stood up, moved to the kitchenette. She put a cool hand on the back of my neck. I flinched—I could feel his slobbering lips moving from my hairline to my spine—but she only reached around and tipped a little of the uncapped bourbon into my glass. Pressed it to my lips like medicine. Her hand on the back of my neck sent tingles up to my scalp and down to my toes, unbearable sparks that fizzled out before they had a chance to catch fire. Trapped between her hand and mine, the imprint of the mark's gluey kisses on my skin.

I slurped at the drink, the sharp sting of the booze the only taste in my mouth now. I finished the watery bourbon and turned to face her. Her green eyes had little flecks of gold in them. She was standing so close to me, I could feel heat radiating from her. She moved her hand from my neck to the side of my face, tucked a dark strand of hair behind my ear.

"Give that to me," I said, and grabbed the bottle from her. I poured a large splash of brown into the glass, topping it with the barest spritz of water, reversing the percentages. Lou's smile grew big, and then it grew wolfish.

"That's my girl," she said. "I'll take one of those."

It was the first time she stayed the night with me. We stayed up for hours talking, drinking—I told her every gory detail, all the meanest things. The zits on his ass. The way he'd let out a series of high-pitched whimpers, like an incontinent dog, between lizard-flick licks. That made Lou laugh so hard she'd fallen backward and knocked her head against my sofa.

"That's a new one," she said, giggling, as she sat upright, massaging her head. "That's perfect. He won't want anyone to know about that."

"What was your first time like?" I asked, trying to think up more things to make her laugh. "When you started working here." Lou crawled to the bourbon bottle that sat upright between us, like the deity we were worshipping, and took a swig.

"Oh, that," Lou said. "My first time fucking for money had nothing to do with working here."

It made complete sense as soon as she'd said it; dominoes that had been lined up in my brain finally fell. After that, Lou pushed another drink on me and laid out the plan for how it would all work, how many weeks I'd spend with the mark, how it would end. He did want to see me again, right?

"Oh yes," I said, looking down at my hands, thinking of the way he'd played with my hair in the postcoital moments, sniffing it. As I'd left, he'd turned to me, the half-darkness of the shade-drawn room drawing a soft slope down his sagging belly, and said, "You're lovely, kid. When can I taste you again?"

At the time, I'd thought the idea of sleeping with him over and over again would be work, real work. But it wasn't. It wasn't that much different than sleeping with a bad date because you had nothing to do or nowhere to sleep or because you wanted to be polite. But this was different—*better*—because I always got to have a secret. Men would buy me drinks, and use their best sweet talk, pull out all the stops to try to tumble me, *trick* me, onto their sheets. And the whole time, I'd be paying attention, jotting down the things they liked or didn't, the things that could make Lou laugh, the things that we could use against them. They were always the helpless ones, in the end. I liked that. I liked that so much.

Lou and I fell asleep in the living room three-quarters of the way into the bottle. I woke up in the middle of the night, spinning, thirsty and bloated, the sugars of the dark drink swelling in my veins. I pushed myself up, feeling like a crust of bread that had been soaked through with liquid—with bourbon—and Lou was snoring a little, her head tucked into the corner between the couch and the fiddle-leaf fig she'd put next to the sliding glass door.

Months later, Lou would tell me, drunk, that the business had never been the same before me, that she hadn't even known she needed me until I was there. That I was becoming indispensable to the Lady. That was the word she used, *indispensable*. "Do you know what that means?" she slurred. "It means you never get to leave me." But that was fine. I never wanted to.

All of that was still a hope, then, as I sat there, watching Lou sleep, wondering why I didn't leave that apartment, call my mother, eat crow. Lou's hair—she wore it short then—was like a silky auburn halo around her head, one tendril reaching for her arrow-straight nose, the kind of nose the Greeks liked to sculpt for posterity. Her eyelashes flickered and she gasped—a bad dream. I reached out and pushed the hair out of her face and Lou sighed, rolled over. I thought to myself, *Now you have a best friend. Now you have a home.* And then I pulled myself to the bathroom on my stomach and threw up for hours.

I thought of all that there, waiting for Carrigan. It had been so long since I'd done a case myself. Once, I'd found it thrilling. I wondered how it would feel, now.

People started to filter into the bar, young professionals mostly. There was a big tilted mirror above the bar's top shelf, which I liked—I could see anyone who came in behind me without being caught looking. Even at four in the afternoon, the bar had a few regular customers, well-dressed women in brightly colored silk blouses, meticulously groomed men. Everyone appeared to be speaking *at* each other, not *to* each other, and no one was looking at me at all.

I made eye contact with the bartender, a pretty woman with a mane of dark curly hair and hundreds of dollars of ink crawling up her arms, and ordered another gin and tonic. A double.

"You don't want to try something more exotic? Our small-batch elderflower syrup is pretty rad." She grinned at me, a gap between her front teeth big enough to wedge a tongue into.

I grimaced.

She laughed and made the double. I studied the campaign brochure Lou and I had swiped from Carrigan's office. I examined his face from as many different angles as the pixelated photographs would allow. I wanted to be sure I would recognize him. I wanted to be sure I wouldn't make any more mistakes.

Behind me, a large group entered the restaurant and seemed to be trying to decide between sitting outdoors in the gray soupy heat or pressing a few sticky tables together inside. It was a different group from the others that had wandered into Sole del Mare—older, for one thing. A man in a gray suit with his back to me talked to a few of his peers, gesturing up and down as he spoke to emphasize his point. An office party? A happy hour group? Or a campaign strategy meeting?

"Another, love?" The bartender broke my concentration on the mirror. I wasn't pacing myself and I'd downed the drink in twenty minutes. I was drinking too fast and I didn't care. I nodded, checked the mirror again.

The man in the gray suit was turning, I could almost see his face—I leaned forward toward the bar. It was possible it was Mitch Carrigan, although I wasn't certain. He was laughing, at his ease. The same dimpled chin from the brochure. The dark and graying hair.

Somehow, he was better-looking in person.

The bartender slid my drink to me. Carrigan was moving toward the bar. He'd stopped to chat with a couple, older, posing for an invisible camera. The man was good. He was always on. I knew that feeling. I scratched my thumbnail along the condensation of my glass as I watched.

As he got closer, I slid my purse off the stool next to me. Now that the bar was full, it was the only empty gap left to order. Carrigan idled up next to me. From the side, he looked like any regular businessman: clean gray suit draped over square-cut shoulders; a head like a block of cement. He cut his eyes toward me, smiled. Friendly, but not pushy about it.

I turned on my stool so I faced him, crossing my legs. I hung a little smile on my face and watched him for a moment.

Carrigan was ordering a round of drinks for the table, and he was ignoring me but not well. He maintained a steady way of glancing around the rim of the bar, like he was taking it all in, but his eyes kept finding my cleavage. After they did, he'd look away and smile a little, sheepish, like he knew he'd been caught.

It took about a decade, but he completed the order for the table, a boss buying shots for his crew, not even asking someone else to do it, that's the kind of guy he was. A man you could have a drink with. A man who would be good for political office. A man who was three points up, with a lot to lose by a very small margin.

The bartender started making the drinks, a trough of alcohol, and Carrigan turned to face me, finally. I grinned at him, full force.

"Hello," he said.

"Hello yourself."

CHAPTER 21

put a stilettoed foot on the rim of the bar stool and pushed it toward him. Carrigan looked down at my legs and then back up at my face. I hid a smile.

"Have a seat," I told him. "You're going to be a while."

"Excuse me?"

"Your drinks," I said, letting my lips spread in a slow smile. "Might be another hour or so before they're ready."

Carrigan was half on the bar stool, the posture of a man reluctant to completely commit himself. One eye shifting back to the party he'd left.

"What's the occasion, big shot?"

He didn't answer that question. Playing hard to get. "What are you drinking?" he asked, nodding at my glass. Deflecting.

"This is water," I said. "But it seems to be making me tipsy."

He looked at my glass and then at me. No smile. "So it does."

Maybe not playing. I finished the drink and made a small show of setting it down next to him. Carrigan looked at the empty glass and then away. He wasn't going to offer.

"What are you drinking?" I asked. Carrigan slapped a palm down on the bar and half-turned. From sweet cross-wearing wifey to Tana the ballbuster, and now here he was, not chatting with me. What did I need to do, stick a hand down his pants? Or maybe he was too scared of Tana.

"Club soda."

Aha. "Not drinking tonight? Scared of revealing yourself?"

Carrigan frowned, cocked his head. Turned all the way to face me, those big blue eyes narrowed. "Excuse me?"

"It's an old Bogart quote," I said, shaking my head a little like I was embarrassed for knowing it. "'People who don't drink are afraid of revealing themselves.' It seemed to fit the bill."

"Maybe I am a little afraid of revealing myself," he said. The bartender finished making the drinks and nodded at Carrigan, who slipped her a card. "Excuse me. Enjoy your evening."

And then he was headed back to his table, his group of admirers, leaving me gaping after him. One shot and I'd missed it. Was I so not Carrigan's type that he couldn't spare even five minutes to talk to me? I knew he liked blondes, but surely his tastes weren't so exclusive.

I tapped the rim of my empty glass, held up two fingers for a double, and the bartender nodded, started to make me another. Had I been too forward? Not forward enough?

Something danced on the bar top in front of me. It took me a moment to realize that it was a cell phone, *my* cell phone. It was Lou. I held it in my hands for a moment, debated answering. I was scared that if I answered, Lou would hear in my voice that something was up, that somehow I'd telepathically transmit Carrigan's presence to her. I was scared that if I didn't answer, I'd never hear from her again. I stared so long, letting the phone ring and ring, that the toothy bartender slid me the drink and asked, "Are you going to get that?"

The phone stopped ringing.

I set the phone down and watched Carrigan's group in the mirror. He was stoic, serious. Smiled when spoken to but looked, perhaps, a little bit bored. The phone started chirping again. I pictured Lou on the other line, missing me. But probably only missing me because she couldn't reach me. It didn't matter. As soon as I pictured her face, I was a goner. I answered, my eyes on Carrigan's party in the mirror. Leading-man handsome. Maybe Lou really would have come out of retirement for him if Ellen hadn't intervened.

"Ignoring me?" I heard a smile in Lou's voice, but it wasn't toothless.

"Sorry, it's not a good time." Behind me, Carrigan checked his watch. Definitely bored. A man that good-looking didn't need to waste his time in bars like this, I thought. Maybe he was eager to get back to Tana—maybe there really were still husbands like that. But he came to happy hour here with the boys every week, or almost. Maybe he didn't even know yet what he was looking for here.

"Oh? You're busy?" A pause. "With Robert?"

I shook my head, even though Lou couldn't see it. I didn't want to be thinking of Lou now while I was trying to figure out Carrigan. I didn't want to deal with her jealousy swings at the Sole del Mare, those moments when she seemed to cling to me. But I wasn't hanging up the phone, either. "What's up?"

"I wanted to see where you were. Thought you might be thirsty, maybe you'd want to grab a drink."

I stared down at my double. "I'm taking a break from drinking. I'm grabbing something to eat."

A beat of silence. "Alone?"

"Yes, alone. Call up Mr. Alibi, he can take you for a drink." My voice sounded bitter. If I closed my eyes, I could see Lou's face staring at me through Jackal's car window, tight and disappointed. In *me*.

"Out getting a bite to eat. I wondered. I didn't see your car parked in its spot."

I blinked. "You're at my apartment?"

"Until five minutes ago. Like I said, I wanted to talk. See how you're holding up." Lou took a deep breath on the other line or blew out cigarette smoke—I couldn't tell which. "Also, there's an unmarked sitting outside your apartment. I circled the block a few times and he didn't move. Just sitting there in the dark. I waited about forty minutes. He's not budging."

My throat started to close up and I shut my eyes, trying to block the humming in my ears. "Thanks for the heads up."

"If he's unmarked, he's not there to arrest you. Only to observe."

"That makes me feel so much better." I took a sip of my drink, putting a hand over the mouthpiece of the phone so Lou couldn't hear the ice rattle on the other side. "You didn't happen to get a look at his face, did you?"

"No." She didn't tell me it would all be fine, that this was normal. I wouldn't have believed her if she had, but I still wanted her to say it. "As long as you don't give him any reason for probable cause, he'll probably stay out there tonight. I'd go to Jackal's if I were you."

Or you could invite me over, I thought but didn't say. *I could stay with you.* "I'll do that," I lied, and hung up.

I told myself I shouldn't be bitter, that she'd come to the canyon; she'd helped me with Ellen when I needed it. I couldn't blame her for the fact that she'd chosen not to stay with me after, that she'd had someone else to hold her while I lay sleepless, Ellen's ghost fluttering over my bed every second. Most of all, I told myself that bitterness wouldn't be attractive to Carrigan. That was what I needed to be focusing on.

If I had any shot with Carrigan left, it would be tonight. Now that I'd already talked to him, I couldn't regroup, try to corner him again—it would look too suspicious. I had to push it, now, see how far I could take it.

If he came back to refill drinks, I'd try again. If he got up to go to the bathroom, I'd follow him down. I pressed my hand to my temple, tried to think, but my hands were shaking. MacLeish was waiting for me. Or Escobar, or someone new, to ask me questions about Ellen.

The woman next to me was starting to get loud and belligerent. ". . . what if it was *murder* all around? Like, so, she kills him, but then someone kills *her* and leaves those bodies in the canyon . . . or maybe someone killed them both, you know? Like don't those producer guys always have mob ties?"

"You watch too many movies."

"Mark my words. *Cosa Nostra.*"

And then I truly couldn't breathe. I was sweating even though we were inside and the heat had started to retreat in the last week—although I couldn't remember, had it been hot the morning of the canyon, had Ellen's body been sitting out in the heat, had her mother had to identify some heat-eaten thing, had she, had it . . .

"Goddammit," I snapped out loud. The woman to my left turned to stare at me. I stood up, plunking two twenties down on the table to cover my bill. I had to get some fresh air. I kept an eye on Carrigan's table—he was still nursing the club soda, nodding at something one of his partners was saying—and ducked outside. I picked a spot near the valet stand where I could gulp the fresh air, pretend to smoke a cigarette, maybe, but where I could still keep an eye on Carrigan's table.

The stars pinwheeled above me, pressing down. The pressure pushed inward on my ears like I was underwater, and I tried to yawn but nothing popped. If we'd gone to the police, Ellen would still be alive. But maybe we would all be in jail right now. If it had been me and only me on the hook, that might've been all right. But it wasn't only me—it was Lou and Jackal, too. The long line of what-ifs stretched out in front of me: I could've picked a different girl. If I'd parked one street over, I might never have met Lou. If I could've looked ahead, I might've told her to get lost after that plate of pie. Or stopped things that night after the first mark, when Lou had been waiting for me. I wished I could unzip my own skin, get out of Jo for a moment.

I closed my eyes, but waiting behind them was the bright picture of Ellen's face with her mouth open, screaming, choking. I gasped and shuddered, covering my face and rubbing, rubbing at my eyes.

"Are you all right?"

My head snapped up. A few feet away, Mitch Carrigan stood on the pavement, eyeing me warily. But not unsympathetically. I didn't trust myself to speak, so I nodded a little. He moved a step closer.

"Are you sure? Maybe I can help."

He was inching forward, like walking toward a wild animal, afraid it would bolt. But it was also the first time he'd looked at me with any real interest all night. His face was kind but serious, his mouth twisted down in sympathy.

"Sorry, I didn't get your name before." His eyes gleamed in the twilight. He brought a whiff of honeysuckle with him as he moved.

Men, I thought, disgusted even as my stomach clenched—in hope. Hardwired to be drawn to the damsel in distress. I blinked rapidly, working up a moistness, and bit my lip. From a nearly forgotten place inside, I heard Lou's voice: *For a certain kind of man, the worse you can make that pretty face look, the better.*

He reached into his pocket and pulled out a monogrammed handkerchief, handing it to me. I dabbed at my eyes with it, noticing that it was both starched and pressed. His eyes were locked on my face the entire time I tidied it with his linen square.

"I'm Mitch," he said. I gave him a watery smile of thanks, and his hand lingered a bit on my own as I passed him back the crumpled and mascara'd handkerchief. "Do you need a ride home?"

He was so close I could almost touch him. Not flirtatious, but I could see it now. I'd learned my lesson in the bar. He had Tana the ballbuster at home. It was the little crucifix-clutching virgin he was missing. I swear, up close his breath smelled like money.

"Please," I whispered.

Carrigan drove a restored '50 Plymouth De Luxe—"a present," he'd said simply, when I'd admired it, and I guessed that meant a present from his wife—and we puttered along the freeway going about twelve miles per hour, but that was fine with me. I was happy for the time alone with him.

He'd wanted the full story once I was in the car. I told him an ex had been following me, someone I was scared of. That I was worried he'd be waiting for me and if Mitch would just drive me home and escort me to my front door, I'd be forever grateful. It was a story with so many holes in it, it could've been a cheese, but Carrigan bought it, or seemed to. I'd laid it on thick, telling him about calls in the middle of the night, hang-ups, that it was starting to drive me crazy, that I wasn't sleeping. That, at least, wasn't a lie.

By the time we got to Tarantula Gardens, he was starting to warm to me—trying to cheer me up by telling me about his campaign. Telling me Bogart was one of his favorites, too, and that it might be an obvious choice, but he preferred *Casablanca* to all other films. It *was* obvious. I didn't say it.

As we pulled into the parking lot, I could feel my stomach tightening again, and I couldn't stop myself from looking around, trying to find

the unmarked that Lou had spotted earlier. I couldn't see it, but that
didn't mean it wasn't there. Or maybe I got lucky, and they went home.

"Do you see him?" Carrigan craned his neck to stare out the window. If I really *was* trying to avoid a jealous ex, he would be a terrible
choice to keep me safe.

"I . . . I'm not sure." I made my voice breathy, like I was trying not
to cry.

"Don't worry," he said. "I'll walk you to your door." He smiled at
me, kindly, but kindliness was not the feeling I was looking to arouse
in him tonight. As he navigated the boat of the car into a parking space
practically a city block long, I slipped off Jackal's bracelet and tucked
it into the valley between the bucket seat and the door, somewhere not
so obvious that the wife would notice it next time she went for a ride.
I needed an excuse to see him again, not for Carrigan to be even
warier of strange women.

Carrigan escorted me past the pool, one hand rubbing soothing
circles on the small of my back, and up the steps to my apartment.
When we got to my door, I turned, pressing my back against the wood.
Trying to shrink like a violet. "Thank you, Mr. Carrigan."

"That's you thanking my father-in-law."

"Thank you, *Mitch*," I corrected. "Nice to meet you."

I hesitated for a moment, thinking the word *bashful* over and over
in my head until it took over me, until I was radiating it, and then
stepped up on tiptoe to kiss him on the cheek. I let my hands skim the
shoulders of his suit jacket, dragging my nails a little so he could feel
them. His cheek was in that in-between state of smooth and stubbly, a
touch oily under my lips. I lingered there, leaving the invitation in the
air. Carrigan gripped the top of my arms to steady me, and I let my
heels hit the ground. A man that handsome, turned on by a scared
little woman—it would be up to him to make the next move.

"Good night," I said, breathless for a second—but not with desire.

Feeling instead the delight of realizing I hadn't entirely forgotten the game. Maybe you never really could. "I don't know what I would have done tonight if you hadn't shown up. It makes me believe good men *do* still exist."

I had my key half in the lock when he threaded his fingers into my hair and, with one gentle tug, pulled me to face him. I let my lips part and my eyelashes flutter, putty in his hands, his for the taking. It didn't last long—not even long enough for him to slip me the tongue— before he was shaking his head and saying, "I don't know what came over me. I have to go."

"Of course," I said, pretending to be in a daze. "Good night."

I watched him walk past the pool, the blue glow illuminating the underside of his face, shadowing his eyes—like a skull, I thought, then shook my head. I'd been morbid enough for one night. He didn't stop once, didn't turn around to look for me. And he hadn't exactly thrown me into bed. But there was something there.

As he walked away, getting smaller and smaller, I rubbed the bare spot on my wrist where Jackal's bracelet had been and felt, for the first time since that night in the canyon, hope. That thing for suckers.

CHAPTER 22

In the morning, I checked the cars on my street. No unmarked now, no one surveilling the place. If Lou was right and had seen someone, he or she was long gone by now—but I was also pretty sure they'd be back. I thought of the slipped bangle, lodged in the side of Carrigan's car. I wondered how quickly I could call and ask to retrieve it.

I was about to head inside, call a taxi so I could pick up my car from Sole del Mare, when I heard her.

"I see you *didn't* sleep at Jackal's."

I whipped around. Lou was leaning against her car door, smiling at me. She didn't seem pissed, or suspicious—just waiting.

"No," I said, stepping toward her. "What are you doing here?"

"I went to Jackal's first," Lou said. "He said he hadn't seen you." She shook her head at my complex. "This place is such a *dump*."

"It's beachfront," I said automatically. "Really, Lou, what are you doing here?"

Lou's smile faltered. She looked tired. I wondered how much

sleep she'd missed last night and who she'd been missing it with. "I haven't been sleeping," she admitted. "I wondered how you were doing."

"That's why you haven't been in the office?" I took a step toward her. Lou nodded. *Bullshit.* Across the hot car, glittering in the morning sun, Lou was tapping her hip against the open car door. Fidgety. That worried me. Drop-in visits weren't her style, not at all.

"Lou, about Chinatown—"

"Forget it, Jo," she said. "Really, forget it. That's not why I'm here, anyway." The corner of her tongue darted out and touched her very pink lips. I closed my eyes for a moment, trying not to remember the feel of those lips pressed against mine. Trying not to think of her face, bone white, in the moonlight, Ellen's body between us.

"Let's play hooky," she whispered. Up close, her eyes looked smeary and her lips were twitching. "Let's forget everything that happened, today only. Okay? We'll forget her and we'll go somewhere else, and then tomorrow, it will be like it happened, but for today only, we're not going to talk about it or think about it or anything. Okay?"

I squinted into the morning sun. Put Ellen aside for the day. In theory, it sounded wonderful. But it would also mean a day of drinking with Lou—it always meant a day of drinking with Lou. I wasn't sure I could handle that. I wasn't sure that two drinks in, I wouldn't be able to stop myself from reciting all the little details I was barely keeping a handle on now—Ellen's favorite color, the plasticky feel of the shower curtain around Klein's body, the candied smell of the drugstore perfume she always wore.

Not to mention Carrigan.

But there was also Lou in the morning sunshine, so still and calm and smiling at me, not moving even when a plane roared overheard. Her eyes trained on me like I held the key to every problem she'd ever had, like there was no one else she wanted to see.

"Where should we go?"

Lou dimpled. "Leave it to me."

Halfway there, I realized. We were headed for Santa Monica. In the direction of Sole del Mare, in fact, or, at the very least, of my abandoned car. If we passed it on the street, Lou might recognize it. Then there would be questions I didn't know how to answer.

"Where are you taking me?"

"It's a surprise," Lou hollered over the sound of the air rushing by, the radio cranked all the way up. She wouldn't answer me when I asked again, kept singing along to the radio. Every so often she'd pause and turn to me and smile, a big one, showing all her teeth. Whatever feelings she'd had outside Tarantula Gardens, she was good at setting them aside. A new thing to marvel at, her ability to compartmentalize.

For once, I wished that we were stuck in our city's most well-known natural disaster, gridlock traffic, so I'd have more time to work on my cover story. I hoped I was wrong, but I knew I wasn't—Lou hated Santa Monica. There was only one reason she'd willingly brave the well-intentioned yogis and tourists.

"The Sole del Mare," I said, pretending surprise. I watched Lou from the corner of my eye as she pulled the car into the lot. It couldn't be pure coincidence that she'd brought me here, today of all days. But I couldn't figure out the angle, either.

"They have a brunch menu," Lou said happily, throwing the car into park in front of the valet stand.

"Since when do you *brunch*? Since when do you pay for valet parking?"

"Since"—Lou willowed her body into the back seat for her purse, brushing against me—"today, my friend. Since today."

My feet were lead, and I didn't bother trying to catch up to her. She was practically skipping into the restaurant ahead of me. At the door, she turned and held it for me, and I smiled at her weakly. She grinned at me and ushered me through, trying to get me to move faster.

I heard Lou tell the maître d', "Two for brunch," but I couldn't stop staring around the restaurant. It was busy, even considering it was a weekday. The curse of Santa Monica. There, the corner where Carrigan had been seated last night. Across from the bar where I'd whiled away some time. Behind it, a woman with a lot of dark curly hair pulled away from her face. Sleeves of tattoos disappearing beneath her T-shirt. I squinted. A gap in her teeth you could lob a tangerine through. *Christ.* Same bartender.

"Do you have a reservation?" The maître d' frowned and tapped at the computer screen ahead of them.

"We'll sit at the bar," Lou offered.

Shit. "Let's go somewhere else, Lou," I said, my mouth dry.

Lou waited until she'd thanked the maître d' for escorting us to the bar to respond. "I should be able to let it go," she said, leaning close to me. "But I can't."

"What? You mean . . . Ellen?"

Lou glared at me. I was ruining her buoyant mood. "I mean Carrigan," she said.

I started to sweat. I wanted to order a drink, desperately, wanted the fuzz that would cloud my mind and make everything feel less sharp and bitter, but I didn't want the bartender to get a good look at me, either. *Don't be silly. She doesn't remember you.*

"It would've meant something to me," Lou said. "You see that name everywhere. It would've been big for us. *Toppling the patriarchy* and all that," she said, adding air quotes to try to convince me she was teasing, but her smile didn't reach her eyes and she coughed gently into her hand after she said it, like the words had bruised her throat on their way out.

"Can I get you ladies something to drink?" The bartender leaned forward on her elbows on the glossy redwood-slab bar. Her T-shirt hiked up an inch, revealing the cluster of bumblebees on her biceps. I looked down at the menu, studying it like she'd quiz me later.

"Coffee," Lou said.

"Make it two," I replied, not looking up.

"Really? Wait a second," Lou said to the bartender, then turned to me, eyebrows raised. "No mimosa, no Irish coffee?"

"I meant it, I'm taking a break from alcohol." *At the Sole del Mare, anyway.*

Lou smiled at me, a megawatt dazzler, and I felt a little warm glow in my chest—the first I could remember since Ellen died. The bartender stared at me for a moment before she turned away. Maybe trying to place me. Maybe curious why Lou had pushed it.

"Anyway, I thought it would be good to come here. I've thought about it since that woman mentioned it. We would've been here tonight anyway, for Carrigan's happy hour."

"*Last—*" I caught myself before I got the sentence out. *Jesus, Jo.* But that was unlike Lou, too, to forget a detail that would've been so important to the case. I coughed, started over, picking my words carefully. "Last I heard, his campaign isn't going well anyway. Less incentive to pay us off," I lied. The last poll still had him up a hair's breadth in the polls. A *perfect* setup for our type of sting.

Lou shrugged. "Yeah, maybe." She didn't sound convinced.

The bartender set the two coffees down in front of us and asked for our orders: Lou picked waffles. I stuck with yogurt, thinking that would be quick to eat. The sooner we finished, the sooner we could leave. Lou thanked her. I didn't say anything. The bartender moved away to put our orders into the kitchen.

"So you didn't go to Jackal's last night after all," Lou said.

I drummed my fingers on the bar. Maybe she hadn't forgotten the standing date for Carrigan's happy hour. "You're very nosy about how much time I spend in Jackal's bed. It's starting to make me wonder."

"Wonder what?"

"Are you jealous of him, or me?" The best defense, and all that.

Lou's fingers froze on the rim of her glass. Her big green eyes met mine—she would've never said it, but I know she liked the question, the challenge of it. I held her gaze for a long beat. She looked away first.

"I'm sure I don't know what you mean," Lou said. She slurped her coffee.

"I'm sure you do." I tried to catch her eye again, but the fun of the challenge had gone out of it for Lou; she wouldn't look at me.

Instead, she unfolded her napkin, placed it over her lap. She let the pause grow long. Then: "You said you went out to eat. Where'd you go?"

"I . . ." I had no answer. My mind was blank, still wishing for an answer from her. Lou stared at me, eyebrows raised.

The bartender saved me.

"Here you are, ladies," she said, pushing the plates forward on the bar top. "Enjoy."

"I went back to that tiki bar," I blurted. "Like you said I would. I guess . . . I guess I wanted to go back to a moment before everything with . . . you know who." *Back to the moment when the only thing I had to worry about was the money I owed the Lady. Back to the moment when Ellen was still a living pain in my ass.*

For the first time that morning, I let myself think of her, really think of her, and it was too much. I knotted my fists into my abdomen, hoping the pain would keep me from sinking back into that Ellen place.

"You lied to me," Lou said, a faint trace of surprise—or amazement—in her voice. She dropped the fork onto the plate, flipping it upside down.

I licked my lips, feeling the pang in my stomach get worse. "I didn't—"

"You said you weren't drinking." Lou shook her head, staring down at her coffee. Like the sight of me disgusted her. She jabbed at the waffles on her plate with the fork tines. "Stupid me. I actually believed you."

She started in on the waffles in silence, drowning the fluffy grids in syrup and hacking away at them with her fork. I stared down at the yogurt, its white clotted texture like scooped marrow. My stomach cramped. I pushed it away. Funny how nothing affected Lou's appetite.

Even if I could work it out with Carrigan—and I wasn't at all sure that I could—slide the money to the police, tie up all those loose ends without Lou or the Lady ever knowing, I'd still be in the Lady's debt. I didn't think I'd ever be able to train another girl without seeing Ellen's face, her bruised neck, her little blue lips. Even if I worked it all out right, it wouldn't change the fact that I'd killed someone.

That *we* had killed someone.

I took a deep breath. "The Lady has to know by now," I said. Lou stopped with a forkful of waffles halfway to her mouth. The bartender had her back to us, racking clean glasses. "About *the last case.* What'd she say?"

Lou set her fork down carefully, busied herself with unfolding her napkin. "She wasn't happy," she admitted. "She wondered if there'd been something we'd missed with Ellen, something we should've caught earlier."

I bit my lip. The bartender dropped a washcloth and bent over to pick it up, revealing a hamsa on her lower back. If it had been a different day, I would've scoffed, pointed it out to Lou. "And me? What'd she say about me? She was impatient for the rest of her money a week ago. It'll be longer, now."

Lou wiped her hands on her napkin and turned to face me. I

caught a whiff of lemons. "A little more time will be all right, under the circumstances. She said she understood."

"*What?* But you said the Lady wanted to . . . retire me."

Lou rubbed her eyes, fidgeted in her seat. She didn't want to talk about it. "Extraordinary times. She's willing to push the debt on to Carrigan, once this all blows over. Really, she does want what's best for us, Jo. She's looking out for us. And I don't know about you, but no one's ever done that for me before."

I frowned. "She turned awfully understanding all of a sudden. Not how you made the situation sound at the tiki bar."

"Maybe I took a little creative license with her words," Lou said carefully.

That didn't make sense. "A little creative license? To threaten me on behalf of the Lady?" I chewed my bottom lip. For some reason, I saw the look of skepticism on Jackal's face as Lou gave the cease and desist orders on Carrigan. "Lou, what do you mean you—"

"Excuse me," the bartender leaned into us again. "Can I get you ladies anything else?"

"No," I snapped. I made the mistake of glaring at her. Instead of being offended, she smiled at me and made a finger gun, snapping it at my head.

"I didn't expect you back so soon," she said.

I glanced at Lou, who was looking between the two of us. "I think you have me mistaken for someone else," I said. "We'll take the check."

"I'm sure I know you," the bartender said. She reached up and pushed a curly lock of hair behind her ear from where it had escaped her ponytail. She grinned at me, stuck her tongue in the gap between her teeth. "I remember that pretty face."

My breath caught in my throat. "Nope, sorry. Not me," I said. "The check, please." I turned to Lou, who was still staring at me with narrowed eyes. But she had something to answer, too. Had it been the

Lady or *Lou* who had threatened me? And if it had been Lou, why had she done it? It didn't make any sense. "Lou, what did you mean when you said—"

"Jo, I think that was a backhanded compliment," Lou said, sliding her eyes to the bartender. Freckles dancing across her nose as she crinkled it. "She remembers your pretty face, only it wasn't you."

"Honest mistake," I said.

At the same time, the bartender said: "Can't blame a girl for trying." She winked at Lou.

"What about my pretty face?" Lou leaned across the table. "Would you remember me?"

I watched them flirt, and it was like watching sand drain through my fingers as the promise of our fresh day of hooky together slipped away. Lou was laughing, giving me the full cold shoulder—still pissed about the "lie" I'd told her, no doubt—tossing her hair. At one point, she reached forward and grabbed the bartender's hand, tracing her fingers over the tattoos on her wrist.

I stood up and made my way to the bathroom. I tried to focus, tried to get back whatever thought had been on the edge of my brain before Lou's flirt fest, but when I closed my eyes, all I could see was Lou's open mouth, laughing, her face lit up by someone else, and then, even worse, Ellen's smeary eyes, her twitching white shoulders, the sound of a car door dinging.

When I rejoined them, Lou had a glass of rosé in front of her and the bartender was snagging it with a fingertip to sneak a sip.

"On the house," she offered. "If you'd like to join us."

Join *us*. "Thanks," I said, "but, Lou, I thought we had plans today." I turned to the bartender and bared my teeth, a smile if you squinted. "Our boss is kind of a demanding bitch."

Lou ignored the bait. "She's not drinking," she answered for me. Not done punishing me yet. "In fact, maybe you'd better go home. It's probably too tempting for you to be here right now. Mischa can call you a cab."

"Don't bother," I said, and grabbed my purse. At the door, I turned and stared back at the two of them, the dark head and the auburn bent toward each other, a little coven of two. I felt a twinge in my heart as I imagined Lou intertwined with her, whispering sweet Lou nothings into the seashell of her ear. I dug my nails into my hand so sharply I started to draw blood. I couldn't make her choose me, I thought, *and that has to be okay*. But then I thought: *Bullshit. Bullshit.*

The sound of her laughter chased me out onto the street, where I turned the corner to my car, the windshield cluttered with parking tickets.

Chapter 23

It wasn't easy to wake up the next morning with the ghost drumbeat of gin horses galloping in my head. I wouldn't be early to the office, but then again, Lou was probably still wrapped around the bartender—*Mischa*, Jesus, what a name.

Ugh. I sat up in bed, massaging my head. Lou would never have what we had with anyone else, though, I thought, not a bartender, not the Lady. She'd never have Ellen's bluing body twitching in the back seat of a car with any other woman.

Be human, Jo.

My stomach roiled as I got out of bed, searching for my phone. We had a three-day no-contact rule, ordinarily, when we ran cases. Gave the mark a long enough time to miss the girl, work up some lurid fantasies, but not so long that he'd forget all about her. Well. No time to play games now.

I coughed a few times to clear my throat before I called Carrigan's office, his direct line. I wanted to sound vulnerable, not hung over.

His voice was brusque, annoyed from the moment he picked up. Not in the mood to be seduced. "Carrigan."

"Mr. Carrigan?" I didn't want to waste his time, but the woman he'd kissed in front of my apartment door was a woman who would be a little unsure about everything, a little meek. "It's Jo. From the bar. The woman you gave the ride to the other night?" I made every sentence sound like a question, like I wasn't even sure of my own name, and I kept my voice soft, like I thought the phone might bite if I startled it.

I caught a glimpse of myself in the small mirror next to my bed—dark hair messy, lips slightly swollen and bearing traces of last night's lipstick. A similar scarlet shade ringing the mouth of the gin bottle next to my bed. My face was creased with sleep, eyelashes tacky with mascara. Some pearl-clutching good girl I looked.

"Yes." He didn't say anything else. I waited. "I remember," he said, finally.

"I don't think I really thanked you properly, it was such a kind—"

"Yes," he said, cutting me off. "It was kind of me. And very foolish, too. I have to go. Please don't call here again."

"But you have my bracelet— I mean, I can't find my bracelet," I said, the words gushing out of me. It wouldn't be impossible to navigate the sting still if Carrigan refused to see me voluntarily, but it would be trickier. Too many coincidences and he'd wonder if I was stalking him. Besides, I was running out of time. "I think I left it in your car?"

There was a pause. I filled it, trying to keep him on the phone. "It's important to me—"

"Not so important you couldn't keep track of it," he said. I could hear him drumming his fingers. "I'll check. Anything else?"

My head was throbbing. I was feeling sick and not only from the gin. I rubbed the spot on my wrist where the bracelet usually sat. "Helluva way to get people to vote for you," I snapped. "I thought the Carrigan name stood for gentility."

There was a pause and my stomach dropped. *Goddammit, Jo, of all the times to lose your temper.* I realized I was clutching the phone in one hand and squeezing the flesh under my elbow with the other.

"Don't call here again," Carrigan said, his voice frosty.

"Please," I said, dropping my voice an octave. There was a real twinge in my heart, imagining never seeing that stupid gaudy gift again. There was a bigger twinge in my heart, imagining not seeing Carrigan again, missing my shot at his money. "It really means something to me."

"Fine," Carrigan said. "I'll check."

He called back not five minutes later. He had the bracelet. I could pick it up anytime I wanted, he said. In fact, that very afternoon, when he'd be out, would be ideal. I bit my lip. *No one can make my Mitch do anything he doesn't want to do.*

"Wonderful," I said. "I'll be sure not to mention that it's jewelry I left in your car the other night."

There was a long pause. I could almost hear his brain clicking through the optics. "On second thought," he said, "I'll come to you. Is tomorrow afternoon good?"

I pinched my inner thigh until it welted, until I was sure I could control the excitement in my voice. "It's perfect."

When I got to the office, there was no sign of Jackal or Lou. But the office wasn't empty.

The door was cracked, and someone had closed the blinds so that thin ribbons of sunlight cut into the ugly orange rug but shaded the corner of the office. A pair of loafers edged out into the sunlight. I gave a little yelp. MacLeish sat in a chair next to a potted plant, reading

Attorney at Law Magazine. Lou's idea of a little joke. I craned my neck, looking down the hallway for Escobar.

"Planned to go to law school once," MacLeish said to me. The chair's leather creaked under him as he shifted.

"That door was locked." I was almost sure of it.

MacLeish focused one eye on me and kept the other on the magazine. An unnerving trick. "One of my skills that wouldn't have been put to good use as a lawyer," he replied.

"You didn't have to break in," I said, my mind working in overdrive. He wouldn't break in alone to serve me a warrant. This had to be extracurricular, coming to collect on the cash.

I took a gamble, tried to throw him off-kilter. "How does it happen that your partner on the force is younger than you and already higher-ranked? It doesn't take a genius to see you're the better cop."

MacLeish tossed the magazine onto the table next to him. "You can lose stripes as easy as you earn 'em."

"Ah," I said. "Because you made a mistake? What kind of mistake?"

"Did you know Hiram Klein had dozens of complaints filed against him over the years?" He stood up, adjusting his belt. MacLeish put his hands on his hips, dipped forward so we were closer to eye to eye.

The abrupt switch threw me. Now I was the one off-kilter. "No, I didn't know that," I lied.

"Mean shit," he said. "And he looked like such a nice grandfatherly type."

"You're here to tell me about Hiram Klein's casting-couch preferences?"

"Dozens of complaints over the years." He shook his head at me, his mouth twisted in a grimace. He wasn't faking his disgust. "And they always went away before we could get around to investigating."

I swallowed. I tried to look casually over my shoulder, check down the hall. If Escobar was nearby, he was sure being quiet about it.

"I see worse all the time. I've got kids burned to death in an apartment building where the landlord didn't want to shell out cash to keep the place up to code. I've got a guy killed his wife cuz she mouthed off. All those people, I'm sorry they're dead. Hiram Klein is one more body to me."

"Why are you telling me—"

"Now, Ellen Howard," MacLeish went on, as if I hadn't spoken. "What bothers me, how did she end up asphyxiated? You hear about people choking on their own guilt, but usually it takes a little longer. And it's a little less . . . on the nose." He shook his head. "It's a shame about that money of hers. She'd be so forgettable, otherwise."

I forced myself to lift my chin so I was looking down on him and calculated my odds of pushing past him to the sliver of open door behind me. But MacLeish seemed to be making a point of letting me keep my personal space.

"This is how it works?" I said. "You get the money back, you look the other way?"

"It's funny what people remember," MacLeish said, still not moving toward me, holding his ground as though he knew what I was thinking. "Not an hour ago, I got a call from a woman, said she saw Klein's car leave the Alto Nido the night of the murder. Recognized the plates right off, he was a man who liked to be recognized. Said she could see two heads in the car, but crime scene says Klein was killed at Ms. Howard's apartment. So who else could be in the car?"

Lou used to tell me my biggest tells were what I did with my hair and my hands. "You toss your head when you're nervous," she told me once, sliding her fingers through my hair and shaking it out, mimicking the motion. "And you drum your fingers when you're scared."

Eventually, she took to cupping her hands softly over my own until I learned to stop.

My fingers were twitching against my blouse like pinned butterflies. I slid my hands into my armpits to hide it. "Give me two days," I said, my voice not steady. "I promise. Then the money's all yours."

MacLeish's mouth twitched. "Here's the thing, kid," he said. "The money that's missing, it's good for the usual. But we've got too many people crawling around, asking questions."

My stomach sank. "Let me guess, squeaky wheels need greasing. How much?"

To his credit, MacLeish didn't make excuses for the shakedown. He didn't pretend to feel bad, and he didn't pretend it was my fault. "Fifteen large. Should do it."

I almost laughed in his face. "Sure," I said. "Would you prefer that in diamonds or gold bricks?"

MacLeish scratched at his chin. He thought for a moment. "I used to think I could help people with this job." He looked almost sad. Shifting back and forth on his toes like he was getting ready to move. I could feel my heart hammering against my palm. "But people have to *want* to be helped." He shook his head again, something almost fatherly in his expression. "This woman you work for, she'll have something on you now. Always her lapdog."

The thought had occurred to me, too. I'd be cultivating girls under the Lady's thumb forever now, seeing Ellen's face in every new girl I trained. But I didn't want to admit that to him. "Sounds like my choice is her lapdog or yours."

"Ellen Howard's dead, there's no coming back from that. And whoever killed her was probably acting on orders," MacLeish said, taking one small step forward. He touched my arm and I flinched. "If she ends up in jail, it doesn't get to the real problem."

I counted to five in my head. "What is it you want from me?"

"The chief wants the money, that's true," MacLeish said with that hangdog expression. "But we both know that dead bodies tend to pile up. You come to me sometime with information that'll bring us directly to your boss, I'll make sure it never rebounds on you. That's all. Would be worth a lot more than money."

"That's never *all*."

MacLeish smiled, a little sadly. "Not everyone's looking to use you. There's no justice in the world," he said. "There might as well be friendship. I can help you. I can get you out. Think about it."

With that, he ambled out the door and down the staircase, taking his time. I watched him walk all the way down, and he knew I watched him. He turned as he unlocked his car and held up one hand, a friendly goodbye.

I closed my eyes. Maybe I reminded him of a daughter, or a woman he'd failed once, or all the women he'd failed all the time in little ways that didn't matter until you looked back over a lifetime. Maybe I didn't remind him of anyone. Maybe he wanted to feel like a hero. I wasn't interested in turning on the Lady—on *Lou*—but he had a point. No matter what, the Lady owned me now, entirely. This time, the debt was more than money.

CHAPTER 24

I spent my lunch easing my hangover with ice-cold highballs, jotting out drafts of my pitch to Carrigan and trying not to consider MacLeish's offer, what that would mean. It would mean the end of my debt to the Lady, for one. I doodled as I drank, thinking.

Even if I was considering MacLeish's offer, I didn't have much to give him. No name, no address, nothing he could use. And I knew better than to think it would be as easy as showing up at the station, announcing that I had a lead for him. Surefire way to end up handcuffed.

But it didn't matter. Because I wasn't going to betray Lou, and that's what this would amount to. I couldn't leave Lou behind. And I knew she'd never leave the Lady willingly. But fifteen grand on top of the eleven that I owed the Lady—even if it all went smoothly with Carrigan, it was a big chunk of change I'd be sacrificing. That did sting. And between the debt and the murder, there was so much about me the Lady knew, while I knew nothing. Even if I'd never give the

information to MacLeish, it couldn't hurt to have something about the
Lady in my back pocket.

And, I realized, I did have something. I riffled through the pages
on my desk, looking for the envelope with the blue fleur-de-lis where
I'd written down the Lady's license plate—the envelope Ellen had
tossed aside to get to the bribe money. I tried to remember if I'd tossed
it out with the rest of the things Ellen had touched, but I wasn't sure—
those days were a soggy blur. It wasn't on my desk. I checked every
drawer and even moved the desk a foot out to make sure it hadn't
slipped anywhere. No luck. My one concrete link to the Lady, van-
ished.

From my office, anyway. Maybe Lou had noticed the envelope
floating around and pocketed it, one more sign of the Lady who swept
away for safekeeping. Loyal Lou, who kept all the Lady's secrets.

I walked to the front door and flipped the lock closed.

I stared at our three office doors. I could almost see the ghost of
Ellen—had it been only a week ago?—outlined in my doorway, steel-
ing her spine to face me and make her demands. Patting down her
fluffy blonde hair with one hand while she rapped on my door with
the other. Thinking about myself at that moment, how the only thing
I'd wanted was to prove to the Lady—to *Lou*—that I was good at my
job, good enough to be let in on all the little secrets they held so close
between the two of them.

*Well, Ellen, back then neither one of us knew we'd turn out to be murderers,
did we?*

I opened the door to Lou's office. One of the benefits of our
office's past as a massage parlor: none of the doors locked from the
outside.

In the unlit office, a disjointed shrub the size of a yacht squatted
on Lou's desk, threatening to topple her sea of notes. I squinted, stepping forward.

The arrangement was a monster, reaching nearly to the ceiling, a bright and gaudy spray of hot-pink calla lilies, dotted through with blood-red roses and choked by baby's breath. It might as well have come with a price tag attached. It hadn't been enough to rub my nose in her exploits with the bartender, Lou had to flaunt roses, too? Probably from Mr. Alibi. I slapped the vase, sending the water sloshing and rocking.

A slim white card fell onto Lou's floor. Of course Mr. Alibi would leave a card. He'd want credit. Maybe he'd included the receipt, too, for good measure. I didn't even hesitate.

> *Dear Lou, thank you for a job well done. I shall keep the Agency*
> *in mind for any future jobs.—Widow in the Sunshine City*

I frowned at the card. It struck me as overly paranoid, to send flowers and sign a card that way, even for our clients. But the sign-off was tugging at some half-forgotten thing I knew, an itch I couldn't scratch or shake. I flipped the card over my knuckles as I sifted through the rest of Lou's notes—some might call it snooping—looking for an envelope with a blue fleur-de-lis.

My eyes registered it before my fingers, and I had to skim backward a few pages before I found it again. The blue fleur-de-lis envelope was identical to the one I was looking for, except instead of a license plate written on the back, Jackal's name was printed on the front. I shook out its contents.

Inside, there was a receipt from the Albatross Coffee Shop in Koreatown, an address not even a mile from our office. I squinted. The receipt was for $713.36. That was a shitload of coffee. There was nothing else in the envelope, but when I flipped the receipt over, in delicate blue pen strokes, there was a note: *Due Nov. 30.* Albatross—I'd seen that on Jackal's desk once before, I remembered. So there was something the Lady was covering up for Jackal. Gambling debts, maybe. A lot of slates she was wiping clean on behalf of her employees. I tried not to imagine what she might have on Lou.

I slid the receipt into the envelope and placed the stacks of paper back on top of it, combing through them one time to make sure I hadn't missed anything. But there were only more notes, magazines, invoices. The Lady Upstairs must've been the last woman in Los Angeles to keep paper invoices. No envelopes. Nothing that looked the least bit useful.

And then it hit me. *The Bride in the Dark City*. Klein's first major film, a critically acclaimed hit that made not only his career but those of a handful of other people associated with the film. Including the leading lady who he'd gone on to cast in dozens of other productions and who, years later, couldn't mention his name in interviews without a veil dropping over her eyes.

I dropped the card, stunned. It shouldn't have been worse to realize Ellen had died only to protect the Lady's organization. Even if I'd known Klein's wife had been the one to hire us, it wouldn't have changed what happened. But still. I would've almost preferred the roses be from Alibi. Because if the widow wasn't so *grieving*, maybe Mrs. Klein wouldn't have asked questions about her husband's death. Maybe she would've even helped us cover it up. If that was true . . . I closed my eyes. I couldn't let myself think it.

I wondered why Lou hadn't mentioned it, that we'd been working for Klein's wife. Helping her ensure a tidy divorce settlement, no doubt. She'd done this for so many years, seeing the very worst in people, *bringing out* the very worst in people. Maybe it no longer struck her as anything special.

I stared at the flowers, trying to think. Such gaudy mourning lilies from the devastated widow, the betrayed wife.

There was an idea.

I went back through the invoices on Lou's desk, carefully this time. It didn't take long for me to find the phone bill. I plucked the sheet off Lou's desk and stuffed it in my pocket.

Later, at home at Tarantula Gardens, I'd circle the numbers that appeared most frequently and try them until I reached the Lady. I was almost positive I'd remember her voice. It was so simple, I could've laughed. Start with the phone records: the original clue to infidelity. *Lou, I'm learning. You'll be proud of me yet.*

I folded the invoice and shoved it into my pocket, fleeing from Lou's flowers, which leered at me like something wild and still living, petals already starting to fall in a bloody pool over her notes.

One last stop before I could go home and get ready for Carrigan the next day. The streets were whizzing by in the inky hot twilight, gray-white streaks of houses and parked cars and family units, and I was thinking, *I'm not even drunk anymore*, and then I was in front of Jackal's apartment, parking the car and tripping up the stairs.

Jackal answered his door looking sleepy and annoyed—looking different, somehow. But maybe I was the one who was different. The feel of another mark on me. It had been so long.

"Aren't you going to invite me in, hot stuff?" I wiggled my shoulders at him. Jackal's frown deepened, but he stepped aside. I leaned forward and grabbed his chin, kissing him hard.

He pushed me away first. "You taste like you've been licking a bathroom floor."

I kissed him again, harder, nipping at his chin, then shucked my shoes off and headed for his kitchen. I ransacked the cupboards until I found a bottle. I held it up, eyebrows raised, a clear offer, and Jackal waved his hand, a no. And I realized what was different wasn't me, but him. He was, of all things, sober. And had been for a few days. His eyes were clear green marbles, no clouds. How strange.

"What's got you so goddamn chipper?" Jackal leaned a hip against the counter, his arms crossed, and watched me dunk a few fingers of warmish tequila into a glass. I looked for citrus to cut the flavor, but Jackal was fresh out of limes, so I settled on a molding orange from the fridge.

"What was the biggest score we ever made?"

Jackal thought a moment, pondering all the bribes it had been his responsibility to turn over to the Lady Upstairs, and I took a sip of my drink. A moldy orange-and-tequila cocktail: I almost gagged it back up again. That didn't taste so great, either.

"I think Lou turned fifty grand one time. Years ago."

Fifty grand. Carrigan could definitely get his hands on that, or more. If he was properly inspired. "And how much of that did we see?" The next sip went down only *feeling* like orange-tinted gasoline.

"The usual. Lou got twenty-five percent, I got another ten. Do the math."

I drained the glass, feeling the buzz of the alcohol and Carrigan's hands on the small of my back, my hips as he pressed me into his lips. Golden fingerprints on my waist, my hips, my ass. A modern-day Midas.

"That's a big percentage the Lady keeps," I said, watching those sober green eyes. Greed was the way to go with Jackal. A man who was feeding a habit by selling photographs on the side wouldn't say no to cash. "On top of what the clients pay her."

"I will have a drink." Jackal reached to pour himself a thimbleful of the warm tequila. He drank it straight. "Carrigan," he said, and it wasn't a question.

"That's right."

"That kind of money doesn't take kindly to blackmail." Jackal closed his eyes, and his nostrils flared against the tequila. "You know better than that."

"Look at you, big man cautious," I said. "That's a hell of a new quality to pull on me now."

"The police have already questioned you once about murder. Better to keep a low profile."

"If you'd *listen* to me, the police won't even be a problem." I did not want to think about murder. I did not want to think about Ellen dead in the back seat of Klein's car. I explained what I wanted, that we had an opportunity to take Carrigan, make a windfall without the Lady being involved. That we could ship enough money the way of the police that they would forget all about Ellen and then it would be smooth sailing for all of us. I left out one or two details.

Jackal stared past me, thinking it through. His tongue swiveled around his lips, and then he shook his head. "It won't work."

"I *know* it will," I said. It had to. Jackal looked skeptical. "Besides," I went on, feeling nasty and liking it, "there's always those photographs. I think the fact that I haven't mentioned them to Lou or the Lady is worth *something*. I think the Lady would be pretty pissed if she found out you were making side money off her business. Doesn't that make you a liability? Particularly now, when we all need to keep a low profile."

Jackal chewed on his lip and avoided looking at me. He kept fiddling with something in his pocket. I tried to think of another time I'd seen him nervous. I couldn't think of any.

Finally, Jackal scratched the back of his head, laughed bitterly. "Oh yes, there's always those photographs, aren't there?" He shoved me out of the way, poured himself another drink. Nearly chewed through the glass to get at the liquor. He needed courage for whatever he was about to tell me. "How about this, sweetheart. They're not for blackmail. Well, not anymore. They're for the police."

"What?" I blinked, gaping at him. "How did this happen? How long?"

He told me the whole story. How one of Lou's marks had lodged a formal complaint, then retracted it, but the police had followed up on the tip anyway, started asking questions about the organization. How Jackal had been stealthily sliding photographs, a few throwaway shots of older cases, undated, to the police in exchange for immunity, should he ever need it.

"But now it doesn't matter. Things have changed with Ellen dead. They're leaning on me for anything I know about the Lady, about the business. If I don't give them what I have in two days . . ." he said, trailing off with a shrug. I heard him, but I was also hearing the heart of the entire condominium. The bones of it creaking and settling. From the next room over, someone coughed loudly, twice. Under that, I could hear the buzz of the fan from Jackal's bedroom. The air sent the dust ruffle of his couch gently waving back and forth. There was a stain on his carpet, brown, in the shape of a heart. Near the sofa. I'd never noticed.

Everything I'd worked for with Lou, and how hard I'd tried to be the woman the Lady wanted me to be, and now: nothing. Even if I got the money from Carrigan on time, the police were already closing in on the Lady's operation. MacLeish was so eager for information on the Lady, but with Jackal's photographs and a sworn statement, he wouldn't need anything from me.

"Two more days," I repeated.

"Two days," he agreed. "And then I'll start over somewhere else. Maybe Mexico. But you could do it, too, you could come with me. You'd testify against Lou, Lou and the Lady, of course. It's the only way—someone has to take the fall. Especially since we don't even have the Lady's *name*, but we could still—"

"Testify against Lou?"

"I know," he said. "I know. But what other option is there?"

I stared at him. "You're not serious." He didn't say anything. I stared down at that heart on the carpet until I could think straight again. Even if the police already knew, I couldn't let him testify against Lou. A small plan started to form, a not-very-good one, but I didn't have anything better. "How much?"

"What?"

"How much," I said, "for you to sell me those photographs before you split town? I'm not leaving with you, and I'm not testifying against Lou. So how much for you not to give those photos to the police? Name your price."

"Jo, you can't possibly think you can *stay* in Los Angeles now—"

"I'm not going to let you do this to her," I snapped. "And I'm not leaving with you."

"No," he said, rubbing his face. He drained the glass, wouldn't look at me. "I didn't really think you would. But don't you ever want to get out of here?" He refilled the glass, then stared at the liquid. Dumped it back out. He met my eyes and shook his head. "I do. Christ almighty, I do."

I sneered at him. Regret was wasted after the fact—I knew that better than anyone. "Good luck finding another boss who'll set you up with a monthly poker stipend."

Jackal's brow folded like an accordion. "You think *I* want that? You think that was *my* idea?" He shook his head, his lip curling. "You ever notice how hard the Lady works to keep us tied to our vices, Jo?"

"*Name your price.* And then once you help me with Carrigan, you can leave town forever if you're so goddamn ready to be gone."

In the end, it didn't take him long to come up with a number. It wasn't even as high as I'd expected. Money eyes. We shook on it and he invited me to stay, but I didn't even dignify that with a response. He didn't speak again until I was almost out the door.

"Jo, look at me." I half turned, could see him out of the corner of my eye. On another man, I would've thought the look on his face was tenderness. He reached a hand out, almost touching me. "Even if you don't leave with me, you should still leave. This job isn't a home, it's a prison. Somewhere, some part of you knows it." I looked down at his hand, still hovering near my waist, then up at his face. He spread his arms. It might've been an invitation for me to step into them. "Look at you. You're drinking yourself to death," he said.

"I'll see you soon," I said, and I shut the door on him.

CHAPTER 25

The anklet was overkill. I decided it as I turned back and forth in the mirror, watching the honey-gold catch the light and wink at me. I liked the way it sliced my leg in two, separating foot from calf, and I liked that it would make Carrigan think of fingers encircling my ankle, the way you only got to do with a person when you had special, intimate access to them.

But it was trying too hard. No woman wears an anklet without an agenda. And I did not want to appear to be a woman with an agenda. I unsnapped it and set it on my bureau, glittering hard in the dying evening light.

I'd dredged out things to warm up my apartment, to seem more like the woman Carrigan was expecting me to be: books, a vase, a few throw pillows I'd bought for cheap that morning. A framed picture of me and Lou, my favorite one: Lou's eyes squinched tight because she was laughing, and I was giving Jackal, perpetually behind the camera, my best tousled-hair *go fuck yourself* glare. A woman with friends, an easy social life.

I'd finished the first gin martini while I was still working on my face, and I told myself that was for the best anyway: it would loosen me up. I made another before Carrigan arrived, and as I slurped at the salty olive juice, I thought: *Piece of cake. Only the rest of your life depends on how this goes.*

Ellen's first night with Klein, I'd gotten her a little drunk, too. "I'm not going to make you do anything you don't want to do," I'd told her. "Even this," I'd said. "It's still early. You can leave, if you want. I can find someone else." And it was true, I told myself. I would've let her go. I would've driven her home and never seen her again. I wouldn't have forced her to do anything, right?

Carrigan's knock at the door was strong and straightforward. I nodded at Jackal, who crept up the stairs to the loft and hid behind the boxes of "books from storage" we'd set up earlier in the afternoon. A perfect direct angle to catch us in the act—so long as we stayed in the living room. So long as I actually *could* seduce him.

I checked my reflection one last time, turning back and forth. When the lamp caught me in the right way, my white cotton dress was completely see-through. I'd picked one with buttons all the way down the front, and I'd pulled my hair up, stitching it in place with a handful of bobby pins. I wanted to give him the illusion of undoing me.

I swung the door open. Carrigan was wearing a fedora, the brim pulled low over his eyes, his hands in his pockets. Incognito verging on ridiculous. He didn't make any move to touch me, not even a friendly handshake hello. Instead, he plucked the bracelet out of his pocket and held it out to me, extending it by two fingers like he was afraid he might accidentally touch me.

"Yours," he said.

I didn't take it. "Come in. Have a drink or something."

"No." His fingers clenched around the bracelet. "Take it."

"A drink, to thank you," I said, "not for any other reason. Please."

He glared at me from under the fedora. A man trying so hard to be good.

"Please," I said again, my voice feather-soft. I reached for the bracelet and put my hand on his, let it rest there. "You've come all this way. Even friends have drinks."

One tug and he was through my apartment door.

Inside, I poured us both a drink of Lou's favorite bourbon—"It's good," Carrigan said, "you'll want to sip it, like this," and he demonstrated, as though I'd never heard of sipping—and clinked his glass in cheers. We sat together on the couch, Carrigan perched so far away from me he was nearly on the arm.

"How's the campaign going?" I took another sip of my drink. I curled my legs under me, propping myself up higher and inching a little bit closer to him.

He looked at me over the rim of his glass, one eyebrow raised. I knew what that look meant. He didn't trust I'd have any head for politics. "That's what you wanted me to come inside for? To hear about my campaign?"

I thought of Tana on TV, all of her opinions on politics. "No. I asked to be nice."

I let him lead the conversation, tilting my head as he spoke, working so hard to find him fascinating. But I had a secret weapon: every time my concentration lapsed, for even a second, I pictured Ellen's face, and MacLeish, and the headlights pouring in through the back windshield of Klein's car. I shivered, but I kept my attention rapt.

Carrigan finished his drink, and I could see him eyeing the door. I scooched closer to him on the couch and leaned forward, grabbing the crystal tumbler from his hand with fingers tipped Size Matters red. We were so close now we were practically breathing the same air.

"I'll take that," I whispered. "Thank you for your company, Mr. Carrigan."

He had reared back into the couch, as far from me as he could possibly get, but it still wasn't far enough. When he answered, his voice was a little breathless, too. "I told you," he said. "That's my father-in-law, that's not me."

I sat back and watched as little beads of sweat appeared on his brow. Twice now, he'd objected to me calling him that. "But it's your name, too."

He grimaced. "Don't remind me."

I wanted to push it, ask him why he'd bothered to take it if he was going to treat it like a burden—no one had *made* him do it. Instead, I said: "All right." I smoothed my dress down and smiled at him shyly, a hopeful virgin on prom night. "Can I get you another drink?"

"Why? Are you trying to get me drunk?" Carrigan scowled at me.

For a handsome man, he sure knew how to make himself look unattractive. I forced the twitch of my lips to stay up. "No, of course not. I'm simply enjoying the pleasure of your company." I reached out and tapped the glass again, moving my knee forward so that it nearly touched his. His eyes flicked down at our almost-touching bodies and then back to my face. "I'm hoping you'll stay here with me a little longer. So, tell me . . ."

I reached down and lightly stroked the flesh of his thigh through his gabardine, scratching with the tips of my nails. His knee jumped and jerked under my fingers. I moved my nails in little circles, inching north. He didn't move—not to brush my hand away, not to lean into me. He was watching me with interest, if not desire—perhaps enjoying the feel of what I was doing, but not yet giving into it. I figured that meant I could keep going.

"What?" His voice was scratchy—maybe with desire; maybe he was thirsty. "Tell you what?"

I didn't actually want him to tell me anything ever again, unless it was him pleading with me, offering any amount of money to keep the photographs of this tryst private. I leaned forward and placed little feather-light kisses on the corners of his mouth, remembering to be soft, to go slow. After a moment, his mouth opened under mine, and I smiled.

"Does that feel nice?" I inched my fingers upward, tracing my fingers lightly, so lightly, over his lap. I put a little smoke in my voice and tried to make him think of tangled sheets. The thought of that money—*fifty K, fifty K, fifty K*—thrummed in me below the waist, but it didn't have the fire I was used to. I closed my eyes, thought of Lou, the lemony smell of her hair that tickled my cheek as she kissed me.

I stole a glance at his face as I started kneading him through his pants, not bothering to be shy now. He'd clamped his eyes shut and tipped his head back. I took it as an invitation to crawl over him, straddling him with my knees as I continued to work. Liking the feel of this man, so wealthy and powerful, splayed beneath me, at my mercy, I began fondling him in earnest.

But it wasn't there. I reached down to stroke him, and he was soft as a lump of clay. I unbuckled him, tried some skin-on-skin contact. Nothing. Carrigan was silent under me, the silence that I knew meant the kiss of death for men: embarrassment. Which would be anger soon, directed at himself and then at me. After a moment, he pushed me away.

"Sorry," he said, with a little laugh. "It's not doing it for me tonight, sweetheart."

Jackal's footage would be a nightmare. There was enough there to show something, enough there that he wouldn't want it to get out, but Carrigan could say, very rightly, that he'd come to his senses, stopped, went home to his loving wife before he did something he regretted forever. These photographs wouldn't scare him enough to cough up $50K, that was for damn sure.

Silently, I scooted off him until there was a little space between us on the couch. I tried not to picture Jackal laughing at me. *Think you're such hot shit now?*

I remembered, then, how the rest of the conversation with Ellen the first night with Klein had gone. "I'm not going to make you do anything you don't want to do," I'd said to her. That much was true. But hadn't I added, after: "But there's plenty of girls who *would* do it, there's plenty of girls I could find to take your place"? And she'd looked up at me with her big eyes and that little *please like me* smile, and that's when she'd said it: "Put me in, Coach." I hadn't even laughed.

I didn't bother to button my dress as I moved to the kitchen to refresh our drinks. I could hear him behind me, moving restlessly on the couch, putting himself back together. I didn't bother to tell him that it was all right, because it wasn't. I added a few ice cubes to the glass of nice-but-not-top-shelf bourbon and thought of what to say.

Baby, it happens to all men. It's not a big deal. We can still have a good time, if you know what I mean. But what sort of good time could we have now that that was worth fifty large?

When I turned around, refilled tumblers in hand, Carrigan was already standing, halfway to the door. Not meeting my eyes.

"Don't go," I cried out, the words coming out more strangled and frantic than I'd meant to sound. Carrigan frowned at me, his shirt half untucked, the pleats of his pants crumpled from the couch.

I had to keep him there, somehow. I had to give him enough time to relax, recover. If he left, I'd never see him again, I was sure of that. I'd be too embarrassing, a moment he'd want to forget—there'd be no other chance. I was starting to panic and trying not to show it. I could think of Jackal above me, packing up his camera equipment. This time, it had been me that fucked it.

Carrigan cleared his throat and I slid a hand down my skirt and pinched my outer thigh through the fabric, on the side where Carrigan couldn't see, working up tears. I waited until I had a really good burn going, my eyes wide to fill better, and then I let the tears spill.

"Please don't leave," I choked out. "You're the first man I've . . . the first man since . . ." I turned my head to the side, letting the little tendrils of hair that had pulled out during our tumble spill across my face. I caught my hands in the tendrils, twisting little snakes out of the locks and watched, through my curtain of hair, as he shifted from foot to foot and debated what to do. But it was a start. He wasn't leaving. Carrigan took one step forward, and I jumped like I was surprised when I felt his hand on my shoulder.

"Your ex? The one you're scared of." His voice was full of a self-righteous anger. A man determined to feel like a hero while cheating on his wife.

I nodded jerkily, still not meeting his eyes. I bit at the corners of my lips to plump them, and before long, Carrigan's arms were around me, whispering soft nothings into the hair at my temples, his lips brushing my skin. I shivered, not because I wanted him.

Above us, I could see Jackal poke his head up from behind the box, moving slowly, frowning down at us. I didn't have to be close to read his expression which was, *You bullshitter.* But one signal from me and he'd hurtle down the stairs. I thought of the first time Jackal and I had slept together—I had been so grateful, in an odd way, that I'd never had to try with him, never had to do anything other than want him. That the very fact of my *wanting* him was a turn-on, that I didn't have to play the game of waiting for *him* to come to *me.* It was so easy. It all used to be so easy.

To my unpleasant surprise, my nose started to burn and real tears began to run. I'd loved this job, once. But I was so goddamn tired of pretending all the time—pretending to want someone I couldn't stand, pretending to want less than I really did. And anytime I shut my eyes, tried to get a break from all that pretending, I was greeted by a ticker tape of images: a rigoring body abandoned to yipping canyon coyotes, fuchsia feathers tickling the night air, scratchy hotel duvets covered in beheaded birds-of-paradise. There was no outrunning it, not ever. I turned my face into Carrigan's shoulder and let myself sob in earnest for a moment.

Carrigan pulled back and cupped my face in between his hands. "Don't cry," he said, his eyes soft. He leaned in and kissed my forehead, my nose, my mouth again, sweet sipping kisses that left me cold. The tears continued to flow, and I could feel him start to harden against my hip. I resisted the urge to bite down on his tongue, draw blood. I knew this man. A trauma junkie. The man who wants to know all about your broken pieces without ever asking about what made you strong.

I let him propel us back to the couch, didn't argue when he started to tenderly undress me from the top down. I feigned little sounds of appreciation every so often, but Carrigan was lost in his own world, a world in which he was healing a broken woman with his magic cock. But none of that mattered if it got me what I wanted. That thought brought a vigor back to my kisses.

Carrigan curled one hand around my ear, stroking the folds, pushing his face into my hair, everywhere at once. I tilted my head into his hand, thinking about Jackal hearing us upstairs, wondering, vaguely, if it turned him on the way it had for me to watch him with that girl, that nothing, on his desk. I closed my eyes and Carrigan kissed me and I was thinking, then, only *Finish it, finish it, finish it.*

"Touch me, touch me, please," I gasped and he did, his face buried in my neck and moving slow, so slow, until he wasn't anymore. Lou's face peeked out at me from the picture over his shoulder, the tendons on her neck bulging as she gasped for breath, laughing hard. Jackal might have run out of battery for all the show that we were giving him. I made sure my head was never in the way. I made sure he couldn't miss the shot.

Afterward, still caged between his arms on the couch, listening to his ragged breathing as he came down, I reached up and kissed his throat. I didn't say anything to him, and he mistook my silence for being moved by the moment. He stroked my face once, then moved off of me, wiping himself off on one of my throw pillows. Carrigan started tucking himself back into his clothes, one sympathetic kiss absent-mindedly shotgunned into the side of my head to show it was more than an afternoon fuck that got carried away. Already making his excuses about how he needed to get going, how he'd be missed at the office already.

I wasn't listening. I was still lying there, staring at Lou's face. I wondered if I would ever tell Lou about this. I wondered if I would have performed differently if it had been her behind the camera.

Carrigan leaned in to give me a proper kiss again before he left, hustling out of my apartment so quickly it was like he knew there were cameras inside. He made some lame *see you soon* attempt, but he thought he'd never see me again. I knew better.

I hoped Jackal had gotten shots of Carrigan holding me, too—in some ways, that was worse than the sex pictures. Those might be worth more than $50K.

I heard Jackal creaking his way in tentative steps down the stairs.

"You got all that?" I asked without turning to look at him. Still staring at Lou's face. *God, you're funny.* I could hear her voice from the night of that photograph, bourbon roses in her cheeks. *You're killing me.*

"You're gonna be rich," he said.

Chapter 26

I was more tired than I'd remembered ever being after a mark, a case—whatever the fuck Lou wanted to call them. Jackal had asked if I'd wanted him to stay, asked if I wanted to review the footage right away. He'd been gentler than normal—didn't try to touch me, didn't snap at me—and I wasn't sure if that was for my sake or for the money. *I'm delicate cargo now*, I'd thought before telling him to go. I didn't kiss him goodbye.

When Jackal left, I turned out the lights so I could slither around in the dark for a little while, adjusting to the feel of another man's hands on my body, the smell of him still on me. God, it had been so long.

I went to the kitchen and poured myself a glass of water—found myself reaching for something stronger. But I still had work to do that night.

I was going to get the money from Carrigan—I knew that much. How much was still up for debate. But with the election so close and

still undecided, he'd pay anything to keep this scandal quiet. Even
with what I'd pay Jackal, it would still be enough to cover my debt and
what I owed the police.

But I couldn't stop thinking of what MacLeish had said and what I
knew to be true, deep in my bones: the Lady owned me now, forever.
The Lady hadn't been the one to take down Carrigan—that had been
all *me*. My plan, my work, my seduction. *Me*. And yet she'd still be the
one reaping the cash from it. Taking the money and telling me it still
wasn't enough. She and Lou would always be a little coven of two.
Because of what I'd done. Because of what *we'd* done.

I pulled the phone bill from my purse where I'd stashed it and
smoothed over the crinkled sheet as best I could. The majority of the
calls were ads, wrong numbers, people who thought we really could
help them with their staffing needs. It was likely Jackal or Lou or even
I had made calls to different people, one-offs, checking restaurant
openings or other things that might be of use in our line of work.
But Lou and the Lady would've talked frequently, a few times a week
at least—daily, for all I knew. I ignored the pang of jealousy that
stirred in me.

First, I got rid of any number from out of state—I couldn't imagine
that the Lady wasn't local, or at least close to Los Angeles. She
had too much knowledge of the city. That took care of most of the
numbers.

I looked at what I had left. I was looking for a number that had
been dialed more than once, and that had called our office more than
once. I circled anything that came close. One of the numbers looked
familiar and appeared over and over again in the records for the past
month. Not the Lady's number, but I felt uneasy. I stared at it. I could

see my fingers punching in the number barely a week before, the crisscross pattern of my thumb on the keys.

Howdy, pardner, what's on the mayhem menu today, Ellen's voice chirped into memory, and then a cackle as she laughed to herself, knowing how much that greeting would annoy me. That same plucky voice pleading, *No, no, please, I won't, I'm sorry, I didn't, it'll be, just let me, no, no, no.*

Ellen's number. Of course. I gulped the water, shaking slightly, then crossed her number out, over and over until you couldn't read it at all. I tore a small hole in one part of the invoice with the pen.

By the time I was done, there were only two numbers left. I wasn't positive that I would remember what the Lady's voice sounded like. I closed my eyes, tried to think. No accent that I remembered. More nasal than husky, more alto than soprano.

Nothing to do but try.

I picked up the phone, cradling the receiver between my shoulder and ear. I dialed the first number on my list. It rang and rang, eventually disconnecting without anyone picking up. I breathed a sigh, somehow relieved. I checked the next number that I'd circled. Another try to find the Lady. I was starting to dial when the phone merengued to life in my hands. I froze. Lou grinned up at me from my phone. How appropriate that she'd want to talk after a case, even if she didn't know it was happening. It would distract me, and I didn't want to be distracted tonight. I brought the glass to my face, tried to cool myself down. But if I didn't pick up, she'd keep calling.

"Hello."

"Hiya." Lou's voice was chipper on the other line. It almost always was, after she got laid. "What are you up to?"

"Lou, what do you want?" I unbuttoned the top of my white dress, crumpled under Carrigan's touch. There were dark smudges near the collar and along the hem. It would never look the same, even laundered. But I didn't need it to.

"Touch-*y*," Lou said, clicking her tongue over the line. "Come outside."

"What? Why?"

She huffed a sigh. "C'mon, do it."

I pulled back my curtains, looked down to the pool in the center of the courtyard. Lou sat on the rim, her toes in the water, jeans rolled up to her knees. The *phit-phit-phit* of night-running sprinklers fizzed the air behind her. A bottle of champagne was tucked against her side, the steam from evaporating chlorine probably warming the glass. I wondered if it could be considered a tradition if we'd only done it twice in two years. She gave me a warm smile, held up a hand. I held up two fingers—*two minutes*—and let the curtain drop, hanging up the phone.

God, this heat would never let up. Even at night. The cotton of the dress chafed against my chest, which was damp, clammy. I stood up, unbuttoned the dress the rest of the way, balled it up, and threw it in a corner. Maybe I'd never have to look at it again. I tucked a towel under my armpits and went down to meet Lou in my bra and panties.

"Look at you," Lou said, giving me an appreciative once-over as I sat down. She handed me the bottle of champagne already opened.

"I thought you were pissed about my drinking." I pulled the edges of the towel down and turned to face her head-on—if she was going to ogle, she might as well get the whole thing. I took the bottle and chugged. I passed it back to Lou, who was making a point of keeping her eyes firmly aboveboard.

"You lied to me," Lou said, taking the champagne bottle from my hand and carefully fixing her lips to the spot where my mouth had been. A shiver twitched my shoulder blades and my nipples hardened. "That's what I was pissed about. I thought we told each other everything."

"Everything," I repeated, thinking of all the lies I'd told over the last few weeks. All of it spurred by the biggest lie—not that Lou would call it a lie, exactly, the fact that she'd kept the Lady from me. But all the same, it was, in its own way. Loyal Lou, who loved the Lady. Loved her so much, she kept her closer than anyone. Even after all we'd done together. "Like the name of the Lady Upstairs."

Lou set the bottle down between us. She studied her toes in the pool, swishing her legs back and forth. The water was a cloudy yellow in the night lights, and it bounced light back under her chin. "It's the only thing I can't tell you," Lou said finally. "You know that."

"The only thing." The champagne was warm, and too sweet, but I liked the burn of the bubbles on my lips. I took two more swigs for courage. "Okay. How was *Mischa* the other night? Was she a good lay?"

Lou gaped at me, then glared. The freckles jumped on her nose as her face went pale. "Great," she said. "I came six times."

I choked on the champagne. "*Six?*"

"Of course not, you asshole," Lou said, still glaring at me. The humidity from the pool was causing her hair to frizz and a fine sheen of sweat appeared on her upper lip, her hairline. Her shoulders dropped and she shook her head. "Christ, do you remember when our conversations didn't always end in arguments? I'm not sure I do." She was silent for a moment, and then she said, more to herself than to me, "How did it all turn out like this?"

I didn't have anything to say to that. The champagne bottle was going more quickly than I'd expected, and I could still feel Carrigan all over me, could still smell him on me. I wondered if Lou could, or what it would make her feel if she did. She'd care because it was Carrigan, of course—would she have cared if it had been anybody else? I stood up, and I could feel Lou's eyes flick up at me. Her mouth dropped open to ask what I was doing, and then I dove into the pool.

I held my breath underwater as long as I could, feeling the water break around me, slosh against the sides of the pool and back again. I opened my eyes underwater, liking the sting of the thickly chlorinated water, and I made for the outline of Lou's pale toes, grabbing her feet, which kicked and jerked, as I surfaced.

"Don't," Lou warned, her face even paler. She'd dug her nails into the grout around the edge of the pool like that would save her if I tugged her in. I let go of her foot, treading water on my own, and she visibly relaxed.

"If she didn't want either Jackal or me to know who she was—if anonymity was so important to her," I said, watching Lou's face, "why did she stop by the office? Why risk it?"

Lou shook her head. "I don't know," she whispered. "Please don't ask me again. Please, Jo. We're so close. It's almost over. Then we can go back to the way that everything was."

Her eyes were big and pleading, and she even leaned closer to me, closer to the water.

But it would never be over, I thought, not for me. There wouldn't be a night I wouldn't see Ellen's face before I went to sleep. That was a given.

And going back to a normal where Lou went home with bartenders but came to me for a midnight chat when she needed to feel like her real self again wasn't going to work, either.

I put my hands, wet, on either side of her legs, soaking her jeans, and when Lou looked down to see what I was doing, I pulled myself close to her so we were almost touching but not quite.

"No more bartenders," I said quietly. Lou's mouth twitched. I took a deep breath; then I pressed myself up until we were nose to nose, my wet legs against her jeans, my mouth hovering only a few inches from her. I remembered the feel of her mouth on mine at the Olvera Street bar, and I remembered Carrigan, having to push him into wanting me, having to pretend to be someone soft and pliant. I was so sick of pretending I didn't want the things I wanted.

So I kissed her.

My mouth must have been salty from the chlorine, and Lou's breath was a little sour from the champagne. When Jackal kissed me, he was all tongue—penetration always. Lou's kisses were softer, breathier, and she was holding herself very still. One slight push from her and I would've fallen back into the pool. Instead, she sat there still as a stone, and let me kiss her.

After a moment, I let myself drop back into the water. I side-stroked away so she couldn't see my face. I'd always thought that Lou was holding herself back from me because she thought it was unprofessional of us to get involved, or because she'd been hurt so many times before. But maybe the truth was she didn't want *me*.

I blinked tears away, ducking my head under the water for cover. *If Carrigan was here, he'd be hard as a rock*, I thought, emptying my lungs in a big air bubble.

From Lou's side of the pool, a big crash. I broke the surface to see Lou, determinedly clinging to the side of the pool, her arms firmly hooked on the asphalt behind her. A slightly terrified look on her face. She bit her lip and stared at me.

"You're my best friend," she started, and then stopped. She wasn't going to say it out loud; she wasn't going to tell me. But I knew.

This time, Lou was greedy, her mouth moving all over mine, down my neck to my ear, which she tugged on with her teeth. A little gasp came out of me, and I threaded my fingers into her hair, pulling her head back to mine. I used my body to keep her upright against the side of the pool, and she wrapped her scratchy wet jeans around my waist. My tongue was exploring the jumping contours of her throat when she whispered something above me. I kissed my way back up to her mouth.

"What did you say?"

Lou's eyes were closed, and her head was tilted back against the asphalt. She didn't open her eyes, but she rolled her head slightly away from me, like she didn't want me to see all of her face as she said it. "Rita Palmer," she repeated, quietly. "That's her name. But promise me . . . you won't tell anyone. Not even Jackal. Promise me, Jo."

My fingertips began to tingle and I kissed her again, harder and deeper, moving my lips all over her now, promising her secret was safe, she wouldn't be sorry she'd trusted me, we were really, finally, *finally* partners now.

I sucked on a salty spot on her neck and came up for air giddy. "God, Lou, thank you—when it's all over, you won't regret this, I promise, we don't need her, we've *never* needed her, it's going to be so much better when we're not under her fucking thumb—"

Lou's head snapped forward, nearly hitting me. She pushed me away, frowning. "What do you mean? Of course we need her. I didn't tell you her name because I wanted you to . . . because . . ."

I bit my bottom lip, swollen from Lou's kisses, and treaded water. Lou was shriveling against the side of the pool with every passing second, staring at me in horror.

"I don't know what I was saying," I said, trying to backpedal. I'd jumped the gun—I hadn't meant to say anything, certainly not yet, not until I had it figured out. Not until I could come to Lou with a plan, with the money. I hadn't even realized I'd made the decision until the words came out of my mouth. "I didn't mean it."

Lou didn't say anything, just turned her back on me and started to haul herself out of the pool. She bent over and grabbed the towel, refusing to look at me.

"Lou, I'm sorry, I swear I won't—"

"No," she said, turning to me finally, eyes blazing, her wet T-shirt clinging to every curve and dip of her. "You won't. You won't say anything to anyone. Or else you'll be sorry." She grabbed my towel and the bottle of champagne, the rusty door separating the pool from the street clanging behind her, and she was gone before I could even ask her what she meant.

Lou had told me once what she owed the Lady—that she'd been the one who'd plucked Lou from the streets, from bad men who liked to hurt her. Sometimes for money, sometimes for love. There was no way Lou would leave the Lady on her own.

Unless.

Unless the choice was taken out of her hands. Unless the Lady was already fingered by the police, with Ellen's and Klein's murders laid at her feet—as they should be. I'd only done what I had to do—what Lou had told me *we* had to do.

It was all so clear now. Lou believed the Lady was the one keeping her from harm, but she hadn't yet realized what Carrigan had taught me: there was no reason we needed the Lady anymore. And she was too dangerous now, too powerful. I just had to explain it to Lou. Lou was a survivor, smart enough to read the changes in the wind.

If the choice was taken out of her hands. If I had a way out. If I had a plan—for us both.

I had a name I could give to MacLeish, along with Jackal's photographs, to make this—all of it, Ellen, the pool, everything—go away. They'd put the Lady away, and Lou and I would be free and clear to do anything we wanted. I'd take the money I earned from Carrigan, money I had no intention of turning over to the goddamn Lady or anyone else, not now, and we'd start over. The two of us, together. Go somewhere until the media furor over Ellen's and Klein's deaths blew over. Maybe, I thought, thinking back to the black-and-white movie, the women in the car, maybe the Mediterranean.

Maybe Lou really would never talk to me again after I did what I now knew I was going to do. But I had to try.

Sleep was still a long time coming. I took a shower, washing the traces of Carrigan and chlorine off me. I fixed myself a drink—

something to help me sleep. I hoped I'd be lucky, that I'd dream of pleasant things, of Carrigan's money, or even of his touch, if it came to that. Of Spain, or anywhere else, any landscape that wasn't the hollow black of the canyons at midnight. Lou's green eyes on a beach, smiling at me, seeing the reason for what I'd done, proud of it. The blue of the water setting her hair even more ablaze, fingers reaching for me. A new and different life. One free of black-eyed corpses.

I hoped I'd be lucky. I knew I wouldn't be.

CHAPTER 27

Jackal had emailed me the photographs first thing in the morning and I'd been right: the best shots he'd taken were the ones of Carrigan holding me, my face buried in the crook of his shoulder. There was an intensity to our intimacy: from a bird's eye view, we really did look like lovers. In the first frames, too many of the photographs centered on my face. We'd have to get rid of those.

I went back through the last few shots, and they were all there, Carrigan unmistakably in the throes of coitus, my own face a big blank, as though I were wearing a mask, or like nothing was happening at all. Even, in that bunch, a few in which Jackal had gone tight on my face, and all there was to see was nothingness. I shivered. Was that always what I looked like having sex? Or only when I was doing it for money?

I stood up, made myself a drink. Before I'd even sat back down, I'd dialed Carrigan's number. He picked up on the fourth ring, his voice irritated. "Ron, can't this wait?"

"Please, I really need to talk to you." I paused, trying not to enjoy it yet. "I really need your help."

"I'm out with my family," Carrigan said. It sounded like he had his jaw, that one I'd licked and nipped not twenty-four hours before, clenched. "Make it fast."

On my desk, one of our photographs stared up at me. I could've been a human blow-up doll for all the expression on my face. I flipped the photograph over. "It's my ex. He's been driving by my house again. I don't know what to do." I quickened my breath. "I couldn't sleep last night."

Carrigan lowered his voice. "Christ, why are you calling me? Try the police."

"Please," I said, letting my voice crack around the *s*. "I'm so scared, I don't know what to do. They won't believe me. They say they can't do anything because it's a public street."

Silence. I held my breath. Then: "What do you need me to do?"

"Tomorrow," I said. "Meet me tomorrow afternoon. Around three. That's usually when he shows up."

"Tomorrow? There's no way—"

I dropped my voice out of the breathy, virginal register I'd been copping, and the relief was immediate, like unzipping a too-tight dress. "Meet me tomorrow with fifty thousand dollars, or else the Friday papers will have photos of you and me doing a dirty tango on my couch. Although I think the ones where you're holding me might be worse. They don't make you look very . . . married. How do you think your prospective constituents would like that? Three generations of Angelenos and adultery." A thick, stunned silence on the other line.

I heard Carrigan say to someone, muffled like he had his hand over the mouthpiece: "I'll be right back, don't wait for me." The shuffling of a phone being moved to another room. Then: "What did you say?"

They never believed you, not the first time you said it. Always thought they could change your mind, charm you back into bed. Like it was something you'd thought up that moment, on a whim.

"Are you seriously trying to—"

"I'm not *trying to*. I *am*. It's nothing personal," I assured him. "But that's the way it is."

"Goddammit, who in the hell do you think—"

"I think my favorite is the finisher," I said brightly. "My poor dress will never be the same, but it's actually quite a beautiful shot." I paused. "If you will."

"Hold on one goddamn second," Carrigan snarled into the phone, and I could hear his huffing breath. I couldn't tell if it was anger or if he was pacing. "How do I even know you have these photographs?"

"That's really a risk you're willing to take, *baby?*"

"Do you know who my father-in-law is? You think he doesn't have connections with the LAPD?"

"Silly me," I said, and I laughed. I'd been paying so much attention to his family name, and I'd missed the forest for the trees. "Silly me," I said again, and I could almost hear Carrigan's relieved sigh on the other end. "It's not your constituents who will care. It's your wife. And her father. Explain to him that not only were you caught playing around on his beloved daughter—the wife who is so *devoted* to you, she gave you that name that keeps opening doors for you—but that you picked someone who photographed you in the act, to boot. I think their blissful ignorance is worth a little more, don't you think? Ignorance is such expensive bliss. Let's call it an even seventy-five."

"There's no *way* I'm—"

"Which do you think would piss Daddy-in-law off more," I said, drawing out the words, making my voice unhurried and low, a tone Jackal would've called my *fuck me* voice, "your cheating or your stupidity?"

"Jesus," he said again, "what a bitch you are," and there was something almost admiring in his tone.

"By tomorrow," I said. I gave him an address—Lou's tiki bar—and told him to meet me there by 8 p.m. I said I'd prefer cash.

"How do I know you'll really destroy the photographs? How do I know you won't keep digital copies floating around somewhere?"

I flipped the closest photograph over on my desk so I didn't have to stare at the blank look on my face. It made me queasy. I didn't want to keep them any more than he wanted them sent to the newspaper.

"I guess you can't trust me," I said. "But I don't want them. I really do not."

The hours had gotten away from me while I'd searched Rita Palmer's name. It wasn't the most common name, so I'd counted on finding something, but there were no records of a Rita, or Margarita, Palmer in Los Angeles in recent years and certainly no one who looked like the woman I'd seen at the office. Lou had either lied to me or been lied to, and I didn't like that I wasn't sure which was right.

I also didn't like that I hadn't heard from Lou this morning—not a call or a text. If she was upset at how I felt about the Lady, I could deal with that. If she regretted kissing me . . .

But brooding on it reminded me. I went back to the list I'd grabbed from Lou's desk, the phone bill, and tried again the two numbers I'd pinpointed as the potential numbers for the Lady. On the first one, the call went straight to voicemail. *Hello, you've reached Graham. Leave a message.* I hung up, wondering if it was Mr. Alibi's voice on the machine.

But the second phone call was a different story. After three rings, someone picked up and waited on the other end, not saying anything.

Breathing loud enough that I knew they were there. My stomach flipped, and I held my breath.

Then, after about ninety seconds: "Why do you keep calling me? Who is this?" The voice was a woman's, a low register made lower by a trace of anxiety. It sounded familiar, but I couldn't be sure, I couldn't be completely positive, that it was *her* voice.

"Hello," I said, trying to think of something to keep her on the line. Until I was sure. "Who's this?"

"Fuck you," she whisper-growled into the phone, her voice shaking. I could hear it now, for real, whoever this was: she was scared. Of me? Or of someone she didn't know having this number? I wondered exactly what Lou had told her about Ellen's death. "*You* called *me.*"

The attitude was right—it was what I remembered and what I'd expect from the Lady. I was almost positive now. *Careful, Jo. Don't assume you're right just because you want to be.*

I took a gamble.

"This is Jo," I said, quietly. "I'm calling with a message from Lou. She needs you to come into the office, tomorrow afternoon. She needs you to meet us there. We have things to discuss."

She was quiet for a very long time. I held my breath, watching cars zip around each other in the complicated braiding of Los Angeles traffic. The air was still sluggish with heat, but it was starting to come down a bit. It was all starting to settle.

"I don't know any Jo," she said finally, her voice very cold. "And I don't know any Lou, but I can tell you if she needs something from me, she can call me *herself.*"

And then she hung up and I stared down at my phone. After all these years, the Lady Upstairs. A phantom with a cell phone. She'd ditch the phone, maybe, if it was a burner, but the police could track the number anyway—it was a start. And if she was as smart as I thought she was, she'd steer clear of the office now, perhaps permanently—but that was fine by me.

I spent some more time searching for Rita Palmer online, looking through pictures, following links. No digital smoking gun, but now I had a name and a phone number for MacLeish. By the time I closed my computer, I was feeling good, confident. It wasn't done yet, I reminded myself. But it was close.

I was locking the door, something resembling a bounce to my step, when a shadow caught my eye. Someone was leaning against my car. For a moment, time froze. *Lou*, I thought, *it has to be Lou*. But I was wrong. Escobar, MacLeish's younger, more senior partner, was flicking through his phone, not watching me approach, although I was sure he knew I was there. Even the sight of a blue leaning against my car couldn't dampen my mood.

"All the crappy condos in all the world and you happen to be waiting outside mine," I said, laughing as I fumbled in my purse for my keys. "What makes me such a lucky girl, Officer?"

Escobar was dressed in plain clothes today, khaki pants and a black button-up, practically choking him. He watched me riffle through my purse with disapproving eyes. One hand was jammed in his pocket, and I wondered, for a moment, if he had a gun in there.

Escobar glared at me. "I wanted to stop by and see if you'd remembered anything else. About the deceased."

"Where's your partner, Sergeant?" I made a big show of looking around. Escobar scowled. If he was going to make much of a cop, he'd have to learn to control his temper better. And maybe that temper would let slip a few details on MacLeish I might be able to use to even the playing field. "And while we're on the subject, how'd he get demoted?"

"I'm working solo today," he said. He wasn't working today, period.

I'd almost bet money on it: this was a visit on his own time. "Where were you the night Ms. Howard and Hiram Klein were killed?"

"I spent the night," I snapped. "With a friend. What else do you want to know?"

"How she wrangled Hiram Klein into the car, for one," Escobar said, squinting now as he watched my face. "Heavy man for one woman. How she ended up strangled is another question I have for you."

"I haven't the slightest idea what to tell you," I said. I'd found my keys, and I unlocked my car door, wondering if he'd try to stop me from opening the door. "Because I sure wish I could answer those things for you, but I really can't help you."

I'd gotten one leg into the car before Escobar caught the door and held it. "What did you do with the gun?"

I looked up at him. He really was a good-looking man. In another moment, in another lifetime, I would've loved spending time counting those long dark lashes. At least that question I could answer almost honestly.

"I don't know what you're talking about. I've never held a gun in my life." This time, when I wrenched the door out of his hands, it slammed shut. Through my window, I could hear him yell something about how I'd be seeing him again, and I held a hand up in a wave. As I sped off, I ticked my fingers down until there was only one left up.

A good cop, I thought as I stared at his shrinking form in my rearview mirror. *How useless in this city.*

Chapter 28

The twenty-four hours waiting to meet Carrigan were torture. If I could've, I'd have spent the night at the tiki bar so I could make sure I didn't miss him. When the time came, he was early to meet me, but by then, I'd been waiting nearly an hour.

Only a handful of patrons sat at the half-moon tables, where germy little handfuls of stale pretzels and peanuts floated in faux-coconut shells next to Technicolor-disaster cocktails. The bar didn't have the same luster as the last time I'd been there with Lou. Now, the ugly décor—the browned and splotched wood of the floor and the exposed beams, the lumpy clientele—was just ugly, not charmingly so. *Jo will tell me she hates this bar, but I bet she loves it.* She'd been wrong, for once. It wasn't the bar I loved.

For the occasion, I'd dressed up: tight black dress that hugged my ass and hips, stilettos, red lipstick. The shoes pinched my toes and the patent leather was scraped in places, but I liked the inches they added to my stems when I crossed my legs. A moneyed woman, I'd thought, looking in the mirror before I left. I'd taken a picture and sent it to Jackal, who sent me back only a full row of dollar-bill signs.

In the movies, Carrigan would've been carrying something ridiculous, like a suitcase weighted down with gold bars. Instead, when he sat down next to me, his expression permanently pickled, he threw a large envelope onto the table in front of me.

"Half cash and a cashier's check," he said by way of greeting. I clawed it open and the sight almost took my breath away: bundles of rubber-banded bills nestled alongside a long white check that might as well have been made out to *Freedom* instead of *Cash*. "Where are my photos?"

Wordlessly, I slid my own envelope across the table. I watched his face while he went through the photos, keeping the manila folder right against his chest, as though everyone in the bar were dying to see them. It took a while. Jackal shot more than he needed to, strictly speaking. Finally, Carrigan folded the envelope in half twice, not carefully, the bump of the USB drive visible through the paper, and shoved the entire packet into his briefcase. I wasn't sorry to see them go.

When Carrigan looked up, he caught my eye and glared at me. "Why are you staring?"

"You look different with your clothes on."

"Fuck you," he said. "You don't have to enjoy it so much." He studied me for a second. "There wasn't even really an abusive ex-boyfriend, was there?"

I ignored him. "I ordered champagne for the occasion. Well, it's sparkling wine, not champagne. But it'll do. I'll even buy."

"I might as well order the bottle then," he snapped, "if you're paying with my money."

"Whatever you want." I could afford to be generous.

In the end, he settled on a ginger ale. I was surprised he'd even bothered to order a drink. I'd expected him to drop the money and bail, threaten to hunt me down, make me pay. Instead, he studied the menu like we were on a date, glaring at the cream-colored card. Once his order had been taken, he rubbed his hands across his face. "How did you ever get mixed up in something like this?"

"I would've expected you, of all people, to know."

The waitress brought my champagne in a little saucer, and I held it up to the candle in the center of our table, flickering through a red glass votive. I twirled the golden juice back and forth, admired the slim line of my wrist and my long nails, now painted blue, in the light. I took a sip. It stuck in my mouth like honey.

"The hell is that supposed to mean?"

"I mean," I said, "when did you find out your wife's last name?"

"Jesus H., you miserable—"

"First date? Third date? Before you got her number?"

Carrigan was silent for a long time. "It's not the same thing."

"Of course not. I only used you for a week, not your whole life. Do me a favor, stop pretending that last name is a burden to you."

Carrigan's mouth opened, and whatever he was going to say was going to be nasty, delightfully so, but I held up a hand.

"Besides," I said, taking another sip of the sparkling wine, letting the bubbles fill my mouth and float all the way to my nose, "you should be grateful. Now you get to feel angry instead of feeling guilty."

Carrigan's face was very sour. "You took a helluva chance I didn't turn you over to the police."

"Not really. But if you like, I can pretend to be scared of you. You seem to want it so bad."

"I won't forget about this," Carrigan said, trying to make it a threat as he stood up from the table. He threw down a few dollars. The edge of one caught the lip of my champagne saucer, and I left it dangling there as I took another sip, smiling up at him. If he was trying to make me feel cheap, it didn't work. Nothing could.

"No," I said, "I wouldn't expect you to."

"You really would've used those photographs? With your face all over them? You really would've sent them to the paper?"

He was looking for a moment of softness from me, some trace of the woman he thought he'd been fucking.

"What do you think?" I said.

The last I saw of him was the line of his shoulders moving for the door. Back to the wife. Maybe this would be a lesson for him. Maybe he'd learn not to go sniffing after strange women to feel like a hero. Maybe he'd go back to that strong wife of his and appreciate her more now. Or maybe he'd learned nothing at all.

I stayed at the bar for another drink or two, watching the clientele get sloshed and then soaked. This time tomorrow, Jackal would be on his way to his new life—whatever that was.

Before I'd left to meet Carrigan, Jackal had suggested one last goodbye drink. I'd told him no, I'd drop the money off in the morning—"What, a lovers' goodbye? You must be thinking of some other woman"—but now I found myself dialing Jackal's number. "I changed my mind. I do want that drink."

"You always do."

"Meet me at my place? Bring something."

There was a pause. "You don't want to go anywhere?"

"Not gin," I said. "Something expensive. Come soon." I hung up.

When Jackal rang my doorbell, he was carrying two nice bottles of pinot noir and an overstuffed file folder of the photographs. "I know you don't drink white," he said.

"Good boy," I said, tucking the prints under my arm. Jackal made a face. I found us two glasses, and then changed my mind, uncorking them both and handing him one of the bottles. He sat down on my couch and started to drink. I put his cut on the table, and he counted it there, his mouth moving with the numbers.

I flipped through the photographs while Jackal drank. I had to admit, he was more than competent at his job: I recognized a judge with a girl who looked underage but wasn't, a famous tennis player with a woman old enough to be his grandmother, and pictures of Lou from every angle, sometimes with the girls, sometimes waiting in the lobby of the hotel, plenty of her in the office. But no pictures of me.

"I'm not in any of these," I said. Jackal didn't say anything. When I looked over, his eyes were closed and his head was slumped against the back seat of the couch. "Jackal. Where are the photographs with me in them?"

"There aren't any."

"What?" I sat up. "Are you trying to pull something on me here? Come back in two months, looking for another score when you blow through this cash?"

Jackal crooked one eye open. "Jesus Christ, Jo," he said. "There aren't any of you because I deleted them. From the SIM card, anywhere. Nothing to tie you to the business. In case."

"In case *what?*"

"In case you changed your mind," he clarified. "If you wanted to come with me. Or even if you changed your mind one day without me." He put a hand over his eyes.

"Oh," I said, not sure what to say. I stared at the photographs in my lap. "That's . . . well. Thank you. I don't need it, but . . . thank you."

Jackal shrugged, eyes still closed.

"When will you leave?" I asked him, reaching out and touching his thigh. Even now, drinking red from a bottle on my couch, Jackal was dressed in a nice button-down shirt, slacks, dress shoes. If I hadn't seen differently myself, I would believe that's what he slept in.

"Tonight," he said, and then took another slug from the bottle. He patted the couch next to him, and I scooched closer, putting my feet into his lap.

"That soon," I said.

"Are you asking me to spend the night?" He popped my right heel out of the shoe, began to massage my foot before sliding the stiletto all the way off.

"No," I said, "I am not."

Jackal uncased my other foot, and I beat time on his thighs with my toes. There was a scar in the webbing between his thumb and forefinger on his left hand, and I pressed the ball of my foot into it, feeling for scar tissue, feeling for the story it would give up. I tilted my face to kiss him, and Jackal gave me a light peck, not trying to start anything. I sank back into the couch.

"Where will you go?" I asked him.

"Somewhere that isn't here," he said, pushing my feet off his lap. I hadn't expected him to tell me. I didn't really want to know. "It's not that much money."

I wondered if he was reassuring himself that the Lady wouldn't bother to track him down for a measly fifteen grand she never needed to know about, or if he was disappointed that we hadn't gotten more.

"Relax," I said. "She'll never know about it."

"Did he give you any trouble?"

"He wanted to," I said. "But no, no trouble. If I'd known it was going to be that easy, I would've suggested independent work years ago."

"With Lou," Jackal said.

I took a drink. I didn't deny it. "If I'd known it was that easy."

Jackal stared at his bottle. He stared at it for a long time, twirling it in his hands, the scar jumping and flexing. He kept it up so long I began to get uncomfortable, wondering what wheels could be turning in his brain, not liking having that question about him.

"I'm not going to ask you about it," he said. "I want you to remember that after I leave, that I never asked you."

"What could you possibly have to ask me about *Lou*?"

"About Ellen," he clarified. "About exactly what happened that night."

"What a hero you are. Isn't this sort of like asking me?"

Jackal shrugged and took a swallow of the wine. Usually it was him watching me drink. Funny that I'd never noticed before. Funny that this was the way things would end.

I tried again to kiss him, and Jackal let me, but again he broke it. I stared at him. "You don't want me? Now that you've seen me with Carrigan?"

Jackal closed his eyes and dropped his head onto the couch back. "It's not that."

"So what, then?"

Jackal's leg jiggled against the cushions. "It's not what I want to remember about you," he said. Then he shrugged. "I don't know what I'm saying."

"The Lady would say you're getting soft," I teased, trying not to feel stung. "I guess it's a good thing you're leaving."

Jackal winced, and I took another sip of my drink. Around us, my apartment was so empty. I thought that if I had plans to stay I'd have to decorate. But the new version of Jo, the one headed for a different country, different life, she'd decorate another apartment. She'd make a home somewhere else.

"Here's some advice: drop the stuff about the Lady," Jackal said. "We don't know anything about her, only Lou. Don't you think that's odd? I've been thinking— Jo, I think—"

"Easy enough for you to say drop it," I snapped. "If you're smart, you'll be in Mexico by sunrise and heading for Brazil in twelve hours. Finding some new rich woman to foot your bills."

"You could've come," Jackal said. "I wanted you to come. Didn't I offer to let you come with me?"

"So generous. Tell me, did you give what's-her-name that option before the Lady had her killed?"

Jackal blanched. He stared at me for so long without saying anything that I almost wished I could take it back. "I'm drunk," I started to say, but Jackal just shook his head. After a moment, I said, "What were you going to say? About the Lady?" I didn't think he knew the name Rita Palmer, but I wondered what he had pieced together over the years.

"Nothing," Jackal said. "What do I know, anyway?"

We both stewed in silence for a bit until Jackal stood up, went to the kitchen, and brought us each a glass of water. "To sober up," he said.

I reached forward and turned on the TV. I curled into him—I wouldn't call it cuddling, exactly, but if you squinted, it wasn't such a stretch to call it a loverly thing to do. He didn't try to kiss me, but he stroked my hair, my back, lulling me into a drowsy half-awakeness. I could feel the *yes* and *no* of him inside me even then, the thing that pulled him close and the thing that pushed him away. Maybe one and the same.

I finished my bottle of wine, and when I was done, Jackal silently handed me his. It was near midnight when he stood up—my head completely soggy by then—and told me it was time for him to go.

I walked him to his car. No long, drawn out goodbyes for us. Three years had taught us both that; it wasn't our style. And it had been only three years. Of what? Nothing worth crying over. Nothing I couldn't do without. Instead, I tried to focus on the car, which was swimming in front of me.

"You have all your things packed in there? How did you manage that?"

"I travel light," Jackal said. "Except for that fifteen large." He unlocked his car and fiddled with the keys.

"Adios, my lovely," I said, making a joke of it. "My best to the woman you'll be screwing tomorrow night. I'll think of you if you think of me."

Even then, Jackal didn't know how to be soft. His fingers crept around the back of my neck, like he might choke me—once more, for old time's sake—and his thumb stroked the hollow at the base of my throat.

He leaned in to kiss me, and I reached up to meet him, then changed my mind at the last second and pulled back. "The St. Leo. Just tell me," I whispered.

"Lou asked me to swing by the Albatross," he said. "Pick up a bill, and then . . . well, you can guess. I really did lose track of time."

"You're a goddamn—" I started, but he leaned forward and caught me in a kiss that didn't end. Finally, he broke the seal between us and took a deep shuddering breath, a serious breath, a one-last-declaration breath, and I thought of what Lou had drilled into me: never get attached, never love someone so much you lose yourself. I ducked my head down, tried to nip at his thumb with my teeth. He jerked his hand away as though it had been scalded. "Everything's always a joke with you."

"Goodbye, Robert," I said.

He walked away, then turned back for one last glance, a hand on the roof of his car. "Think about what I said. You should get out."

"I'll be fine," I said. I could tell he didn't believe me. "You should go," I said. "Wherever you're going has a lot of miles between here and there."

"I'll still buy you that last drink sometime."

"Sure," I said. "That'll be nice. I'll be waiting for it."

He started the car, the engine loud and whirring. It didn't sound healthy. It didn't sound like it could take him far. He rolled down the window and said something to me. I couldn't hear it, or pretended I couldn't, and waved one more time and turned and walked back to my apartment.

Chapter 29

Red lipstick looked wrong for the occasion—too celebratory, perhaps—and I couldn't get the line right. I kept frowning at myself in the mirror, trying to figure out where I'd gone wrong. This close, my reflection was always choppy, like none of the parts of my face fit together. One arch of my lip was higher than the other, giving me the look of a demented Kewpie doll, and there was a shadow of Hell Hath No Fury beneath my lower lip.

I didn't have many superstitions, but one thing Lou had taught me was that looking the part was the first step to feeling the part. Had I ever told Ellen that? I couldn't remember. I hoped I had. Not that it mattered anymore.

When I stepped into the police office with the name of the Lady, the selection of Jackal's photographs that didn't showcase Lou, and the phone records, I would be wearing my power lipstick. I would feel confident because I would look confident, and that's what they would see. Not a murderer, or a working girl, or someone with something to hide.

I grabbed the bullet and tried to even out the lines, but I couldn't stop my hands shaking, and I realized, quickly, that I was making it worse rather than better. I took a deep breath and stared at myself in the rearview mirror. *Now or never, Jo.*

The heat had started to clear a little, and the trees with their banana leaves shimmied a little with the cool breeze. If you waited long enough, the heat on anything went down. You got used to living like that in the city. I grabbed my purse from the back seat and locked my car, wondering if it would be impounded if I was arrested, and stepped into the station. The station was a good-looking building downtown that might have once rivaled Dohony's mansion for opulence. Above the entryway, a gold statue of Lady Justice welcomed entrants with a blind blank stare: her eyes had been gouged out. I blinked, looked again—but no, just the usual blindfold this time. A few anemic trees gave the illusion of landscaping outside the front doors. Healthier-looking blue agave cracked apart the dry brown soil, bursting from the ground like heads of buried pineapple.

Inside was less striking than the exterior: an open floor plan of rows and rows of identical cubicles. Justice is a bureaucracy like any other. I made eye contact with every blue I passed and smiled, as though I weren't the least bit concerned to be there. How I imagined a woman who hadn't murdered anybody would look at a police station.

I gave MacLeish's name to the bored-looking receptionist and waited while she picked up the phone and let him know he had a woman at the front. I tried to ignore the way she eyed me, as though she could smell the sex for money on my skin, and looked past her to the small square of the station floor I could see. After a moment, I caught a flash of a face I recognized. Escobar and I realized it at the same moment. His jaw dropped and he caught my eyes and held them, but before either of us could move, MacLeish appeared behind the secretary and gave me a warm smile.

"Jo," he said, friendly as I could've hoped for. "What a pleasant surprise. How can I help you?"

My mouth had gone dry. I peeled my gaze away from his partner, whose eyes were darting between us, and tried not to feel triumphant just yet. "Turns out, I do have some information that may interest you."

MacLeish escorted me past the receptionist, past Escobar, who said, "William, what are you—" but then we were beyond him and into a small room at the very back of the station, a fluorescently lit room with a single plastic table and two uncomfortable chairs. An interrogation room straight out of central casting.

"Are there cameras behind that one-way glass?" I asked, thinking of Jackal and his recording equipment as MacLeish pulled a chair out for me.

MacLeish didn't answer, but he did reach under the table and pull out a recorder. "You're in the nick of time," he said. "The St. Leo turns over the security tapes tomorrow. I wouldn't be able to do anything for you, then." He punched the recorder on, and nodded at me in encouragement.

I leaned down and grabbed my purse and pulled out the photographs, along with the phone records.

"What you said, about being under the Lady's thumb. You're right. I don't want to live that way anymore." I nodded at the photographs, telling myself I was doing the right thing. Even if I gave the Lady the money, Lou and I were too much at her mercy now. Knowledge is power, and she had too much of both. "This should be proof enough about the type of operation she's running. I have a name, too."

MacLeish stared at the photographs and, with one finger, spread them out across the table, a patchwork *Kama Sutra*. He mouthed the names of the men in the photographs as he looked at them. "Jesus," he breathed softly, and then his eyes flicked up, away from the photographs, directly into the one-way glass. He kept them there for one long moment, and then he looked back at me, eyes full again of that hangdog sadness. He reached across the table and softly punched the recorder off.

That's when I realized I'd made a mistake.

From outside the interrogation room, there came a swift two-knock. MacLeish crossed to the door and opened it. I expected his partner to walk through the door, but it seemed I couldn't get anything right.

A man entered, dressed in black jeans and a white button-down shirt. Sleeves rolled up. Nice-quality shoes, black leather shined to mirrorlike proportions. The shoes always give the game away.

"Jo. My boss, the chief of detectives, Graham Lafferty," MacLeish said. It was the most formal sentence I'd ever heard him pronounce. *Graham.* A little sound came out of me but I managed a nod.

Chief of Detectives Graham Lafferty stood a little over six feet tall, with a face a mother might've struggled to love. He stood and moved with the most perfect posture I'd ever seen, like he might be photographed at any time.

Mr. Alibi, I presume, I thought but didn't say. It would only matter if I made it out of the room uncuffed. And I hated to admit it but it was another of Lou's smart moves, an extra insurance policy. But if I was here, that meant he hadn't cracked her—or that Lafferty didn't know she was part of the Lady's operations.

He turned his head to MacLeish and said, "A moment alone with the young lady?"

MacLeish stood up. He didn't even look back. My palms started to sweat. When was the last time I'd been nervous to be alone in a room with a strange man? I couldn't remember. That thought brought me back. There wasn't a man alive who couldn't be manipulated if you could find the right pull. *Wear the con like a coat, hide in the spotlight, Jo.*

Lafferty stared at me, not smiling and not friendly, until he finally said: "So tell me what happened. With the dead girl and the producer and the Lady."

I stared at the tape recorder. Lafferty hadn't bothered to turn it back on.

"Now, let's be clear with each other," he went on. "For whatever reason—and I'm a nice man, I won't ask questions—our monthly stipend got lost somewhere. Okay, that happens. It's not great business, but we have bigger problems now. Now, we have a body. *Two* bodies. Good people."

I scoffed, trying to remember what a confident woman would say. "Define *good*. Klein was rich, certainly. I didn't—"

Lafferty tucked his finger against his lips, the universal *shhh* sign, and shook his head. "It doesn't really matter to me what you *did* or *didn't* do. You're going to keep selling the story that Howard *wasn't* one of your girls? Or, rather, the Lady's girls." At the mention of the Lady, Lafferty's gray eyes took on a brighter glow.

"Here's a theory," Lafferty said. "The two of you were working Hiram Klein, had yourselves a little party. All three of you together. Something went wrong, and he winds up dead. The two of you move the body, but Ellen gets squeamish, wants to call the police. You can't have that. Now the dead bodies perform a miracle and multiply."

I was still watching the tape recorder, looking for a little red light. Could they have rigged it to record without suspects ever knowing? They had it out on the table. You couldn't pretend you weren't informed about it. I licked my lips. I could see myself, suddenly, as he saw me: so confident, thinking I was such hot shit with my photographs—but what was that worth if he knew I'd been involved in Ellen's murder? Nothing.

"If that was the case," Lafferty went on, "you'd be looking at twenty years, give or take, a jury sends you, twenty-five years max. You're pretty, you can cry on command I'm sure—so no jury gives you max. You might even get light, ten, fifteen years. No priors, after all. Some sob story about no money, no man, had to do what you could. All sorts of ways it could play, if that's how things go. But that's still likely a decade of your life we're talking about. If that's how things go."

"If," I repeated.

"I believe Detective MacLeish told you his views about the victim," Lafferty said, "As it happens, I share them. Hiram Klein had a lot of money, and his death is taking up a lot of ink, but he lived large and he crossed the finish line a lot better off than most will. But Ellen Howard matters, to me."

"You're some sort of feminist," I said, "threatening me here in this room."

"Ellen Howard matters because she's one of your girls," Lafferty said, "isn't she."

It wasn't a question, so I didn't answer it. I crossed my arms and then unhooked them and scooted my chair closer. "What do you want from me?"

"I'm a reasonable man," Lafferty said. "I bet your Lady likes the anonymity for her work, makes her feel more powerful. I can understand that. I'm not looking to take that away. Not entirely.

"But this Klein case isn't good for business. The bodies, the publicity. Your boss needs to be brought to heel. I don't mind a nice lady playing in the field, but I do mind when she overreaches herself and makes it messy for us all. I want a say on all the cases she takes from now on."

"You don't *mind?*" I said. "That's big of you. I'm sure she appreciates your permission."

A say on all the cases she takes on? I'd been hoping that when I gave them the photographs and her name, they'd lock her up and throw away the key, and Lou and I would be free to waltz off into our own new, shiny lives with the Carrigan cash. Not this. Not a partnership with Lafferty. Christ. She'd be even more powerful with closer ties to the police. And she'd know that I'd ratted—and, worse, that Lou had given me the name to do so. Retirement parties all around. I hadn't counted on that. I licked my lips nervously, not sure what to do with the new information.

"You and MacLeish understand each other well," I said, stalling.

Lafferty smiled, like a teacher who'd finally gotten his slow pupil to a passing grade. "He used to be my partner. When we met your girl Lou."

I jerked a little in my seat and tried to disguise my surprise. One glance at his face and I knew he'd caught it. So he did know she was involved. I thought of Lou's stress the last few weeks, the details she'd let slip. Maybe Lafferty had been hounding her from the other side, and not just about the murders.

"Six years ago. Sitting across from me in this very room. MacLeish there." He nodded at the corner. "We were the first investors in your business, you might say."

I had a flash, a sudden certain vision of a younger Lou sitting in this same chair, scared but not too much, in control of the situation, or trying to be. A plume of blue smoke from her cigarette covering her face like a veil.

"Then why isn't Lou here, answering these questions?"

"Because Lou isn't the one who was with Ellen Howard at the St. Leo. And because she has an airtight alibi for the night Ms. Howard died."

Airtight. I tried not to picture his fingers on Lou's body. "Okay," I said slowly. "Tell me what you want to know."

Lafferty cracked his neck, his eyes flicking up to the one-way glass above us. "I want your boss's name," Lafferty said. "I want anything you know about her. I want her address, I want her shoe size, I want her sitting here across from me. Or else I book you as a suspect in the Klein murders."

It was no different than what I'd half expected from the moment MacLeish left me alone, but I still felt my stomach drop at the threat. "Then I guess I've made my decision," I said. "But I want MacLeish in here, too, when I tell it." I wanted a friendly face. I wanted no confusion about the deal I was getting.

Lafferty's eyes flicked, almost imperceptibly, to the one-way glass. "I'll be right back," Lafferty said.

I took a moment to gather myself, breathed deeply, thinking about it all. Six years before, Lou had had a run-in with the cops—a case gone bad, probably, and she'd made an arrangement. Maybe more than one. Lou had taken so many lucky gambles in the Lady's name.

When Lafferty came back, he brought with him a glass of water and MacLeish, looking unhappy but resolute. I tried to make eye contact with the detective, but he wouldn't meet my eyes, instead stood behind his boss and smoothed his salt-and-pepper hair, brushing up the bristles of it, over and over.

Lafferty set the water down very delicately, as though he were worried about it splashing my face, a new form of police brutality. "Your boss," he prompted. Neither one of them went for the tape recorder.

I hesitated, unsure where to start.

"Give it up," Lafferty said. "Why are you protecting her? We know what happened. She gave you the order to kill Ellen once Klein was dead, didn't she, Jo? Couldn't have those loose ends around. Had to make sure that everything stayed on the up-and-up for your little staffing agency. So she told you to kill Ellen Howard, and stage the bodies to look like a murder-suicide. And this is the woman you're protecting, Jo? The woman who made you a murderer?"

I didn't like the way he kept saying my name. I didn't like the shape of it on his tongue. It was a tactic I'd used before, a way to instill comradeship, build trust in the person across from you. I didn't like it one bit.

"She didn't make me a murderer," I snapped, "because I didn't kill anybody." And I wished, so badly, that were true.

"It doesn't matter," MacLeish said wearily. "Don't you get that? It doesn't matter if you did or not. It looks an awful lot like you might have. It looks enough like that that you should start talking."

"This is what I have," I said, gesturing at the photographs, the proof of our blackmail. "And I've met her. Peroxided hair and a blue tattoo on her wrist. Her name is . . . Rita. Rita Palmer." The name came out of me before I'd fully given it permission, and I coughed, almost in shock, after I said it. Self-preservation was a more powerful reflex than I thought. I tapped the phone bill. "Her phone number for you, too."

Lafferty leaned forward and studied the pictures. MacLeish jotted something in his notebook. After a moment, and without a word between the two of them, he grabbed the phone bill and left the room.

"Where's he going?" I half stood up out of the chair, craning my head after him. Lafferty put a hand on my shoulder, pushed me back into my chair, not roughly.

Unlike his former partner, Lafferty hadn't taken notes of anything that I'd said. I had the feeling that all this information was more useful to him on a personal level. But now, Lafferty stretched out a hand and pressed the record button on the machine. "And how does the business work?"

I summarized for him our work—that the names came from the

Lady, hired by someone, we didn't know who, or picked by her as the occasion dictated. That they were always men, rich men, usually rich and despicable men, and that it was my job to find the girls who would most appeal to them, who would help me leave a trail that we could use. That most often we let them pay for the photographs, but that occasionally—and, I suspected, most closely associated with those names most personal to the Lady—we sent them to the paper. Or the man's boss. Or his wife.

MacLeish came back in, threw two photographs down on the desk.

"Is that her?" he asked.

I blinked a few times, staring at the picture on top, a mug shot. She was younger than when I'd met her, but rougher, too, her skin worse, her eye makeup thick and cakey and looking down her face. A woman who had seen too much. But it *was* her, the Lady Upstairs. I bit my lip, and then, before I could second-guess myself: "Yes, that's her. That's the Lady."

Lafferty and MacLeish exchanged a glance. Finally, MacLeish said, almost gently, "No, it isn't."

"She isn't anyone named Rita Palmer," Lafferty added, pushing the second photo forward. Another mug shot of the Lady, but this one with the words *LOS ANGELES, PROSTITUTION, DAWES, EVE* across the bottom. "She's another lackey, like you, brings us the money every month. We've tailed her before, has a nice house in the Hollywood Hills—not the nicest part. But she ain't your boss, kid. She's answered these questions, too. And more convincingly, I might add."

I reached for the water to wash the acid and bile out of my mouth, then thought about my fingerprints on the glass, the DNA from my lips on its rim. Two red lip prints like a smoking fucking gun. I wrapped my arms around myself and tried to keep from shivering. It wasn't working.

"You're wrong," I said.

MacLeish shook his head. "The phone number tracks back to Eve Lowenstein, née Dawes."

"Eve Dawes," Lafferty said. "Arrested her, oh, six or seven years ago, working a street corner downtown. She's an ex–working girl your Lady turned out. There must be someone in her life she doesn't want knowing about her past." I thought of that yacht of a diamond ring, and Lafferty went on: "I imagine that's how your boss keeps her ferrying cash. If you don't believe me, look her up yourself. She's not hard to trace. And she's not your boss."

She wasn't the Lady. Or maybe she was, and she was a better liar than I. But the police seemed so sure and that was what mattered—they had to believe I'd given them the Lady, and they didn't. Maybe there was a Rita Palmer and Lou hadn't lied to me, but I sure as hell hadn't found her. Maybe she'd made the name up completely. Christ. I was back to square one. I hadn't given them anything they could use. My new life with Lou was slipping away, and there was nothing I could do about it.

I shook my head, and once I'd started I couldn't stop. "But that doesn't make any sense," I said, my teeth chattering. None of it made any sense. "That's her, that's the Lady, that's her."

"Aw, she doesn't know anything," MacLeish said to Lafferty.

"For her sake," Lafferty said, "I hope that's not true." Like I wasn't even in the room with them. He leaned across the table and switched off the recorder once again, and told me to stand up.

"What—what are you—"

"Stand up," Lafferty ordered. "Turn around."

"Are you *arresting* me?" I cried. "Because I can't give you my boss's name?" I'd gotten so close. But it wasn't enough.

Lafferty stood up, and I clutched the side of my chair with both hands, trying frantically to make eye contact with MacLeish. "Wait," I said, "wait, please." I took a deep breath. *One last gamble, Jo. Nothing left to lose now.*

"Give it up, Jo," Lafferty said. "You have nothing left to bargain with."

But that wasn't entirely true. "Give me twenty-four more hours," I said. I had to get out of that room. I would've said anything. "I can bring you—I can bring you fifty grand. And I'll tell you everything that happened with Ellen and Klein. Everything. I swear. And I'll . . . I'll try to find her for you. Please. I can find out more."

Lafferty and MacLeish exchanged another glance, and I could see how they'd been partners once, that it was like a dance, or the lyrics to a song—once they'd learned it, they'd never quite forgotten.

"So now you do know something about it," Lafferty said. "Convenient. How do we know you won't skip?"

"You were right," I blurted out. "The Lady wanted Ellen dead. Trust me, I want her held accountable for that as much as you do. You'll never be able to find her without me, she's too well-connected, she's too smart. But if you give me one more day . . ."

Lafferty looked at me, his eyebrows raised. Wanting me to know he doubted me even as he was thinking it over. But MacLeish was the one who broke the silence first.

"Come on, boss," MacLeish said quietly, ever the good cop. The harder role to play. "We can give her twenty-four hours, can't we?"

Lafferty nodded, his gray eyes never leaving me. "You're lucky my detective wants that money," he said, pretending like MacLeish had changed his mind, like this wasn't a part they were both playing. "But this is a one-time deal, you hear me? If you don't come back in twenty-four hours with fifty large and a name, you're on the hook for the Klein/Howard murders." He gave his old partner one last look and then turned on his heel. When he got to the door, he turned around and said to me, "I overestimated. You're not that pretty. You'll do the full twenty-five."

I stood up on legs that didn't feel fully solid, and moved toward the door of the interrogation room. MacLeish kept a sympathetic eye on me, then said, softly, "Come on, kid. Don't make us book you."

I shook my head over and over. There were too many things that didn't fit. Too many pieces of a puzzle I'd gotten some glance at but couldn't put together. But nothing made any sense; nothing led anywhere that would help me. I was out of time and out of clues.

To my horror, real tears came to my eyes, and I covered my face. MacLeish handed me a handkerchief, which I waved away. He kept it under my nose until I took it, dabbed at my face, and handed it back to him, stained with mascara. I sniffled and said, trying to get myself back together, "The bribe is for you? Not Lafferty?"

"It's frowned on for police chiefs to take bribes," MacLeish said. "That's how people get fired. It's how people lose stripes."

"What?"

"Works out better this way for us both," MacLeish said. "Even if I had to take a hit for it. Still a better paycheck. But I tell you what, it stings when you realize your old partner calls your shots." MacLeish shook his head, his forehead creasing in anger. "That one takes some getting used to."

My scalp tingled, some shadowy glimmer of an idea pressing at my brain, but I couldn't think; I couldn't touch it. I didn't say anything but got up on rubbery legs and made for the door. MacLeish touched my arm as I passed. "The chief's a reasonable man, I promise you that," he said. "Find a way to give him what he wants, and I promise it'll be okay. I only want to help you, kid. Give him the money and a name and then be a good friend to yourself and get out of this line of work."

Instead of saying anything, I nodded in his general direction and stepped back out into the station. I could barely see a foot in front of my face, but I clocked Escobar watching me all the way out. I wondered if he'd be thrilled to see me in cuffs or disappointed that he hadn't been the one to do it.

Lafferty was waiting for me by the door. He wasn't done with me yet. As I passed by him, he called after me, "Any information you get—any way you get it—is appreciated. Remember that, Jo," and that froze me in my tracks for a moment, trying to process the ramifications of it, but then I squared my shoulders. They were letting me leave. I had one more chance, and I had to use it.

I had to be Jo for a few hours longer.

CHAPTER 30

ilver sky again. Hot night air blowing through the window of my car, which I'd unrolled halfway to Lou's house. While I'd been inside the station, the sun had gone down. The moon lounged like an actress getting ready for her close-up, and the stars bit little holes into the blanket around her.

Lou had left me a message, but I hadn't gotten it until I'd left the interrogation room. There had been no reception there, as though they'd encased the place in concrete. Nowhere for the signal to land.

When I called, she said she needed to see me. She said it was urgent. She said please.

I needed to see her, too.

I zoomed through the streets away from the police station, being very careful not to think my thoughts. Above me, the gray-green palm trees zipped by like silver streamers guiding my way. I was going too fast or the cars in front of me were too slow, and I had to pull into the other lane to pass, nearly kissing the bumper of the car in front, the pop of the headlights like small explosions that blinded me even as I pulled back into the blue twilight of my own lane.

I kept checking the rearview. I couldn't see any headlights that kept after me. But I couldn't be sure. I couldn't shake the feeling that MacLeish or Escobar would be keeping tabs on me for the full twenty-four hours until I brought them the cash.

There was no way they were getting that money.

I parked the car in Lou's driveway, in front of a bed of fat, white hydrangea globes. Lou's small bungalow was immaculately manicured, with miles of quality turf rolling up to the front door. The grass looked like it had been cut with the precision of nail clippers. In the middle of the lawn, a small cherub puked water into the bowl at his feet.

Lou pulled the door open, hip leaning against the jamb. Her fingertips were painted a bright vermilion nearly identical to my now-flaky power lipstick. Her dark red hair was damp and curled around her shoulders. Sometime not too long before, she'd taken a shower and slung on a slinky black kimono, which hugged her in all the interesting places. Lou's face cracked into a smile, as though she hadn't spit my tongue out of her mouth and stormed off the last time I'd seen her, and she reached in for a hug.

"Hi," Lou said, her voice breathy and shy. "Come in. Have a drink."

I stared at her. Her voice on my machine had sounded desperate, wounded. And then there had been that kiss. And even though she didn't know it, I was a marked woman living on borrowed time. "I guess," I said. It was as good a place to start as any.

"Come in, come in," Lou said, guiding me inside so we could get down to the business of drinking. She steered me to the kitchen, where, on the island, she'd already placed a bottle of Hendrick's, uncapped, and two tumblers made of thick purple glass that shined in the moonlight beside it. A lime wedge, lying belly up, between the two.

There were details of Lou everywhere in the house, but nothing that told you anything. On the mantel in the living room sat several pictures of Lou smiling openmouthed with people who had her same coloring, close enough to pass as family. One sad photograph of a little girl, hands folded beneath her chin like an angel. I didn't want to know where she'd gotten that one. Unlike me, and unlike Jackal, Lou wanted her place to pass for a home.

But every single piece of furniture was exactly the same age. If you took the books down from the bookshelf, you'd notice that all of the spines were uncracked. Most of them were expensive, shiny-jacketed hardbound copies or else rare auction pieces. Each cheap frame on the mantel had come from the same store, and not a single one was chipped. Almost all of the pictures of Lou, the little girl not-withstanding, were of the same age, too.

"Are we celebrating?" I sat down at the table, my hands trembling in my lap. I took a sip to steady myself. The gin wasn't particularly chilled. She must have had it out, waiting for me, for some time. "I don't feel much like celebrating."

Lou watched me as I sipped. "I know these last few weeks have been hell," she said, "and the last time we spoke, it ended poorly. But I have missed you so much."

I looked down at the drink. In the fluorescent light, I could see the slight cast of blue prismed in the gin. Blue gin, blue fleur-de-lis, blue corpse, blue Lou. I threw back the rest of my gin. I was searching so hard for an angle, and I had nothing but round edges. Nothing left, nothing left.

"I spent the day with a few old friends of yours. Lafferty and Mac-Leish." My voice caught, and I coughed, trying to hide it.

Lou put her drink down. Her face was so white I could've counted her freckles if I wanted. She chewed on her upper lip as she worked it out. "You wouldn't be here if you'd been booked for murder."

I laughed bitterly. "They didn't book me." I stared at the table. I couldn't get the words out.

"Jo," Lou said, a mask sliding over her face, her eyes a big blank. Keeping herself shuttered to me. "What did you tell them?"

I laughed again, rubbing my eyes. I wanted all that gin in my veins. I didn't want to have to think about anything else for a long, long time. Thinking, and doing, had gotten me nowhere anyway. Ellen, Carrigan—none of it would matter, in the end. Lou would hate me. There was no way she wouldn't hate me.

So I told her. Everything. Starting with Ellen at the St. Leo and finding the cash from the Lady—or Eve fucking Dawes—and holding it for her. Well, meaning to hold it for Lou. Slipping Ellen the bribe from the police. I didn't have any other option. I hadn't known what was going to happen. I told her everything about Carrigan and Jackal's help—I didn't figure it would hurt, now that he'd skipped town. I told her I had one last shot to give the cops the cash from Carrigan and the Lady's name or else I'd be on the hook for the murders. And after everything, that money was mine—*ours*. Our only option was to go. *Now*. It was only a matter of time before the Lady knew I had turned on her, before the cops came for us.

Lou's eyes popped when I mentioned Carrigan, but I pushed on, telling her how I'd gotten the money from him, $75K (even then, it was hard not to feel a little proud of it, and I checked Lou's face to see if she was proud of me, too, maybe a little, underneath everything), which would be more than enough for us to run away together.

"And, Lou," I said, finally. "I know."

Lou's eyes turned wary. "You know?"

"About Lafferty. Mr. Alibi." Lou's face shifted, almost relieved, and I went on, "It was a smart move. But don't you get it? He won't help you now. Not anymore."

Lou's mouth opened and then closed. She nodded. "Of course,

you're right. That's over." She stared at me for a moment and then she said, her voice hushed, "You took Mitch Carrigan." I couldn't tell if she was proud or angry. "You really did it?"

"I know," I said quickly. "I wanted to do it with you, Lou, but it was my mess to fix."

Lou nodded, not looking at me. "Did you tell the police . . . I mean, did you mention Rita Palmer's name?" Lou nibbled on a fingernail, her gin untouched in front of her. She didn't like gin, I remembered, had told me once it tasted like Christmas tree piss.

Maybe she was trying to get me drunk.

"I had to, Lou," I said, my fingers jittering against the glass of the tumbler. Maybe she hadn't understood me; maybe she didn't realize how bad this was. The name hadn't gotten me anywhere. "But it didn't mean anything to them; they didn't believe me. They thought I was making it up."

Lou was looking past me out the window, her face still frozen. Those lovely big eyes, dark and blank. "They wouldn't have let you know if they believed you," she said, her voice low. "Rita Palmer. Well."

"Didn't you hear me? We have to go now, *tonight*. If we don't get the money and leave *right now*—"

"I heard you."

She snapped herself back from whatever mental void she'd fallen into and smiled at me. It wasn't her usual smile, and it wasn't very convincing, but it was better than nothing.

"I heard you," she said again, leaning forward to pour me another tipple of gin. The silk robe moved with her, tugging open down her chest. I closed my eyes, knuckling my fists into them so I could concentrate.

"Lou, please, you have to understand, I didn't have any *choice*—"

Lou scooched the drink to me across the marble countertop of the kitchen island. "Okay," she said softly. "We'll go tonight." She met my eyes briefly—shyly, almost—and I stopped talking, not sure I'd heard her right.

"What?"

Lou nodded, and then she knocked back the gin she hadn't touched yet, grimacing. "You're right—you're always right, Jo. There's no point staying anymore. We'll go."

In my wildest dreams, I hadn't imagined that it would be so easy, that Lou would agree with me so quickly. But I'd always known she was the survivor, capable of seeing the writing on the wall. There was nothing left for us with the Lady, now. It was exactly what it had to be. I slumped in relief against the countertop.

"Where should we go?" I asked. I hadn't packed anything—we'd have to stop by my apartment, for me to pick up my things. And the money. But MacLeish and Lafferty were probably watching my apartment, I thought, the panic starting to rise in me. They'd be suspicious if I came there with Lou, grabbed anything.

I closed my eyes, trying to think it all through. When I looked up, Lou had taken a step closer to me, silk wrinkling and flexing with each move. I closed my eyes, and I could smell the lemon in her hair without even trying. When I opened them again, she was standing right in front of me, her face tilted up to mine. Her eyes didn't look flinty now, only sad and wet. Her face twitched and the freckles on her nose jumped and danced.

"We'll go," she whispered, her breath light against my lips, "anywhere you want." And then she shrugged off her robe, putting her arms around me. I could feel my heart drumming in my chest and her own answered, and I was thinking to myself, *Was that all it took? A simple murder and some blackmail?* And then she was kissing me, moving her hands across me, and the only thing I was thinking was, *Finally, finally, finally.*

A fterward, upstairs in her bed, Lou shook a cigarette out of her case
and lit it, stretching like a cat and flipping herself upside down before taking a drag. The smoke drifted down for half a beat, toward the
carpet, and then back up. I touched her toe, near my head, and Lou
smiled.

"How ugly is this bed?" Lou lifted her head, which had been purpling from hanging off the edge of the mattress, and watched herself
make small circles with dusty feet on the virginal white of her headboard. A lock of hair had fallen into the corner of her mouth, and she
didn't bother to move it.

My limbs were full and drowsy and my head was cloudy—from
the gin, from Lou, the tangy taste of her still on my lips. "We could
torch it," I said. "On our way out of town."

"Yeah," Lou said dreamily, walking her feet across the quilted
satin, back and forth, a half-assed Charleston. "We could."

I sat up in bed, tucking the sheets under my armpits. We should've
been on the road hours before, as soon as she'd agreed, but I couldn't
make myself regret what had happened. "The money," I said, and Lou
looked at me, cricking her neck upward to meet my eyes. "We have to
go back by my apartment for the rest of Carrigan's cash. And then we
could go—Palm Springs, maybe. For the night. We can come up with
a better plan tomorrow."

Lou nodded slowly, her eyes unfocused. She liked the plan, I could
tell. The desert drive, the night wind in our hair. Lou flipped over,
onto her stomach, making a figure-four shape. Her toes dug into the
pale flesh at the back of her knee. She placed her chin onto her over-
lapped hands and stared at me, then nodded, another of her quick
decisions.

"I'll drive," she said, suddenly all brisk business. She sat up, letting the sheet fall, and I caught my breath—she was so beautiful. Statues were made of bodies like hers.

"But first, let me make some coffee to help me sober up for the trip. You stay there," she said with a wink as I tried to sit up, reach for her. "I like this view." She crept down the stairs, not bothering to cover her nakedness with a stitch of clothing.

Goofy grins are for chumps, not murderesses on the run, but I couldn't help myself. I was under no illusions: running away with Lou wouldn't be easy. Being on the run was, I imagined, its own special kind of hell. Having to always look over your shoulder. The strain wouldn't be easy on Lou and me, either, I figured, whatever we were, or were becoming. And it would be made worse by the dreams of Ellen. Those weren't going away. If I closed my eyes, I could see her and Klein in the car. His sagging, wrinkly body. Her face unmarred by so much as a laugh line. Both rotting.

In our line of work, we trafficked only in the young or the wealthy. Even when you slept with an old man, you thought of the money, each caress of wrinkled flesh making you more grateful for the elastic quality of your own. I hoped, very hard, that I would never grow old, that some terrible car crash would end it for me, leaving my body mangled but *young*. Death should come sudden or not at all.

Perhaps Ellen had been lucky, after all. Perhaps I'd made her lucky.

I pushed the thought out of my head. Below, I could hear the steam of Lou's kettle and her soft voice, maybe talking to herself. Maybe singing. I couldn't keep the goofy smile off my face for anything after that.

I pulled myself out of bed, despite Lou's instructions, slipped my clothes back on, and began hunting around for a suitcase or a duffel bag—I could help her get a head start on packing. We could splurge tonight, I thought. Pick some fancy resort in the desert, order room service tomorrow morning and sleep in. And then maybe Mexico.

Maybe, I thought, my mouth twisting, we'd even cross paths with Jackal again. Wouldn't that be something.

Lou's closet was a mess. I should've expected that, the way she kept her desk. I pulled a few of my favorites of her dresses and tossed them on the disheveled bed. But I couldn't find a suitcase underneath the piles of her shoes and old magazines.

I got down on my knees and flipped the bed curtain up. Bingo. Pressed so far back it was nearly against the headboard, an old beige suitcase was gathering dust. I pulled it out and flipped it open, ready to start packing for Lou.

But it wasn't empty.

Inside, there was a magazine and an oatmeal-colored cardigan—a color I'd never seen Lou wear. I frowned and lifted it out. Embroidered on the collar were the words *Good Vibes!* in pink thread. Not Lou's style at all. *Good Vibes*—I'd seen that before. Ellen's shower curtain that we'd wrapped Klein's body in. I frowned, uneasy, and lifted the sweater to my nose. A faint trace of plasticky, candy-smelling perfume. I knew that smell.

Frantic, I threw the cardigan on the bed and clutched the magazine, a glossy tabloid that screamed coverage of the Klein-Howard murders. Something a murderer might keep, if she was sloppy. A trophy. Underneath it, case notes in my handwriting, with Ellen's name on them.

Underneath that—the tip of a gun resting on a bed of white. I thought of what Escobar had asked, what I'd done with the gun. I hadn't seen it since that night. And yet here it was.

But the gun wasn't the worst of it. My fingers trembled as I pulled one of dozens of the Lady's embossed fleur-de-lis envelopes from Lou's suitcase. The Lady's special stationery—in *Lou's suitcase.*

Before I could process it, the door creaked open and Lou, still naked, handed me a tumbler.

"What the hell is this?" I asked, setting the tumbler on the bedside table so I could hold the envelope out to her.

Lou glanced at the envelope and then at the spread of evidence on her bed. Her expression didn't change. She grabbed the silk robe from the foot of the bed where she'd abandoned it, turning away from me to cinch the belt. I watched the long line of her neck bent over her task.

Maybe there was a simple explanation for it all—the gun, the envelopes, a piece of clothing doused in Ellen's perfume. Maybe the gun was for safekeeping. But the envelopes . . . "Lou, why do you have the Lady's stationery?"

Lou sighed and turned to face me, eyebrows raised. The faint marks my lips had made against her skin were starting to bloom, and a pulse in her neck ticked as I stared. She didn't look like my Lou. But then: she'd never been my Lou, never. I closed my eyes, feeling sick.

"Come on, Jo," she said, still turned away from me. "You must've guessed."

I thought of the Jo I'd been that morning: nervous, unsure where the day would take me. I thought of MacLeish telling me without telling me what I already knew. I thought of plane tickets to Spain that would never be purchased and Jackal trying to warn me and Lafferty saying I needed to bring him the Lady and the crinkle in Lou's nose when I made her laugh and Ellen's dead weight in my arms and lemony Lou lying next to me in bed for a few short minutes.

She'd never been my Lou, but she'd always been my Lady.

CHAPTER 31

wanted to tell you," she said, her arms crossed over her silk robe. She didn't sound particularly regretful that she hadn't. Until she said it, I had been holding out hope that I was wrong.

"But you never quite got around to it." I could feel the shadow of the gun on the bed behind me, a black, throbbing presence. "And it would've been so hard? Take me out for a drink, say, *By the way, I'm really the Lady Upstairs?*"

Lou gestured to the tumbler on the table. "You might like a sip of that. It might make you feel better."

"You were so cool, giving me orders. But they never seemed like orders, did they? They always seemed like suggestions. Good advice. All of it, from the pie diner to that night with . . . Ellen."

Lou's green eyes sparkled, as though I'd told her a joke. "I'm surprised Jackal didn't say anything, I know he was on to me by the end. The way he wouldn't talk to me." That one stung. She narrowed her eyes and smiled a little. "You know, I always wondered if he'd be able to do it, if I asked. *Take care of you.*" She must've caught the look on my face because her smile blossomed. "Oh yes, he was much handier than he looked. You can convince that man to do just about anything for an afternoon at the racetrack. And he was so good at keeping the girls quiet." Lou's face softened a touch, and she took a step toward me. "But I never really wanted you dead, Jo."

Jackal, the Lady's—*Lou's*—hitman. I wasn't sure which was worse: that he'd never told me, or that I'd never guessed. Jackal, the man with nothing under the surface. If only I'd known, I thought. Murder was something we could've bonded over. I could've laughed except it was so unfunny. I wondered how many over the years, who and how and when. The room tilted on its axis and started to realign itself in unfamiliar ways. Monsters, all of us, I realized. Not only me. All three of us.

I licked my lips, tried to look away from her, and my eyes landed on the still-open luggage, the gun. *Fuck.* I couldn't remember if I'd touched it or not. "The police told me you bribed them years ago, when a case went wrong," I said. "That's how it started?"

Lou laughed bitterly, taking a step forward, still between me and the door. "That wasn't half a mess. One of my very first cases—back when I was doing it all myself, you can imagine what a disaster that was—and the mark called my bluff, went to the police with the photos and the note and everything. Said he didn't care about the photos in the paper, he wasn't going to let some little cunt run his life."

Lou laughed again. It sounded like she was gargling glass. Despite everything, my heart ached at the idea of her, alone and scared, trying to run the grift on her own.

"That one had quite the mouth on him. Nasty, nasty man." She shrugged at me. "So I talked my way out of the situation. I invented a boss, someone powerful, someone who could keep the police from taking advantage of me. Another layer of protection."

Lou had to have a good reason for keeping the gun. Maybe she didn't know how to get rid of it without being sure the police would find it. Maybe she'd panicked, thought it was safest to keep it. I could come up with a million excuses for her, in my mind. The twist of my stomach told me something different.

"Why didn't you *tell* me?" I said, my voice cracking. I was surprised how much that one hurt, how that was the thing that hurt most after all. "Did you think I wouldn't keep your secret?"

Lou's feet made soft indentations in the carpet as she crossed to her purse, bending over to snag a pack of cigarettes from her bag. She cupped her hand over a cigarette and sparked the lighter with the other.

She took her time with the smoke, luxuriating in it while I shivered and waited. Finally, she said: "You used to be so good at your job, Jo. What happened? All of a sudden, there were so many little slipups. Little things matter. They *matter*. But you couldn't stop drinking, you were taking too long on the cases—it shouldn't have taken you more than a year, *tops*, to pay me back. And that's not even the worst part." She shook her head, disgusted. "I saw so much potential in you. *So* much. That day at the diner and then . . . after. I knew I couldn't let you walk away from me."

She slid me a sly look and my stomach dropped. None of it had been a mistake—even the debt had been a ploy to tie me closer to her. Somehow she'd let slip a detail to the Asshole that made him able to trace it all back to me. They'd been alone in that conference room for twenty minutes—who knows what she'd said while she tied him up, while she straddled him. I'd always assumed it had been my fault he'd found us. Because it couldn't have been Lou. It could never have been Lou's fault.

"I want you to know I wouldn't have done this if you hadn't forced me," Lou said. Lou, or maybe really Rita Palmer. Unless that had been a lie, too. "You started to make such a mess. I asked Jackal to go to the Albatross that day because—well, because I know him. I knew what would happen, he'd never show up. And then I'd have a reason, you know? I could justify it with Jackal. You'd fucked up so *bad*, over and over again—I don't know if you got sloppy or lazy or—"

My head was pounding, and I could hear my blood beat in the spaces where I should've been able to hear my own breath. It felt like I hadn't taken one in minutes, hours. I backed up until my legs bumped the bed, jostling the suitcase with the gun nestled inside.

She could've thrown it in the ocean. That would have been so easy. But no. She'd kept it for a reason. For *this*.

"Or if you're so in love with me you can't see straight anymore." Lou looked at me, very level, very steady, one hand supporting the elbow of her cigarette hand. She blew out a plume of smoke. "What's our one rule with the girls?"

I reached a hand back and found the edge of the suitcase to steady myself. "Lou, what are you—"

"One rule, Jo. You get attached, you start to fuck up. How could you forget that?" She smiled a little. Like she was enjoying herself. That pretty face of hers, all angles, all sharpness where once it had been soft toward *me*, always soft to *me*. "I'm not going back to the streets, just me. You think you know tough? You don't know anything about it."

"I'm going to be sick," I said.

"Be my guest. The police should be here any minute. I called them from downstairs just now. I told them I felt *obligated* to help in their search for justice." She gave me a little smile and wink. "Don't you think Ellen deserves justice?"

The police. I had one small chip left to play. "MacLeish told me that the St. Leo turns over the security tapes tomorrow. Going back months. You were there with her, Lou. Remember? If I go down for this, you do, too. But we could still go. Start over somewhere new. Let's go, please let's just go."

For the first time, a small shadow passed over Lou's face, and then she shook it off, her cheeks creasing in dimples. "Looks like Mr. Alibi will be coming in handy for more than an alibi," she said with a wink. "Tapes get erased all the time."

I gagged on the taste of gin still in my mouth. I'd never drink gin again after this, I promised myself, after this very moment I was done with juniper, Lou was right, it did taste like Christmas tree piss. My vision was pinwheeling to a small point, like Lou was the only thing I could see. I couldn't stand to look at that face, that beautiful, terrible face.

Lou took another drag of the cigarette, shrugged. That same little smile. "Not so tough now," she said.

I took a breath and forced myself to take another one, and another. I nodded and nodded and nodded, and then I swung the gun up from behind me and pointed it at her face. She froze. "Move, Lou. Get out of my way."

That got a reaction from her, finally. "Put the gun down, Jo. It's too late." But her face was pale, the freckles bright against her nose. She took one small step toward me, still between me and the door. "Jo, listen to me."

I'd never held a gun before. The metal was slick against my palms, which were sweating, and I had the urge to tap the trigger just to make sure it really worked.

"Put it down," Lou said, taking another step toward me.

"Stop it," I warned, but she moved another step closer. I flinched and gripped the gun with both hands. She put her hands up, but she took another step. Lou's face was soft again, and if I let myself, I could almost believe that she hadn't really meant everything she'd said, that she was only scared. I could understand that. Anyone could.

"Think this through," she said. "The police will be here any minute. Would you really shoot me?"

I'd been trying to avoid asking myself that question since I'd grabbed the gun. She didn't want to go back to the streets. I could still leave tonight, go to Palm Springs without her.

It wouldn't take MacLeish more than twenty minutes, tops, to get to her place, less if he was speeding, and at least ten, maybe fifteen had passed since she'd called them. If they got here, it would be her word against mine. A coin toss.

Except I was holding a gun on her.

"I don't want to," I admitted, and cocked the gun. "So please, Lou, please, get out of my way."

She stopped moving, her hands in the air, and bit her lip, a genuine flare of fear in her eyes. I thought about what she must have been like before this life, before she'd started being the Lady. I thought of the picture of Eve Dawes, yanked off the street, scared and alone in a justice system that told her she was trash, that punished her but none of the men who had used her. I wondered if Lou had a similar picture anywhere in her file. That kind heart of hers couldn't have been entirely faked. It must have made her easy pickings for the world, once upon a time.

"Did you ever care about me?" I asked, knowing it was stupid. I was wasting time.

She took one very small step closer, still smiling that little smile. She was too close now—I could smell her. Some of her lemony brightness had faded, and underneath it was a musky, animal smell, a stink. "A little," she admitted. "I love all my marks, a little."

I reared back, my cheeks burning as if she'd slapped me.

Lou took the opening, throwing herself on me, barreling me backward. I bounced against the bed and twisted off it, Lou's knee connecting with my stomach and spiking the air out of my lungs. Stunned, I could barely get my arms up to push her away as she clawed at my hair, climbing up me to get to the gun I was still clutching. "You're not going anywhere," she huffed into my neck, her breath tickling my ear, and finally I kicked at her, managing to knock her off for a moment, and then she was back, scratching at me, reaching for the gun.

I let my fingers loose, trying only to throw the gun far enough that I could push her away from me and scramble for the door, but she was too quick, she caught my hand on the way, pinning my arm down and growling as she clutched at it, grabbing the gun from the ground and thumbing back the hammer, trying to hold me down and wriggle it away, both at the same time. But I was bigger than she was, too strong, and I flailed my free arm, trying to get her off me, and my fingers caught the tumbler on the bedside table, showering us both with stinging gin. I only meant to stun her, I only meant to give myself a fighting chance, which was all Lou had ever wanted for herself, too, a chance to take control of her life, but then I was bringing the tumbler down just above her ear and an unholy crack came from the side of her face, that beautiful face I couldn't stand to look at anymore, crunching against the floor as a thin line of blood ran down from her skull, as she looked up at me, her eyes big with surprise and, oh God, sadness, and her mouth dropped wide and then there was a roaring coming out of her that was worse than anything, worse, even, than the rattle that had come out of Ellen in the back seat of the car, a syrupy *herk, herk*, as if she'd tried to will oxygen back into her lungs.

And then I was bringing the tumbler down against her head again because if I didn't make that sound *stop* I really was going to go crazy and then it did stop and the only sound in the room was my ragged breathing.

"Lou?" I whispered, pushing her away from me. She didn't move. She didn't make a noise. Oh God, what had I done, I hadn't meant to do it, I hadn't really meant to do it. But there was a little voice in my head that disagreed, that had been screaming since I'd seen the suitcase, since I'd heard her say it, *I love all my marks, a little*, since even, maybe, Ellen.

I pressed a hand to my hammering heart and sat up, staring down at her slumped body. *Stupid, stupid. Get out of here. When she wakes up in two minutes, you'll have missed your shot.*

But I didn't listen to myself. I turned her over. Lou's face was frozen, lips parted, the blood seeping slower now but still covering her face. Her open eyes. That perfect porcelain face, lifeless and cracked and red and white.

It had been the only thing I'd stared at the entire time I'd choked Ellen from the back seat of her own car, Lou's hands holding Ellen down with all her might, her face like a slice of bone-white china in the moonlight. The entire time, while Ellen had flailed like a fish on a hook, twisting and raking at Lou's eyes, never quite reaching her, I'd stared at Lou's face. *One, two, three*, I'd counted, trying to see if I could match all the pale freckles on Lou's nose with the count I was keeping up as I willed Ellen into unconsciousness, the seat belt wrapped around my knuckles. Making a mythology of her face as Ellen stopped struggling, until it was really and truly over.

I straightened up, breathing hard. My hands were shaking and I stared at them, counting to ten over and over in my head. I could hear the light buzzing from the bathroom, like water rushing in my ears.

I knew it was useless, but I probed under her chin for a pulse. No luck. I stared at her body, numb, the body that not an hour before, I'd been . . . I shook my head. If I let myself think about that, I'd go crazy. I wasn't sure I wasn't going to go crazy, anyway, but I had to get myself together. I had to think.

Lou's body. The police on their way. If I closed my eyes and concentrated, I thought it was possible I could hear the sirens approaching.

The light buzzing from the bathroom gave me an idea. I gulped down a gag and grabbed Lou's body under the armpits, dragging her to the bathroom. I set her carefully against the toilet and ran a bath. I didn't have enough time to fill the tub so I pushed her in with it only halfway full. It wouldn't fool anyone for long.

As she slipped into the water, I remembered what she'd told me once, that she couldn't swim. I pulled her head up, above the water. Some of the blood was already drying and tacky around the split in her skull, but some of it had turned the water pink. I cradled her head in my hands and stared at her. *Lou, why did you do it?*

If she'd come with me when I'd first asked, we could have been halfway to Palm Springs by now. I closed my eyes. The slideshow of images of what could have been: holding her hand across the gearshift, a midnight swim. *Well, she got that*, I thought, and then I started to laugh; it was so horrible and perfect. My ears caught the faint wail of a siren, and I knew I wasn't imagining it this time.

If it was Escobar, I was completely fucked. If it was MacLeish, I had options. She'd been drinking. She'd fallen in the bathtub, hit her head. It happened, I knew it did.

But I wasn't so sure I wanted options. Jackal was gone, Lou was gone. Ellen. All gone. Was there anything left for me, now, that was better than being locked up? The Lady's business, for all it had been about taking down bad men, had left so many dead women in its wake. And I was a part of that. Maybe it was better for everyone if they caught me. Maybe that was the only end left, the best end left, for dangerous women like Lou and me.

I left the bathroom and picked up Lou's gold lighter from the bedroom floor, where she'd dropped it in our struggle. I wanted something of hers close to me as I did what I knew I had to do. It wasn't a trophy. It wasn't that.

I clicked it with each step back down her stairs, dropping the hammer like a tiny guillotine. I glided my hand over the polished mahogany handrail for the last time. My prints were all over the place anyway.

I descended the staircase. Through the fogged glass of Lou's front windows, I could see the pulse of blue and red lights, hear the slap of car doors closing. My breath was tight in my chest, and my hands were cold and soggy with Lou's pink blood, and dripping red with Ellen's, even if I was the only one who could see it. Through the window I saw shapes moving closer, two, but I couldn't tell who they were. MacLeish and Escobar, MacLeish and someone new?

One of the shapes was close to the door now, and as he raised an arm to knock—the other hand moving to his hip—I took a deep breath and flipped the lock, placing my hands securely on my head in supplication, and then I waited.

I didn't have to wait very long.

What had been our biggest rule? Oh, Lou, if you didn't believe you taught me anything, believe this: I won't make the same mistake twice.

CHAPTER 32

The alarm went off: 6 p.m. Officially time for a drink. I was proud of myself; I'd been managing to wait longer and longer every night. It was even dark now.

I poured myself a little bourbon from the bottle that I kept under the sink in what had been Jackal's office and dropped two sweating ice cubes into it. The heat had cooled but hadn't left completely, even as we'd passed Thanksgiving and Christmas was on the horizon. Not that I had anyone to buy gifts for this year.

I read the paper as I sipped. Nothing fickler than a daily newspaper. There'd been a stir when Joel Klein was arrested on suspicion of his father's and mistress's murders. Multiple witnesses, among them a certain leading man, had reported a loud altercation between Junior and Ellen at a cemetery party just a day before the bodies were found. And while he'd never be convicted—money like that never was—it was a terrible marvel to realize that, in the end, Ellen had created the perfect cover for me. For us.

It would've made Lou laugh. Maybe she *was* laughing, wherever she was now.

A few days before Joel Klein was arrested, one of the local papers, not even the *Times*, dedicated a thumb's width of space to the decease of a local woman, née Rita Palmer, at her home.

It made it worse, almost, that the name hadn't been a lie. It made me wonder what else might have been true. But I'd never get those answers, so I pushed it away.

> The deceased was found in her bathtub, with an injury to the head that had been sustained after a night of drinking. Investigating police officers said there was no sign of foul play, and the death was being investigated strictly as an accident.

That was all. That was all the article said. Nobody mentioned Ellen's suitcase. Nobody mentioned it because it would never be found. MacLeish had been thorough in his favor, erasing all signs of me from the house. I tried not to think of what he'd done to stage her so well. Had he undressed her, lit a candle, splashed gin in the bathtub? No one else knew she hated it. *Jo, be human.* In the end, no justice for Ellen, no justice for Lou.

The day after that notice appeared, I'd called Lou's phone carrier and asked that any calls that came to her phone, either cell or home, be redirected to my number. I explained the situation—a friend of mine had committed suicide, and I had no way of getting in touch with her family. But I wanted them to hear the news from a friendly voice before anyone else. It had taken all of three minutes to connect.

As the days went by and no one called, I felt a sadness deeper than any I'd known even when Ellen died, when I first realized what I was capable of. Lou had no one. Only me. And she hadn't even wanted that. She'd preferred being alone to my company, at the last. And unlike Ellen's death, her demise had inspired no speculation, no court reporters banging down her mother's door. Only me. I supposed, in a way, that made her finally mine.

I'd gotten everything I wanted, hadn't I. In the end. I stood up and poured myself another drink.

I'd kept coming into the office because there wasn't much else I could think of to do. I was waiting, but I didn't know for what. I'd moved Lou's chair out of her office—it had a better cushion than mine—and I'd flipped through her desk, looking for anything with my name on it. I'd found nothing, which should've been a relief but wasn't. I did find dozens of pictures of a younger Eve Dawes with six or seven different men. Staring at them, I understood why she'd kept ferrying Lou's bribes to the police in order to keep them secret. They were truly lurid, but it was the look on her face she'd want to protect, I thought. The blankness in her eyes that made you wonder. It didn't square with the woman she was trying to be now. It must have seemed worth the price of acting as an extra layer between Lou and the police. To keep being used by Lou.

The phone rang when I was on my second glass of bourbon. On the other end, a voice I'd never expected to hear again. "You must really not be scared of me," Carrigan said. "You didn't even bother to change your phone number."

"I was sorry to hear about the election," I said. I was a little surprised to find I meant it. "But at least you know I had nothing to do with it."

There was a pained pause, and then Carrigan said, tightly, "Thanks. I don't dwell in the past."

"And yet here you are," I said, "calling me."

"I'd like to engage your services," Carrigan said.

"I don't fuck for money."

"Since when?" he fired back. "Anyway, that's not what I meant. I'd like to employ *all* of your services. I assume you're still . . . in business?"

It was a good question.

I'd gotten lucky. MacLeish, not Lafferty or Escobar, had been the one to pull open Lou's door that night. When he saw me, soaked and shivering, he'd shouted to his partner to phone it in, a 10-16. Whoever it was trudged back to the car, and MacLeish shut the door and looked at me, those droopy hangdog eyes, and said: "We'll have five minutes, tops. Go out the back. Where is she?"

That's how long it took us to reach a new understanding.

Later that night, MacLeish had called me from a number that showed up on my phone as *Unlisted*. He hadn't bothered with pleasantries.

"The chief wanted me to pass something along," MacLeish said.

"Yeah?" I thumbed Lou's lighter, back and forth, back and forth. Trying to place my fingertips right over the dulled fingerprints I could catch in the light. If I pressed hard enough, maybe I could feel them pressing back.

"Said if you had a moment, he'd love an in-person meeting with the Lady. A few details to iron out."

"I'll bet," I said, wondering how much Lafferty minded his partner covering up his girlfriend's murder. "But there's no Lady anymore. You fished her out of a bathtub tonight."

"Chief thought you might say that," MacLeish said. "Told me to tell you, if that changes, he'd appreciate a call."

"I can't imagine," I said, closing my eyes as I said it, "what you owe him now. On my behalf."

MacLeish sighed. "The chief's not a sentimental man, I'll say that much. But it wasn't painless. And Jo"—and his voice got deeper as he said it—"one day I *will* collect."

I nodded, even though he couldn't see me. That was the problem of some future woman. Who knew who she'd turn out to be, what she could handle.

Another pause. A longer one. "Give the chief a call if the Lady's ever back in business."

"All right," I said, and hung up before he could press it again. I flipped the lighter, dropping the hammer again and again. It really was a pretty thing. All cheap Art Deco imitation gold and black enamel, nothing of value but pretty all the same. It was almost enough to make a woman consider taking up smoking.

The irony wasn't lost on me, that I'd sold out our sisterhood to a man, to a cop. That in the end, I'd chosen to put my life in his hands, the way I'd once laid everything at Lou's feet. One day, there would be a heavy price tag. I knew that. Nothing is free—not kindness, not friendship. Certainly not favors. The implications unfurled before me, unending and evil. Maybe I'd spent too much time with Jackal, I thought, because I'd learned to gamble. Someday, I'd hear from Mac-Leish again.

I hadn't expected to hear from Carrigan first.

"What exactly did you have in mind?" I asked him.

"You know what it takes to win elections these days?"

"Money," I guessed. It was a pretty safe guess. It was true for most things that had to be won.

"Money," he confirmed. "Money my lovely little wife's family didn't feel *comfortable* sharing. So now that my political aspirations have been, so to speak, doused in gasoline and lit on fire, I've turned my mind to other things. I don't think I was well suited for office anyway. Too many public appearances, too many babies to kiss."

"We charge by the hour and that counts for phone calls, too," I reminded him.

"My father-in-law," Carrigan clarified, "told me he couldn't support my campaign because he had something grander in mind for me

than public service. Said I was the son he'd never had, that he'd turn
the business over to me someday. All bullshit. He won't retire before
he dies. Unless someone forces him to do it. I'd like to speed his time-
line up, a little."

"You could just ride it out. Law office no longer fulfilling?" I was
doodling on my notepad, not taking notes the way Lou had trained me
to. Instead, I'd doodled a constellation of stars—or freckles—and I
was working my way between them, connecting everything together.

Carrigan cleared his throat on the other end of the phone. "No
one has come right out and said it to my face, but I know they're happy
I lost the election. You know my firm never even bothered to put up a
poster? Not one single poster," he said, and there was an edge to his
voice. "That's reason enough for me."

"I see," I said.

"Could we grab a drink sometime?" Carrigan asked. "Go over the
particulars?"

I thought about it. I thought about his wife and his big house and
his even bigger bank account, and I thought about fucking him with
Jackal's eyes on me in his apartment, the way he'd shivered as I cried.
I thought about the red blinking light on my answering machine
that morning. When I'd clicked it, the voicemail button squishing under my fingernail like a ladybug, an unfamiliar voice had filled my
office.

"Hi, um, hello? We met—well, no, we didn't exactly meet, I guess,
you left your card for me a few weeks ago at the, um, at the St. Leo.
The hotel. I was there with a man, and he was, well, ha, you know. I
spilled a beer into his lap. Jesus, Laura, shut up, you're rambling! Anyway. You left your card for me. That's all. You left your card for me and
told me to call you if I wanted, um, a free drink? And, well." A breathy
little laugh. "Here I am. Calling."

At the time, I'd rewound the tape, played it again. Wrote down the number she'd left me on my notepad and stared at it for a long time, wondering what to do about it. On the phone with Carrigan, I thought about that pretty young girl at the St. Leo, a million years ago, and what she might be able to do to the career of an old money man like Carrigan Sr. I thought about how I wouldn't have to split the money with the Lady Upstairs, and about how grateful a man like Mitch Carrigan would be for my help. I thought about the power I had now over this girl's life, if I called her back.

I thought about all of that and then I said, "Yeah, okay. I'd like that."

We hung up, but not until after we'd agreed to meet the next week for a drink. I wondered what his company would be like when I wasn't playing defenseless. I told Carrigan to pick someplace expensive. I told him to consider it an investment.

Somewhere during the phone call, I'd finished the bourbon. I crossed to the bar cart, uncapped the bottle, and poured a little more brown into my cup. Topped it off with a squeeze of lime juice from a warming green plastic bottle shaped to look like the fruit. A spritz of club soda on top of that. A proper cocktail.

Lou had asked me once, early, whether I thought what we did was evil. Testing me, maybe, when I was green and tender-fresh. "Not evil," I'd said, surprising myself by how much I meant it. "Everything is currency." And it was true: everything was currency of a sort. A smile applied at the right time like a crowbar—that was currency, a kind word the same. My body was mine to spend as I wanted. It wasn't evil to not have good intentions with sex. I didn't owe men pure motives. It wasn't kind, what we were doing, it might not have even been right, but it wasn't evil. Not then.

And some part of me still believed it. We'd done evil things. But that didn't mean the game was flawed from the ground up. Not when men who shot their wives in the face could plaster their names all over the city and be remembered as *good* men, not when men's potential was considered more important than women's bodies, not when the game was so rigged against us all.

I'd learned things from Ellen, invaluable things. I would do it differently this time. I wouldn't give this new girl, Laura, the chance to feel too much. You left someone in the orbit of charisma and of course she'd fall for it. It wasn't her fault. It didn't matter how tough she was; sometimes it couldn't be helped. Particularly if she was heartbroken, or lonely, or borderline homeless, sleeping out of a car.

I'd watch Laura carefully. I'd take my time, make sure she was ready for it all, that she was more than ready for it: that she wanted in on it, too. I'd drill Lou's one good lesson into her head: *Never love anyone more than yourself.* I'd be straight with the police. I'd send the pictures right to the papers. I wouldn't give Garrigan Sr. a chance to barter his way out of it. This time, there'd be no Jackal, no other partners to complicate things, to play their own games in the dark. No distractions.

Before, there had been the beginning of something special with our work. But I'd learned from Lou's mistakes, and from my own. It was why I was still there, in that office, watching the twilight settle over the city. It was why it wasn't me six feet under, staring up at the sunset and looking for the living to play the part I'd outlined. The script was all mine now, not some faceless dead woman's.

Maybe Lou had started out with good intentions, too. Maybe she'd thought she was building a sisterhood, a place for women to take back power using the weapons men haven't learned how to defend against. That was the dream she'd sold me. Or maybe she'd only needed to protect herself at a moment when she had no other options. Maybe it was both. I'd never know. But her failings had taught me everything I needed to make sure that tiny glimmer of possibility, that glittering picture she'd painted for me one morning in a diner, became the reality. The artificial into the true, the alchemy of Hollywood. I'd take

Lou's vision, and I'd perfect it. And in the end, that would be Lou's true legacy. In the end, a little piece of her would last forever.

I took a sip of my drink and watched the daylight purple and melt into twilight, become renewed with the dark. The sun was setting earlier these evenings. The heat that had plagued the city for weeks was mostly behind us—or long in front of us, if you wanted to think of it that way.

I went to the balcony at the back of the office and stood in front of the iron railing, drink in hand, and watched the lights of all of the city's people flicker out, brief and bright, before me. As soon as one blinkered off, another one took its place, so it was never true dark. The night sky was clear and glittered hard, but not with stars. People read so damn much into the stars—star-crossed lovers, love like galaxies, written in the stars, all that jazz. In my city, we'd gotten rid of all that and in its place put something brighter and harder that never went out, so you could barely even see those stars at all.

I preferred it that way.

ACKNOWLEDGMENTS

First, I want to thank my wonderful agent, Sharon Pelletier, for her incredible vision for this book and her help in getting it there. It is a dream come true to work with you. To my editor, Danielle Dieterich: thank you for taking a chance on me and Jo, and for your heavy lifting in sculpting this novel. To my team at Putnam—Ivan Held, Sally Kim, Brennin Cummings, Alexis Welby, Monica Cordova, and Erika Verbeck—thank you for making this experience even better than I dreamed it would be. And another huge thank you to Kristina Moore for taking this book places I'd barely let myself dream it might go.

To my Otis College cohort, thank you for all your work in helping me bring this book to life, and in particular, Esther Lee, Heather John Fogarty, Krystle Statler, Kevin Thomas, Guy Bennett, Marisa Matarazzo, Jen Hofer, and Marisa Silver. A huge thank-you to Peter Gadol, who taught me so much about craft and who spent one very memorable afternoon storyboarding with me. It was one of the honors of my life to study with Paul Vangelisti, one of the great noir poets, who made grad school so much more fun than my future children will ever one day believe.

This book is inextricably linked with Olivia Batker Pritzker, who deserves a whole chapter of thanks. From Trader Sam's Tiki Bar to sneaking into Disneyland (invaluable research into the art of the con!) to your unending patience for talking through every question and insecurity I threw at you (along with the multiple charts you drew), this book would not be the same without you.

It is not hyperbole to say this book would not exist without the loving editorial eye and support of Layne Fargo, who plucked me out of the Pitch Wars slush pile. Thank you for taking me and Jo in hand and helping me figure out exactly the right way to break the book to make it better. You are truly the fairy godmother of this book, and the best part of Pitch Wars is knowing you.

A huge thank-you to my loving family and friends, in particular, Samantha Omana, Tara Donohoe, and Leah and Lorraine Esturas-Pierson, the best cheerleaders a girl could ask for (and to Wilder Esturas-Pierson, who did not do very much cheerleading this time around, but I will let it slide). And finally, batting cleanup: my parents, Kim and Jeff Sutton, who never even once told me they thought it was a bad life plan to become a writer. Thank you for bribing me to read as a kid, and for nurturing and encouraging me as an adult. I love you very much.

The Lady Upstairs

Halley Sutton

Discussion Guide

A Conversation with Halley Sutton

BOOK
ENDS

PUTNAM
— EST. 1838 —

DISCUSSION GUIDE

1. Discuss the ways in which *The Lady Upstairs* does or does not fit into the noir genre. What noir tropes do you see in the novel? How does the author subvert the more typical conventions of this genre?

2. How did the first-person narration in the novel affect your reading experience? Did you always trust Jo as a narrator? How does viewing things through her eyes change your perception of the events in the novel?

3. Jo is determined to take down men who treat women badly, and yet it could be argued that she herself does not always treat women well. What do you think of Jo's attitudes toward other women? Do those attitudes change over the course of the novel? Would you consider her to be a feminist?

4. Take a look at Jo's romantic relationships, particularly those with

Jackal and Lou. How were these relationships different? How was Jo herself different in each of them?

5. Compare and contrast the different ways that characters in *The Lady Upstairs* command power over others. How do traditional definitions of power—whether political, financial, or professional—compare to the kind of power that Jo, Lou, and the Lady create?

6. What do you imagine Jo's past looked like, before she joined in with the Lady Upstairs? Additionally, what do you imagine happens to Jo after the novel's end? Is history doomed to repeat itself?

7. Many of the characters in *The Lady Upstairs* believe that money will solve their problems. Which instances in the novel support that idea and which undermine it?

8. Did you guess the identity of the Lady Upstairs while you were reading? If so, when?

9. Consider the different moral codes that guide each character. Who do you think bears the most responsibility for Ellen's murder? How are "good" and "evil" defined?

10. Did you ultimately find Jo to be a sympathetic character? Discuss the different consequences of her actions. Did the ends justify the means?

A Conversation
with Halley Sutton

The Lady Upstairs is your debut novel. Can you share a bit about
your experience as a first-time author?

It's a strange thing to have your childhood dream come true in the
middle of a global crisis. I would say that the best part is having access
to the writing community and to writers whom I admire, in a different
way than I did before. For example, I've attended Noir at the Bar
events for years—getting to read at one of those, from my own book,
is a life highlight I won't easily forget. Along with seeing my name on
a book for the first time!

What inspired you to tell this story?

I wanted to write a story about power and sex and heartache and regret. It doesn't get more noir than that.

Jo's first-person voice is so unique and powerful. Where did that voice come from? Which came first, the character of Jo or the plot of the novel?

I had Jo's voice in my head early; I knew I wanted to spend more time with her. I didn't have a story for her yet, but her voice was definitely the first thing that grabbed me and made me think, *I could spend a novel untangling this person.* She didn't spring into my head fully formed, but her snappy, snarky voice was always there, sort of parallel, narrating events in my head all day long. Maybe she was just waiting for her chance to find the right story to waltz into.

The Lady Upstairs is a modern take on the classic noir genre. Did any particular noir authors impact your writing? Do you have any favorite noir movies or novels? How is this book different from a traditional noir story?

If you're writing about LA noir, there's no escaping Raymond Chandler, and *The Long Goodbye* is one of my favorite books. Nobody packs as much pain per ounce as James M. Cain—he can do more with one hundred pages than most authors can in a trilogy. Dashiell Hammett, Dorothy B. Hughes, Jim Thompson. But the writer I return to over and over is always Megan Abbott, particularly her novel *Queenpin.* Sara Gran's *Dope.* Vicki Hendricks is another favorite—I don't think anyone spends enough time talking about what a fantastic book *Miami Purity* is. Whenever I feel like my writing needs better rhythm, I pick up Elmore Leonard (my particular favorite being *Gold Coast*, featuring one of Leonard's many compelling leading ladies named Karen). For films: I watched *Body Heat* almost daily while writing

The Lady Upstairs (frighteningly, that's only the tiniest bit of an exaggeration). *Gilda* and *Jackie Brown* were movies I returned to again and again, and it doesn't get much more hard-boiled dame than Linda Fiorentino in *The Last Seduction*. *Devil in a Blue Dress*—both the Walter Mosley book and the film starring Denzel Washington. Steph Cha's Juniper Song books were great modern noirs I turned to repeatedly.

As for how this book is different from a traditional noir story—I wanted to take all the noir tropes that I love and shift the spotlight. I wanted to create a femme fatale who was the center of the story—and a *literal* femme fatale at that. What if women had weaponized the anxieties of classic noir to work for them, to take back a little money and power for themselves?

The city of Los Angeles feels so alive on the page—it is almost a character itself! What is your own personal experience with LA and why did you choose to set the novel there?

Los Angeles was actually the missing piece to Jo's story! I moved to Los Angeles for grad school and didn't know that much about the city. When I first started trying to learn about the history of Los Angeles to make sense of my new home (admittedly, mostly via murder bus tours, which are not necessarily the same as diving into peer-reviewed research or history), I was struck by how much it felt like the myth of the city eventually just became the history of the place. I thought a good way to approach understanding LA might be to dig into it through a cultural lens, which refired my love of noir. Once I figured that out, I realized that Jo was a perfect femme fatale voice, and the rest of her story clicked into place for me.

Were there any particularly challenging scenes or characters that you encountered while writing? Were there any surprises during the writing process?

Jo's scene seducing Carrigan was the hardest in the novel for me to get right. I probably wrote more than twenty drafts of that scene, each one maybe a little better than the last (*maybe*), but none of them right. It was the scene I was working on the longest in the book, but once it was the right version of itself, I knew. That was a very, very satisfying moment.

Did current events or the rise of the Me Too movement have an influence on your writing? Would you define *The Lady Upstairs* as a feminist novel?

Not as much as you'd think, or at least not in the sense that it was written with the Me Too movement in mind. It's not like men abusing power or women started with #MeToo, but the movement did put a specific stamp on it. I started writing *The Lady Upstairs* in 2015, and stories about sleazy Hollywood men capitalizing on the casting couch to assert power over women have been around since Hollywood began. They probably started when the first couch was made, to be honest.

   To me, *The Lady Upstairs* is a feminist novel because it centers on the experience of women—broken, jagged, fucked up women. That said, they're also working within the patriarchy, and much of their work and lives *do* revolve around men—they haven't broken free of the structure, even if they're subverting it for personal gain. Jo often prioritizes herself or Lou above the well-being of other women. I don't know that I think Jo would describe herself as a feminist. *I* would not describe Jo as a feminist, either.

Sexuality and sex work are forms of both currency and agency in the novel. Why did you want to explore these themes? And why was it important for you to depict queer characters on the page?

In the noir genre, there is almost nothing more dangerous than the sexually empowered woman. I wanted to take that fear and danger and make it explicit for my femmes fatales—what if they really *were* using their sexuality to destroy men? It felt like both a timeless and a timely idea.

I think representation in fiction is always important. But I also think when writing about sex it wasn't possible to imagine some of my characters not being fluid in their sexuality—that's just not true to life, and it didn't feel true to Jo or Lou, either. But I don't think I ever specifically label them in the book, because I don't think Jo would label herself as *anything*. It's not Jo's relationship to sex or to being queer that's hardest for her to deal with in the novel; it's the fact that she has feelings for Lou (and Jackal!) at all, that it's not actually possible for her to be the hardened woman she's always striving to be.

What do you hope readers take away from Jo and her story? What lessons can we learn from Jo's example?

At the end of the novel, Jo speculates that the business started as a way for women to take back power, before pivoting into another way to assert power, and that original idea isn't *flawed* per se. But eventually, if you're working within an institutionalized system that prioritizes money over people, any good that might have happened along the way becomes secondary. I think there's strength in community and standing up to power and the patriarchy, but I don't know if it's possible for that not to be corrupted when it becomes about the individual.

What is next for you?

Hopefully twenty-five more books with my name on them.

Photo of the author © 2019 by Faizah Rajput

HALLEY SUTTON is a writer and editor who lives in Los Angeles. She is a frequent contributor to CrimeReads and a mentor for Pitch Wars, a program pairing published authors with up-and-coming writers. She holds a bachelor's degree in creative writing from the University of California, Santa Cruz, and a master's degree in writing from Otis College of Art and Design. *The Lady Upstairs* is her debut novel.

Visit Halley Sutton Online

HalleySutton.com
🐦 Halley_Sutton